Victor and Nora

a gotham love story

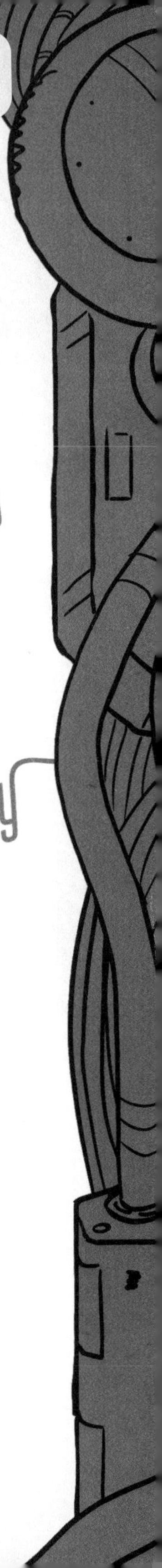

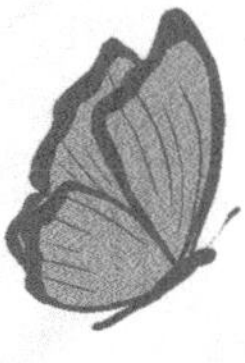

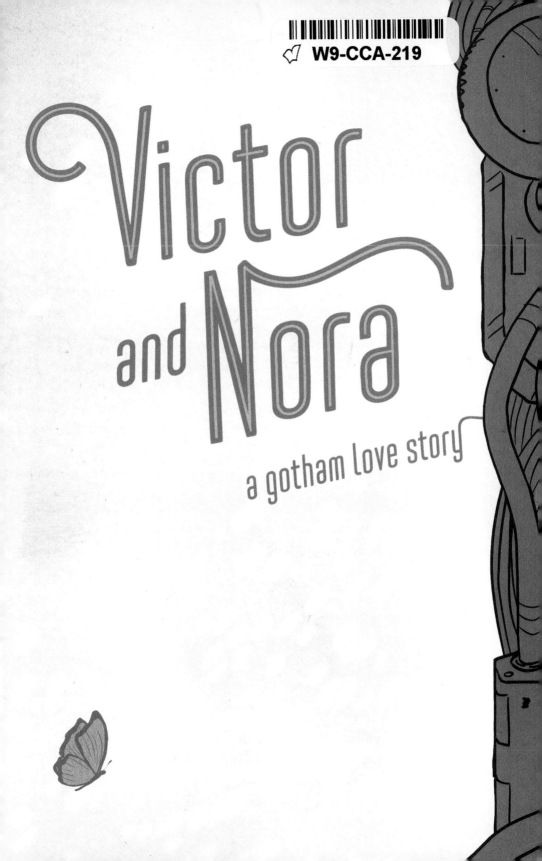

WRITTEN BY
LAUREN MYRACLE

ILLUSTRATED BY
ISAAC GOODHART

COLORS BY
CRIS PETER

LETTERS BY
STEVE WANDS

Victor and Nora

a gotham love story

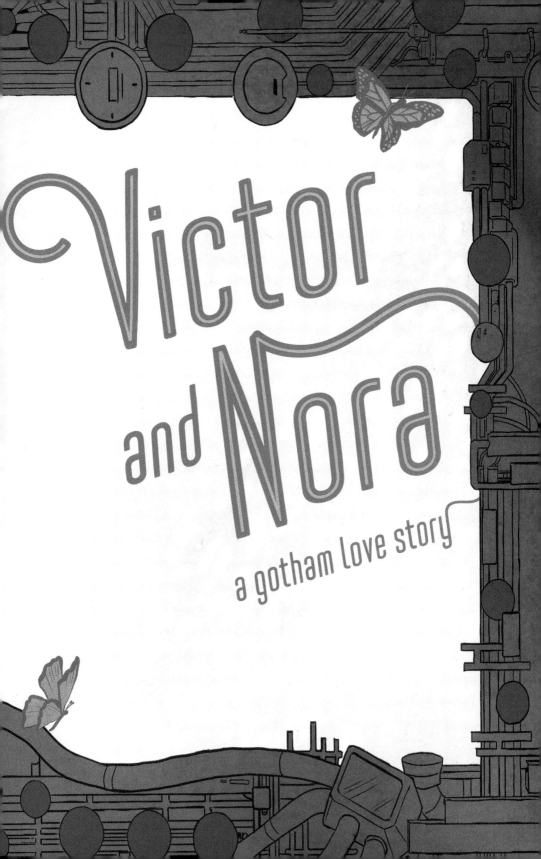

Diego Lopez Editor
Steve Cook Design Director – Books
Amie Brockway-Metcalf Publication Design

Bob Harras Senior VP – Editor-in-Chief, DC Comics
Michele R. Wells VP & Executive Editor, Young Reader

Jim Lee Publisher & Chief Creative Officer
Bobbie Chase VP – Global Publishing Initiatives & Digital Strategy
Don Falletti VP – Manufacturing Operations & Workflow Management
Lawrence Ganem VP – Talent Services
Alison Gill Senior VP – Manufacturing & Operations
Hank Kanalz Senior VP – Publishing Strategy & Support Services
Dan Miron VP – Publishing Operations
Nick J. Napolitano VP – Manufacturing Administration & Design
Nancy Spears VP – Sales
Jonah Weiland VP – Marketing & Creative Services

VICTOR AND NORA:
A GOTHAM LOVE STORY

Published by DC Comics. Copyright © 2020 DC Comics. All Rights Reserved. All characters, their distinctive likenesses, and related elements featured in this publication are trademarks of DC Comics. The stories, characters, and incidents featured in this publication are entirely fictional. DC Comics does not read or accept unsolicited submissions of ideas, stories, or artwork. DC – a WarnerMedia Company.

DC Comics, 2900 West Alameda Ave., Burbank, CA 91505

Printed by LSC Communications, Crawfordsville, IN, USA.

9/25/20.

First Printing.

ISBN: 978-1-4012-9639-1

Library of Congress Cataloging-in-Publication Data

Names: Myracle, Lauren, 1969- writer. | Goodhart, Isaac, illustrator. | Peter, Cris, colourist. | Wands, Steve, letterer.

Title: Victor & Nora : a Gotham love story / written by Lauren Myracle ; illustrated by Isaac Goodhart ; colors by Cris Peter ; letters by Steve Wands.

Description: Burbank, CA : DC Comics, [2020] | Audience: Ages 15+ | Audience: Grades 10-12 | Summary: After Victor Fries and Nora Faria meet at a cemetery outside of Gotham City, their summer quickly spirals into a beautiful romance, and Victor's cold heart is able to thaw, allowing him to begin to enjoy life again after his brother's death, but when he learns of Nora's incurable illness, he is driven to try to find a scientific solution to keep from losing another person he loves.

Identifiers: LCCN 2020030691 (print) | LCCN 2020030692 (ebook) | ISBN 9781401296391 (paperback) | ISBN 9781779507280 (ebook)

Subjects: LCSH: Graphic novels. | CYAC: Graphic novels. | Love--Fiction. | Fate and fatalism--Fiction.

Classification: LCC PZ7.7.M98 Vi 2020 (print) | LCC PZ7.7.M98 (ebook) | DDC 741.5/973--dc23

LC record available at https://lccn.loc.gov/2020030691
LC ebook record available at https://lccn.loc.gov/2020030692

PEFC Certified
This product is from sustainably managed forests and controlled sources
PEFC
PEFC/29-31-337 www.pefc.org

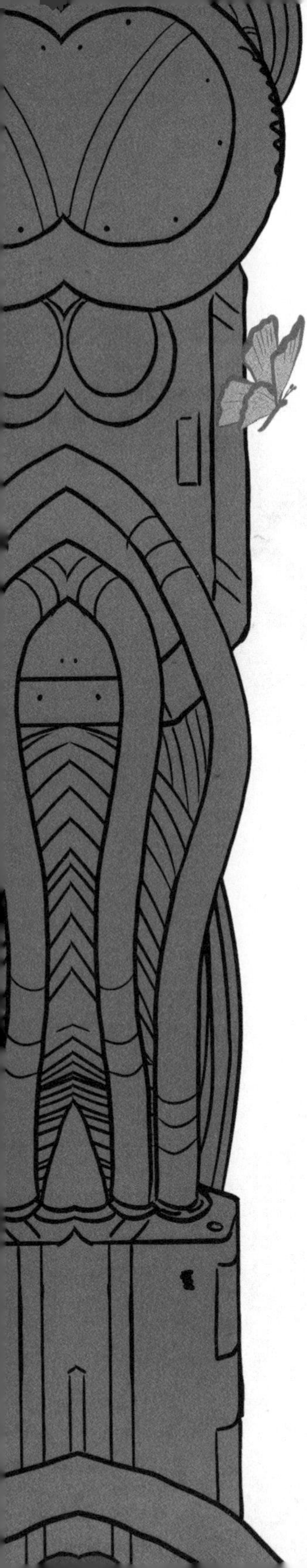

For Randy, because if anyone could reanimate me from a frozen state, it's you. (But let's not put it to the test.)

—Lauren

For Danielle, my biggest inspiration.

—Isaac

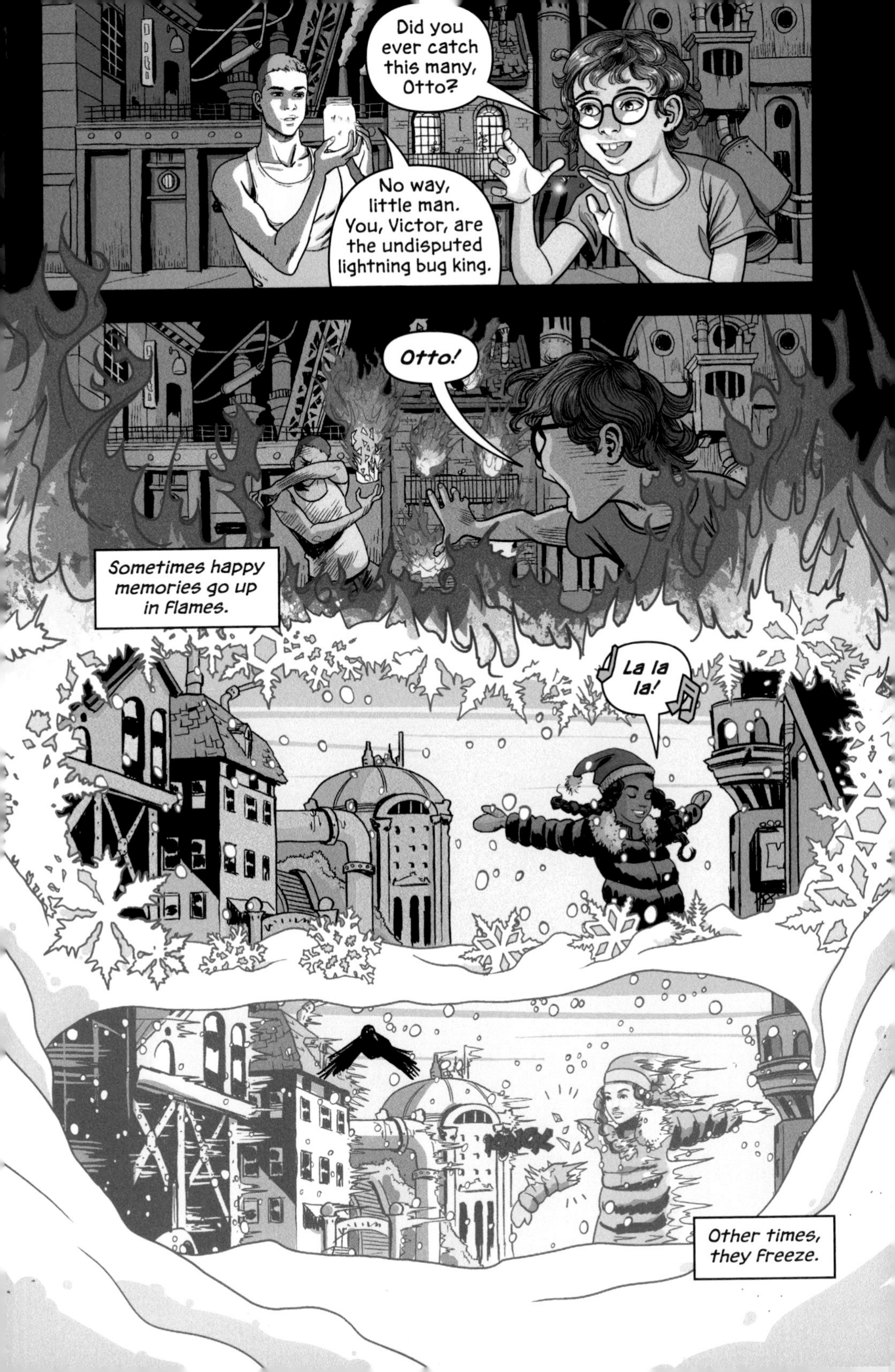
Did you ever catch this many, Otto?
No way, little man. You, Victor, are the undisputed lightning bug king.
Otto!
Sometimes happy memories go up in flames.
La la la!
Other times, they freeze.

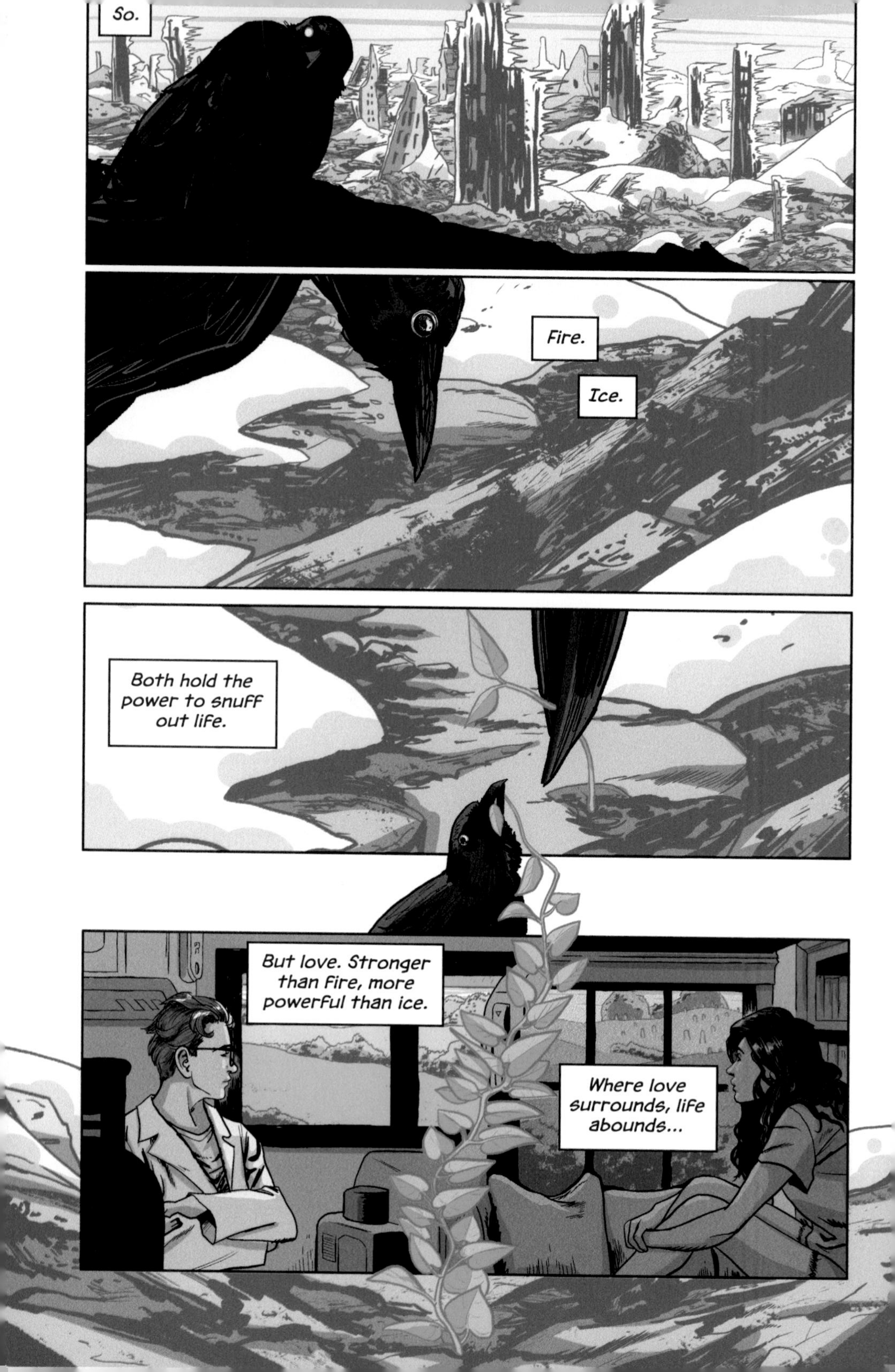

So.
Fire.
Ice.
Both hold the power to snuff out life.
But love. Stronger than fire, more powerful than ice.
Where love surrounds, life abounds...

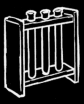

The Boy Who Hates Death

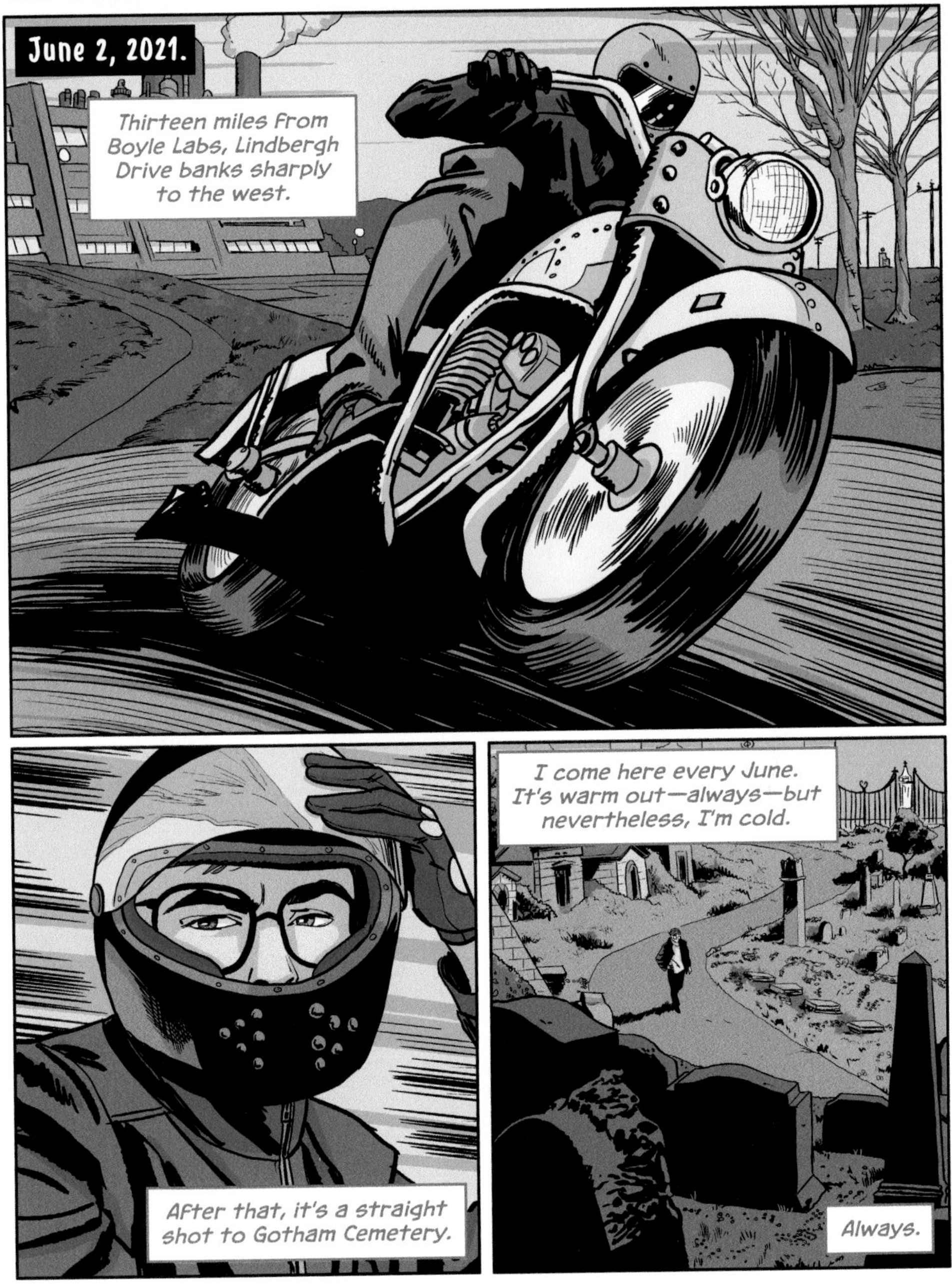
June 2, 2021.
Thirteen miles from Boyle Labs, Lindbergh Drive banks sharply to the west.
After that, it's a straight shot to Gotham Cemetery.
I come here every June. It's warm out—always—but nevertheless, I'm cold.
Always.

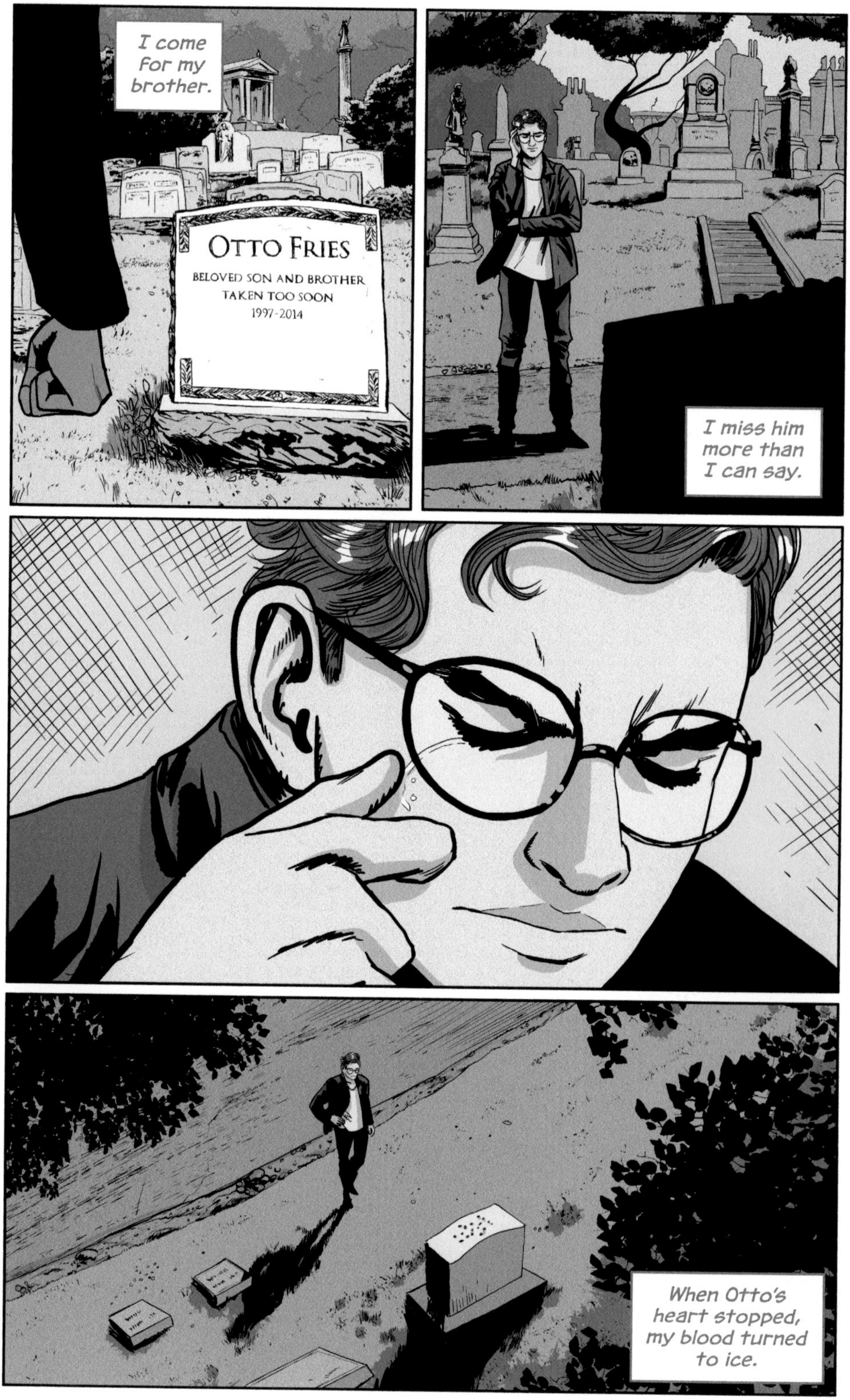
I come for my brother.
OTTO FRIES
BELOVED SON AND BROTHER
TAKEN TOO SOON
1997-2014
I miss him more than I can say.
When Otto's heart stopped, my blood turned to ice.

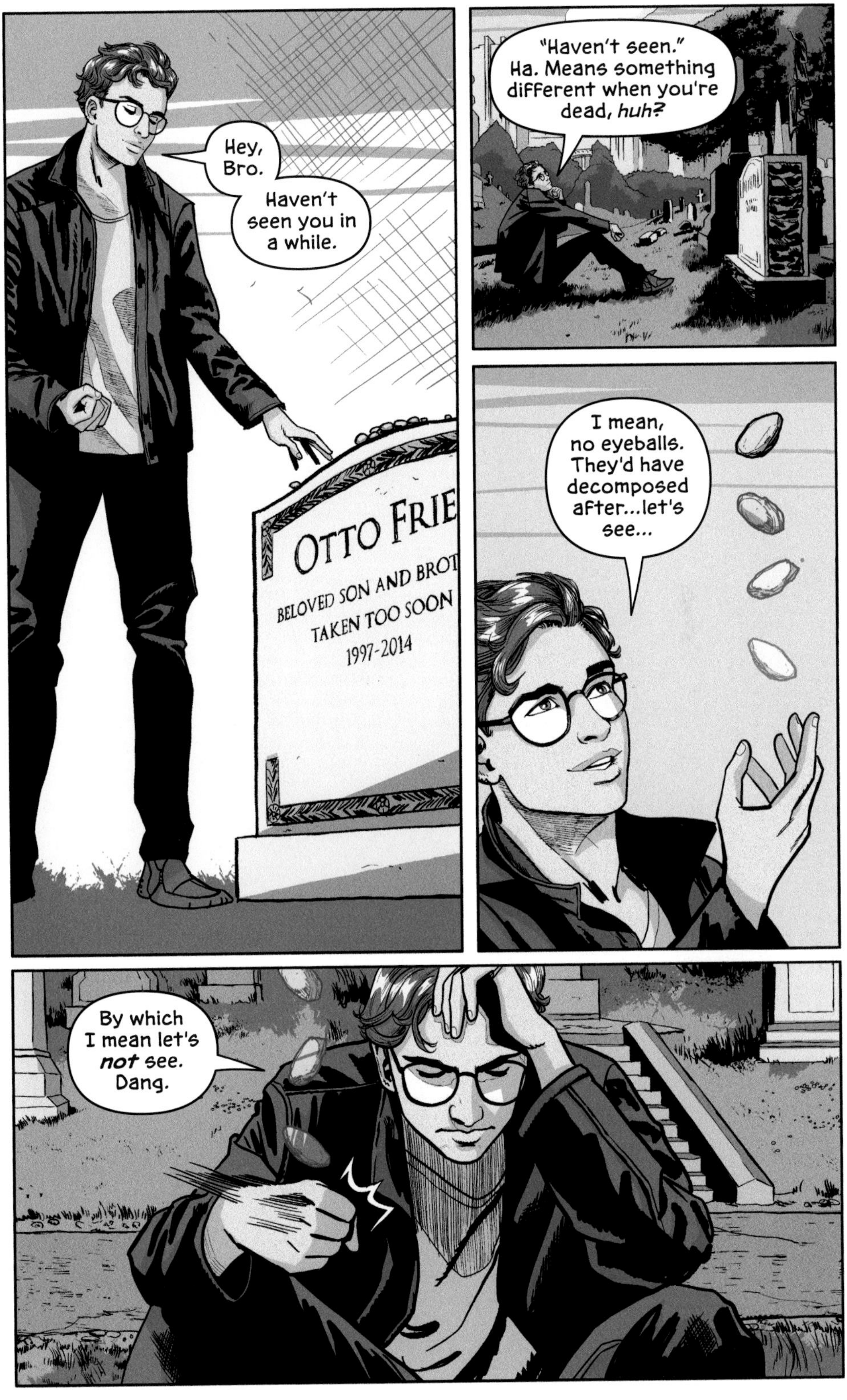
Hey, Bro.
Haven't seen you in a while.
OTTO FRIE
BELOVED SON AND BROT
TAKEN TOO SOON
1997-2014
"Haven't seen." Ha. Means something different when you're dead, *huh?*
I mean, no eyeballs. They'd have decomposed after...let's see...
By which I mean let's ***not*** see. Dang.

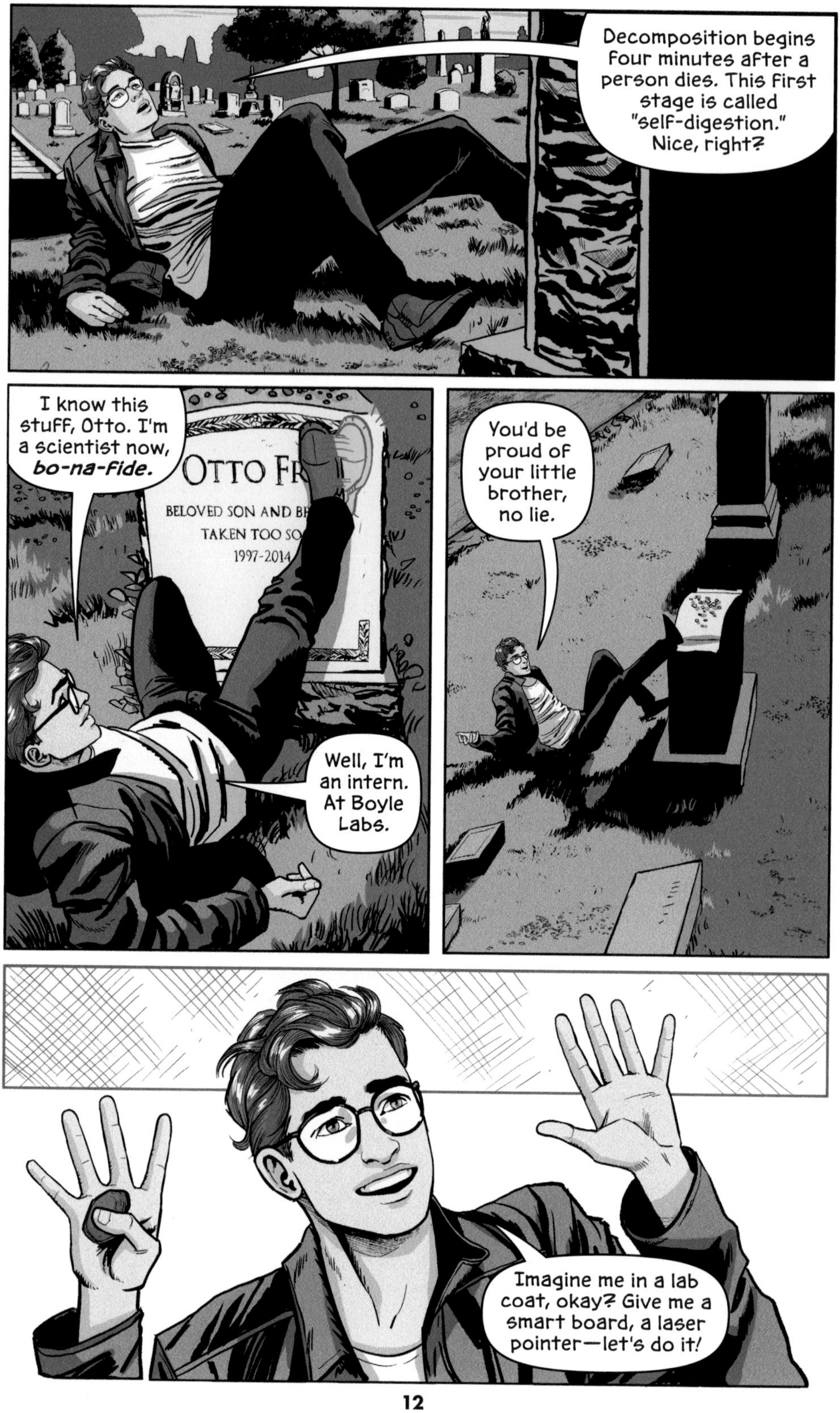
Decomposition begins four minutes after a person dies. This first stage is called "self-digestion." Nice, right?
I know this stuff, Otto. I'm a scientist now, *bo-na-fide.*
OTTO FR
BELOVED SON AND BR
TAKEN TOO SO
1997-2014
Well, I'm an intern. At Boyle Labs.
You'd be proud of your little brother, no lie.
Imagine me in a lab coat, okay? Give me a smart board, a laser pointer—let's do it!

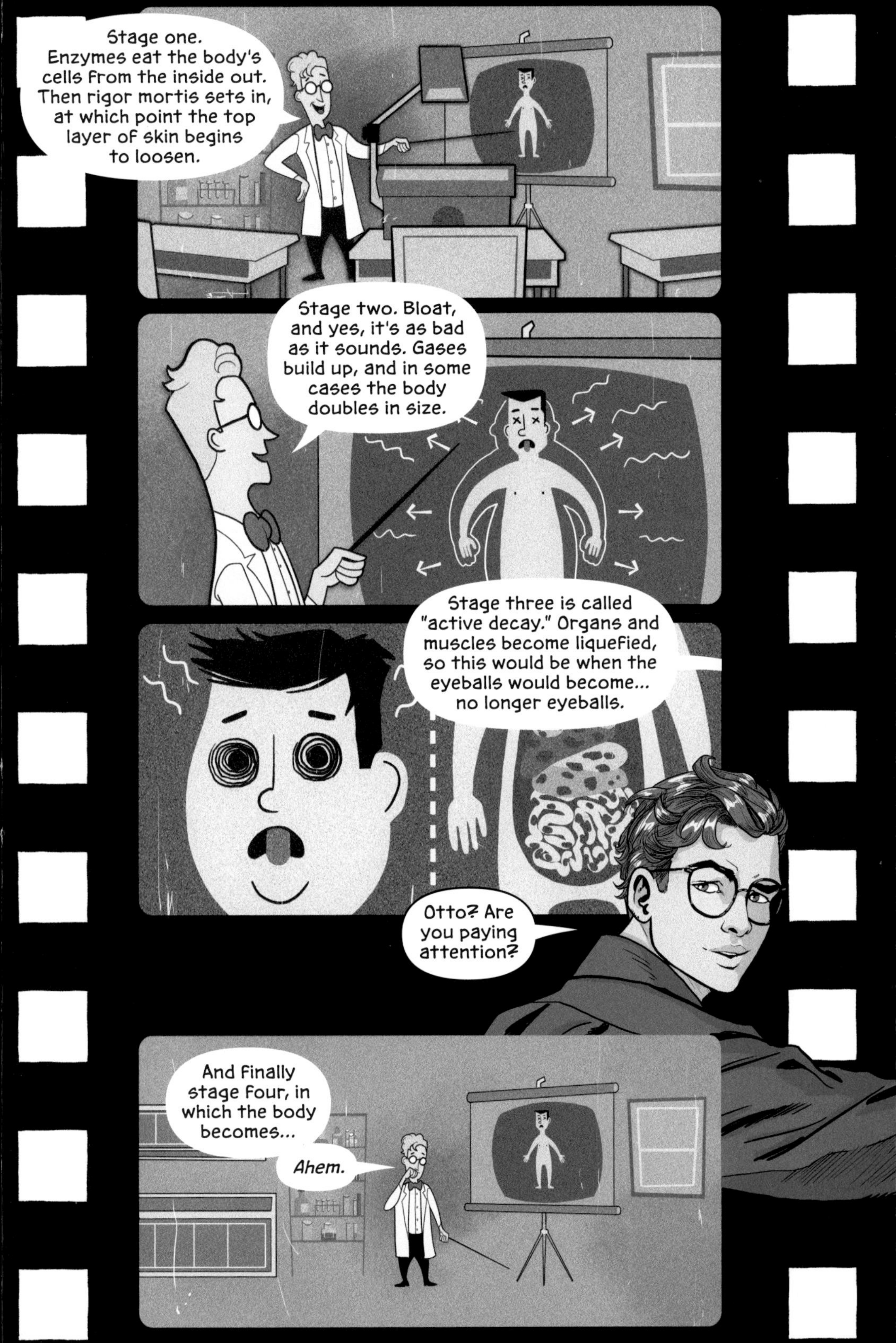
Stage one. Enzymes eat the body's cells from the inside out. Then rigor mortis sets in, at which point the top layer of skin begins to loosen.
Stage two. Bloat, and yes, it's as bad as it sounds. Gases build up, and in some cases the body doubles in size.
Stage three is called "active decay." Organs and muscles become liquefied, so this would be when the eyeballs would become... no longer eyeballs.
Otto? Are you paying attention?
And finally stage four, in which the body becomes...
Ahem.

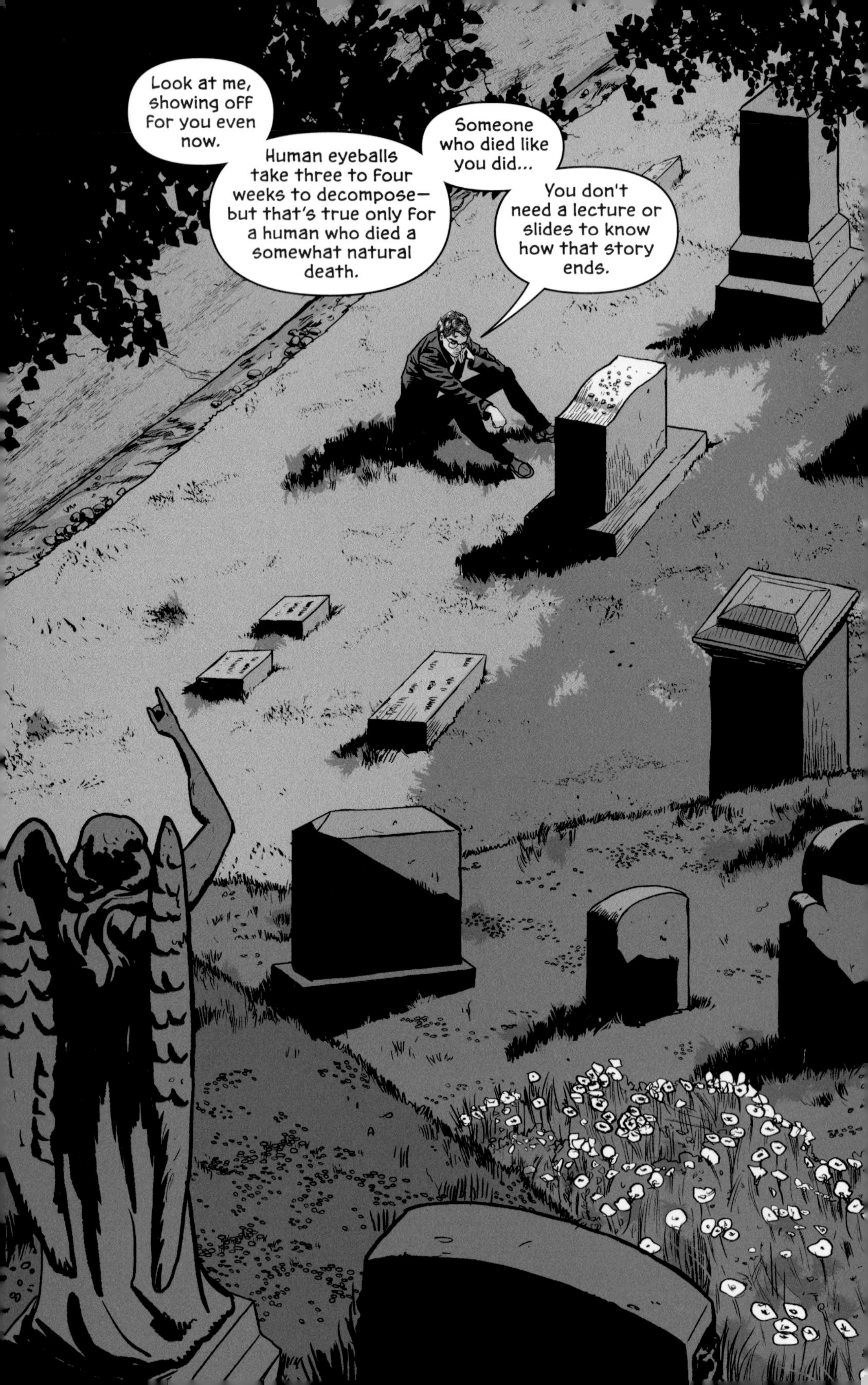
Look at me, showing off for you even now.
Human eyeballs take three to four weeks to decompose—but that's true only for a human who died a somewhat natural death.
Someone who died like you did...
You don't need a lecture or slides to know how that story ends.

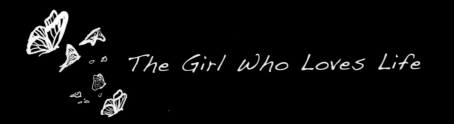

The Girl Who Loves Life

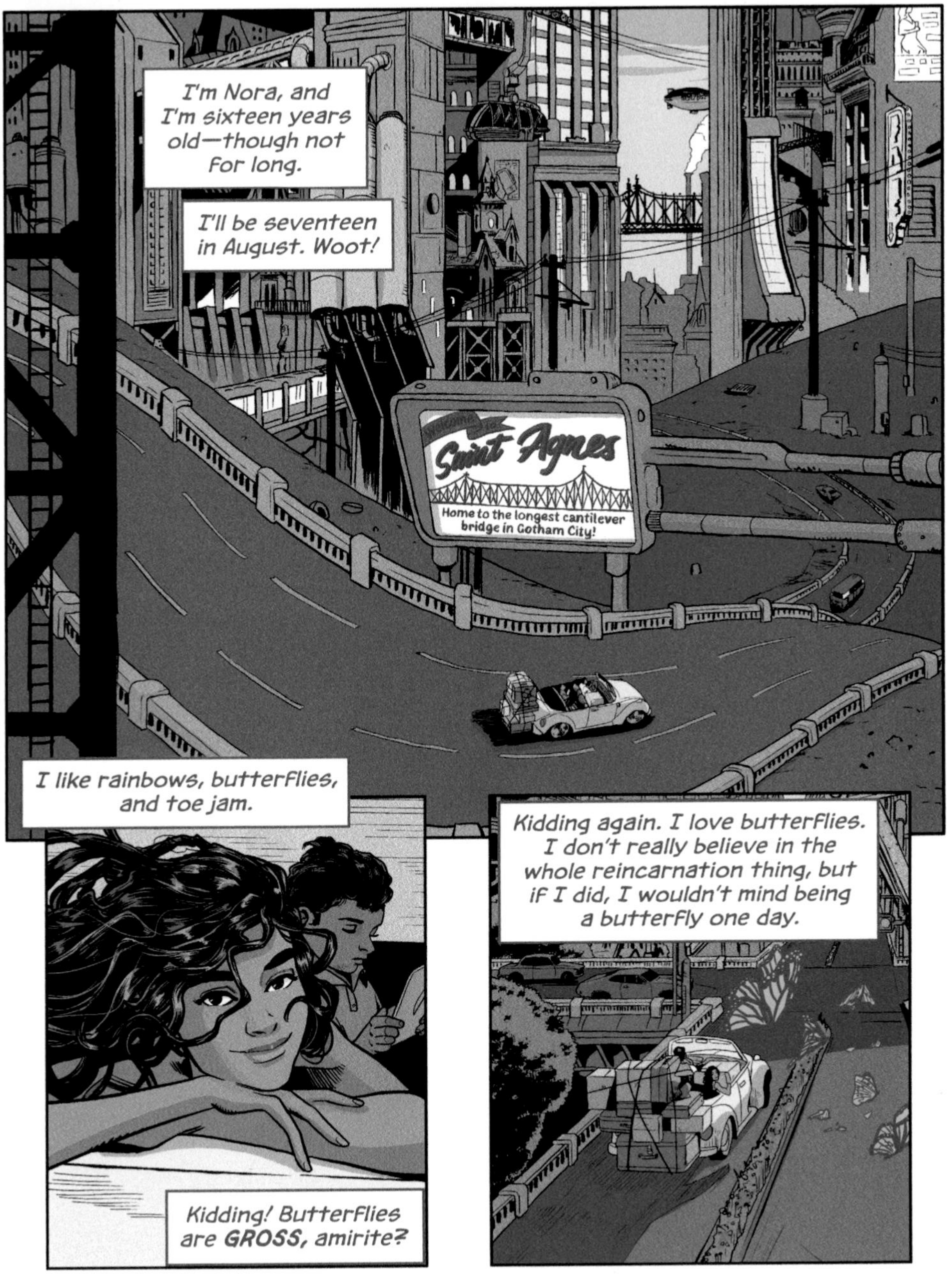
I'm Nora, and I'm sixteen years old—though not for long.
I'll be seventeen in August. Woot!
Saint Agnes
Home to the longest cantilever bridge in Gotham City!
I like rainbows, butterflies, and toe jam.
Kidding! Butterflies are **GROSS**, amirite?
Kidding again. I love butterflies. I don't really believe in the whole reincarnation thing, but if I did, I wouldn't mind being a butterfly one day.

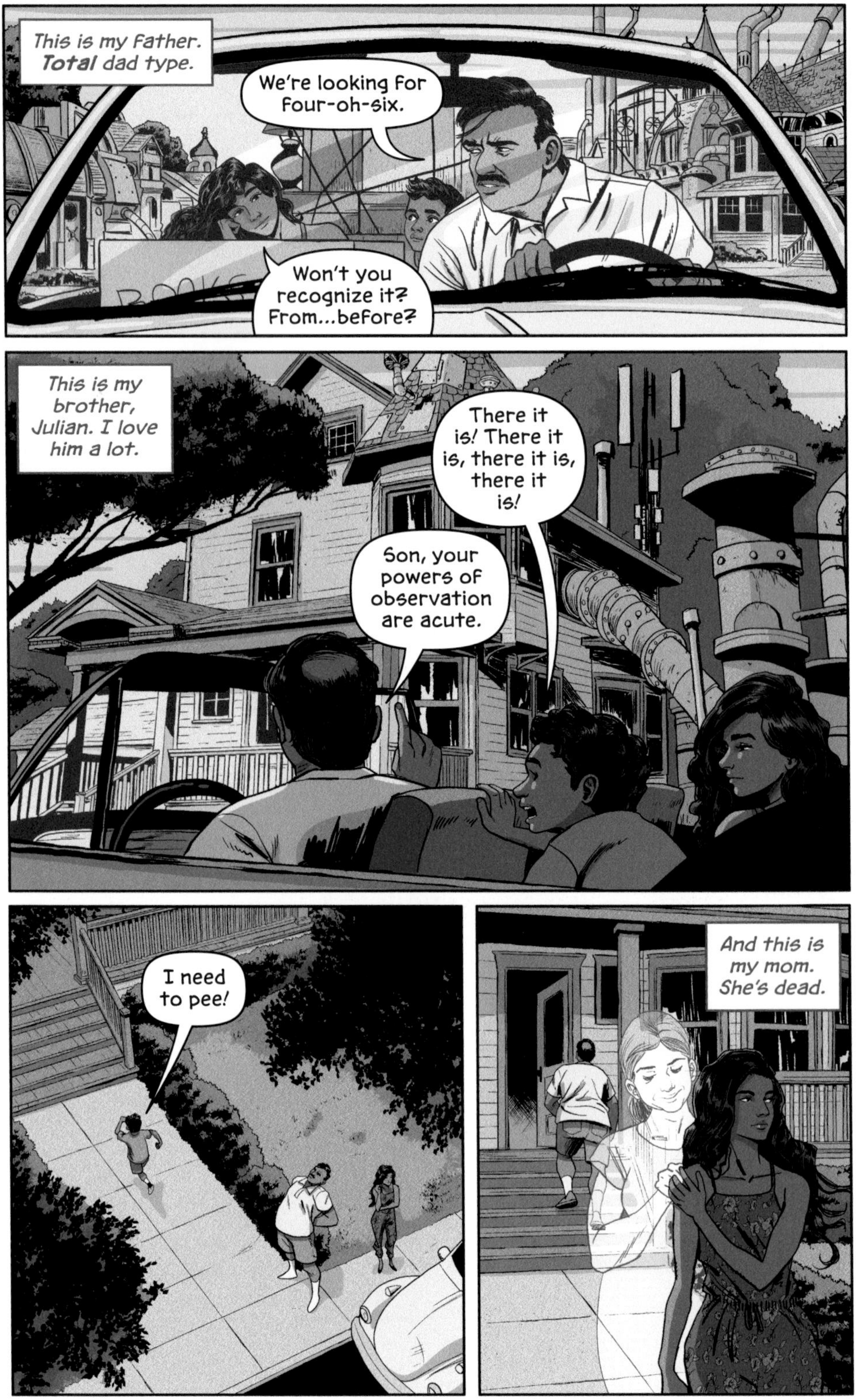
This is my father. Total dad type.
We're looking for four-oh-six.
Won't you recognize it? From...before?
This is my brother, Julian. I love him a lot.
There it is! There it is, there it is, there it is!
Son, your powers of observation are acute.
I need to pee!
And this is my mom. She's dead.

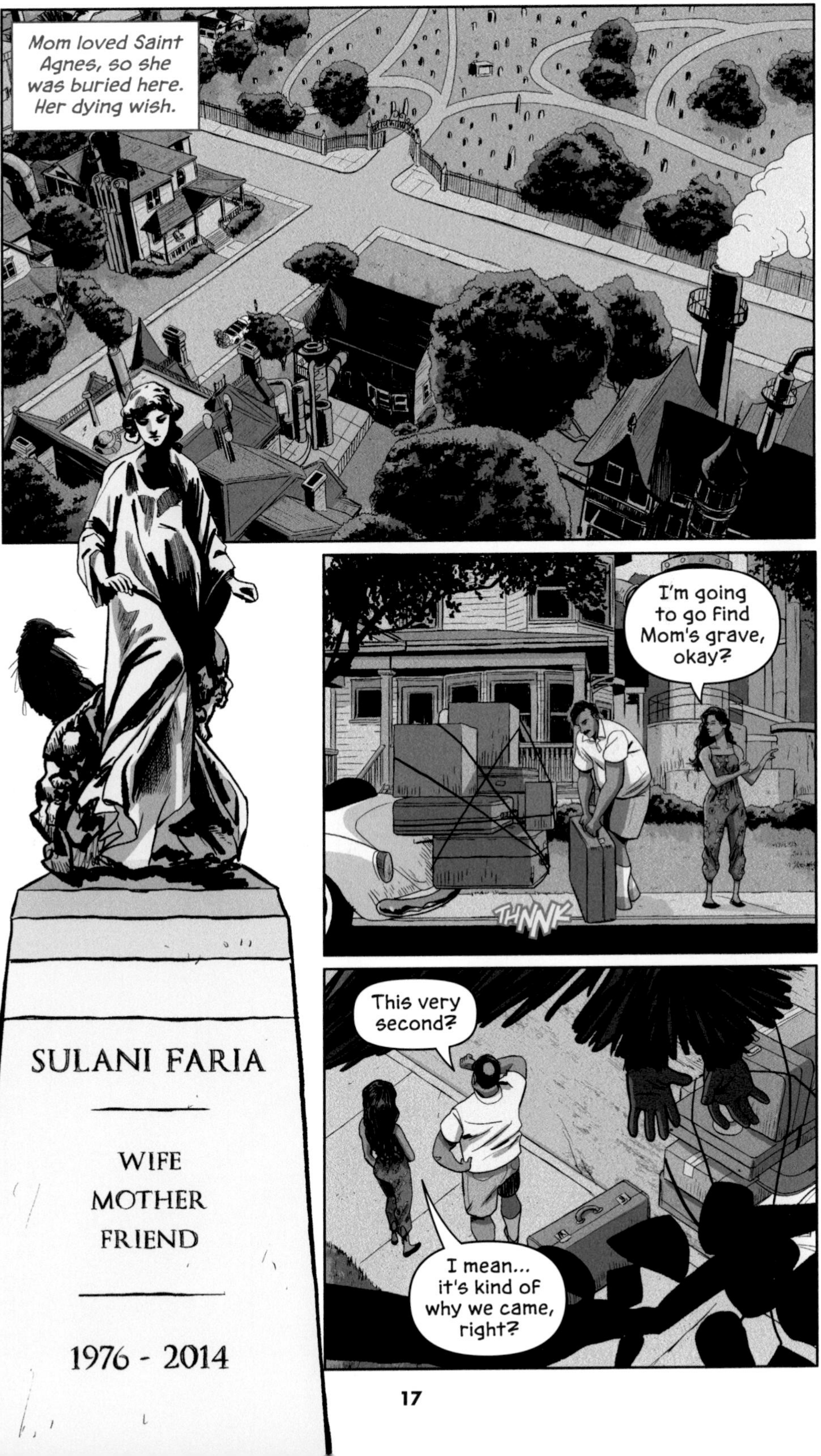
Mom loved Saint Agnes, so she was buried here. Her dying wish.
SULANI FARIA
WIFE
MOTHER
FRIEND
1976 - 2014
I'm going to go find Mom's grave, okay?
THNNK
This very second?
I mean... it's kind of why we came, right?

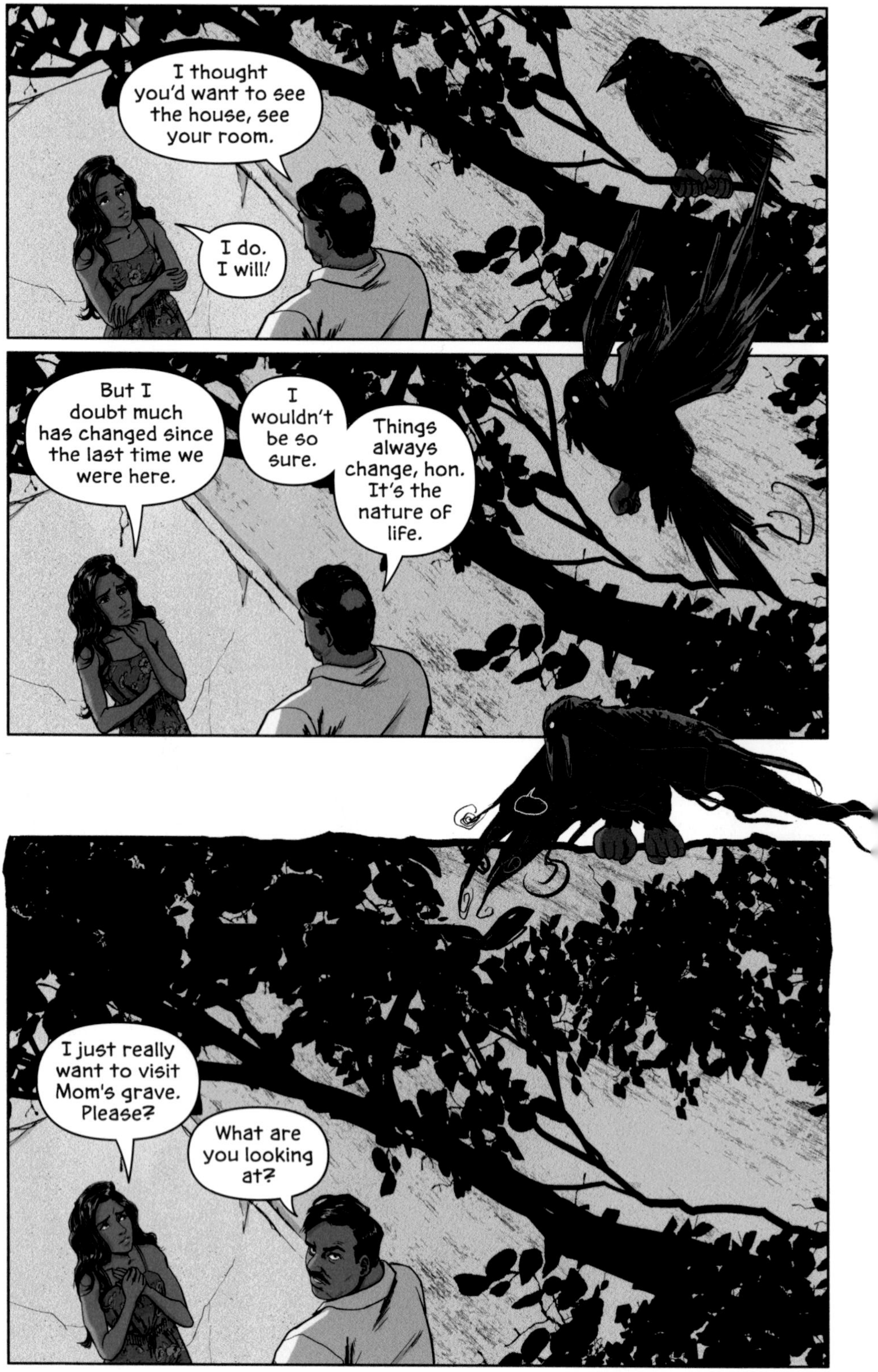
I thought you'd want to see the house, see your room.
I do. I will!
But I doubt much has changed since the last time we were here.
I wouldn't be so sure.
Things always change, hon. It's the nature of life.
I just really want to visit Mom's grave. Please?
What are you looking at?

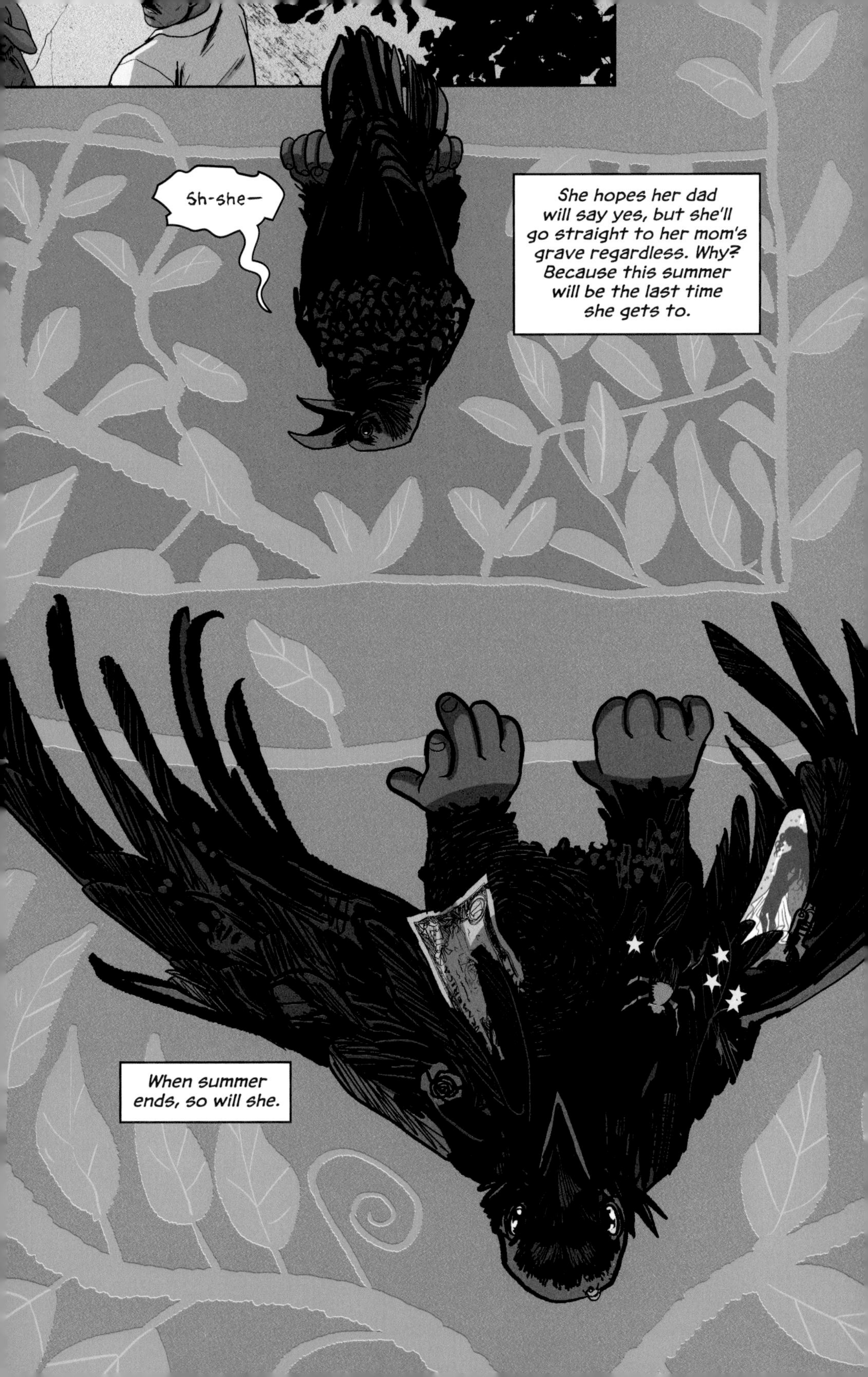
Sh-she—
She hopes her dad will say yes, but she'll go straight to her mom's grave regardless. Why? Because this summer will be the last time she gets to.
When summer ends, so will she.

The Boy Who Tries to Move On

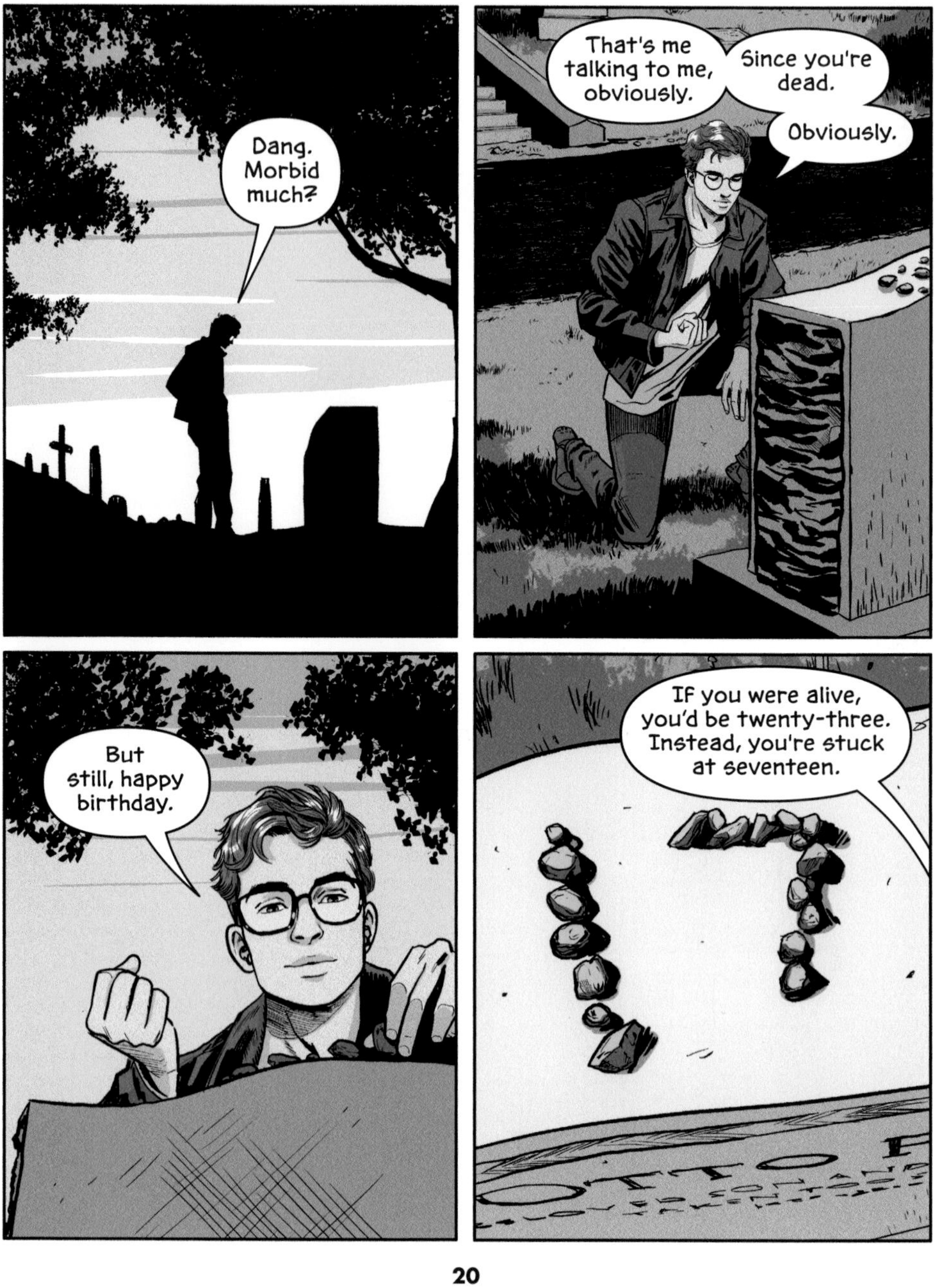

Dang. Morbid much?
That's me talking to me, obviously.
Since you're dead.
Obviously.
But still, happy birthday.
If you were alive, you'd be twenty-three. Instead, you're stuck at seventeen.

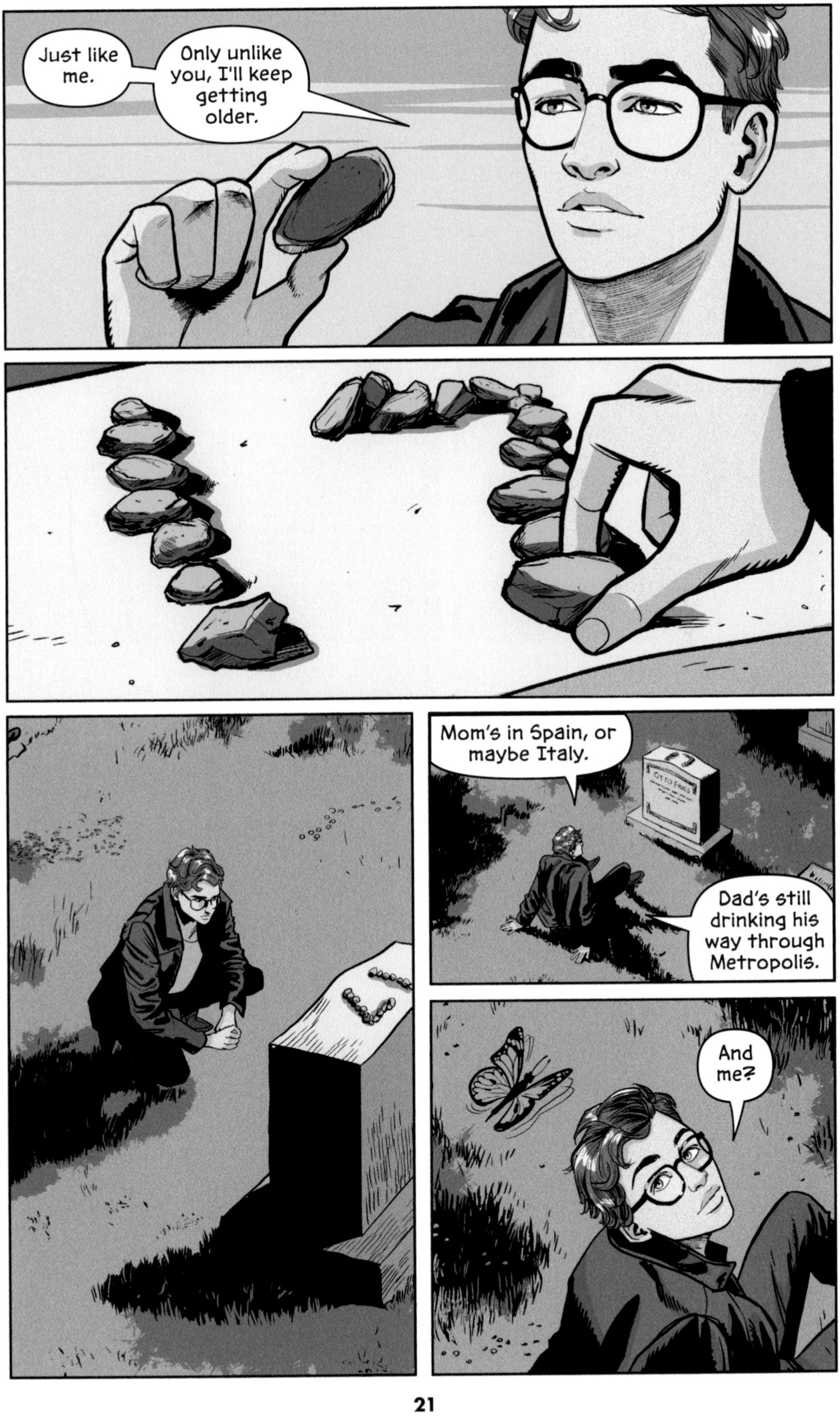
Just like me.
Only unlike you, I'll keep getting older.
Mom's in Spain, or maybe Italy.
Dad's still drinking his way through Metropolis.
And me?

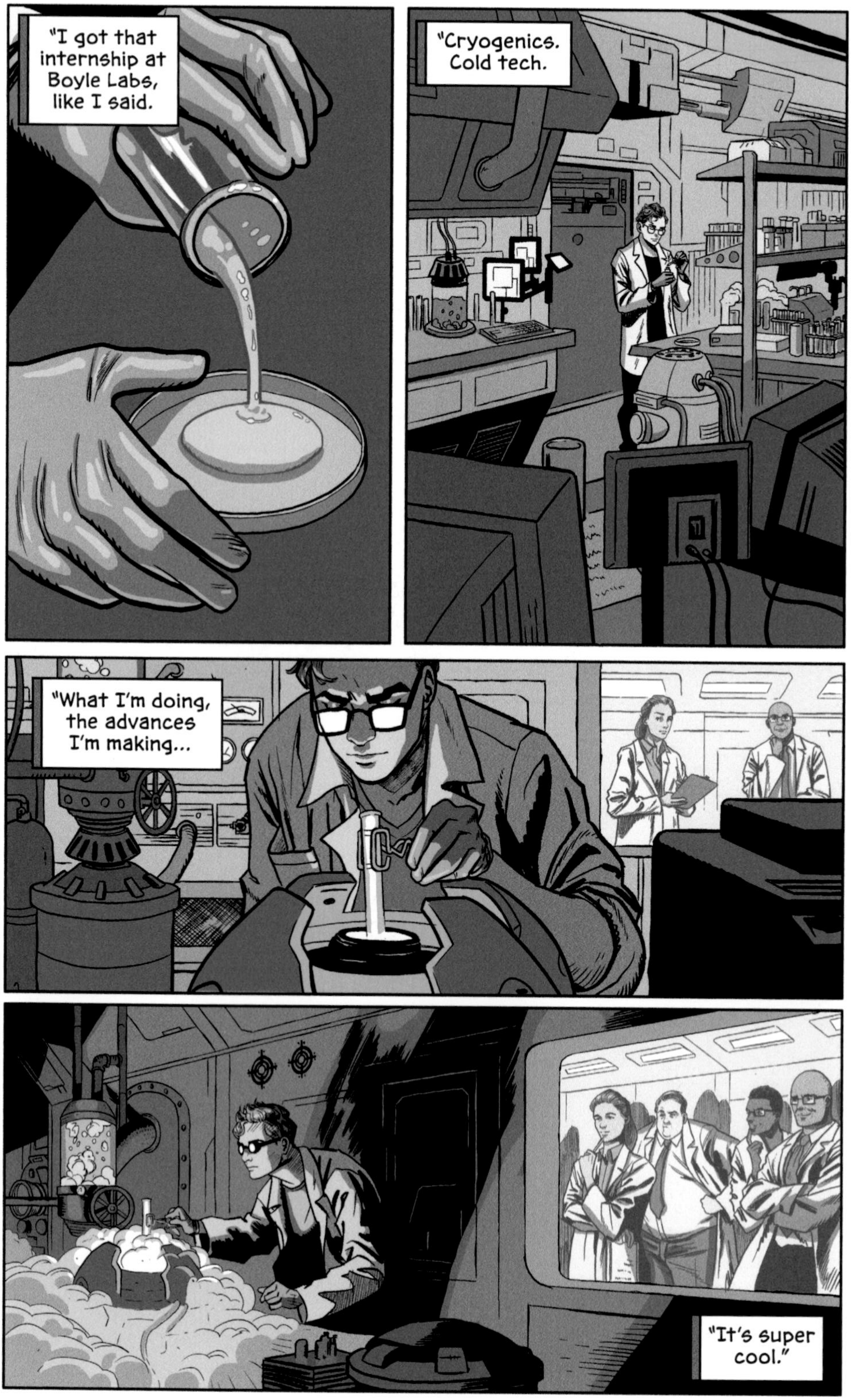
"I got that internship at Boyle Labs, like I said.
"Cryogenics. Cold tech.
"What I'm doing, the advances I'm making...
"It's super cool."

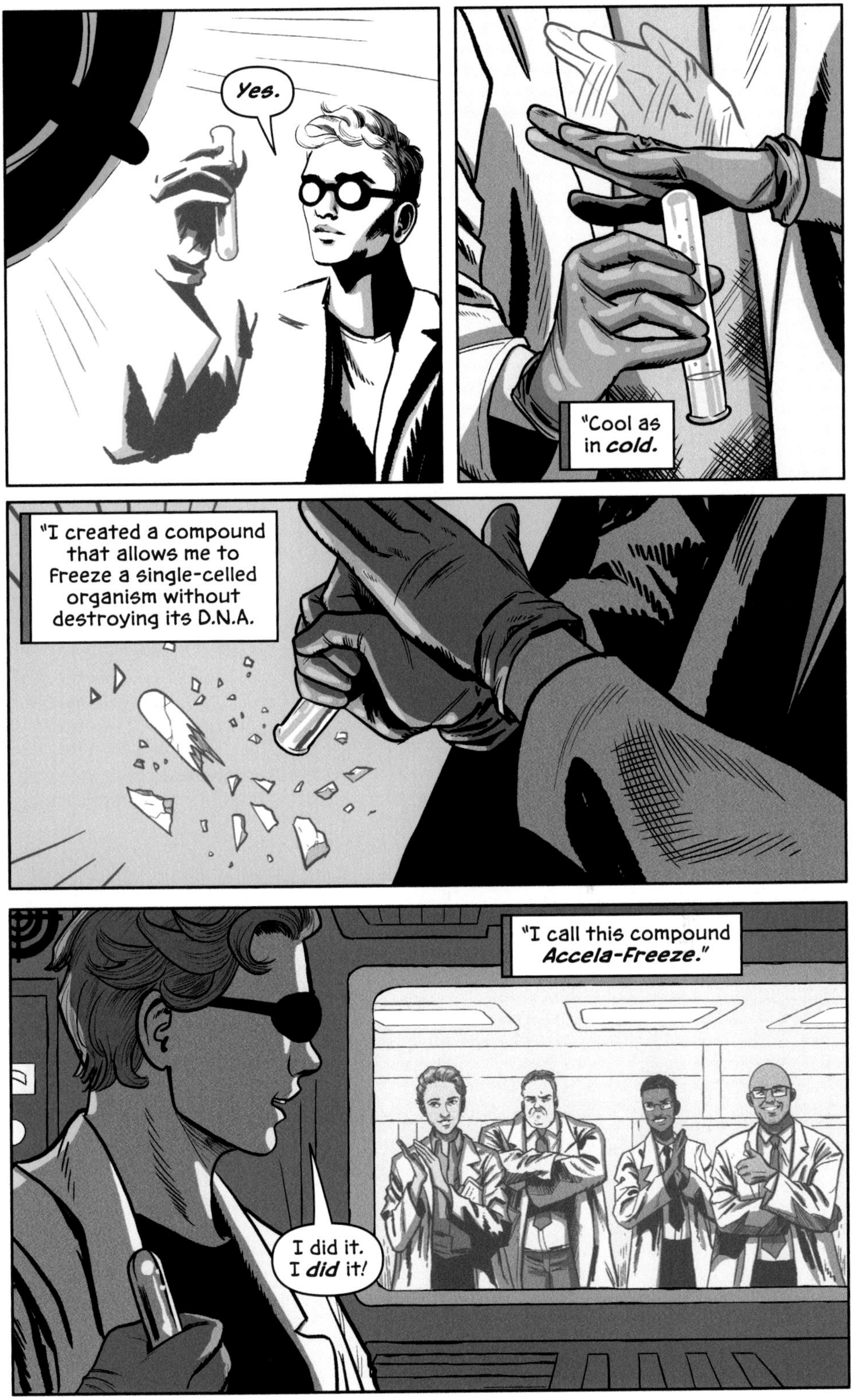

Yes.
"Cool as in *cold*.
"I created a compound that allows me to freeze a single-celled organism without destroying its D.N.A.
"I call this compound *Accela-Freeze*."
I did it. I *did* it!

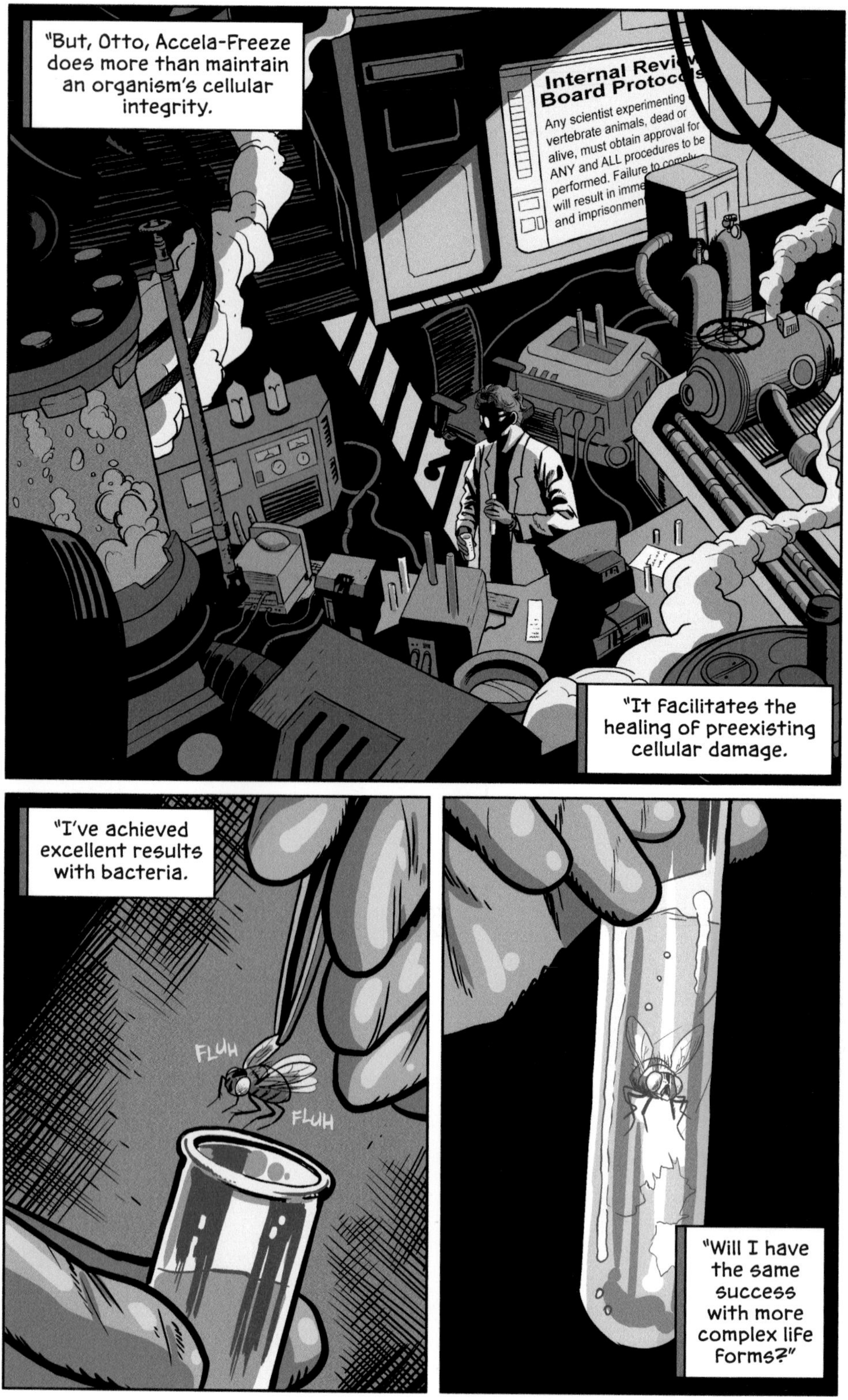
"But, Otto, Accela-Freeze does more than maintain an organism's cellular integrity.
Internal Revi
Board Protoc
Any scientist experimenting
vertebrate animals, dead or
alive, must obtain approval for
ANY and ALL procedures to be
performed. Failure to comply
will result in imme
and imprisonment
"It facilitates the healing of preexisting cellular damage.
"I've achieved excellent results with bacteria.
FLUH
FLUH
"Will I have the same success with more complex life forms?"

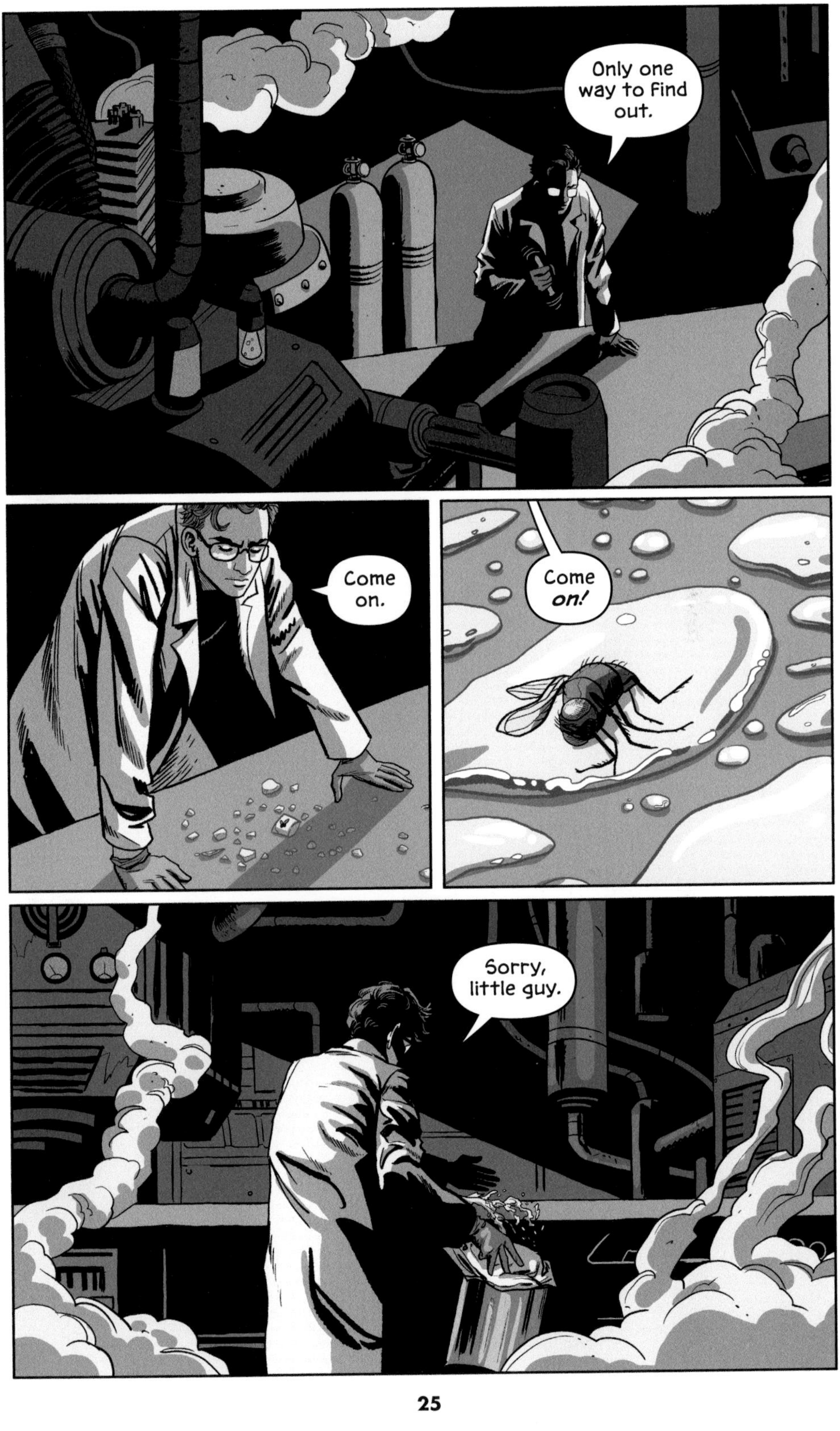
Only one way to find out.
Come on.
Come on!
Sorry, little guy.

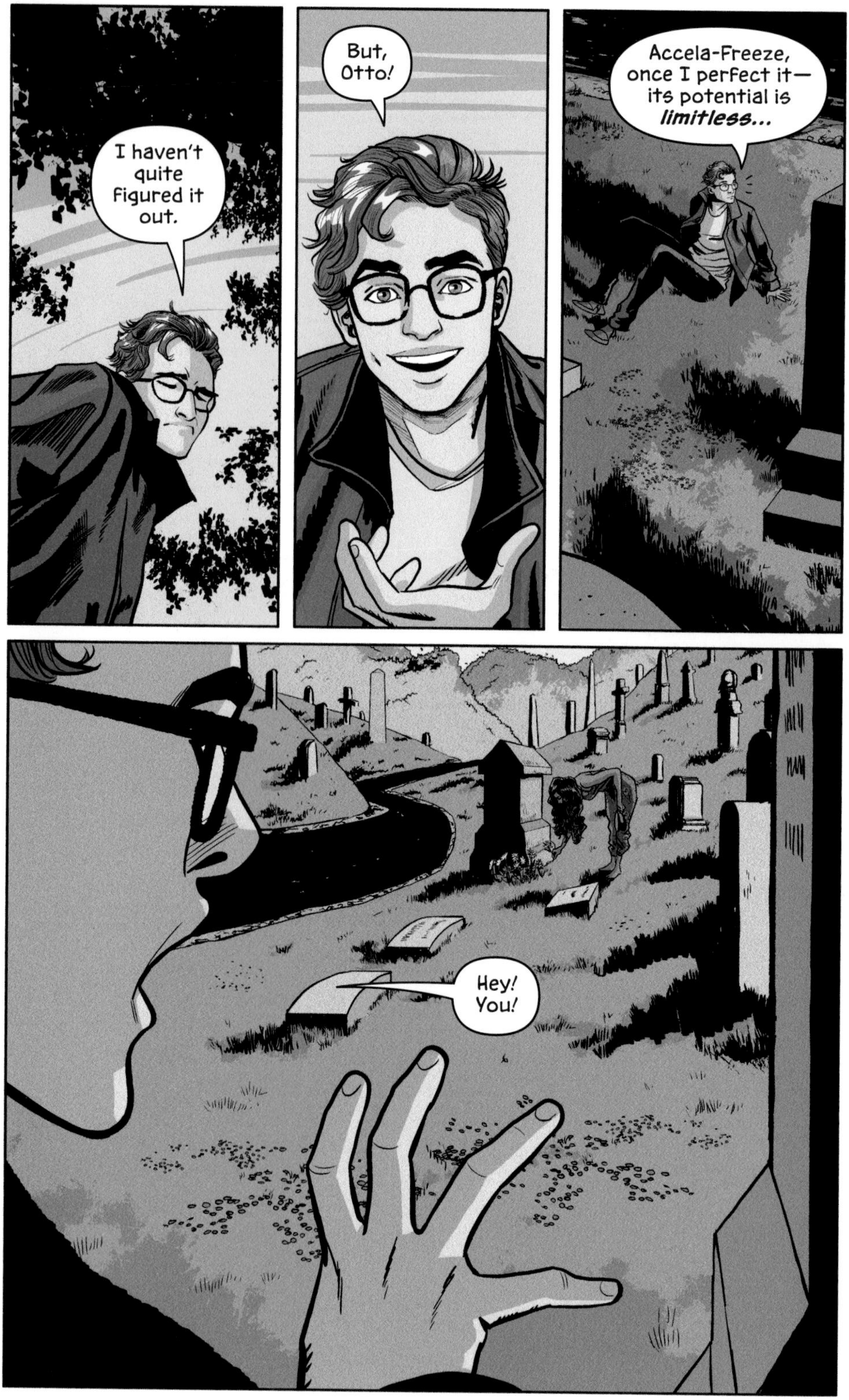
I haven't quite figured it out.
But, Otto!
Accela-Freeze, once I perfect it—its potential is *limitless...*
Hey! You!

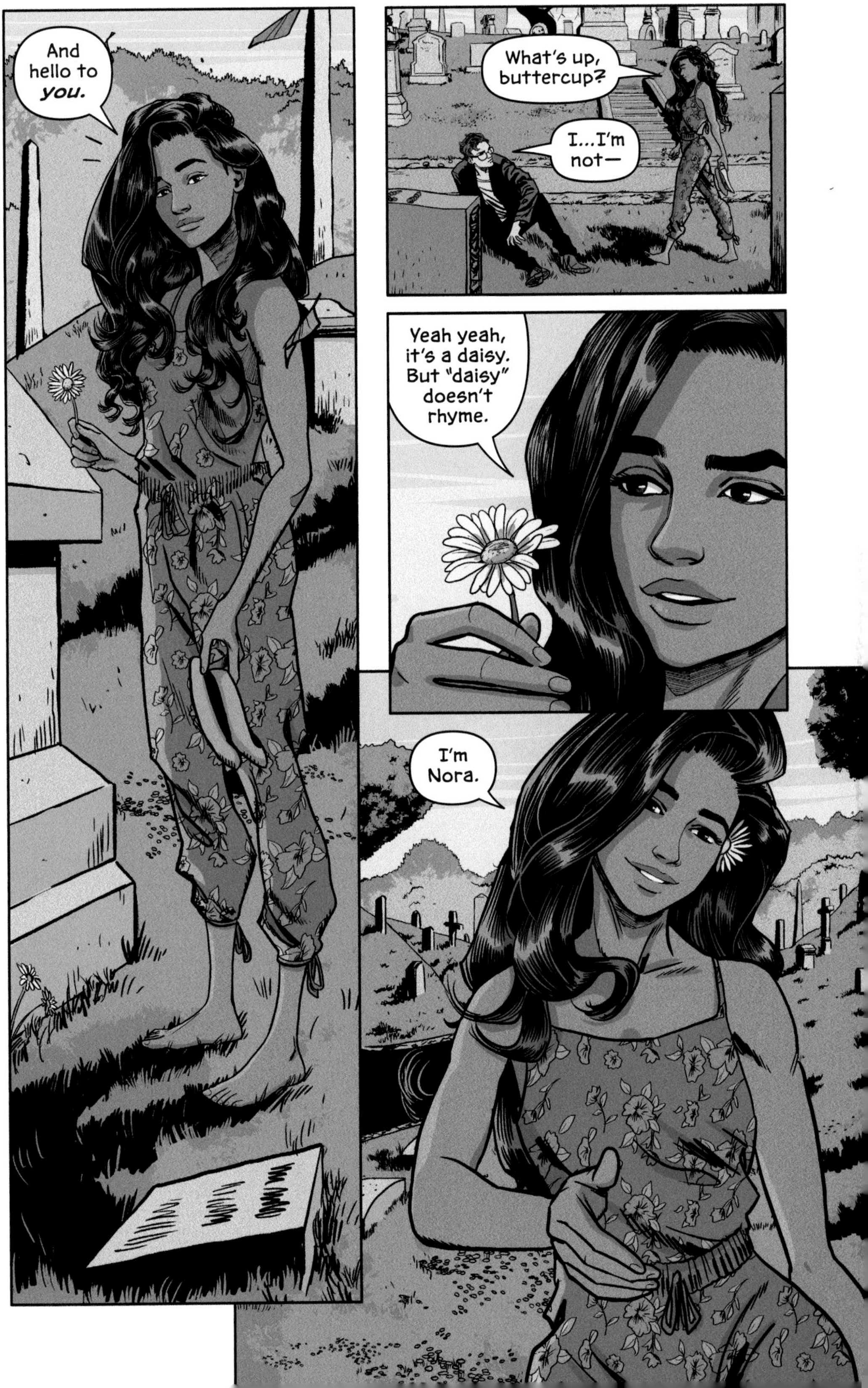
And hello to *you.*
What's up, buttercup?
I...I'm not—
Yeah yeah, it's a daisy. But "daisy" doesn't rhyme.
I'm Nora.

The Girl Who Refuses to Look Back

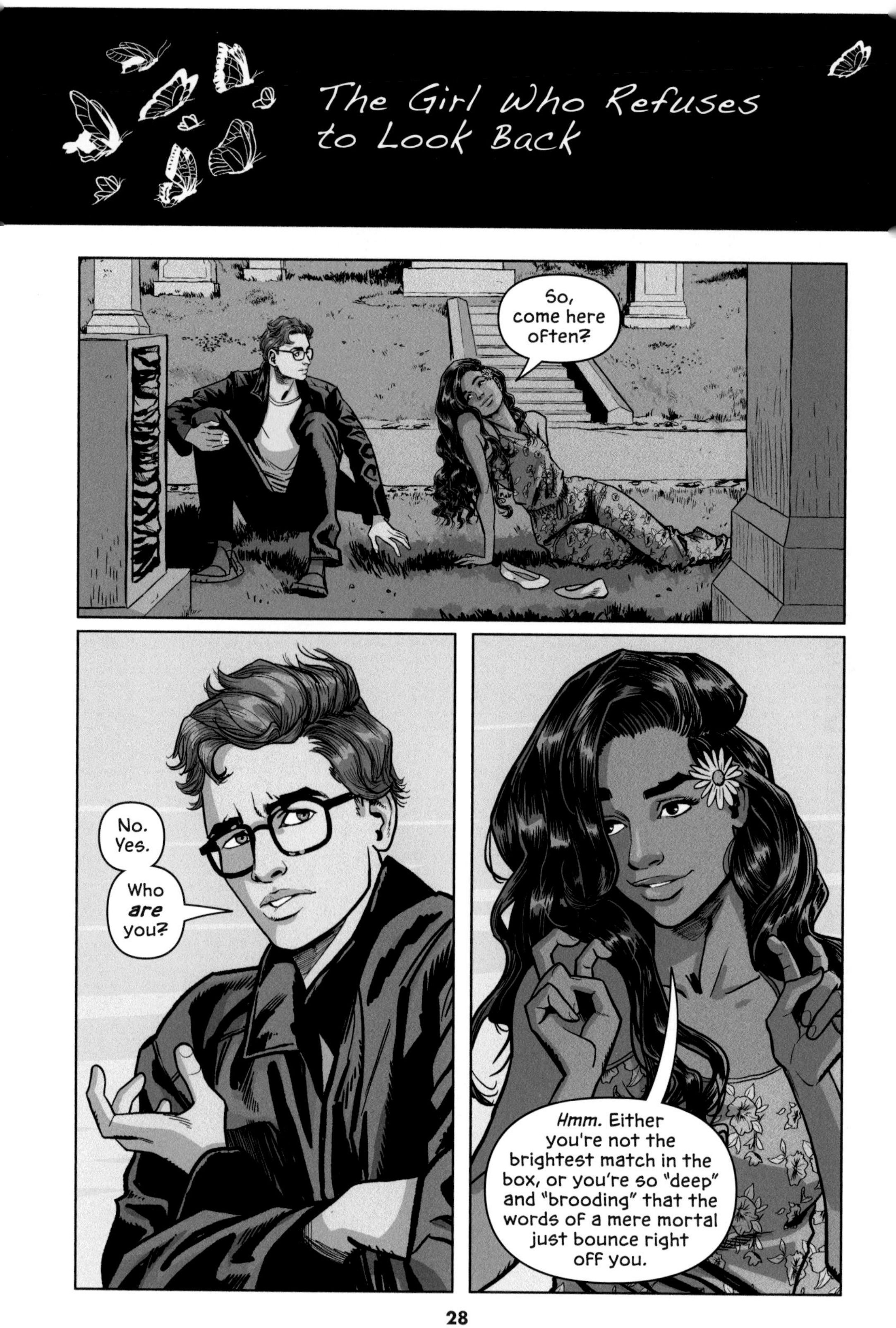
So, come here often?
No. Yes.
Who *are* you?
Hmm. Either you're not the brightest match in the box, or you're so "deep" and "brooding" that the words of a mere mortal just bounce right off you.

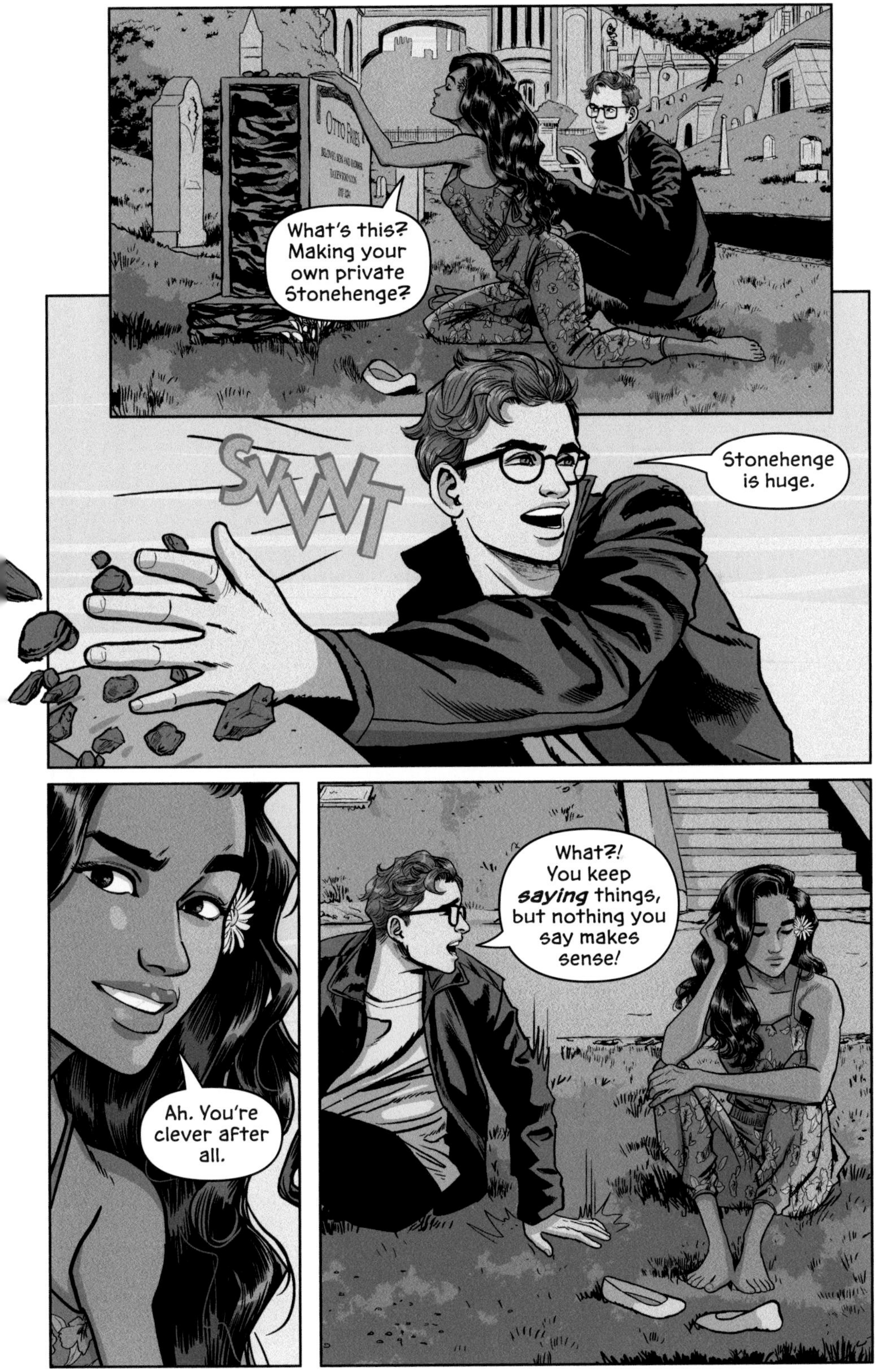
OTTO FRIES
What's this? Making your own private Stonehenge?
SVVVT
Stonehenge is huge.
Ah. You're clever after all.
What?! You keep *saying* things, but nothing you say makes sense!

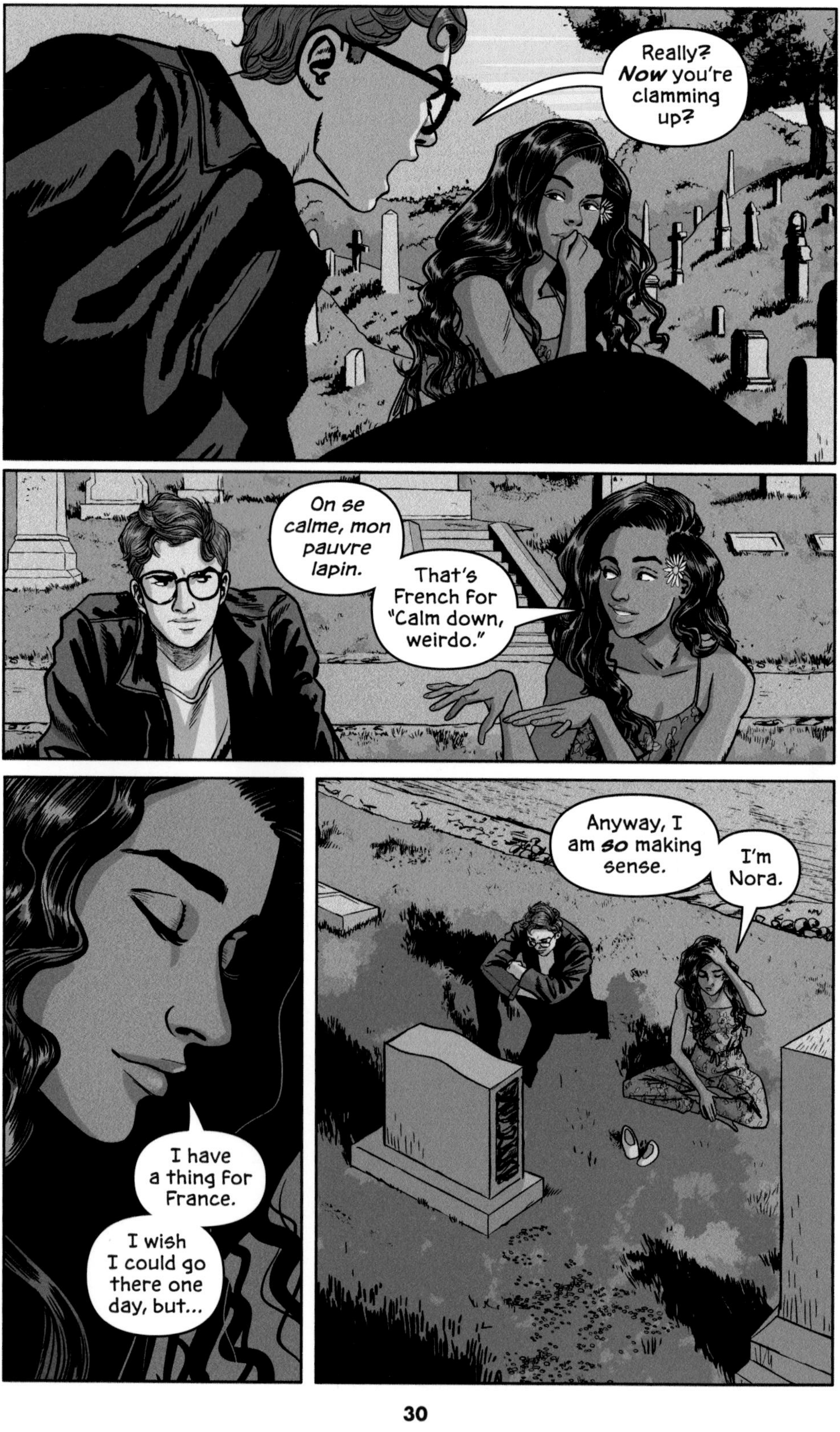
Really? *Now* you're clamming up?
On se calme, mon pauvre lapin.
That's French for "Calm down, weirdo."
I have a thing for France.
I wish I could go there one day, but...
Anyway, I am *so* making sense.
I'm Nora.

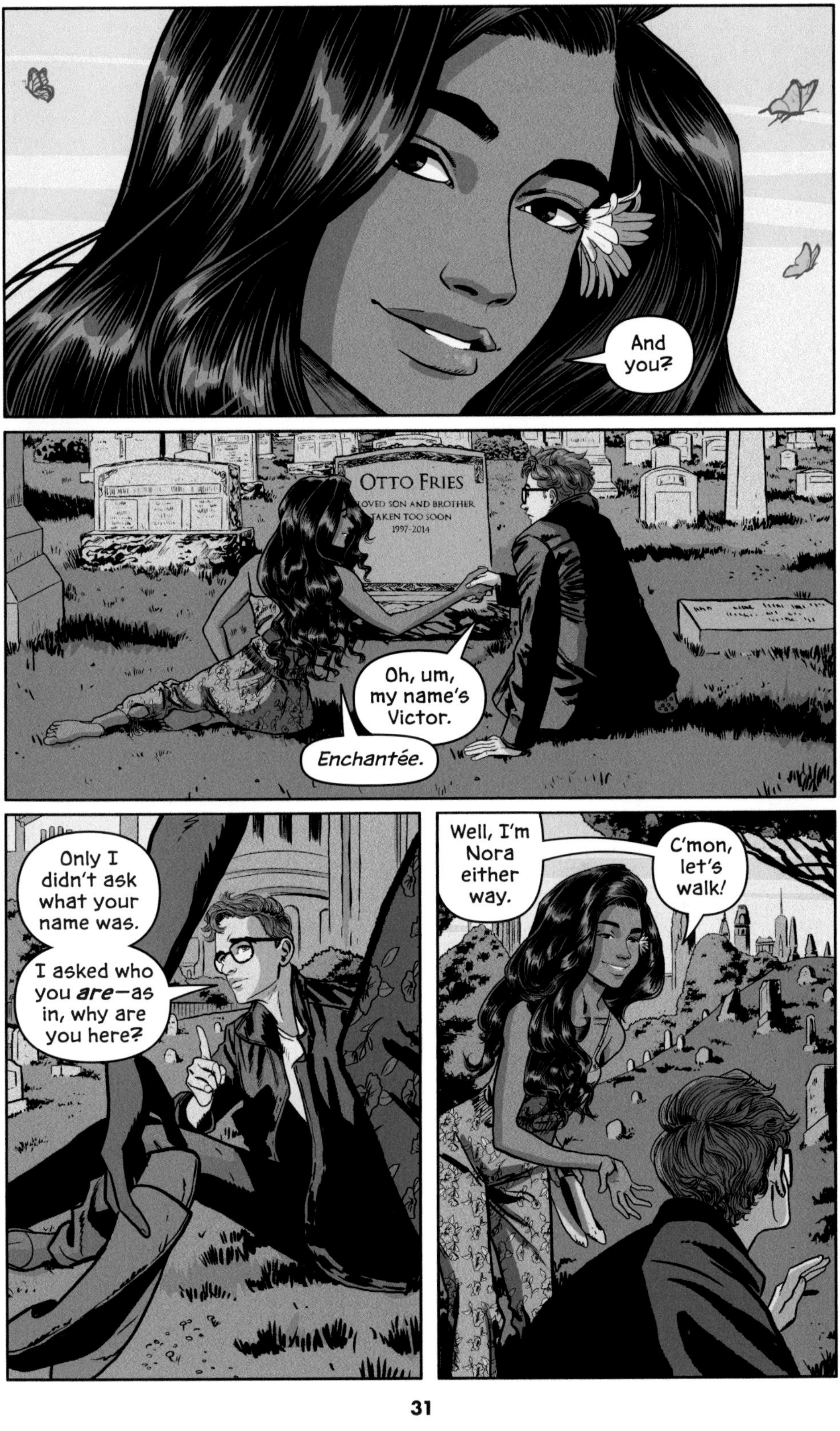
And you?
OTTO FRIES
LOVED SON AND BROTHER
TAKEN TOO SOON
1997–2014
Oh, um, my name's Victor.
Enchantée.
Only I didn't ask what your name was.
I asked who you *are*—as in, why are you here?
Well, I'm Nora either way.
C'mon, let's walk!

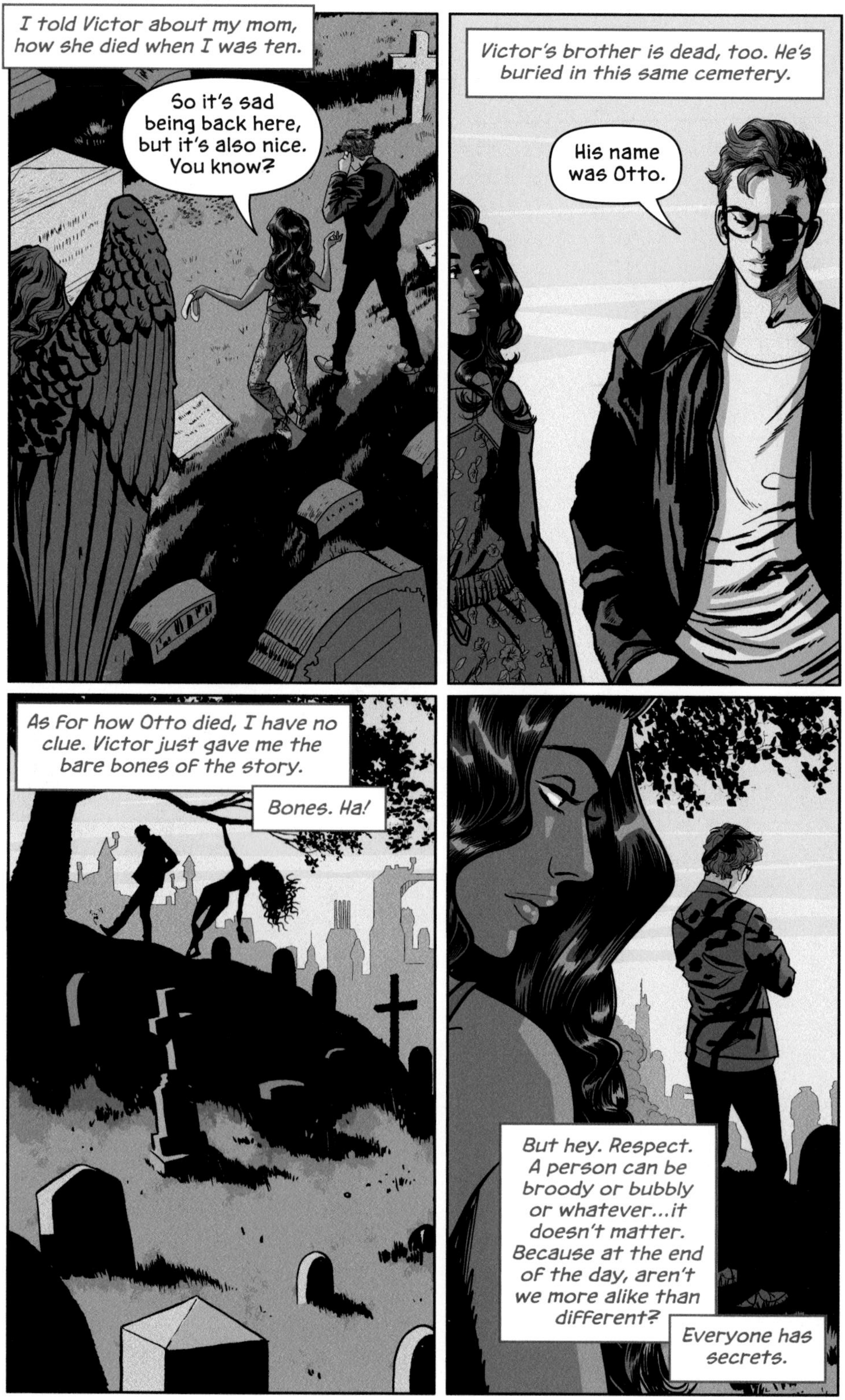

I told Victor about my mom, how she died when I was ten.
So it's sad being back here, but it's also nice. You know?
Victor's brother is dead, too. He's buried in this same cemetery.
His name was Otto.
As for how Otto died, I have no clue. Victor just gave me the bare bones of the story.
Bones. Ha!
But hey. Respect. A person can be broody or bubbly or whatever...it doesn't matter. Because at the end of the day, aren't we more alike than different?
Everyone has secrets.

The Boy Who Lives in His Head

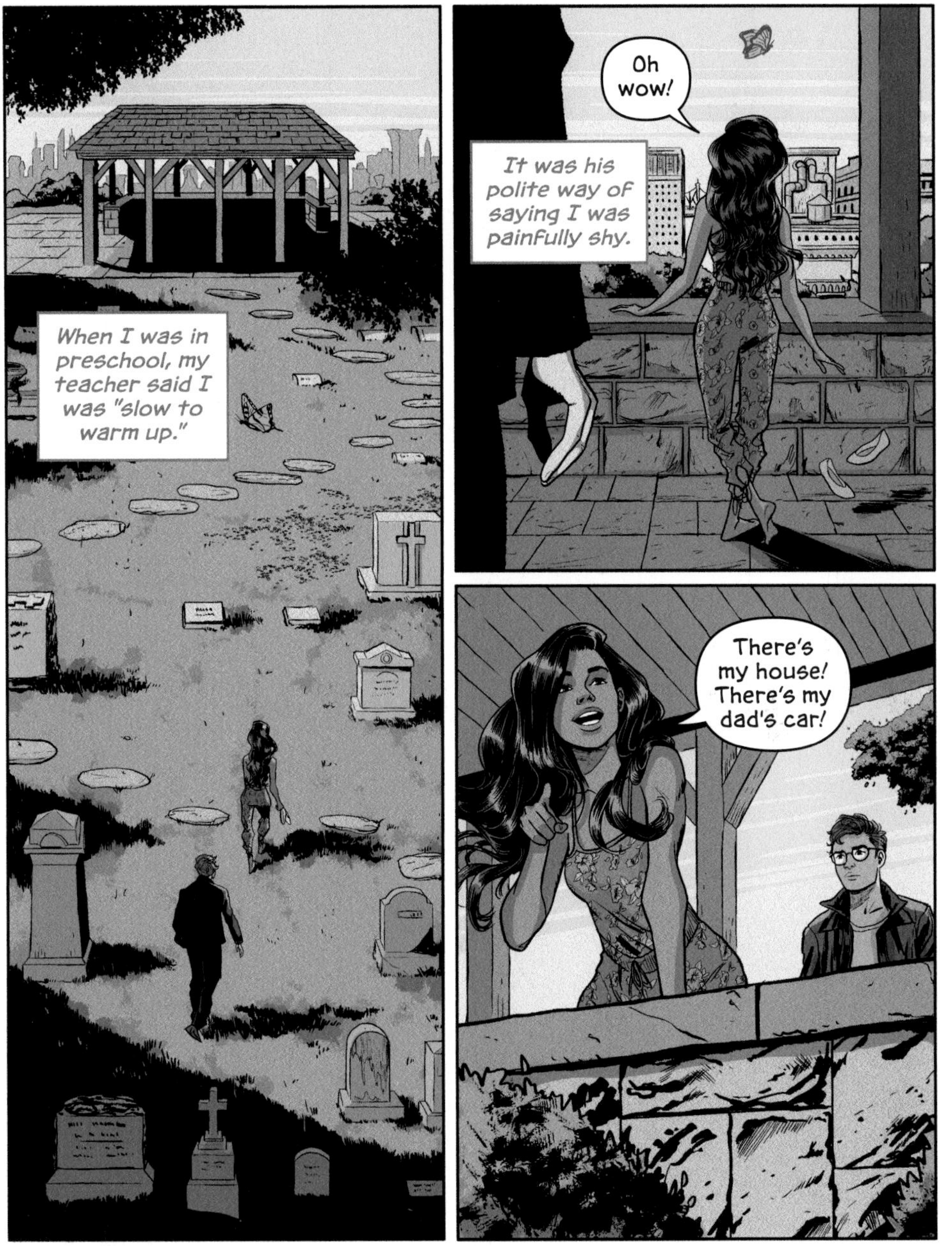
When I was in preschool, my teacher said I was "slow to warm up."
Oh wow!
It was his polite way of saying I was painfully shy.
There's my house! There's my dad's car!

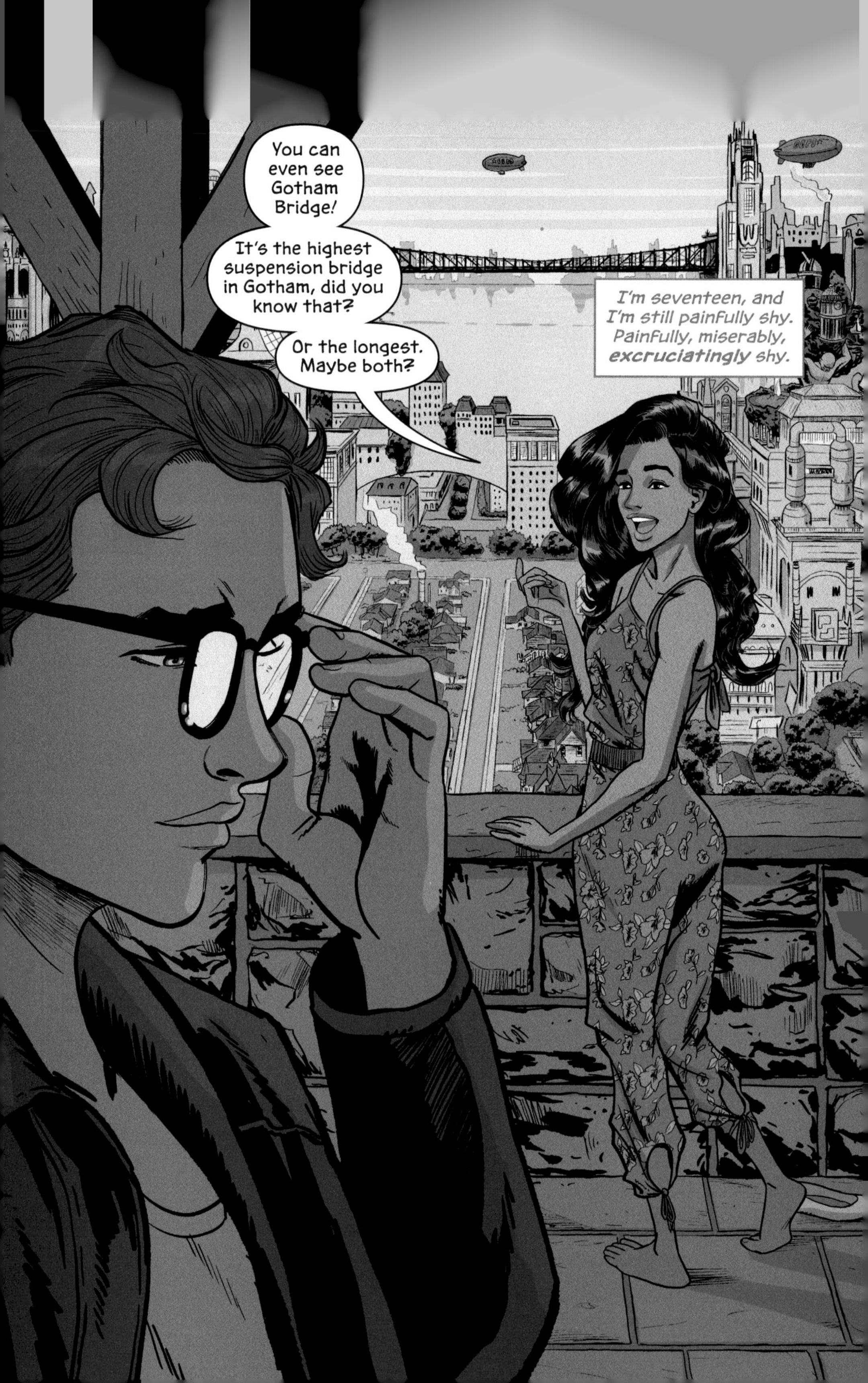
You can even see Gotham Bridge!
It's the highest suspension bridge in Gotham, did you know that?
Or the longest. Maybe both?
I'm seventeen, and I'm still painfully shy. Painfully, miserably, ***excruciatingly*** shy.

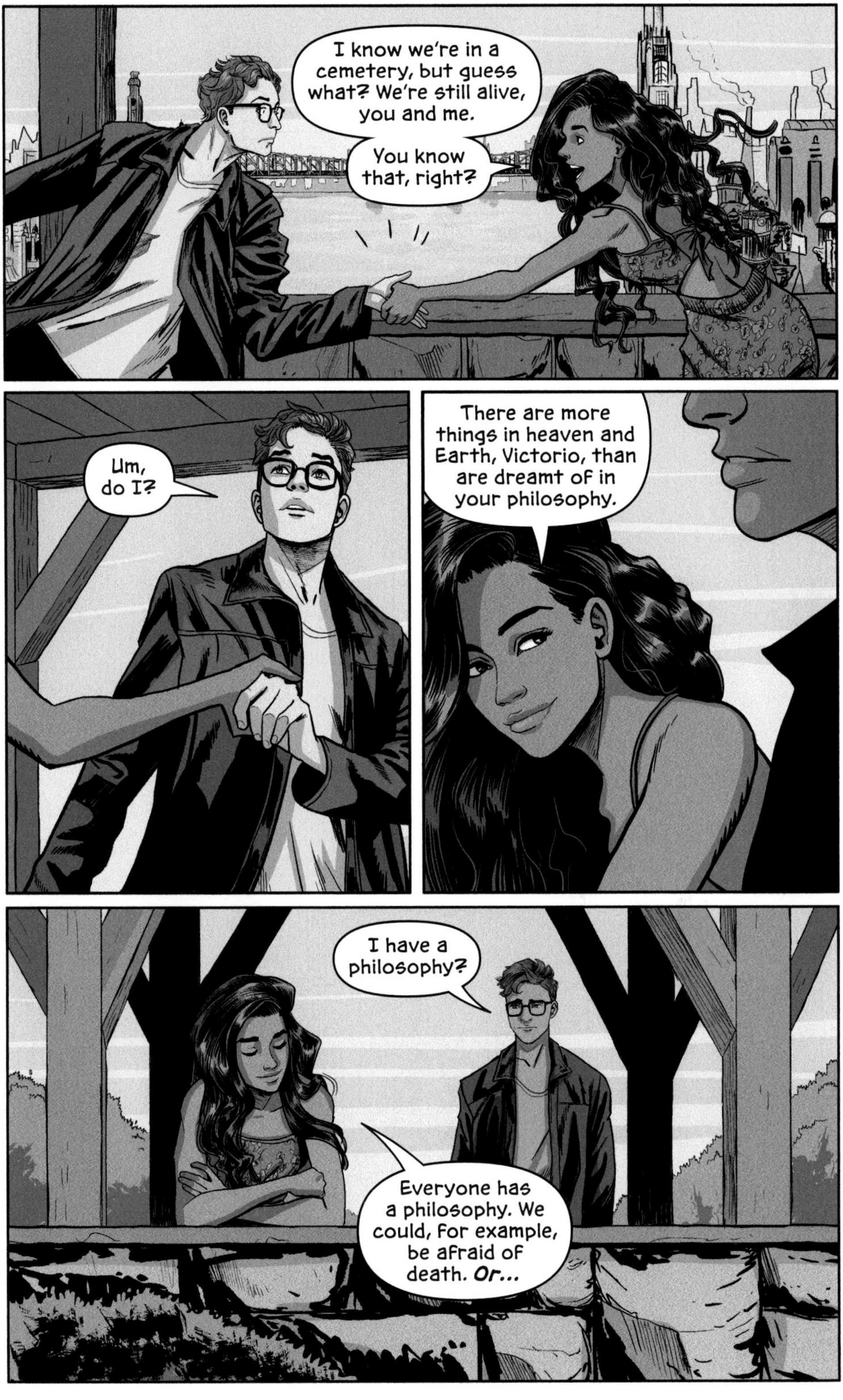
I know we're in a cemetery, but guess what? We're still alive, you and me.
You know that, right?
Um, do I?
There are more things in heaven and Earth, Victorio, than are dreamt of in your philosophy.
I have a philosophy?
Everyone has a philosophy. We could, for example, be afraid of death. *Or...*

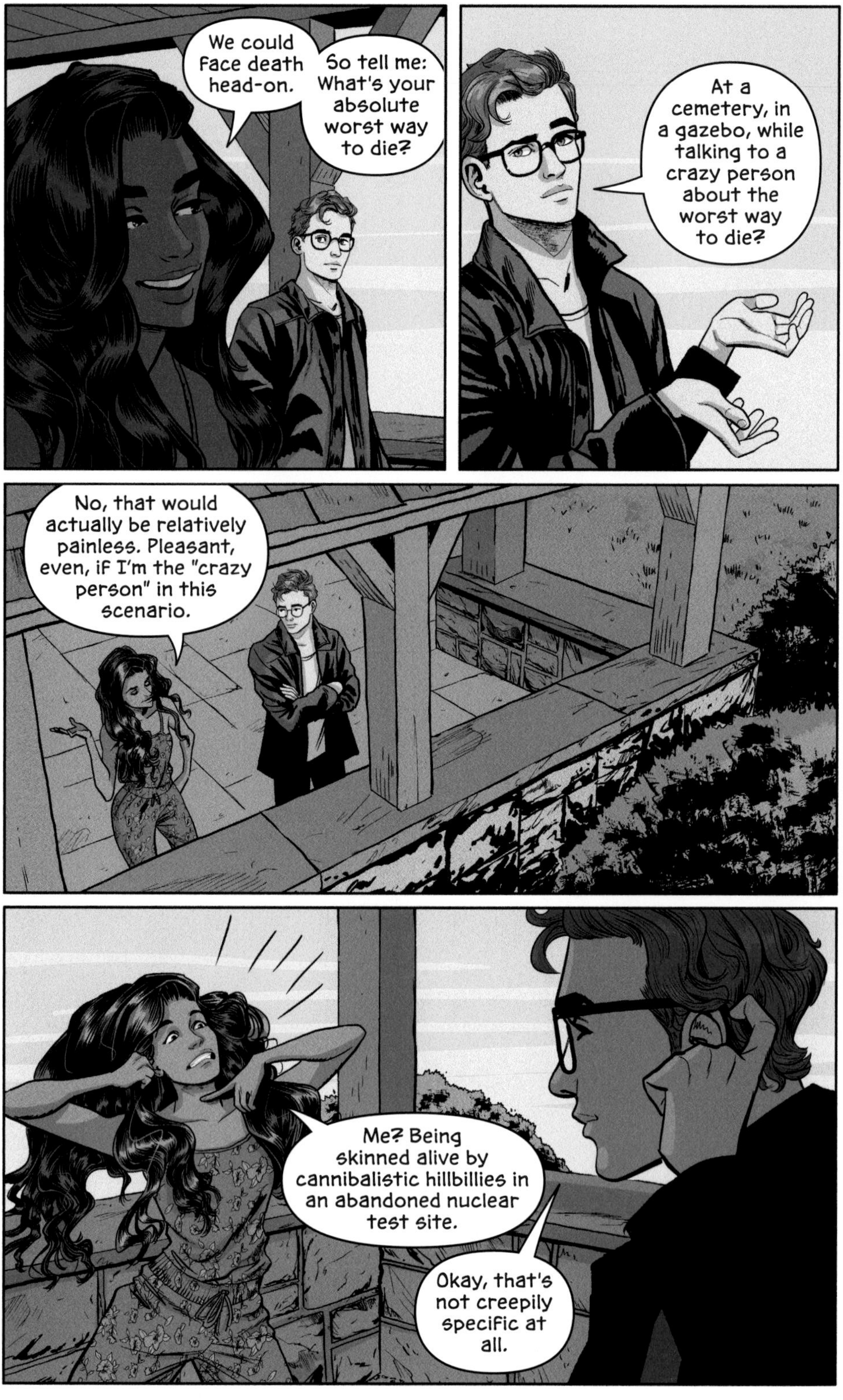

We could face death head-on.
So tell me: What's your absolute worst way to die?
At a cemetery, in a gazebo, while talking to a crazy person about the worst way to die?
No, that would actually be relatively painless. Pleasant, even, if I'm the "crazy person" in this scenario.
Me? Being skinned alive by cannibalistic hillbillies in an abandoned nuclear test site.
Okay, that's not creepily specific at all.

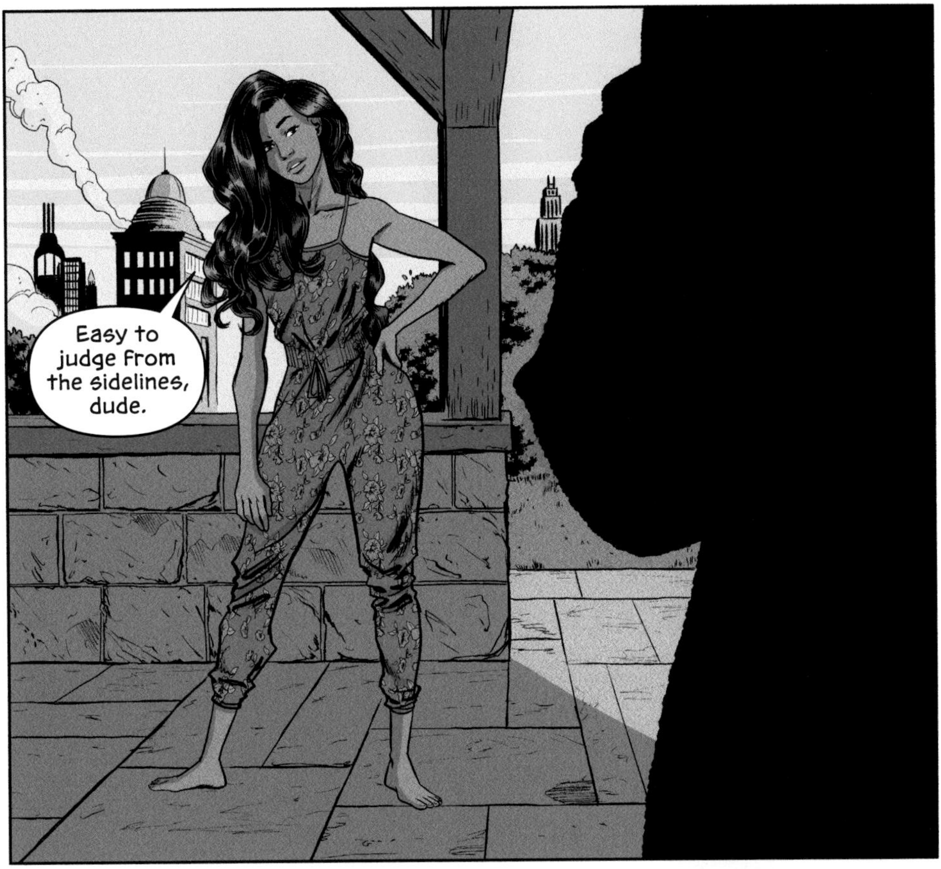
Easy to judge from the sidelines, dude.

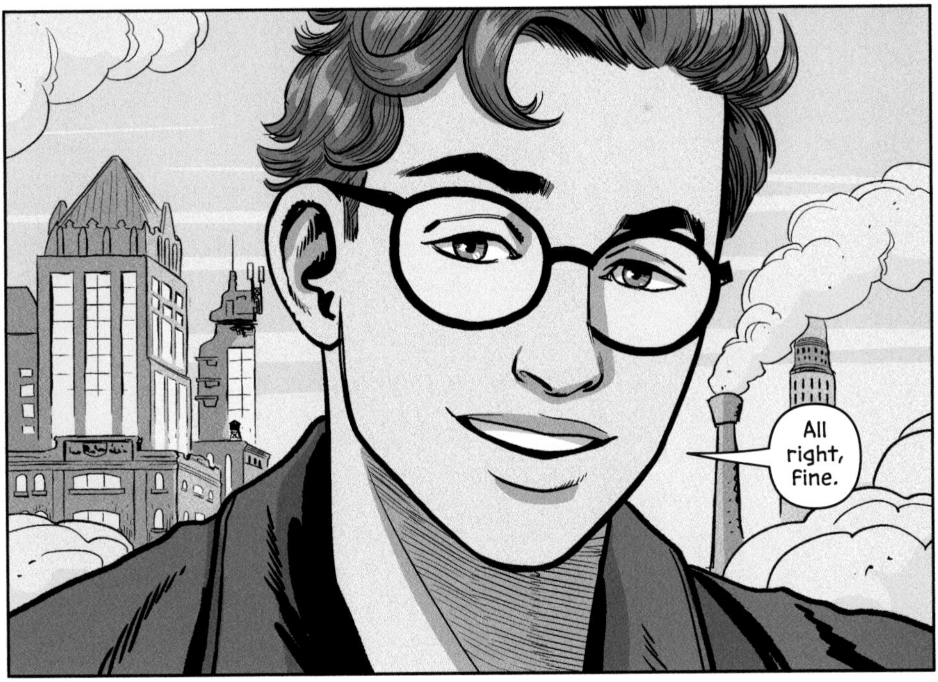
All right, fine.

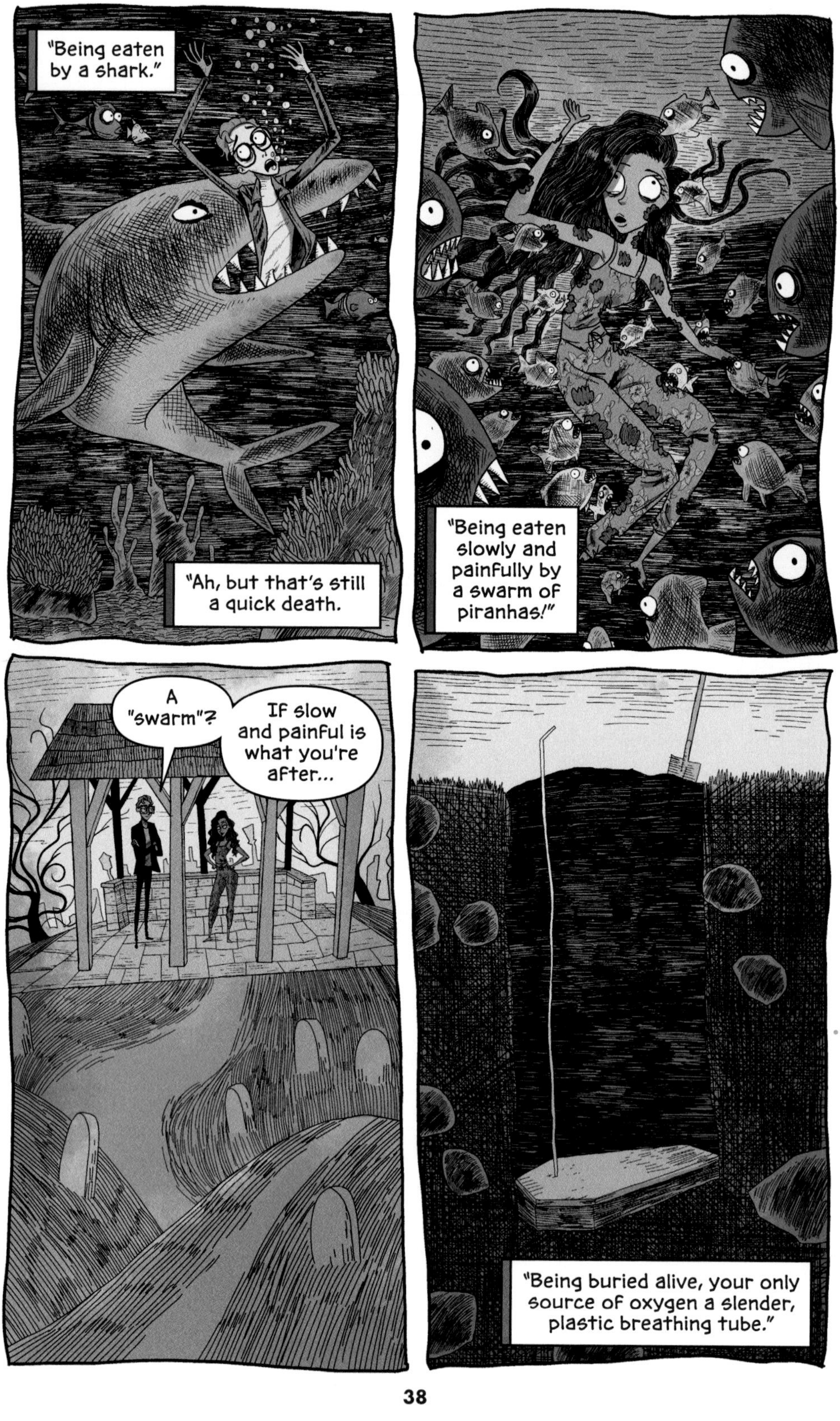
"Being eaten
by a shark."
"Ah, but that's still
a quick death.
"Being eaten
slowly and
painfully by
a swarm of
piranhas!"
A
"swarm"?
If slow
and painful is
what you're
after...
"Being buried alive, your only
source of oxygen a slender,
plastic breathing tube."

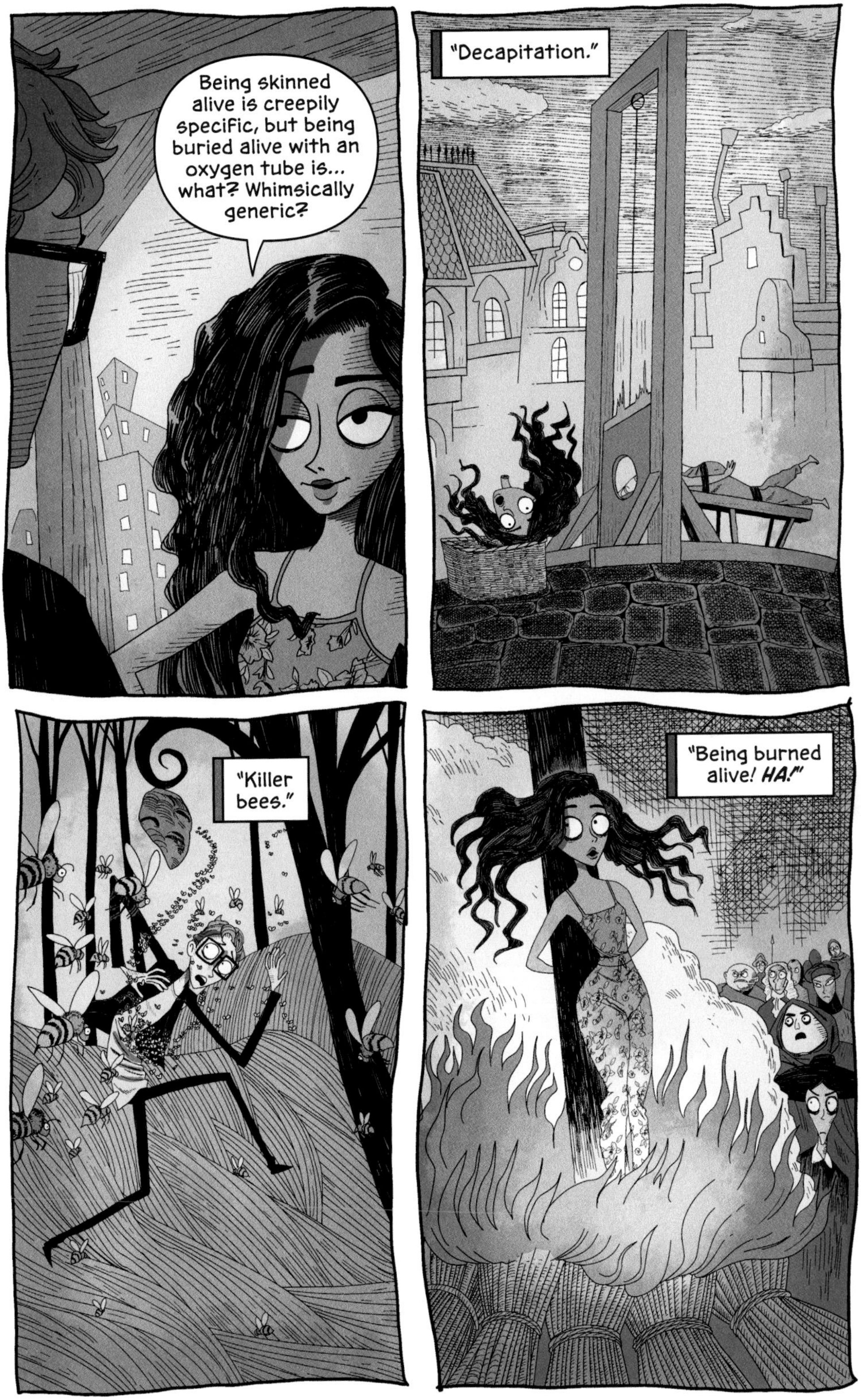
Being skinned alive is creepily specific, but being buried alive with an oxygen tube is... what? Whimsically generic?
"Decapitation."
"Killer bees."
"Being burned alive! HA!"

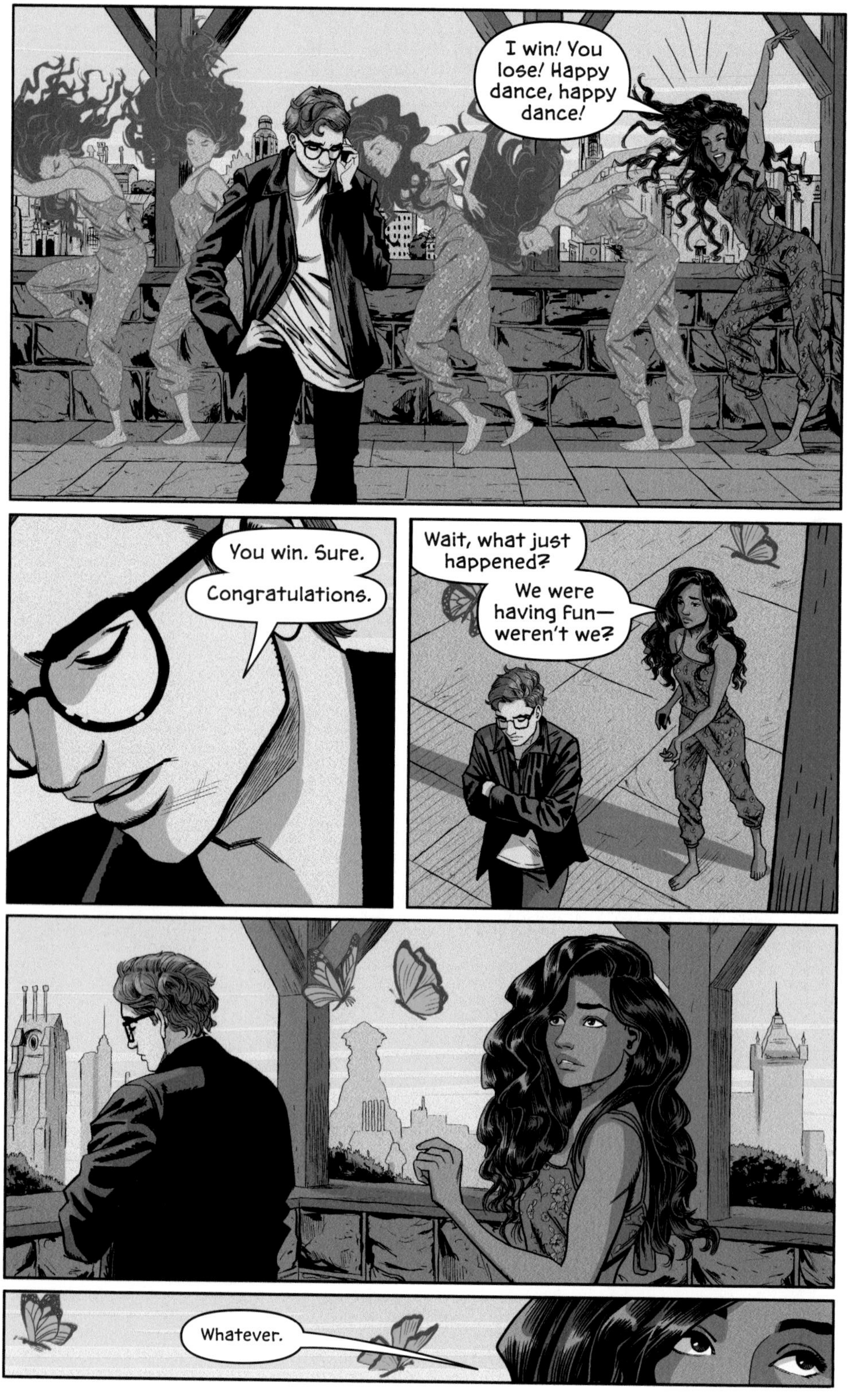
I win! You lose! Happy dance, happy dance!
You win. Sure.
Congratulations.
Wait, what just happened?
We were having fun—weren't we?
Whatever.

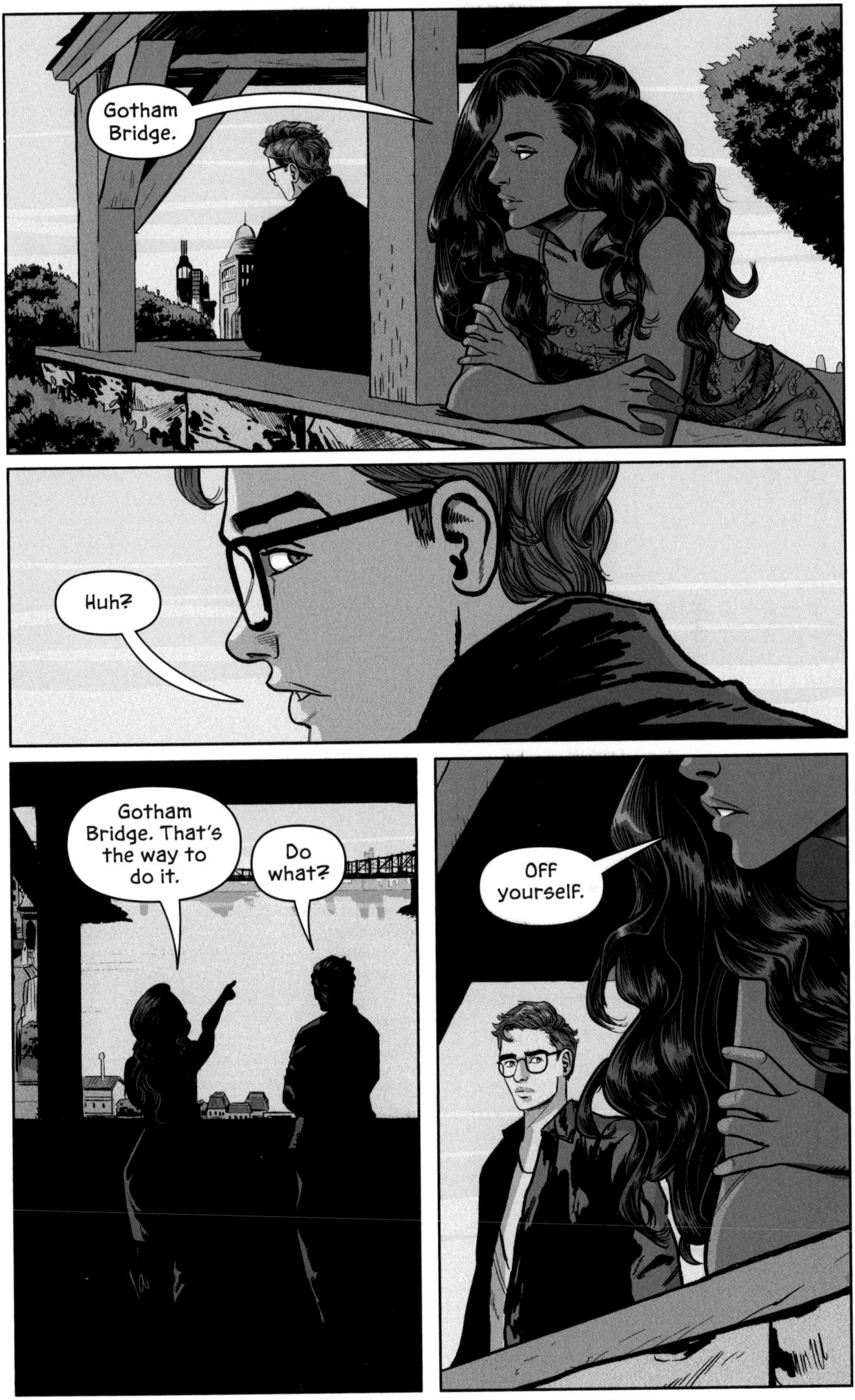
Gotham Bridge.
Huh?
Gotham Bridge. That's the way to do it.
Do what?
Off yourself.

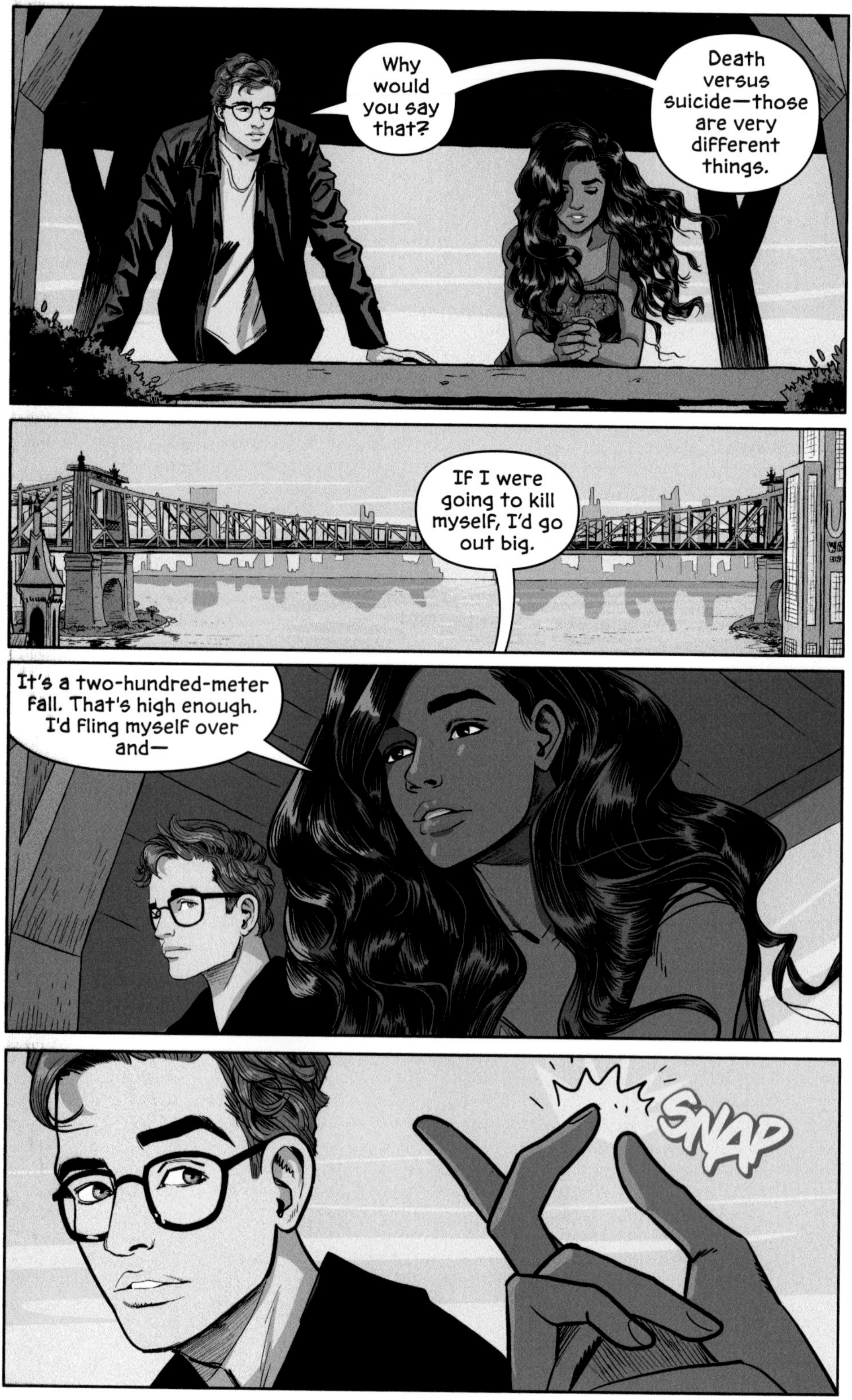
Why would you say that?
Death versus suicide—those are very different things.
If I were going to kill myself, I'd go out big.
It's a two-hundred-meter fall. That's high enough. I'd fling myself over and—
SNAP

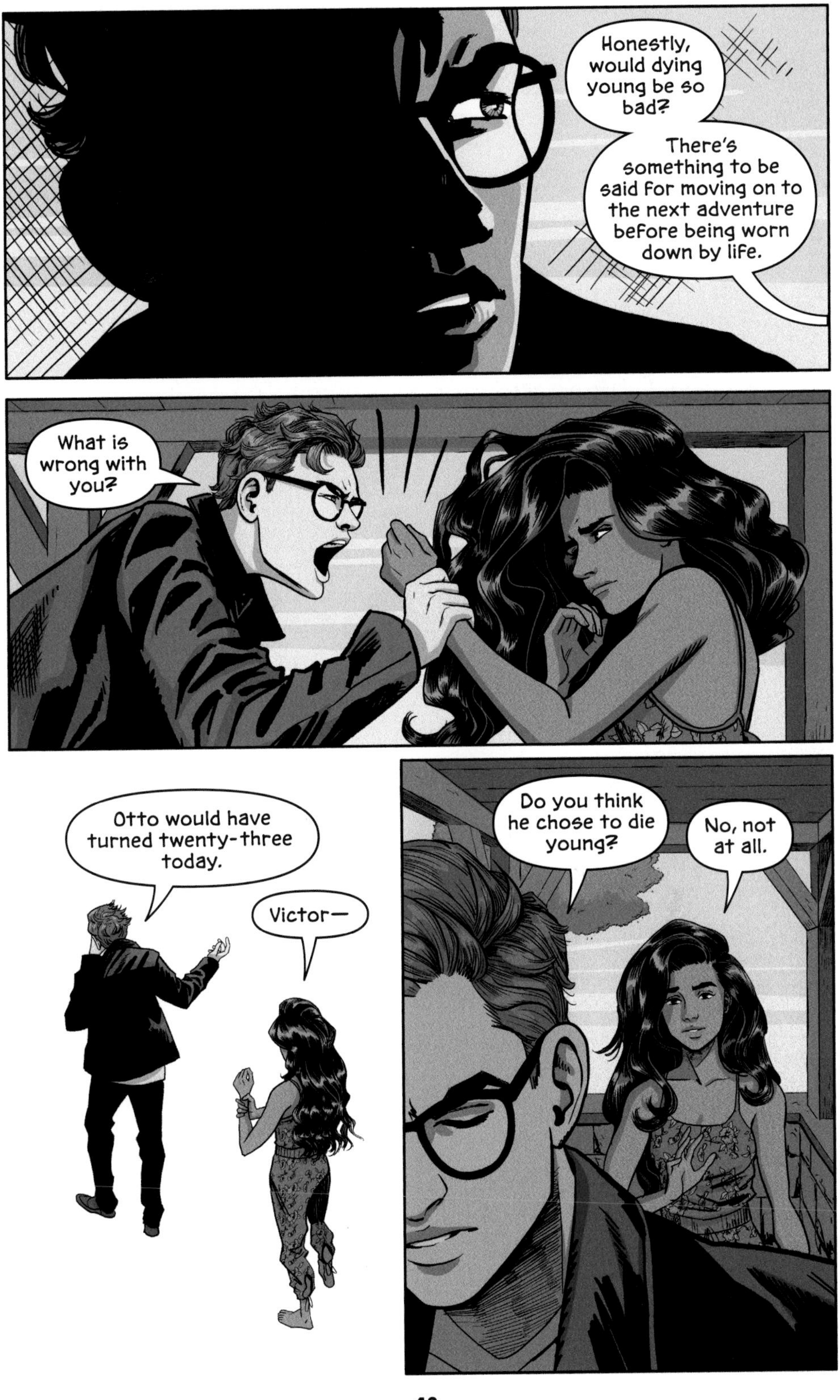
Honestly, would dying young be so bad?
There's something to be said for moving on to the next adventure before being worn down by life.
What is wrong with you?
Otto would have turned twenty-three today.
Victor—
Do you think he chose to die young?
No, not at all.

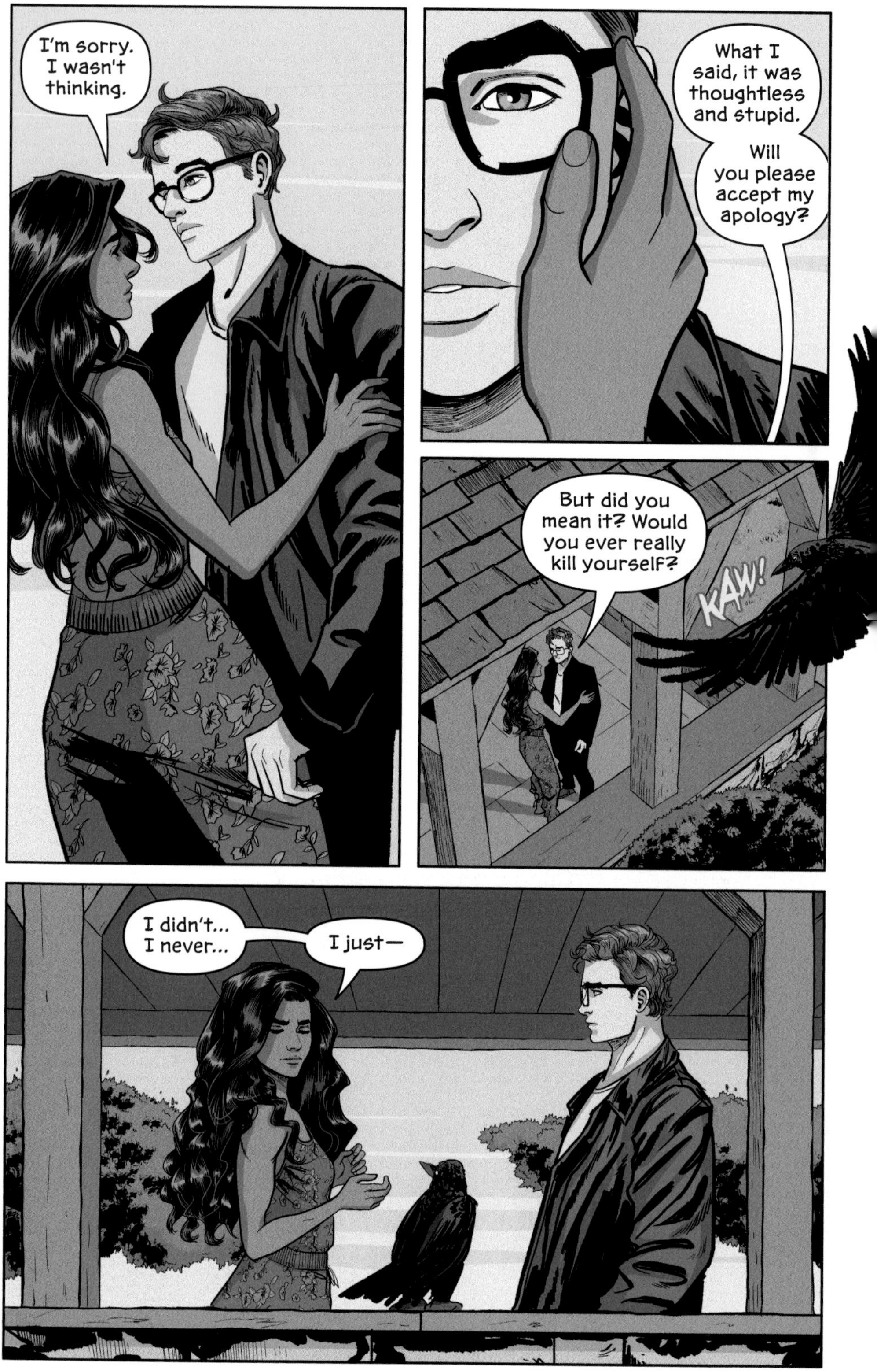
I'm sorry. I wasn't thinking.
What I said, it was thoughtless and stupid.
Will you please accept my apology?
But did you mean it? Would you ever really kill yourself?
KAW!
I didn't... I never...
I just—

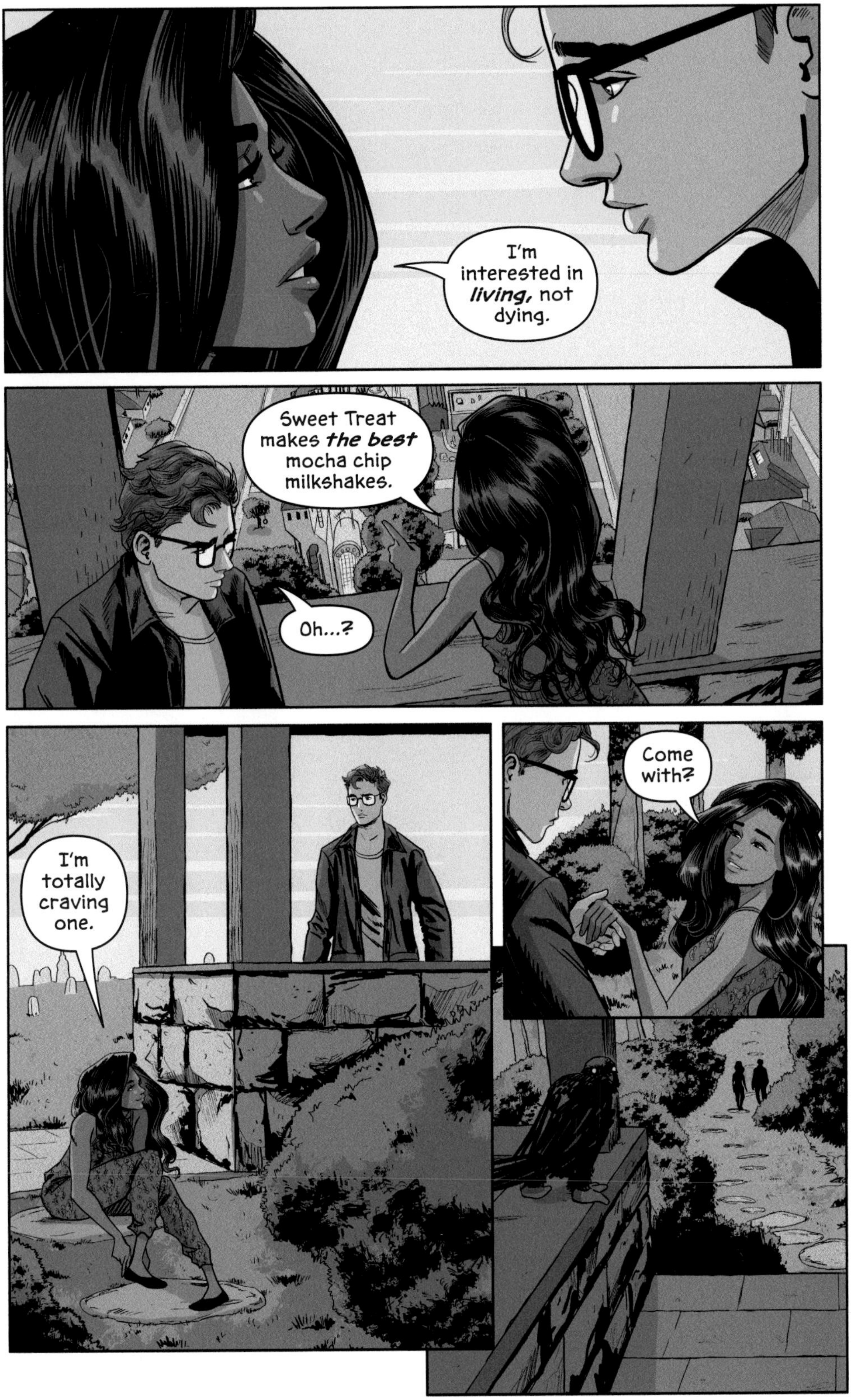
I'm interested in *living,* not dying.
Sweet Treat makes ***the best*** mocha chip milkshakes.
Oh...?
I'm totally craving one.
Come with?

The Girl Who Is Heading for a Fall

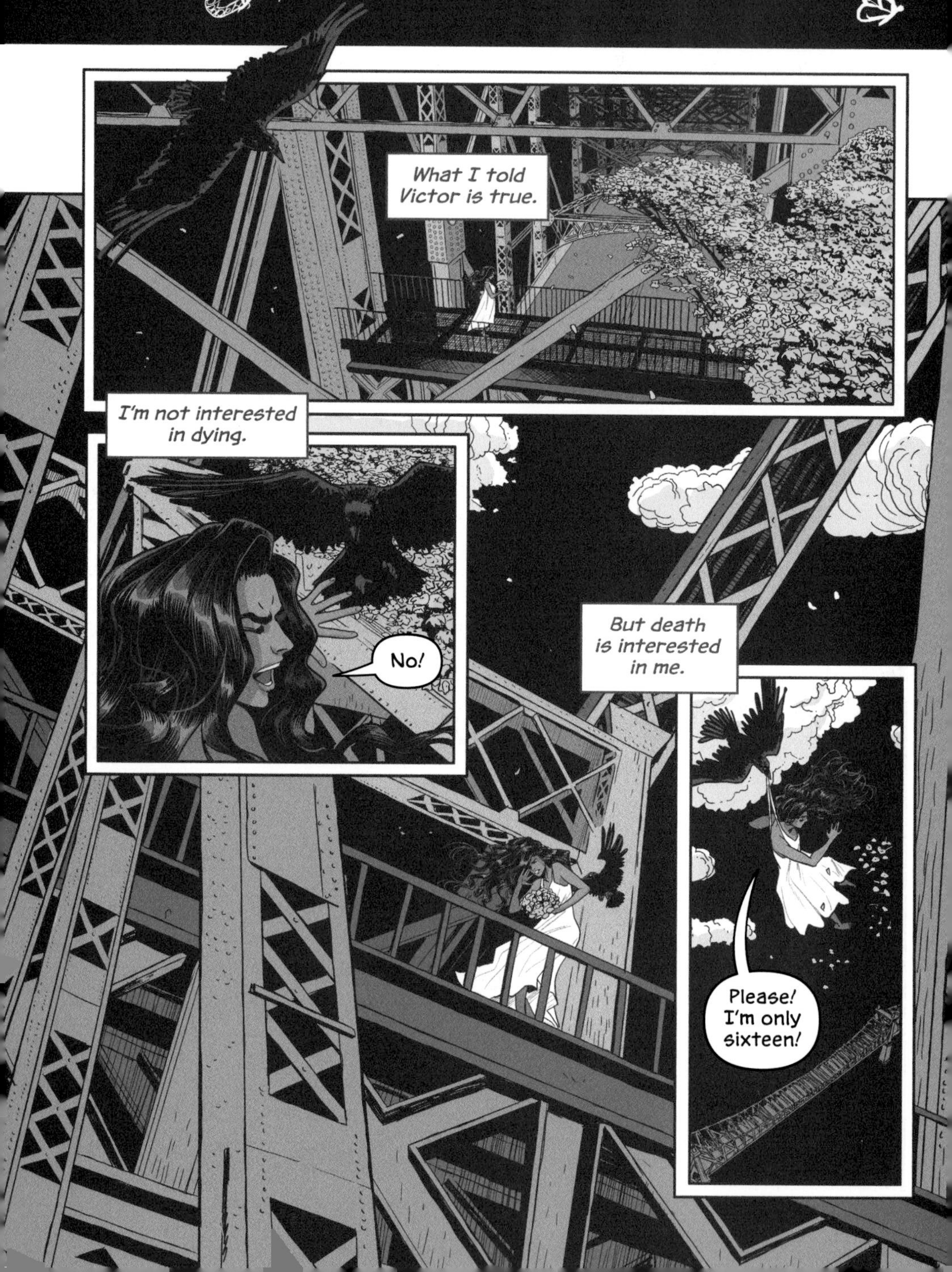
What I told Victor is true.
I'm not interested in dying.
No!
But death is interested in me.
Please! I'm only sixteen!

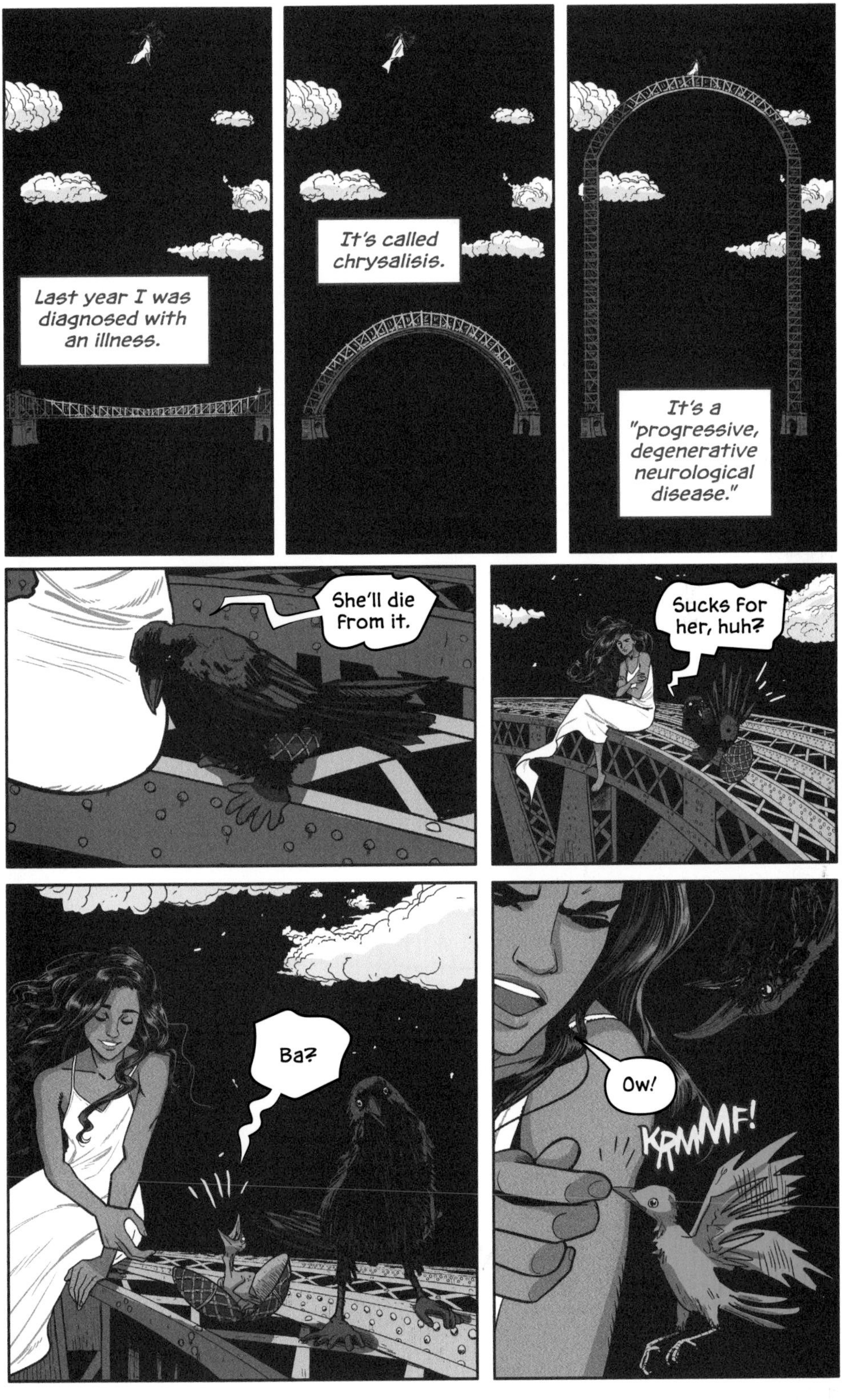
Last year I was diagnosed with an illness.
It's called chrysalisis.
It's a "progressive, degenerative neurological disease."
She'll die from it.
Sucks for her, huh?
Ba?
Ow!
KRMMF!

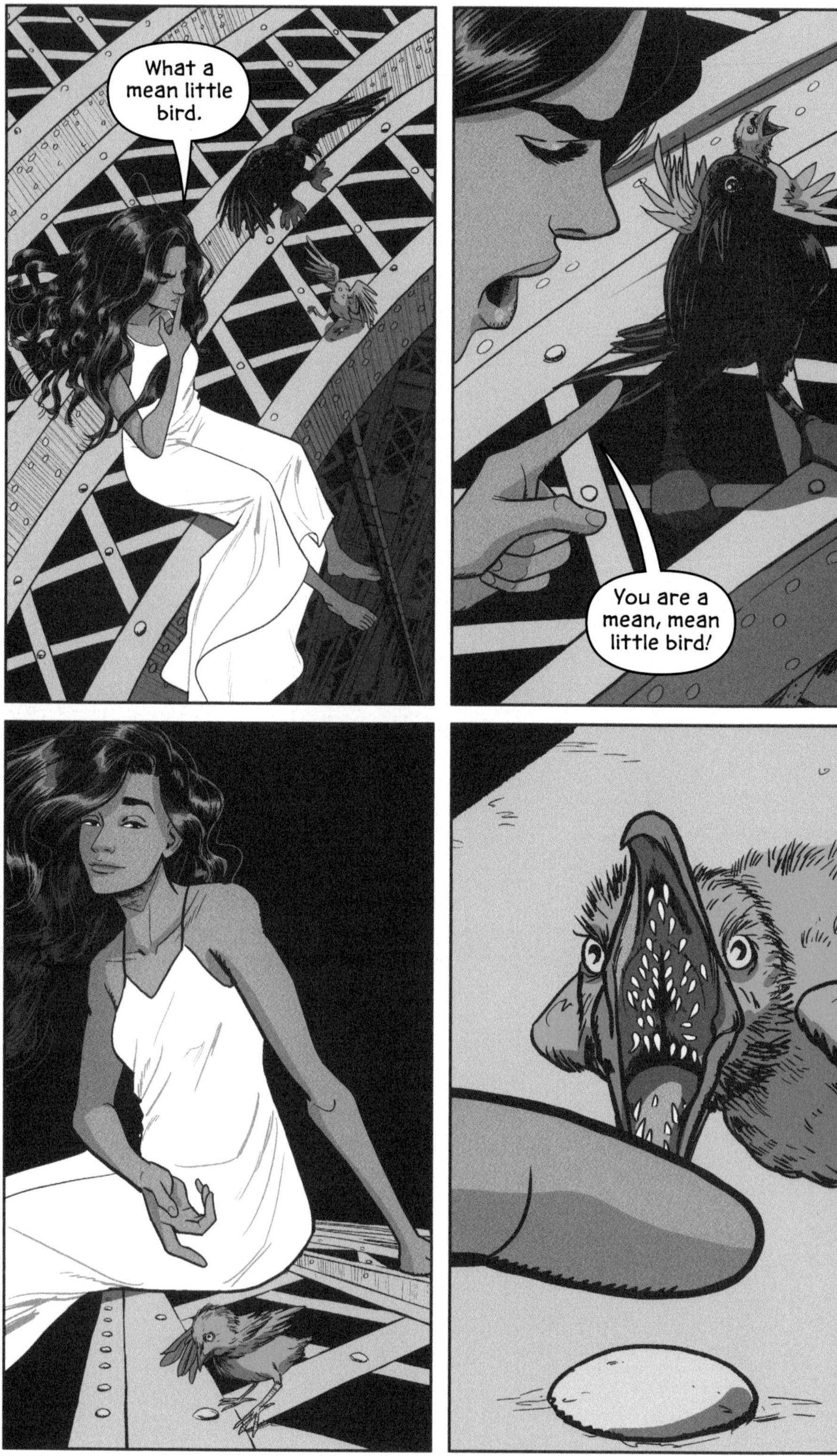
What a mean little bird.
You are a mean, mean little bird!

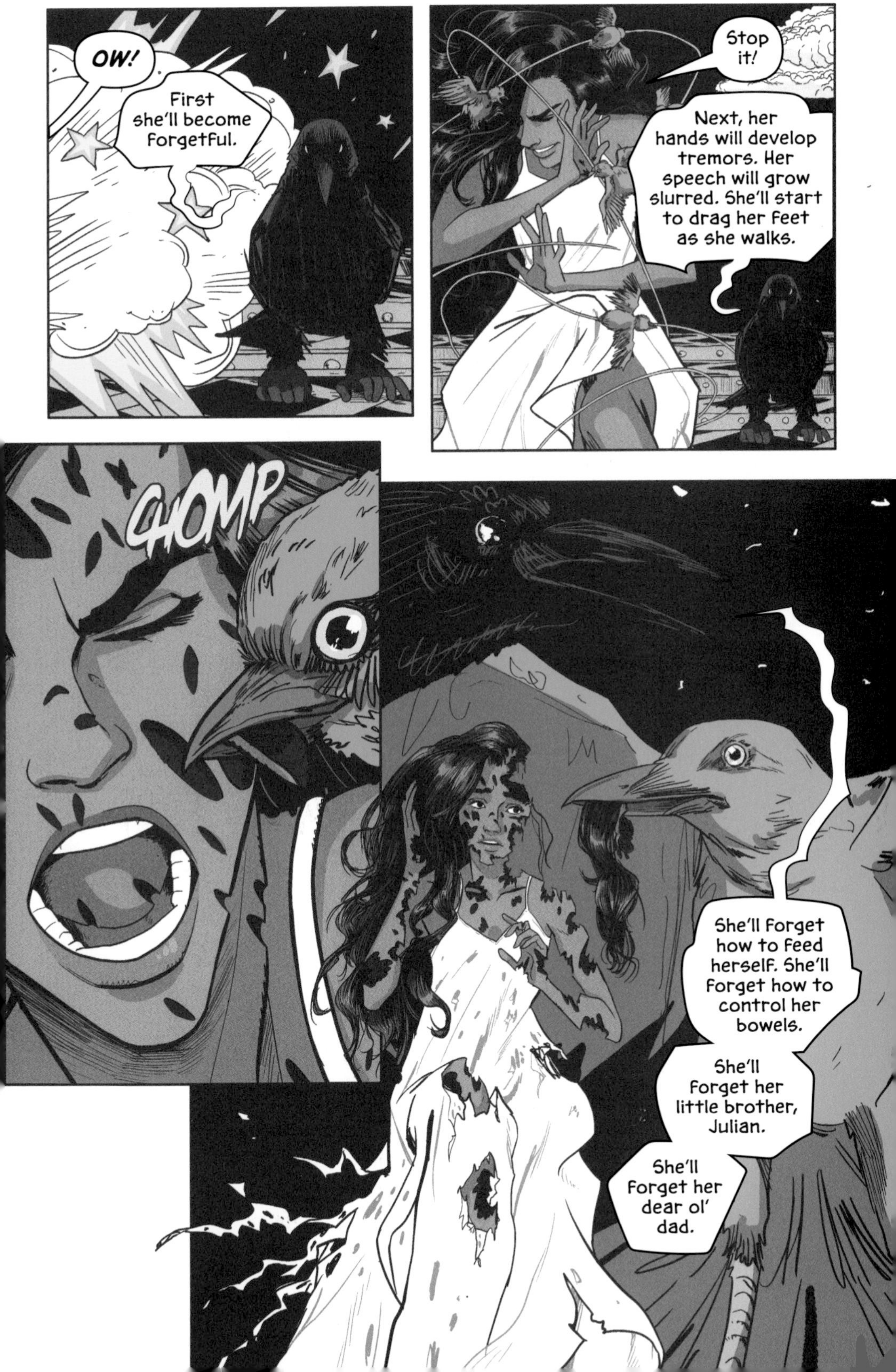
OW!
First she'll become forgetful.
Stop it!
Next, her hands will develop tremors. Her speech will grow slurred. She'll start to drag her feet as she walks.
CHOMP
She'll forget how to feed herself. She'll forget how to control her bowels.
She'll forget her little brother, Julian.
She'll forget her dear ol' dad.

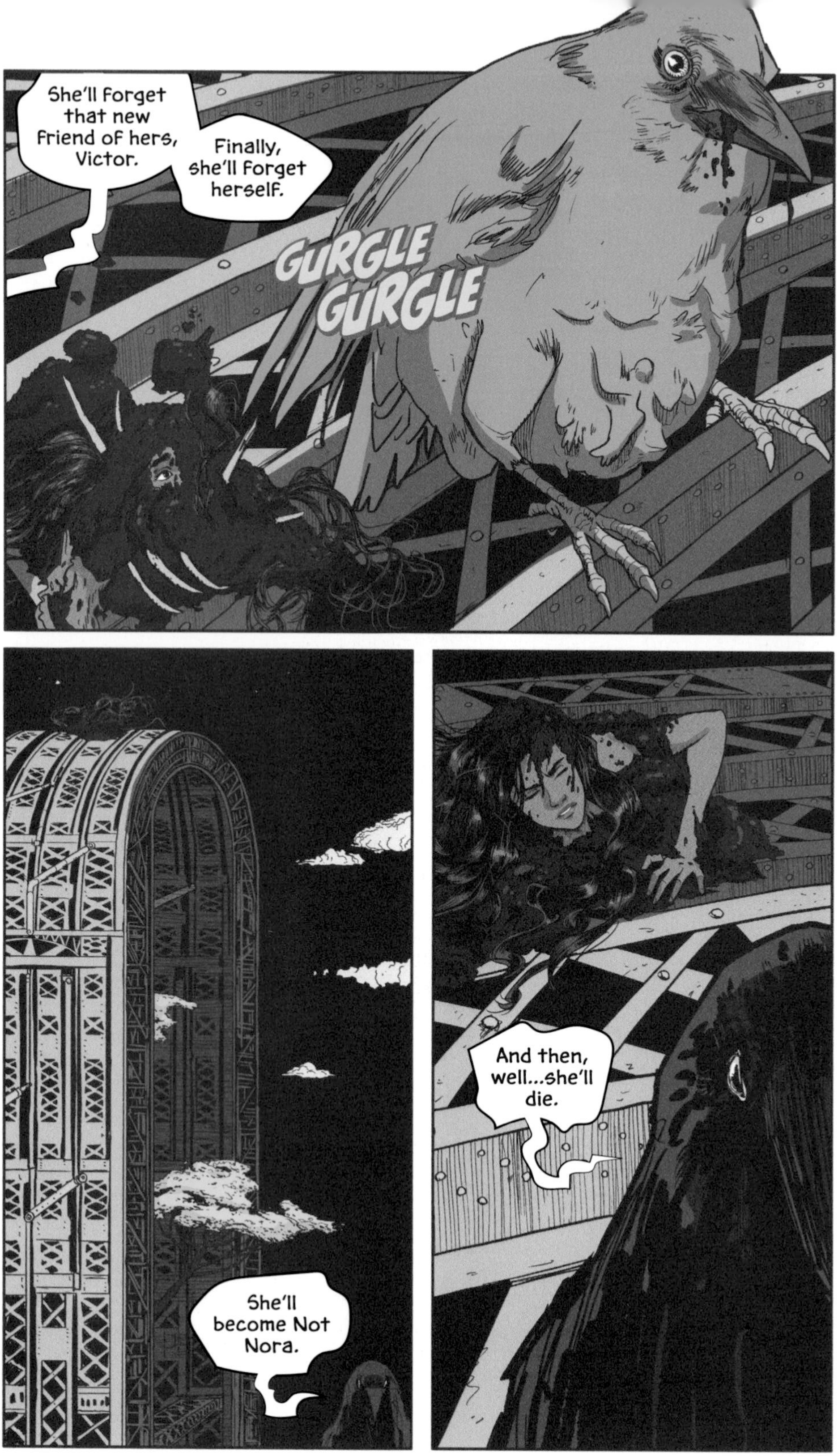
She'll forget that new friend of hers, Victor.
Finally, she'll forget herself.
GURGLE GURGLE
She'll become Not Nora.
And then, well...she'll die.

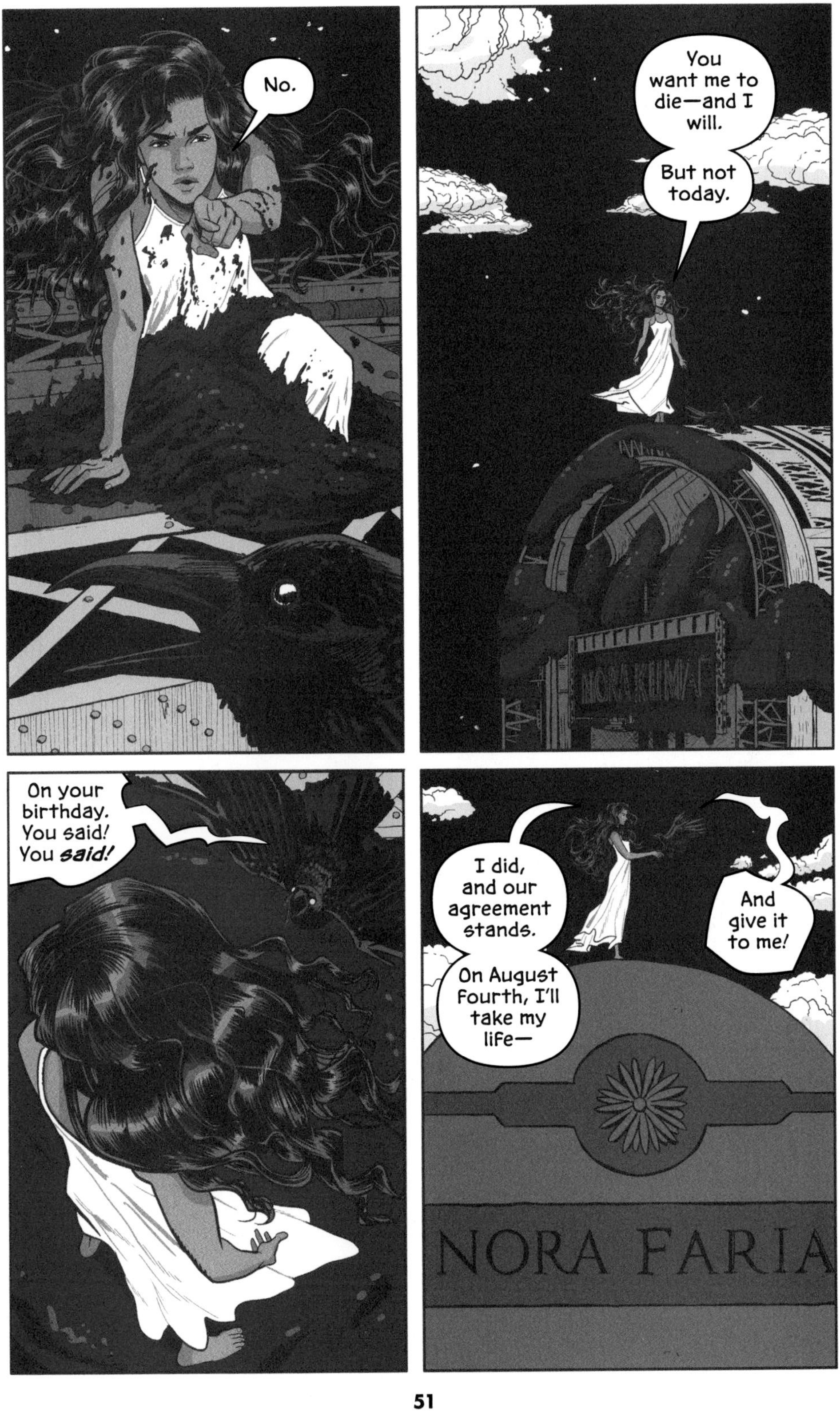
No.
You want me to die—and I will.
But not today.
NORA KUMAR
On your birthday. You said! You ***said!***
I did, and our agreement stands.
On August fourth, I'll take my life—
And give it to me!
NORA FARIA

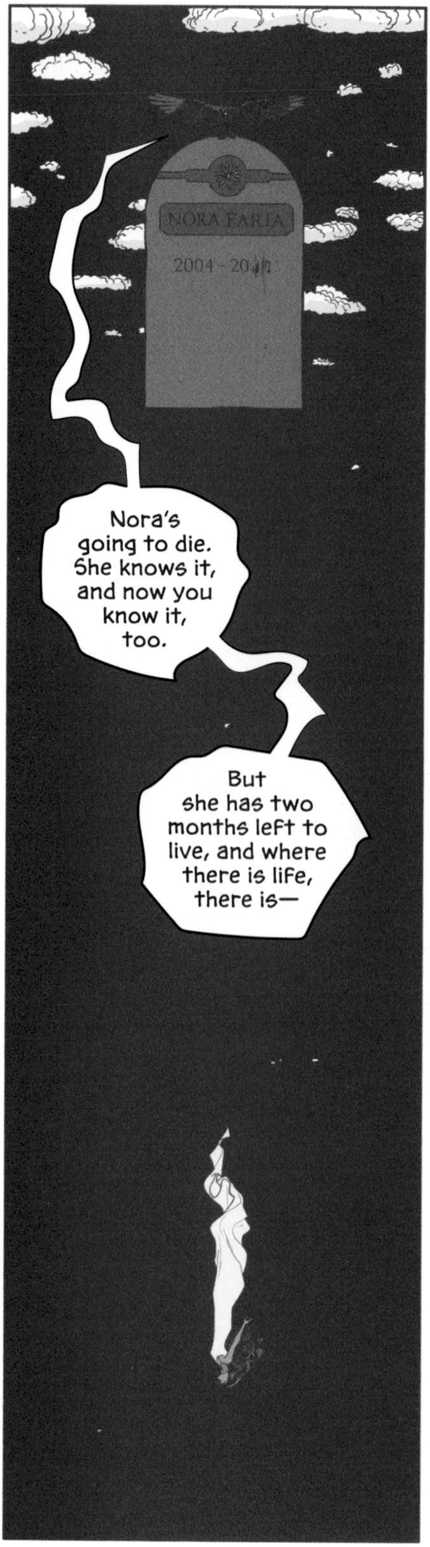
NORA FARIA
2004 - 2041
Nora's going to die. She knows it, and now you know it, too.
But she has two months left to live, and where there is life, there is—

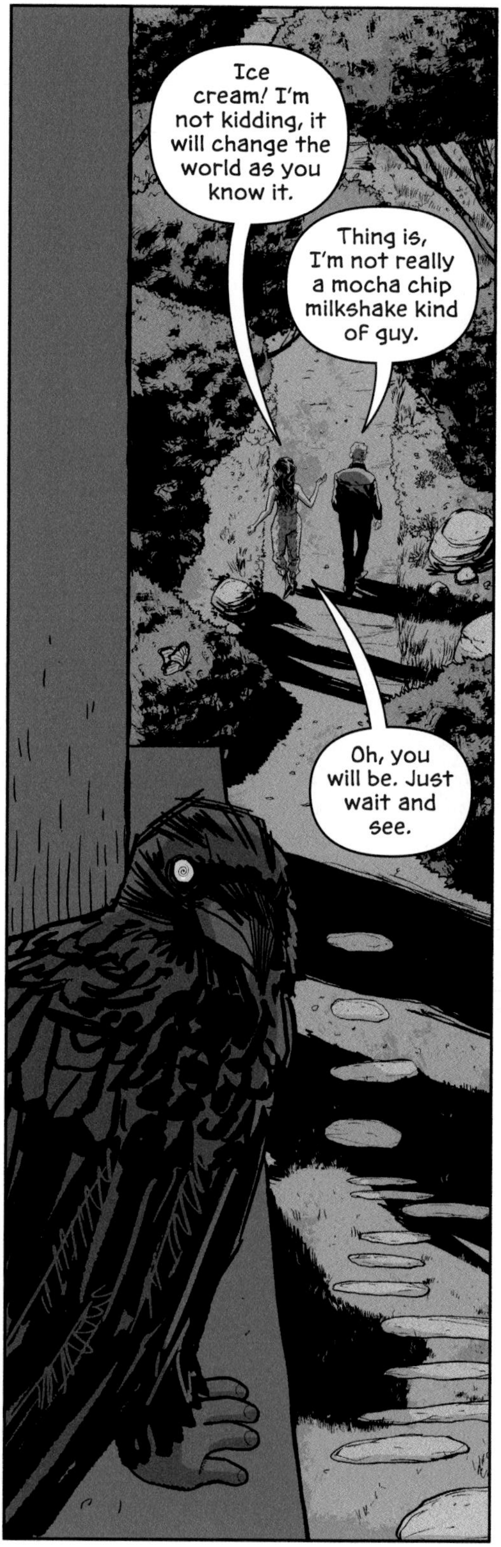
Ice cream! I'm not kidding, it will change the world as you know it.
Thing is, I'm not really a mocha chip milkshake kind of guy.
Oh, you will be. Just wait and see.

The Boy Who (Nervously) Embraces Adventure

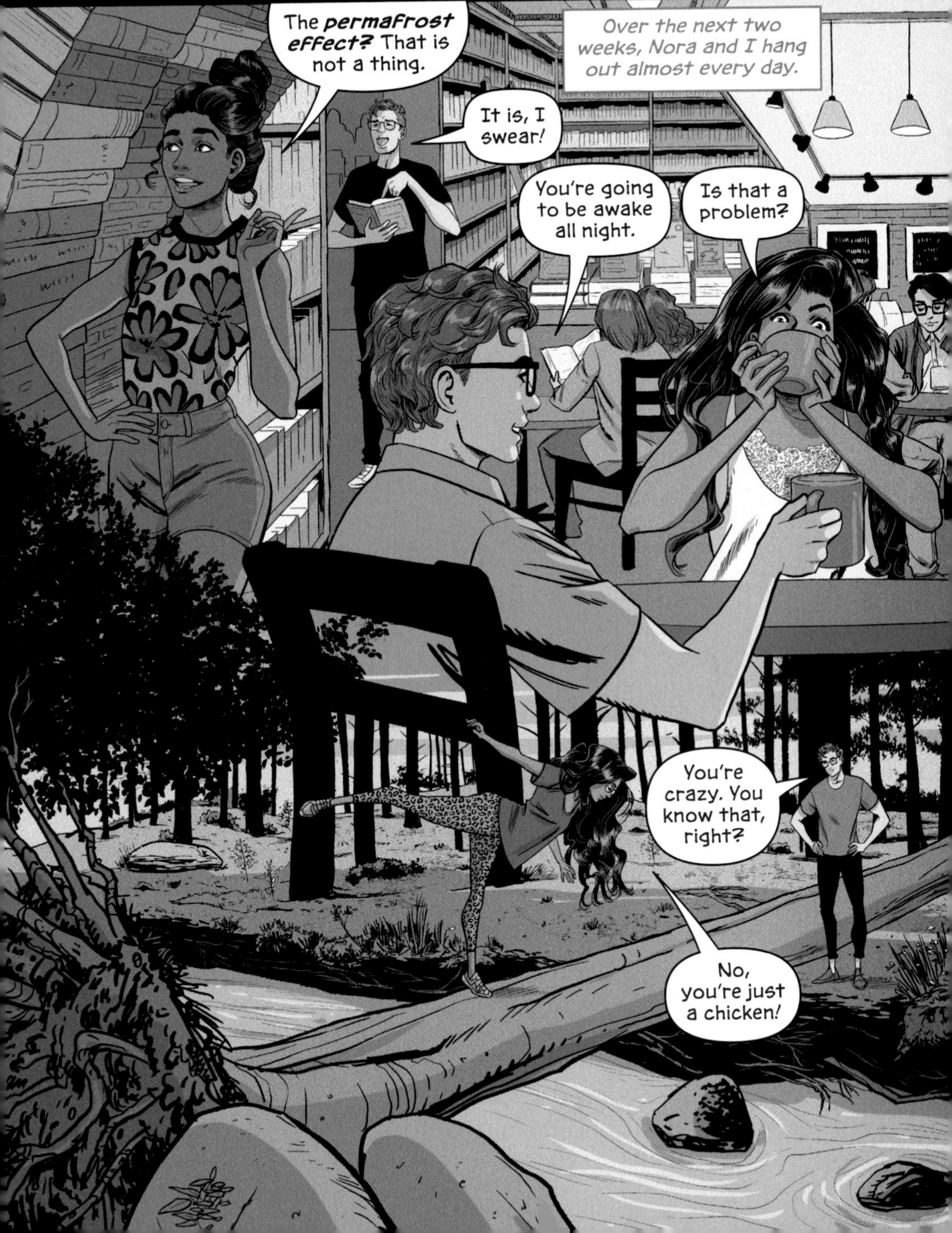

The **permafrost effect?** That is not a thing.
It is, I swear!
Over the next two weeks, Nora and I hang out almost every day.
You're going to be awake all night.
Is that a problem?
You're crazy. You know that, right?
No, you're just a chicken!

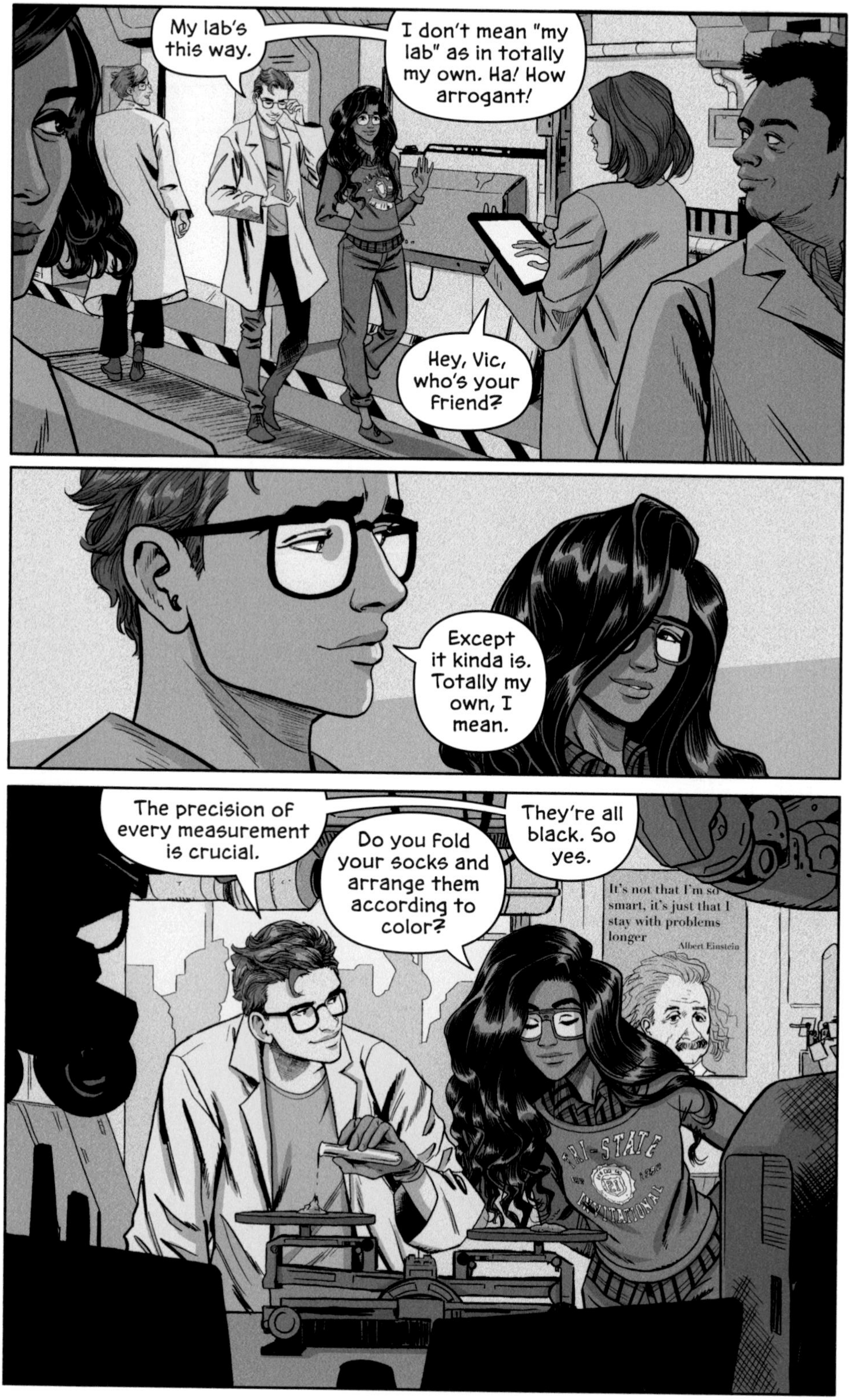

My lab's this way.
I don't mean "my lab" as in totally my own. Ha! How arrogant!
Hey, Vic, who's your friend?
Except it kinda is. Totally my own, I mean.
The precision of every measurement is crucial.
Do you fold your socks and arrange them according to color?
They're all black. So yes.
It's not that I'm so smart, it's just that I stay with problems longer
Albert Einstein
TRI-STATE
INVITATIONAL

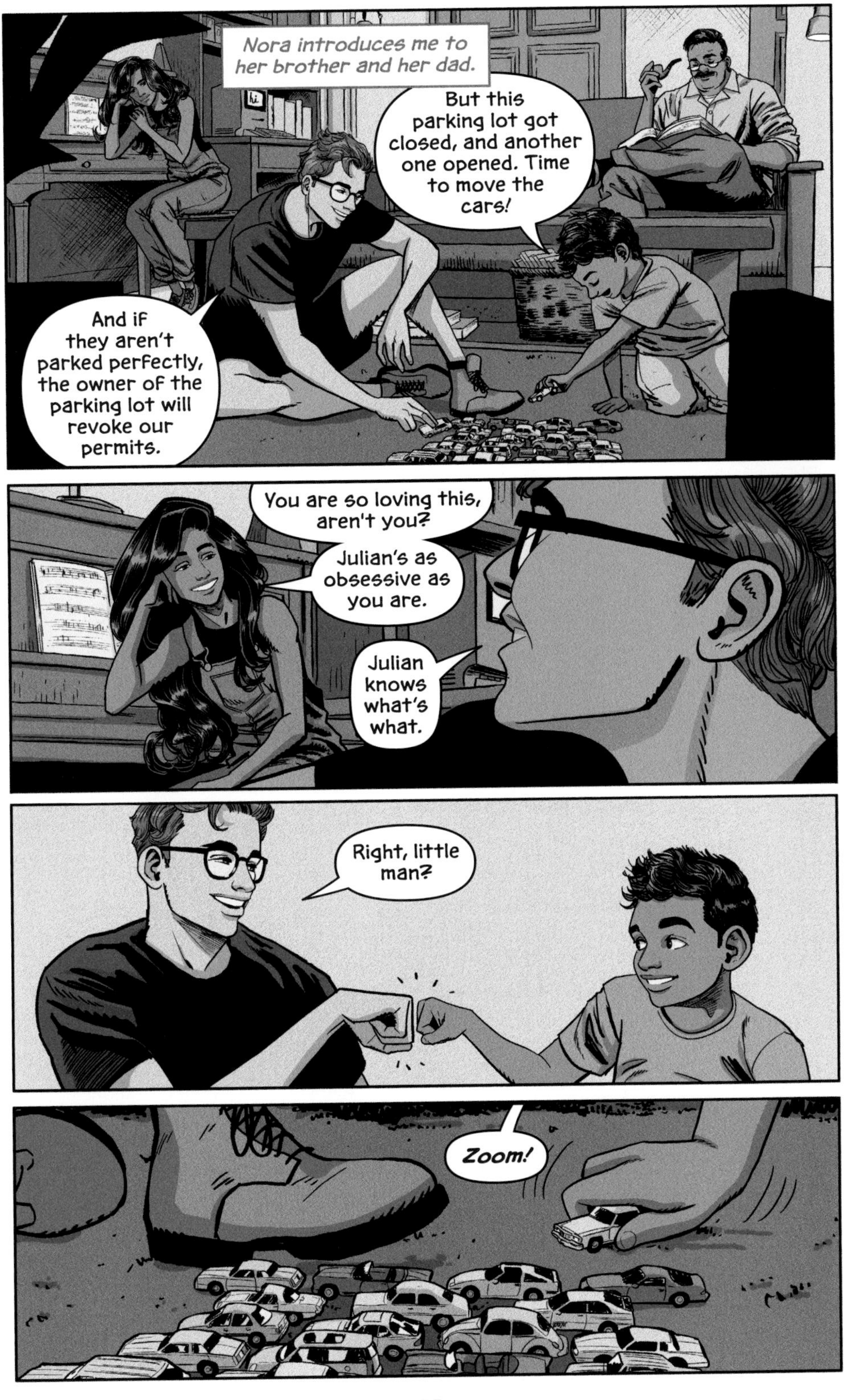
Nora introduces me to her brother and her dad.
But this parking lot got closed, and another one opened. Time to move the cars!
And if they aren't parked perfectly, the owner of the parking lot will revoke our permits.
You are so loving this, aren't you?
Julian's as obsessive as you are.
Julian knows what's what.
Right, little man?
Zoom!

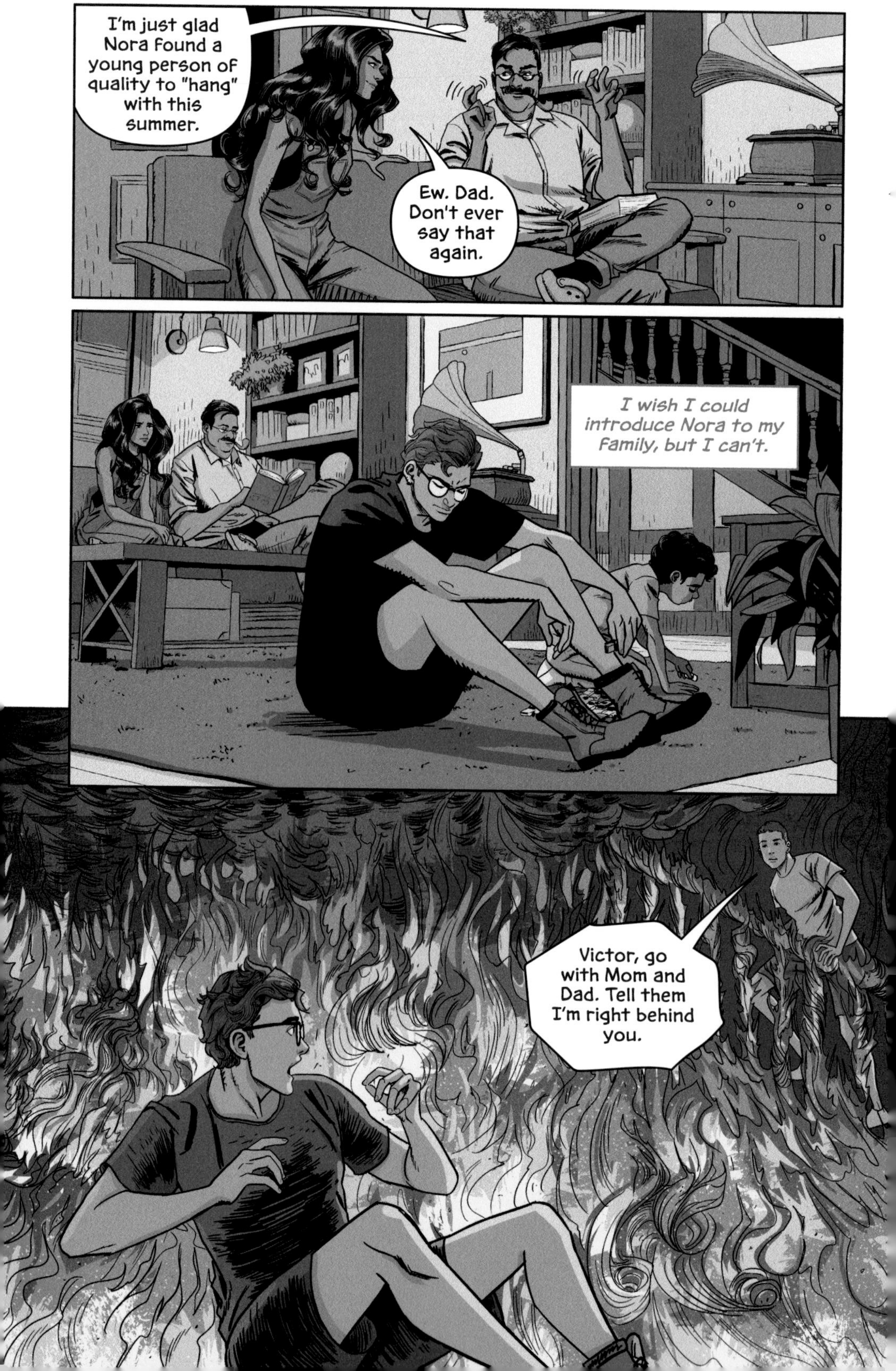
I'm just glad Nora found a young person of quality to "hang" with this summer.
Ew. Dad. Don't ever say that again.
I wish I could introduce Nora to my family, but I can't.
Victor, go with Mom and Dad. Tell them I'm right behind you.

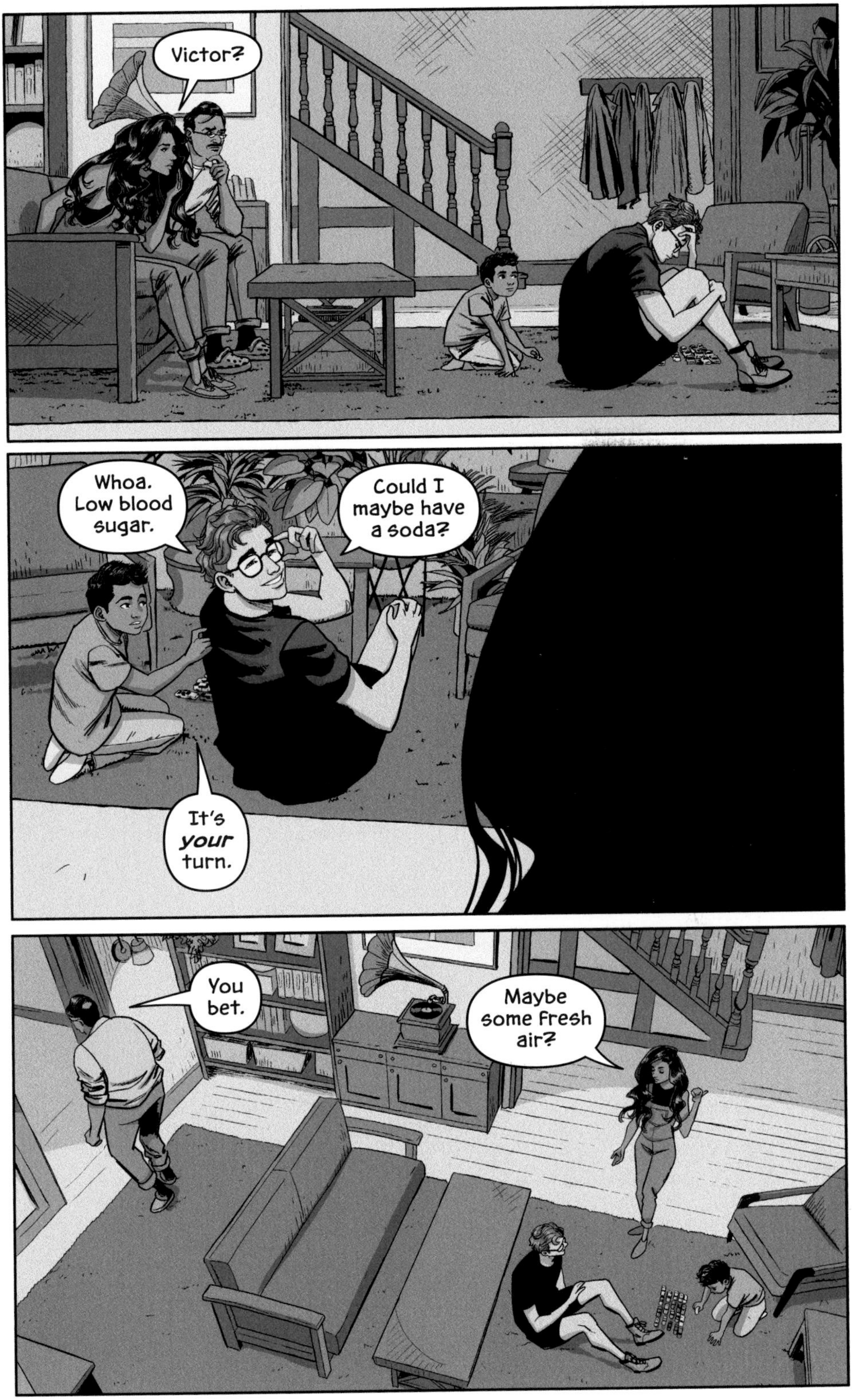
Victor?
Whoa. Low blood sugar.
Could I maybe have a soda?
It's *your* turn.
You bet.
Maybe some fresh air?

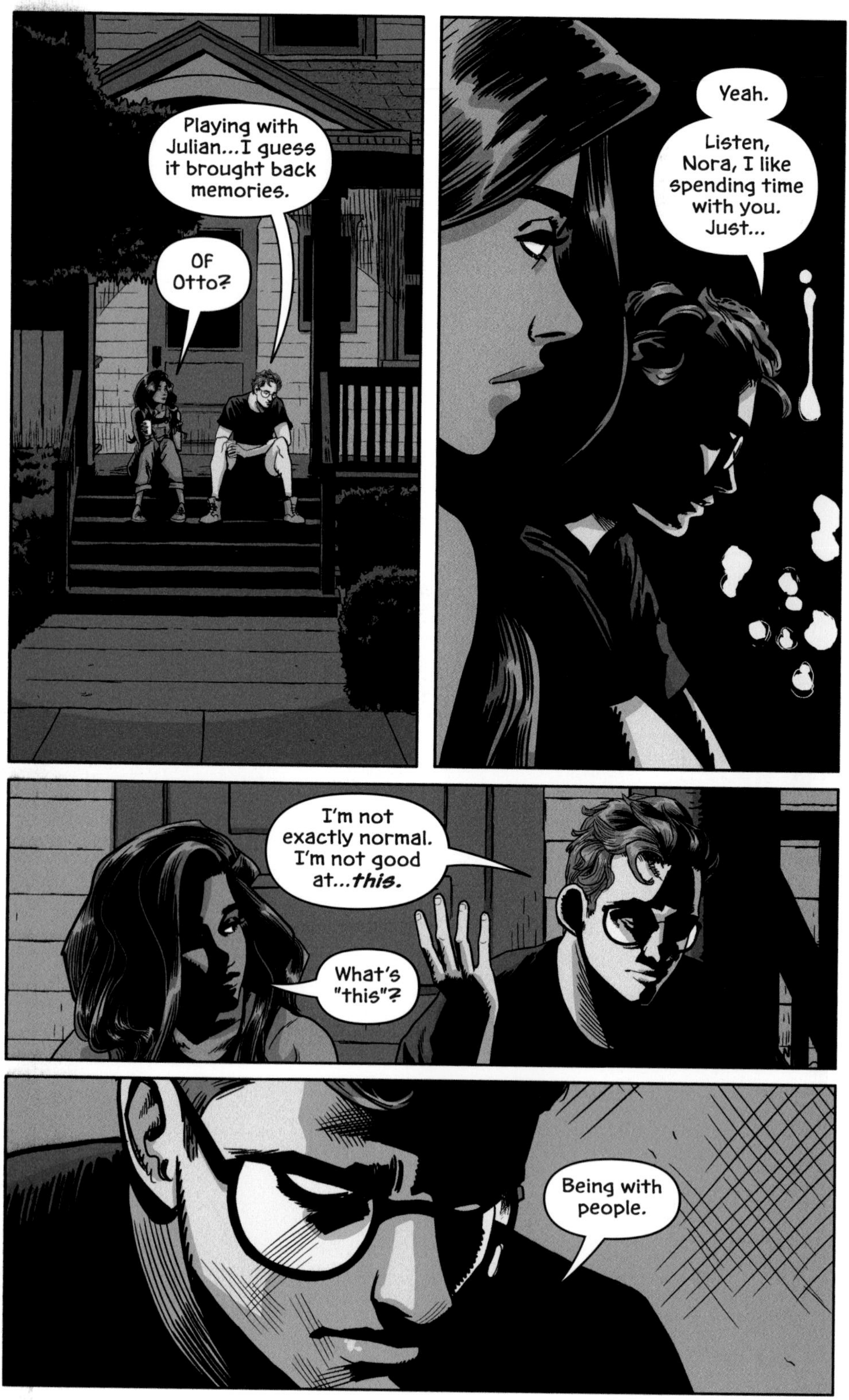
Playing with Julian...I guess it brought back memories.
Of Otto?
Yeah.
Listen, Nora, I like spending time with you. Just...
I'm not exactly normal. I'm not good at...*this.*
What's "this"?
Being with people.

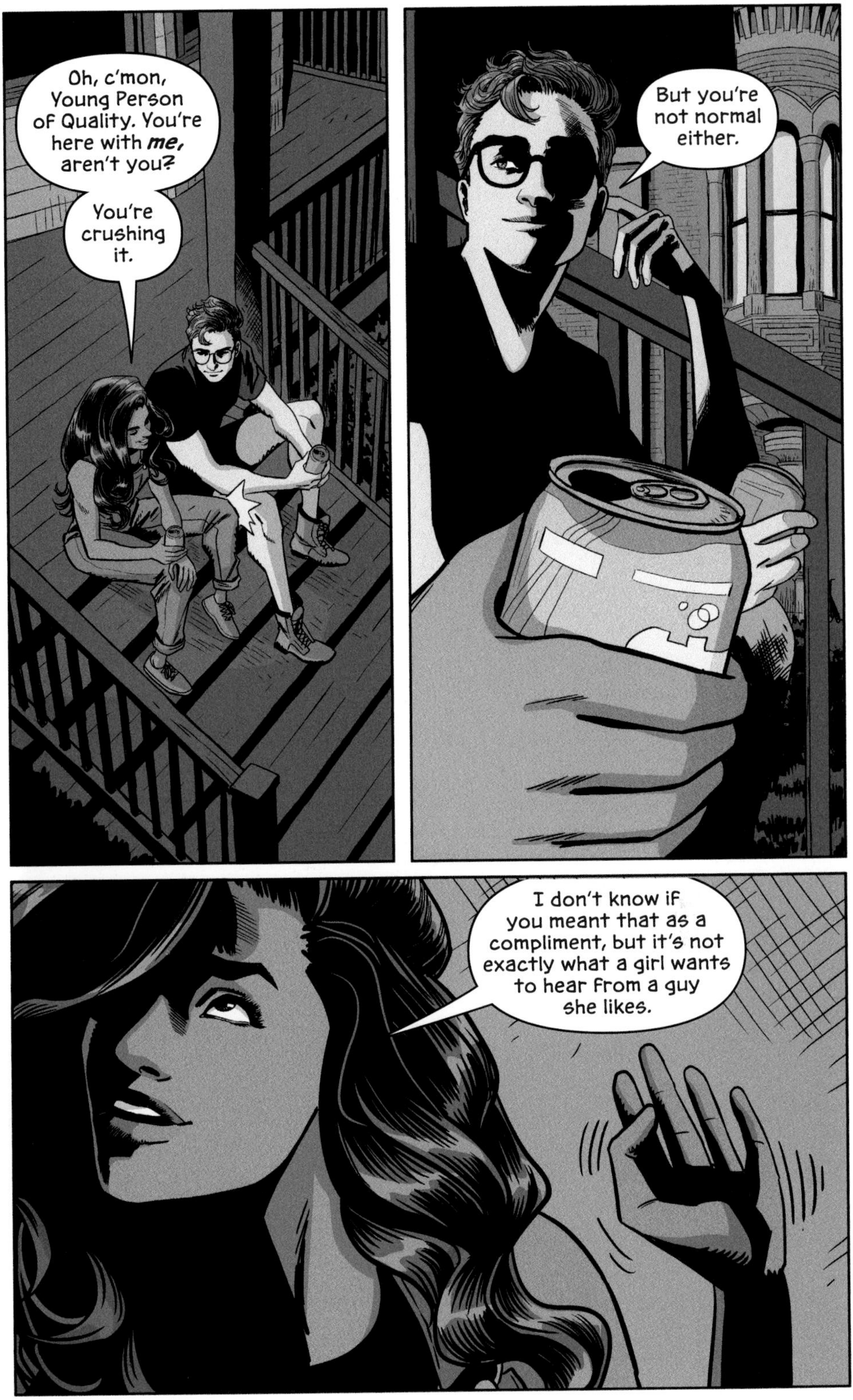
Oh, c'mon, Young Person of Quality. You're here with *me,* aren't you?
You're crushing it.
But you're not normal either.
I don't know if you meant that as a compliment, but it's not exactly what a girl wants to hear from a guy she likes.

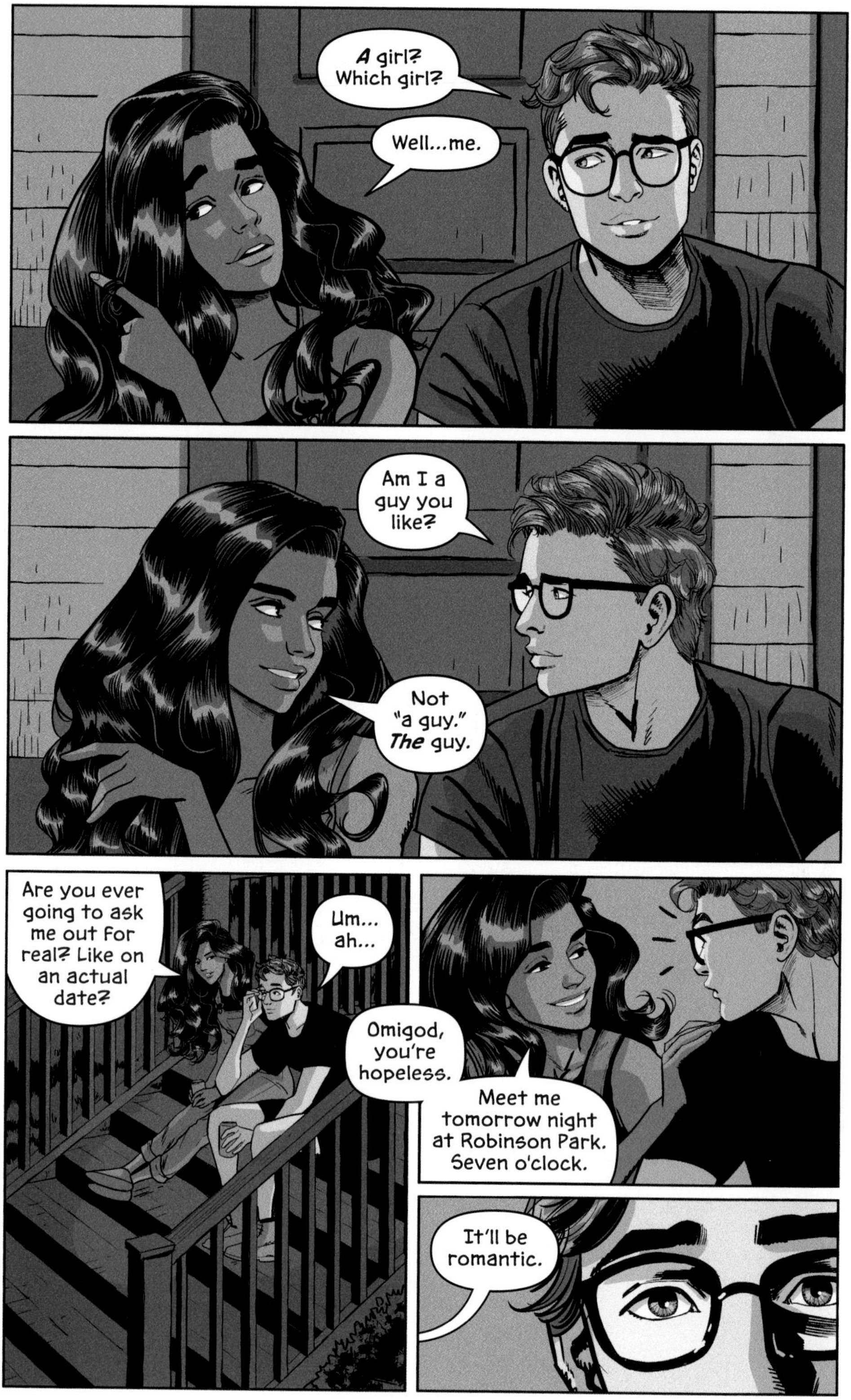
A girl? Which girl?
Well...me.
Am I a guy you like?
Not "a guy." *The* guy.
Are you ever going to ask me out for real? Like on an actual date?
Um... ah...
Omigod, you're hopeless.
Meet me tomorrow night at Robinson Park. Seven o'clock.
It'll be romantic.

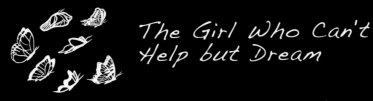

The Girl Who Can't Help but Dream

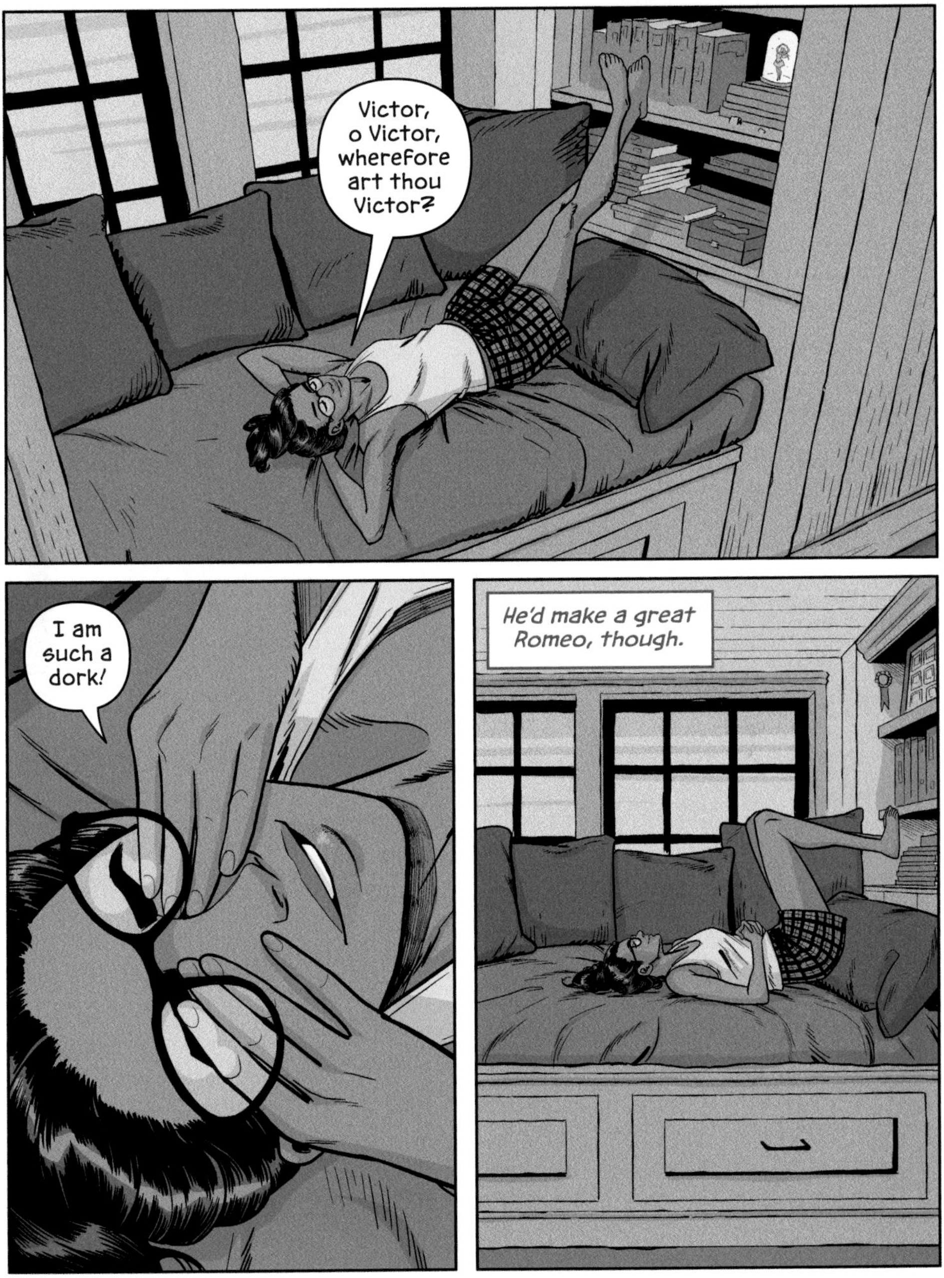
Victor, o Victor, wherefore art thou Victor?
I am such a dork!
He'd make a great Romeo, though.

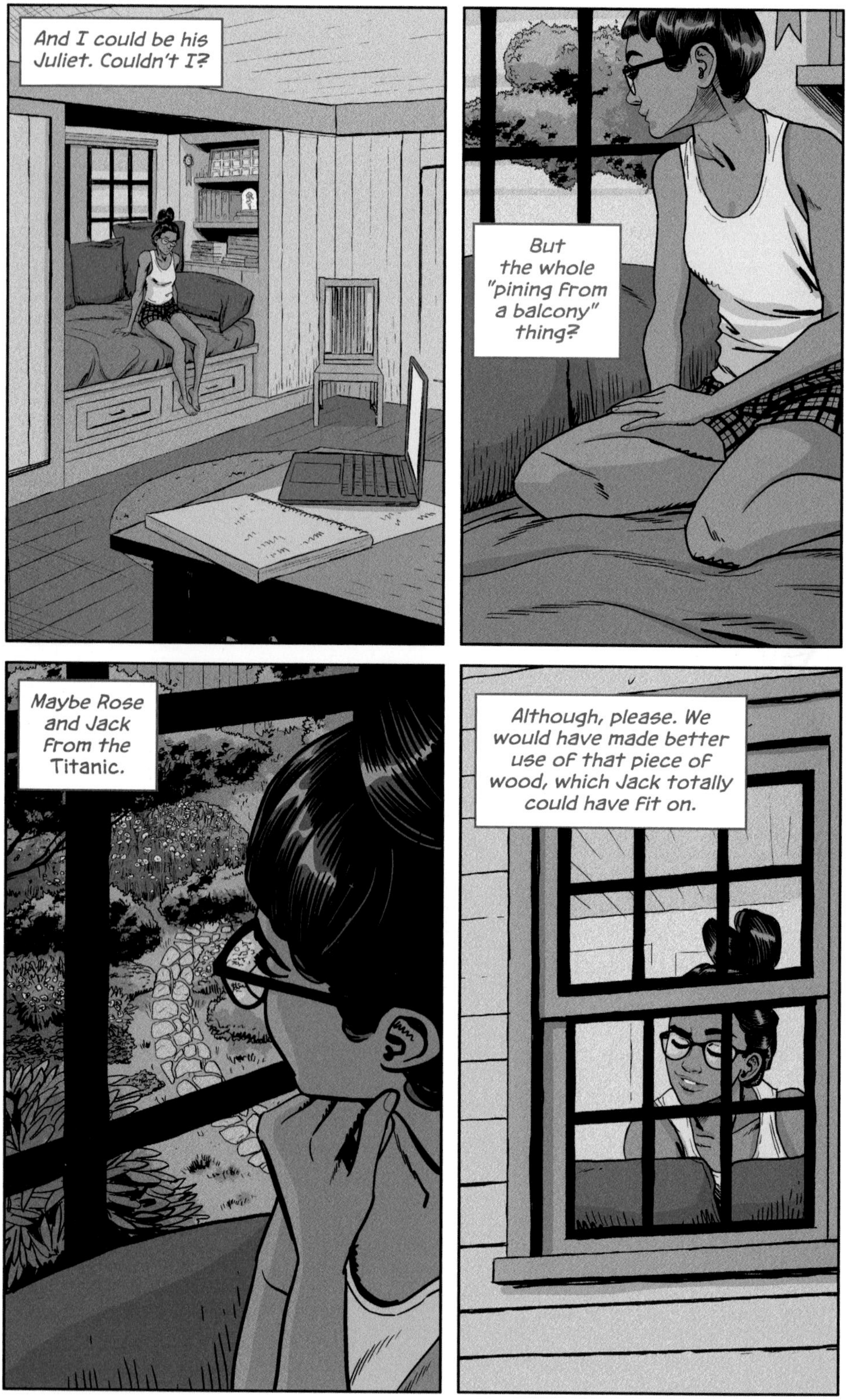
And I could be his Juliet. Couldn't I?
But the whole "pining from a balcony" thing?
Maybe Rose and Jack from the Titanic.
Although, please. We would have made better use of that piece of wood, which Jack totally could have fit on.

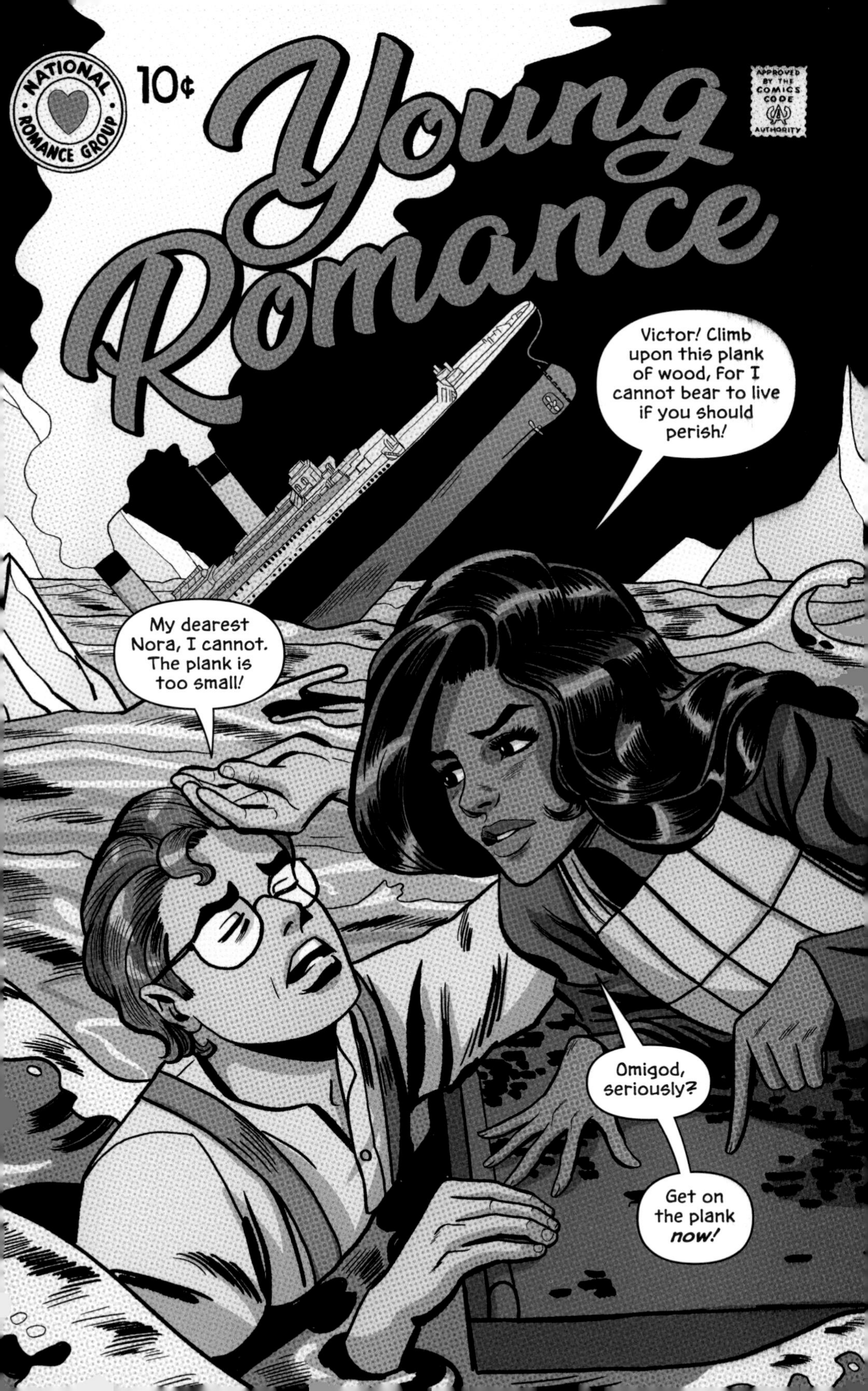
NATIONAL ROMANCE GROUP
10¢
Young Romance
APPROVED BY THE COMICS CODE AUTHORITY
Victor! Climb upon this plank of wood, for I cannot bear to live if you should perish!
My dearest Nora, I cannot. The plank is too small!
Omigod, seriously?
Get on the plank *now!*

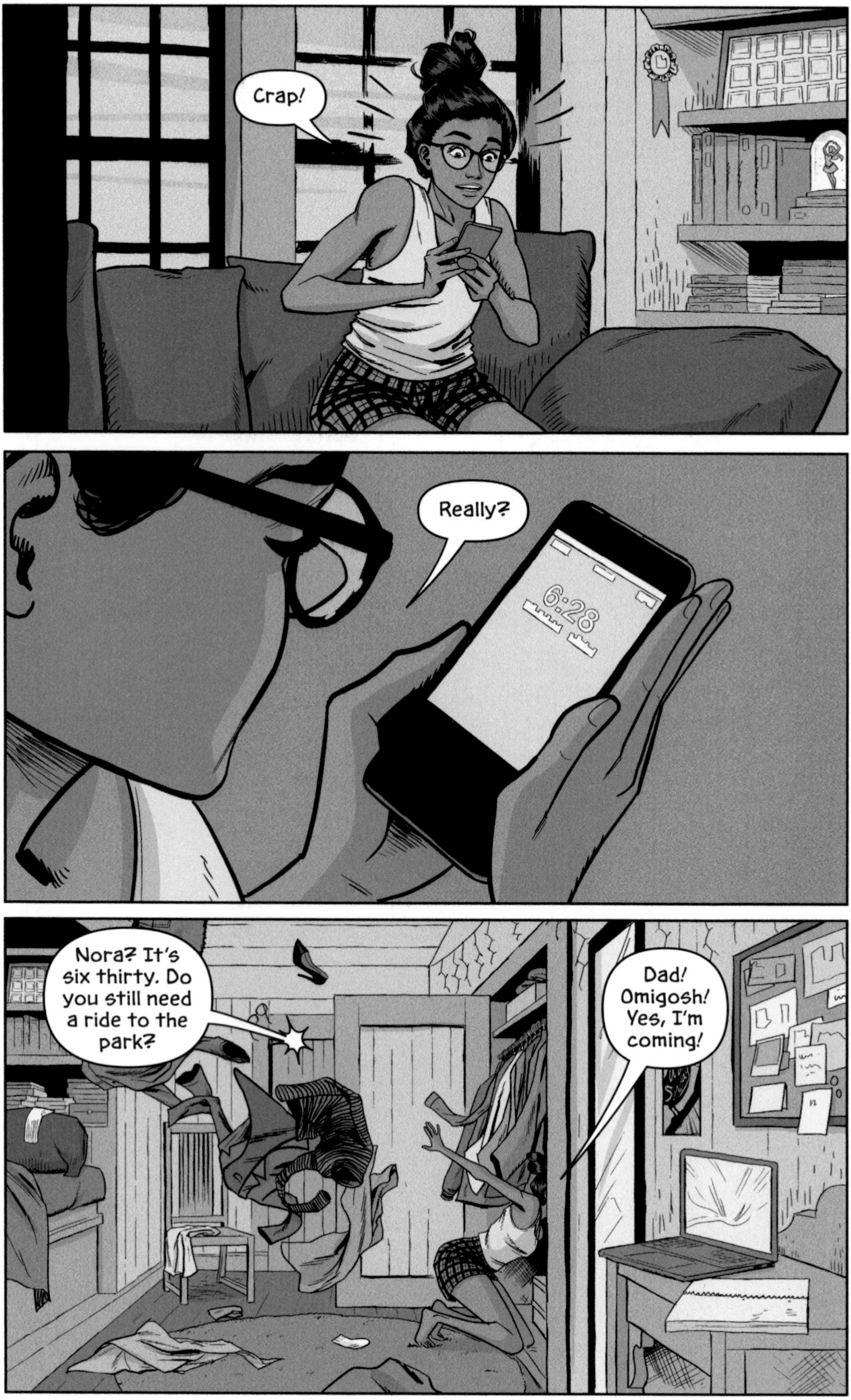
Crap!
Really?
6:28
Nora? It's six thirty. Do you still need a ride to the park?
Dad! Omigosh! Yes, I'm coming!

The Boy Who Seeks the Cold

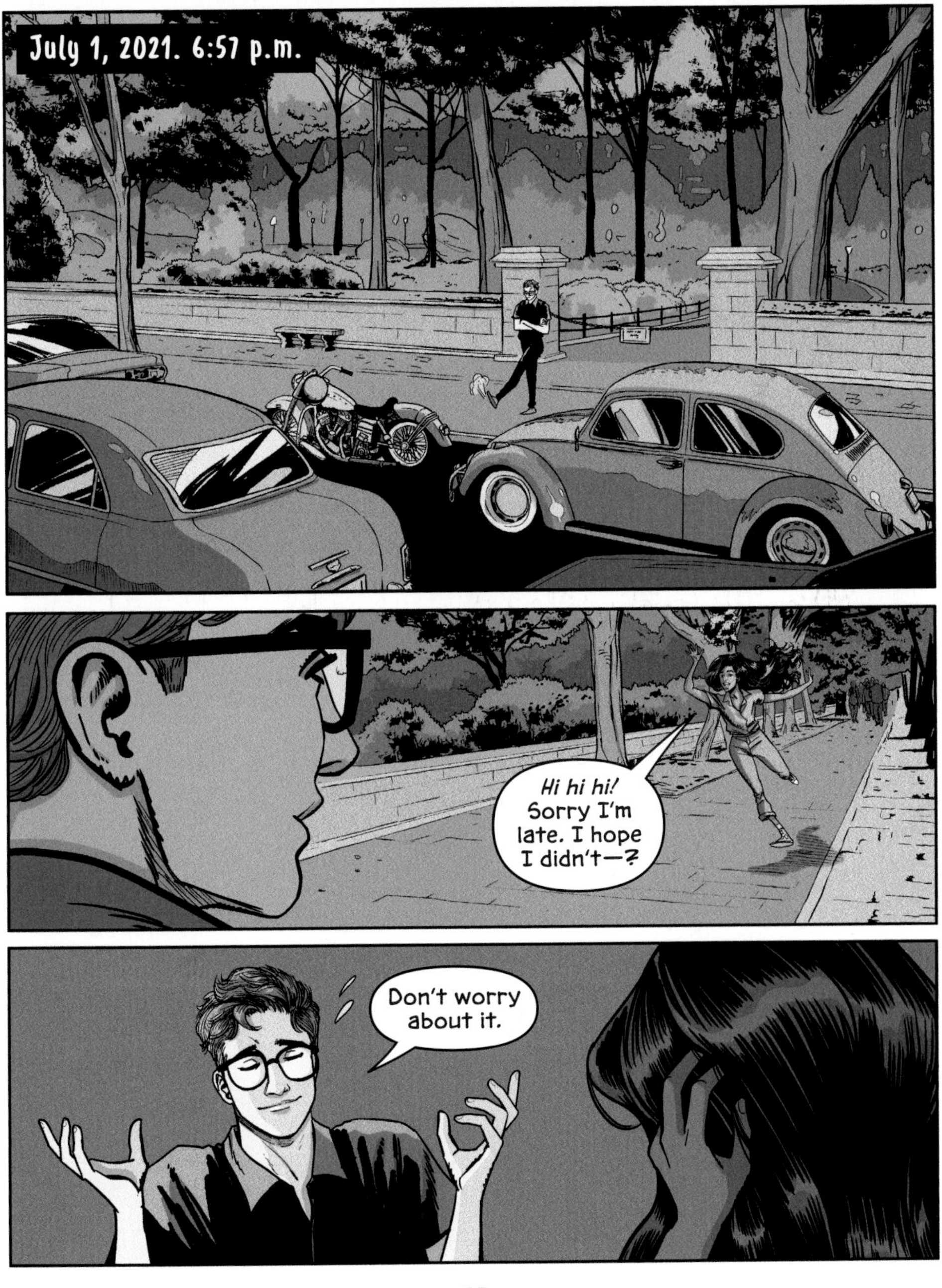
July 1, 2021. 6:57 p.m.
Hi hi hi! Sorry I'm late. I hope I didn't—?
Don't worry about it.

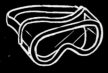

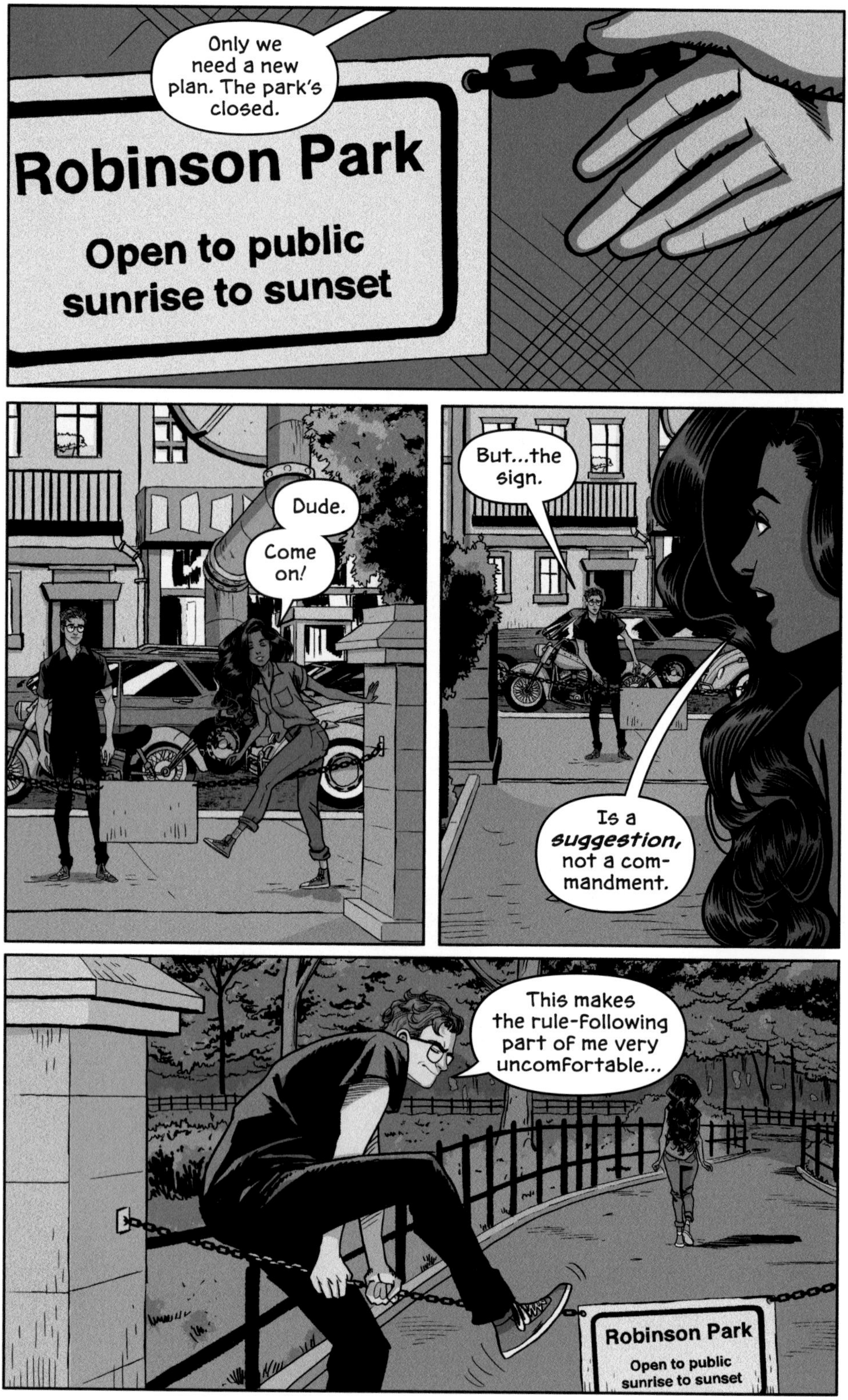

Only we need a new plan. The park's closed.
Robinson Park
Open to public sunrise to sunset
Dude.
Come on!
But...the sign.
Is a *suggestion,* not a commandment.
This makes the rule-following part of me very uncomfortable...
Robinson Park
Open to public sunrise to sunset

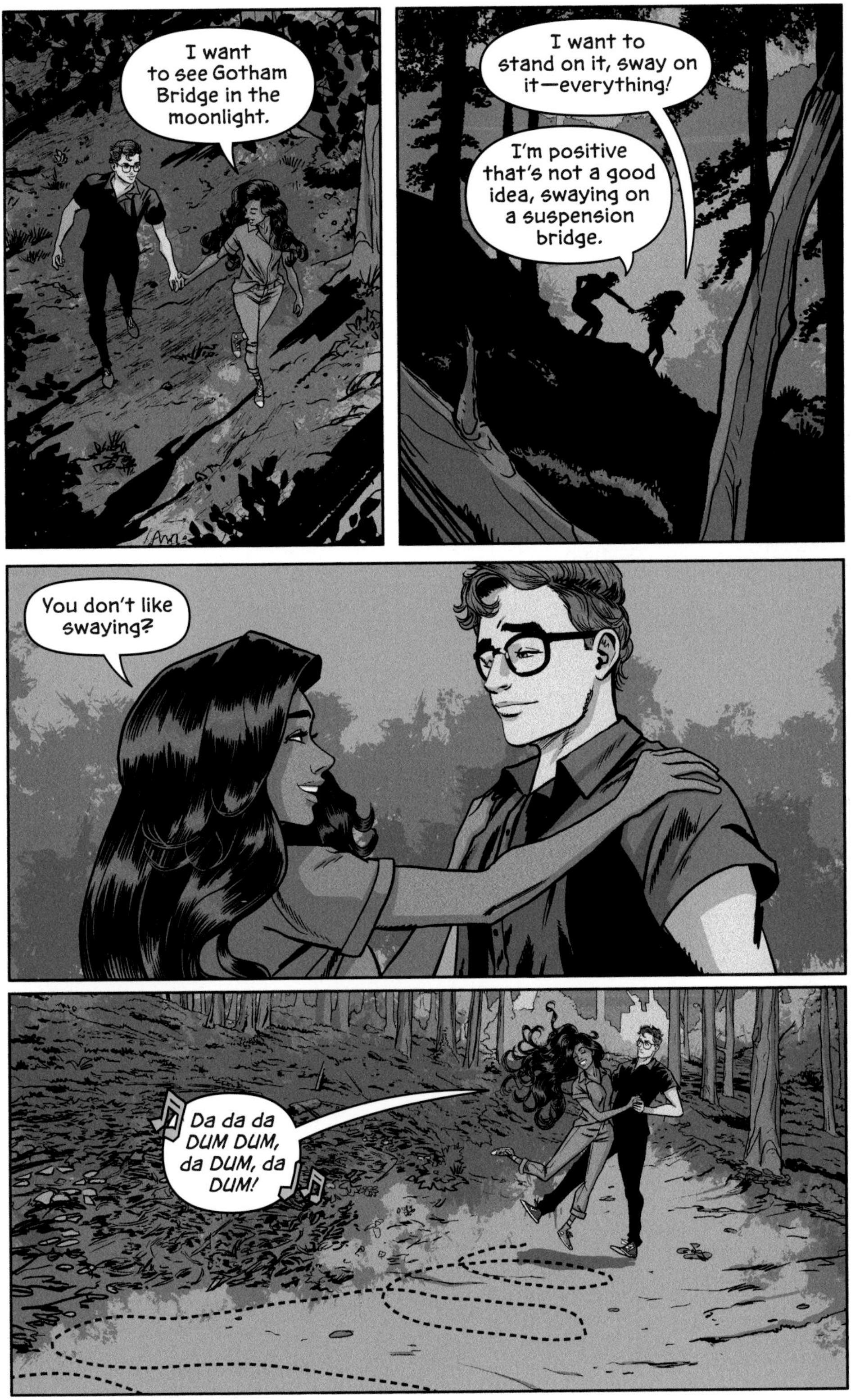
I want to see Gotham Bridge in the moonlight.
I want to stand on it, sway on it—everything!
I'm positive that's not a good idea, swaying on a suspension bridge.
You don't like swaying?
Da da da DUM DUM, da DUM, da DUM!

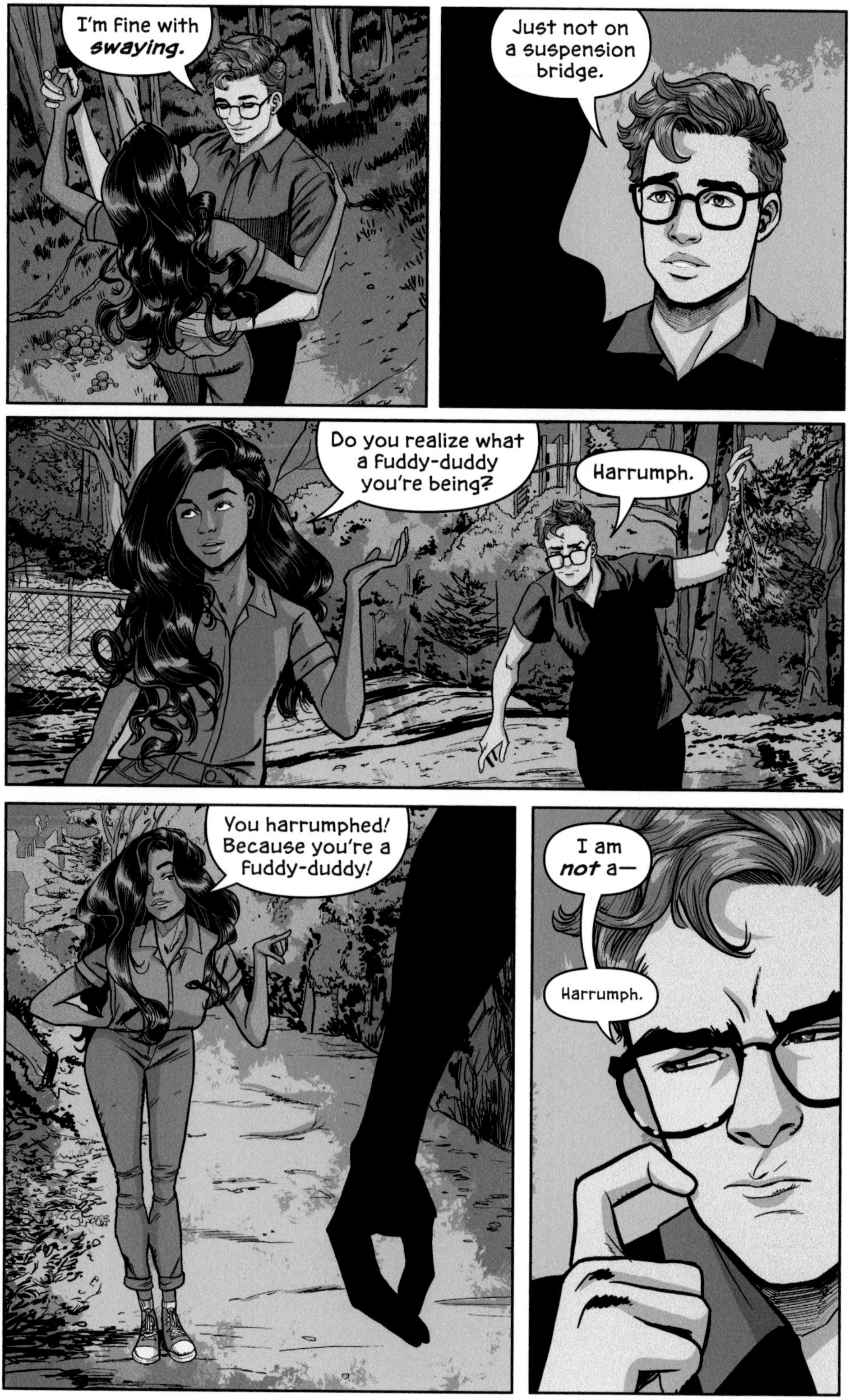
I'm fine with *swaying.*
Just not on a suspension bridge.
Do you realize what a fuddy-duddy you're being?
Harrumph.
You harrumphed! Because you're a fuddy-duddy!
I am *not* a—
Harrumph.

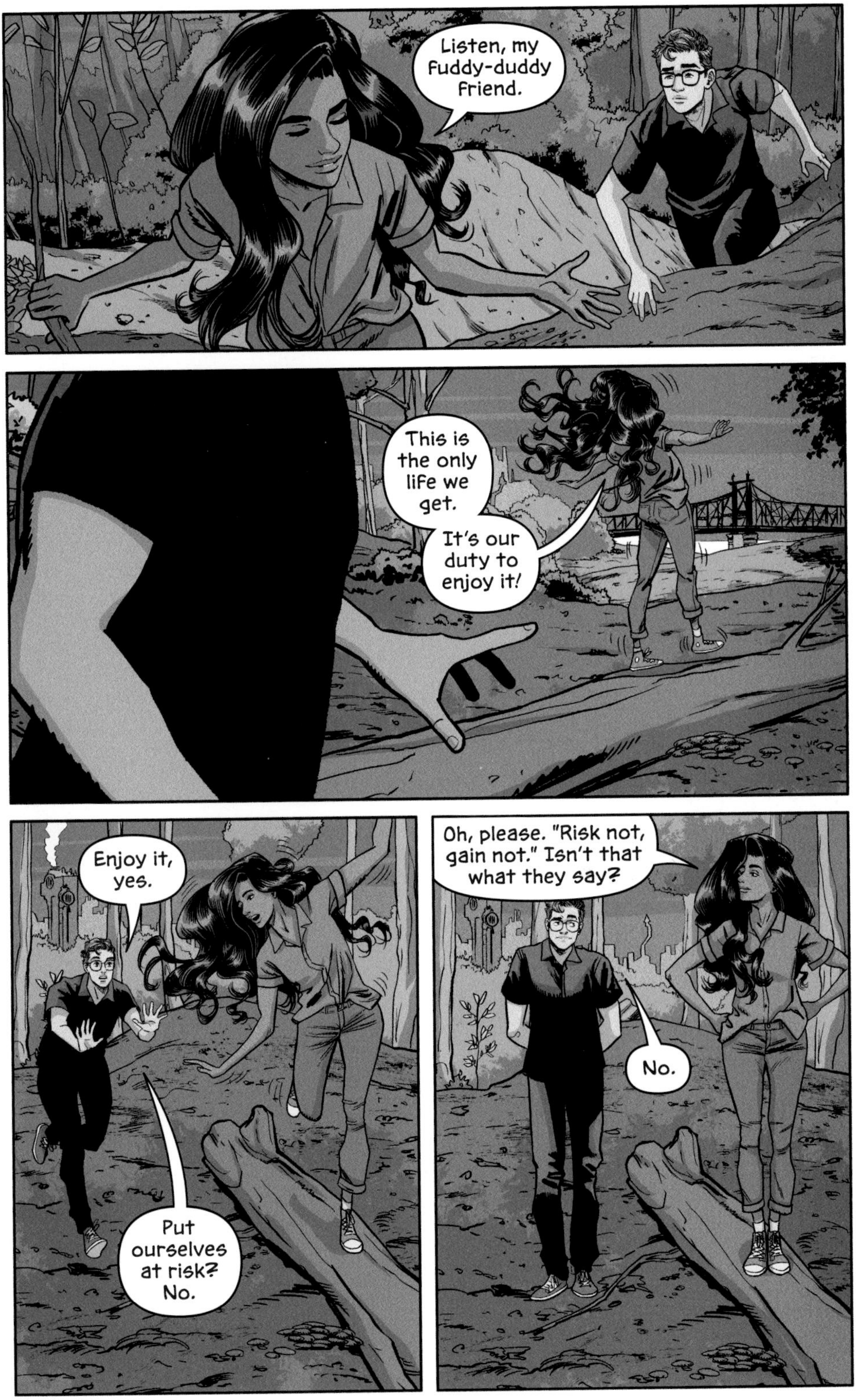
Listen, my fuddy-duddy friend.
This is the only life we get.
It's our duty to enjoy it!
Enjoy it, yes.
Put ourselves at risk? No.
Oh, please. "Risk not, gain not." Isn't that what they say?
No.

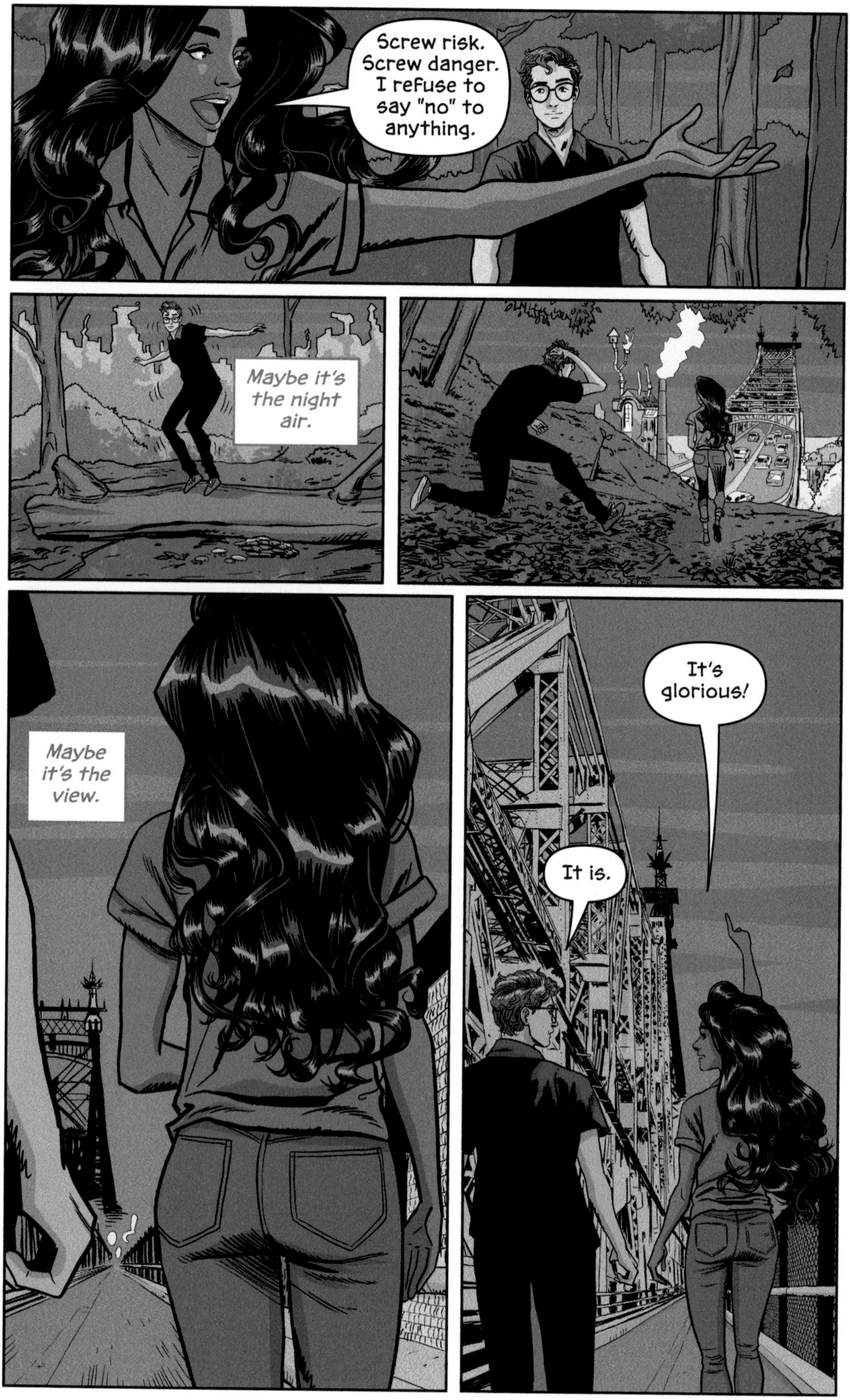
Screw risk. Screw danger. I refuse to say "no" to anything.
Maybe it's the night air.
Maybe it's the view.
It's glorious!
It is.

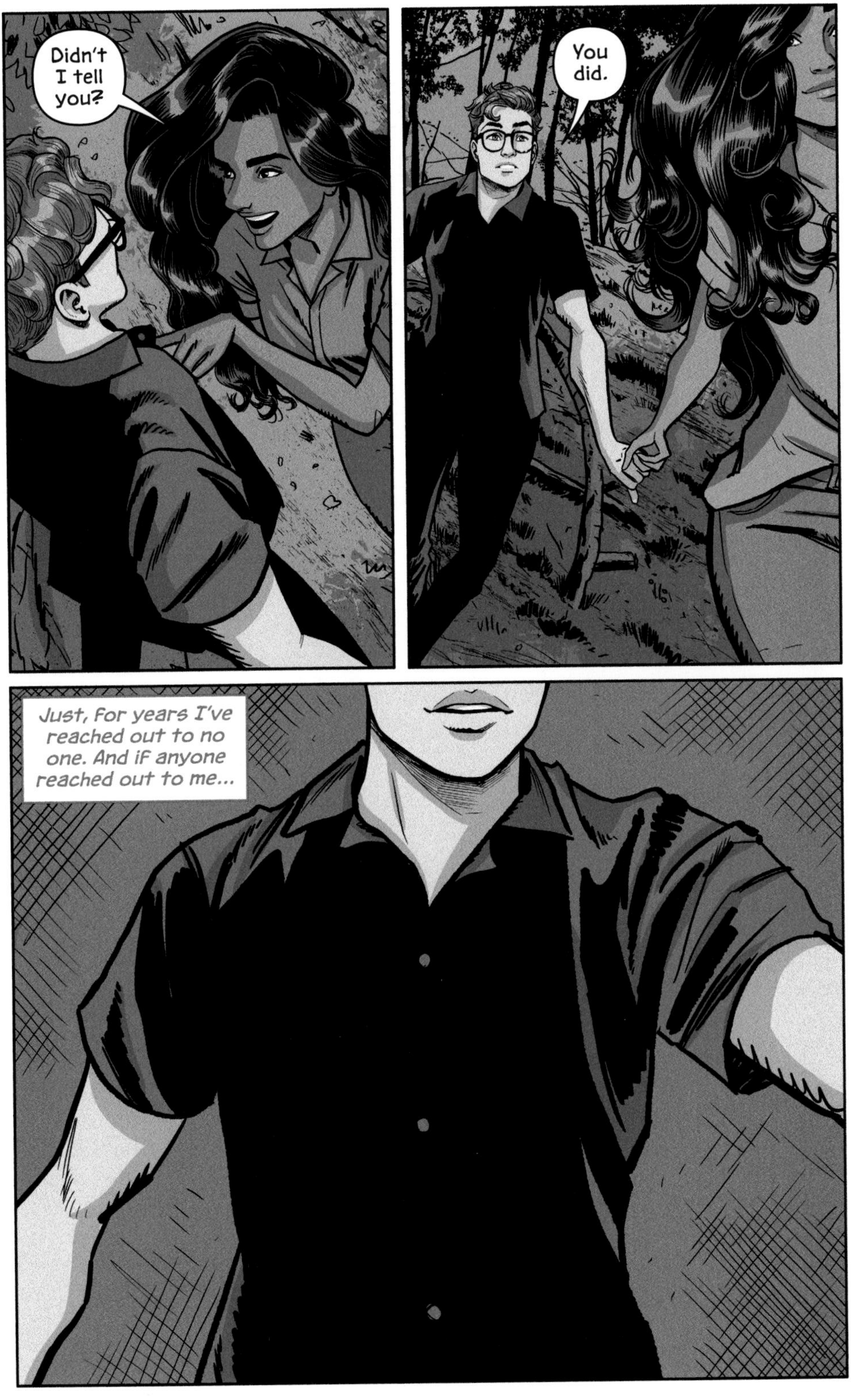
Didn't I tell you?
You did.
Just, for years I've reached out to no one. And if anyone reached out to me...

Well, I made sure to keep my heart protected.
First thoracic
First lumbar
And then this girl comes along.
Nora.
And... and...
She melts me.
KA-THUMP KA-THUMP

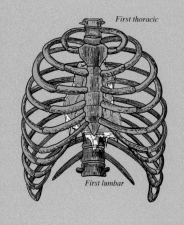

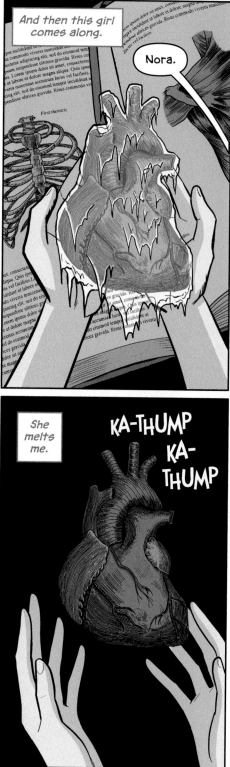

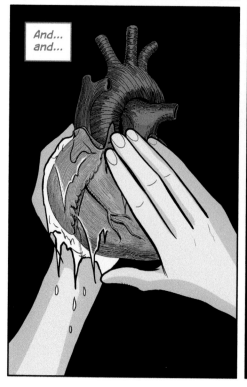

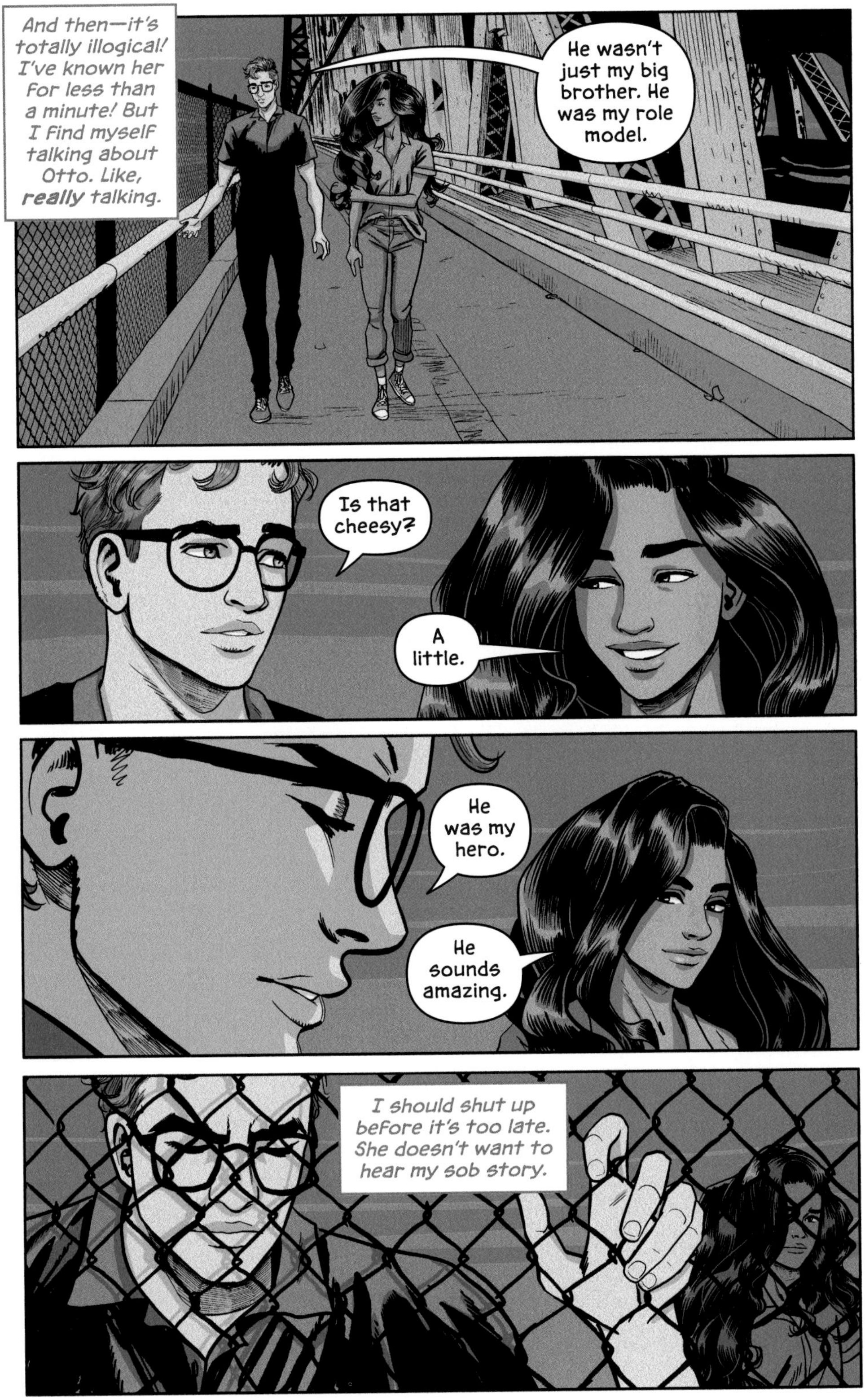
And then—it's totally illogical! I've known her for less than a minute! But I find myself talking about Otto. Like, *really* talking.
He wasn't just my big brother. He was my role model.
Is that cheesy?
A little.
He was my hero.
He sounds amazing.
I should shut up before it's too late. She doesn't want to hear my sob story.

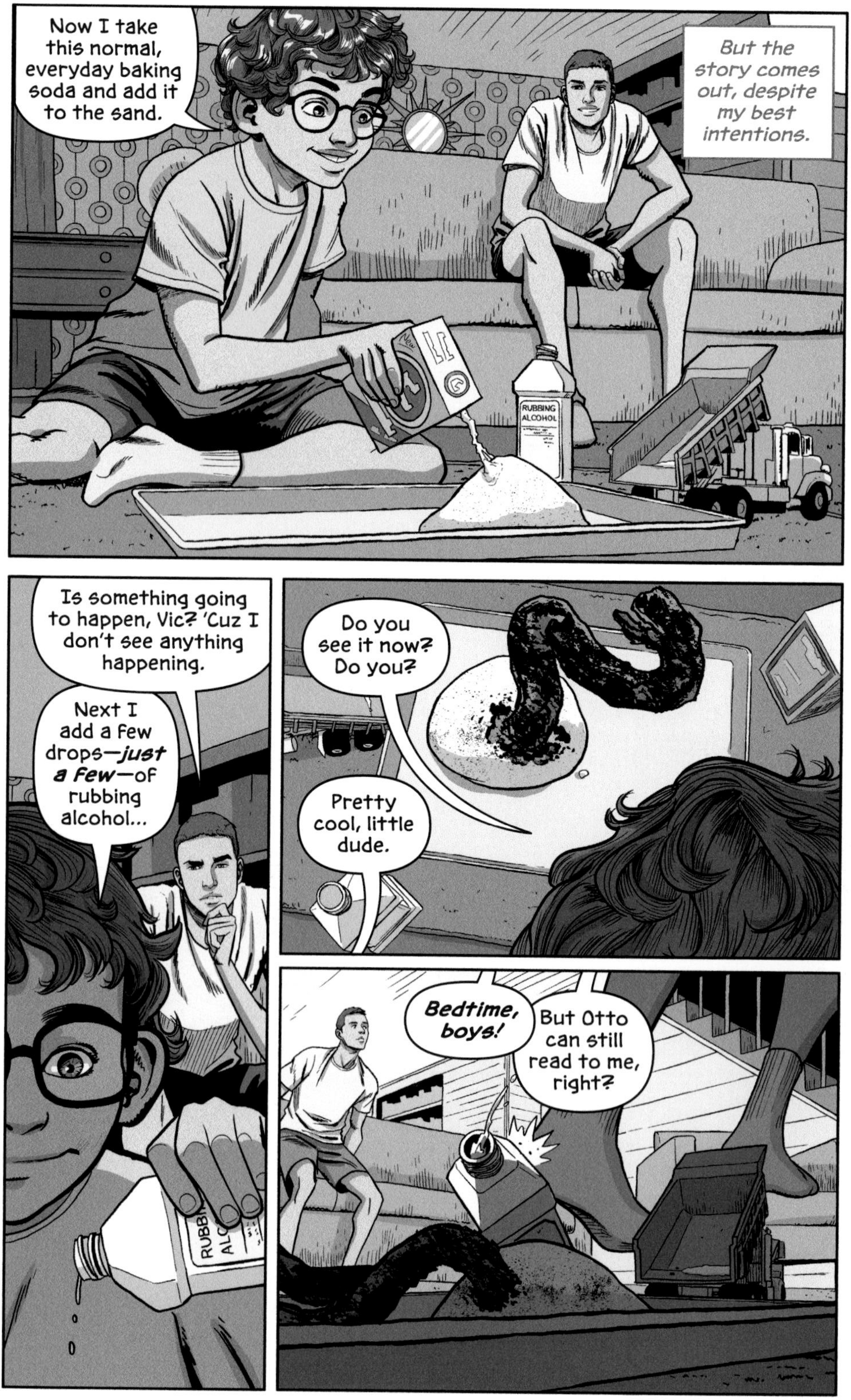
Now I take this normal, everyday baking soda and add it to the sand.
But the story comes out, despite my best intentions.
RUBBING ALCOHOL
Is something going to happen, Vic? 'Cuz I don't see anything happening.
Next I add a few drops—*just a few*—of rubbing alcohol...
Do you see it now? Do you?
Pretty cool, little dude.
Bedtime, boys!
But Otto can still read to me, right?

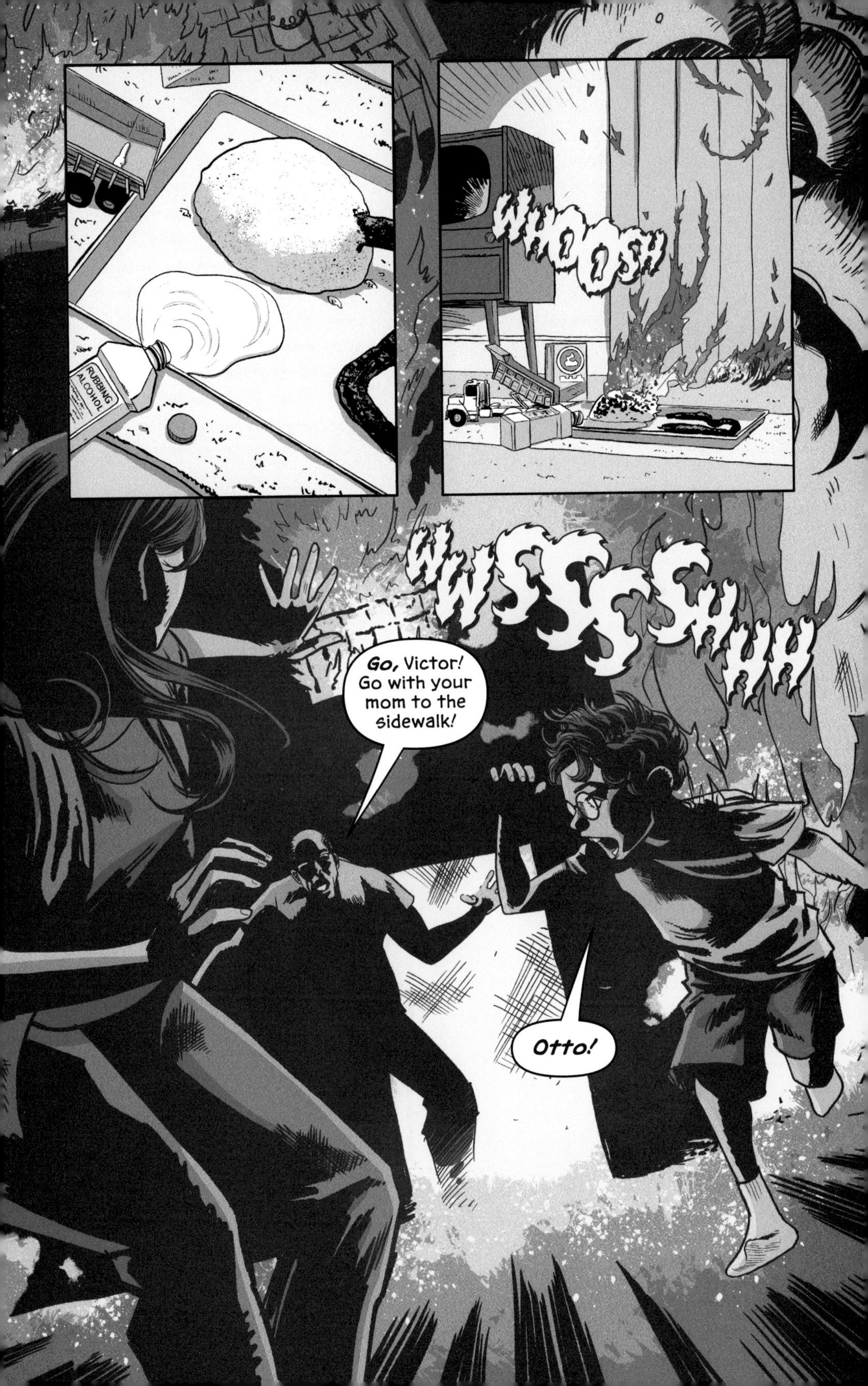
RUBBING ALCOHOL
WHOOSH
WSSSHHH
Go, Victor! Go with your mom to the sidewalk!
Otto!

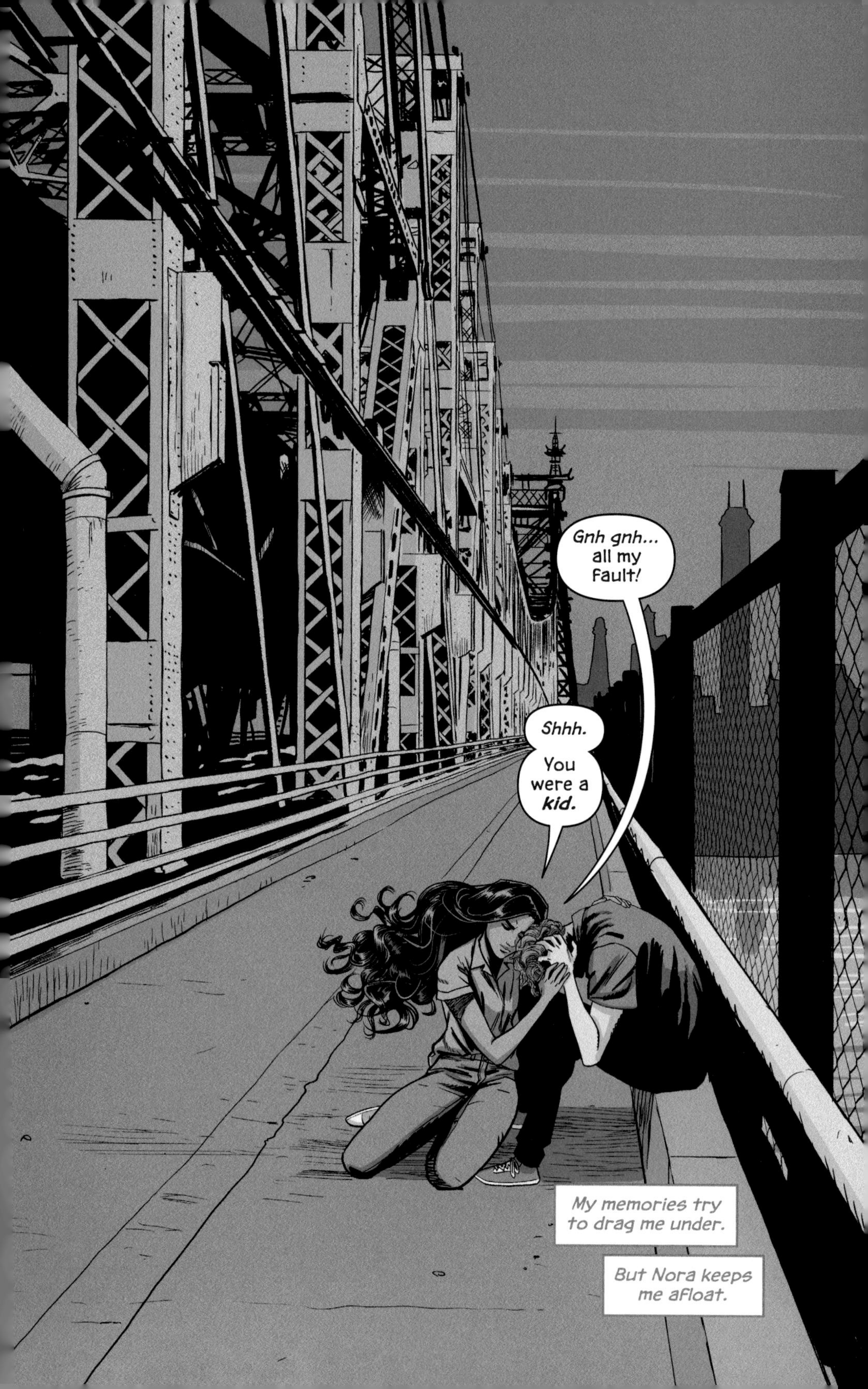
Gnh gnh... all my fault!
Shhh.
You were a *kid.*
My memories try to drag me under.
But Nora keeps me afloat.

The Girl Who Is Surprised

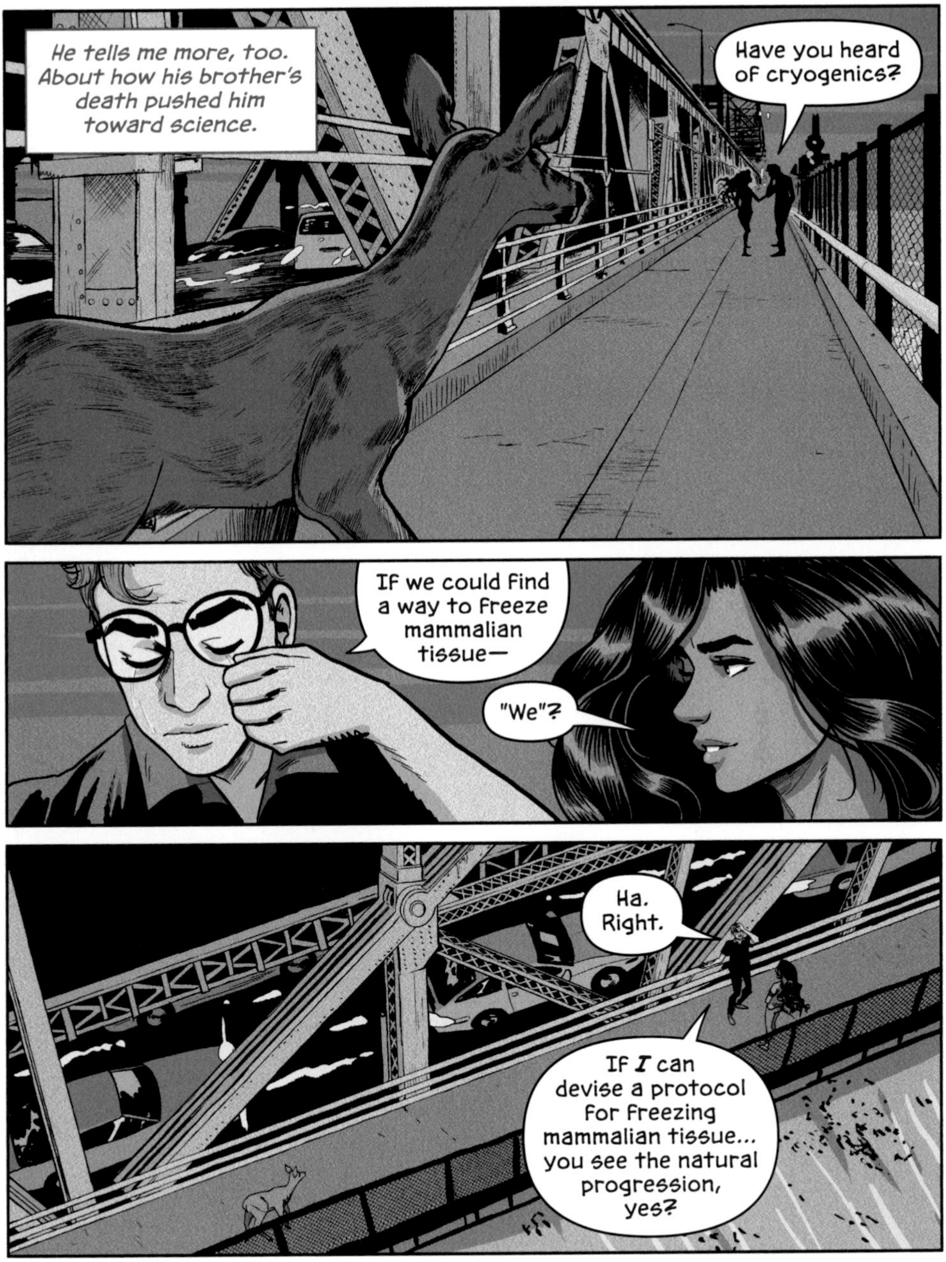
He tells me more, too. About how his brother's death pushed him toward science.
Have you heard of cryogenics?
If we could find a way to freeze mammalian tissue—
"We"?
Ha. Right.
If *I* can devise a protocol for freezing mammalian tissue... you see the natural progression, yes?

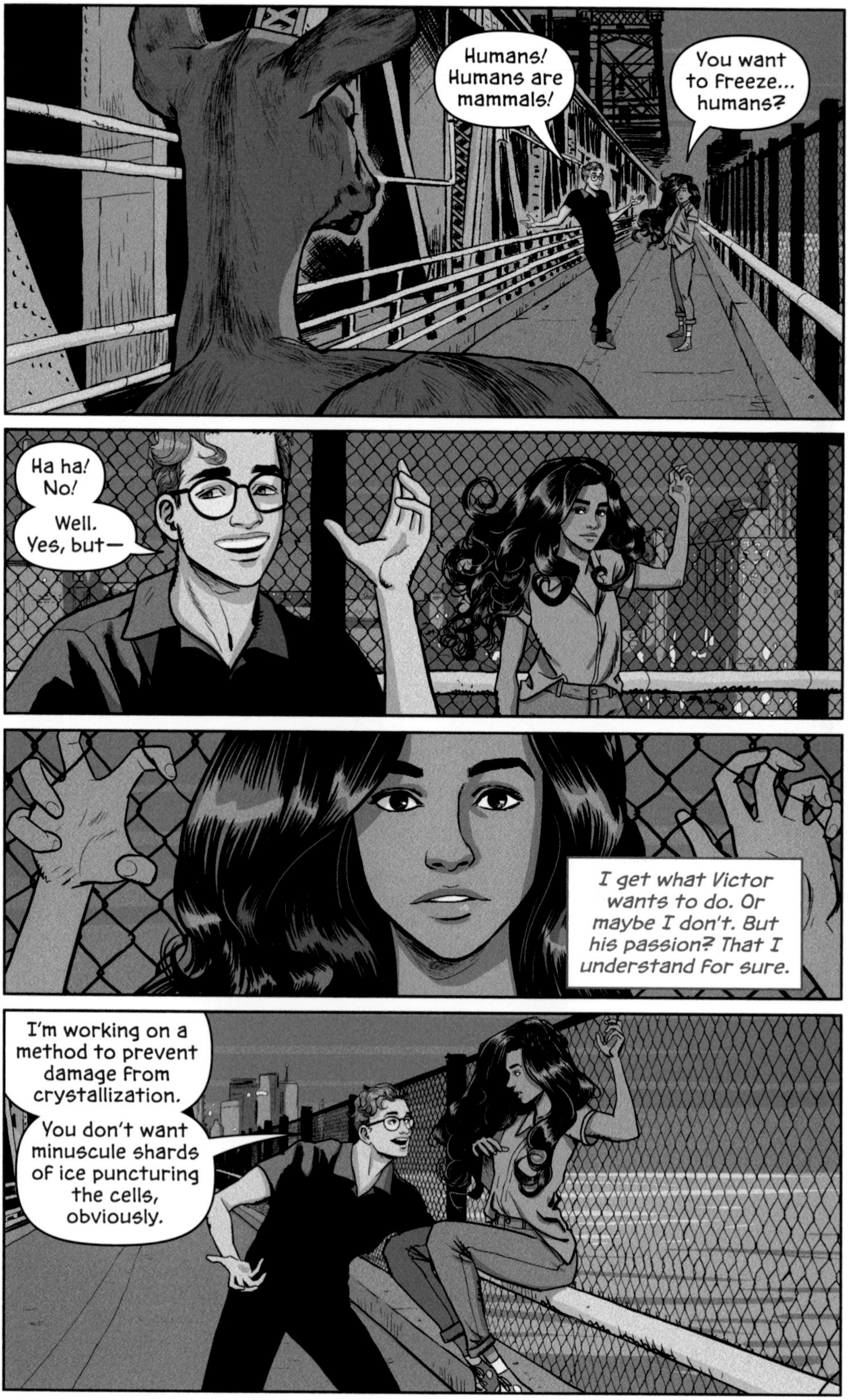
Humans! Humans are mammals!
You want to freeze... humans?
Ha ha! No!
Well. Yes, but—
I get what Victor wants to do. Or maybe I don't. But his passion? That I understand for sure.
I'm working on a method to prevent damage from crystallization.
You don't want minuscule shards of ice puncturing the cells, obviously.

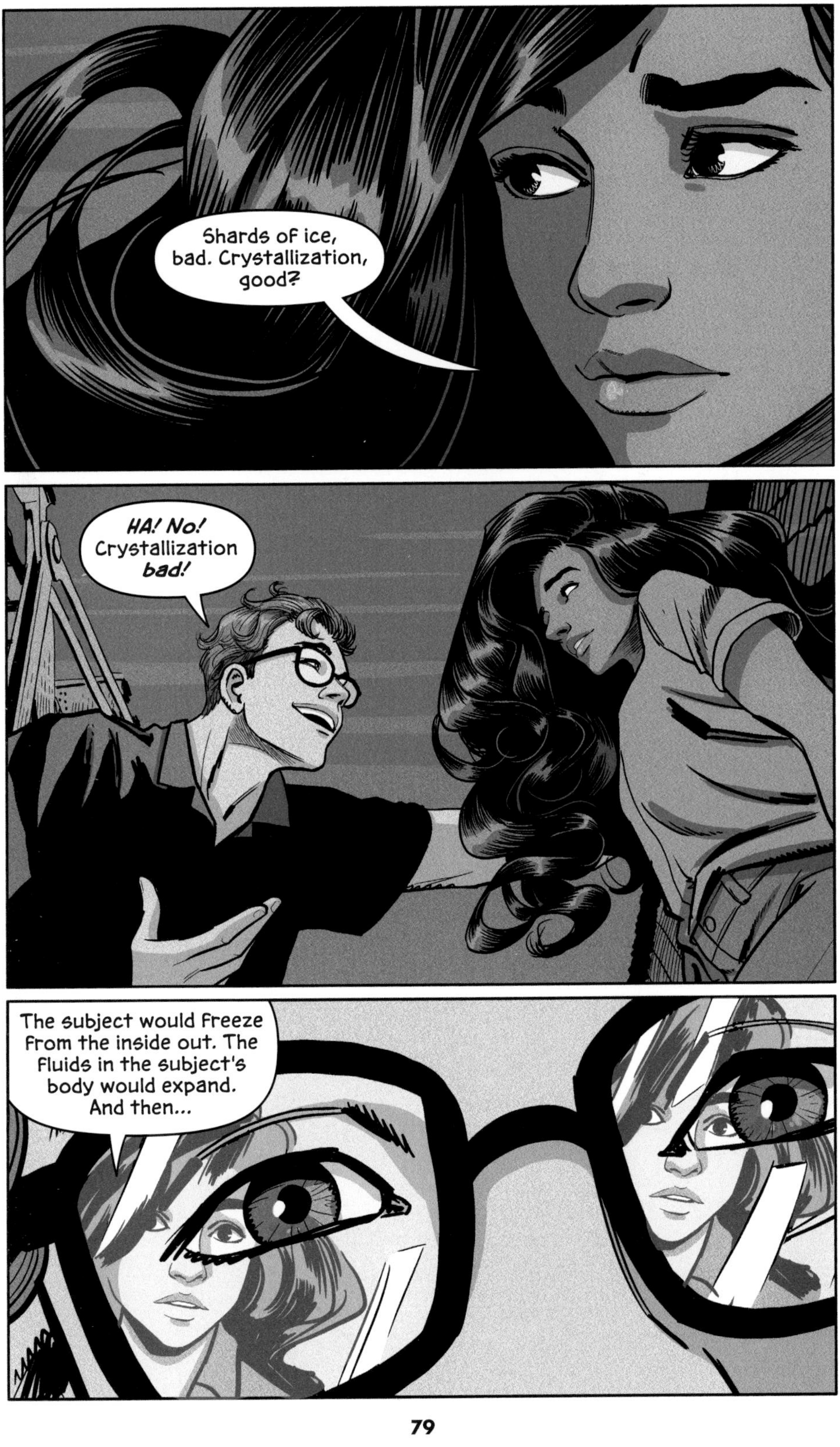
Shards of ice, bad. Crystallization, good?
HA! No! Crystallization *bad!*
The subject would freeze from the inside out. The fluids in the subject's body would expand. And then...

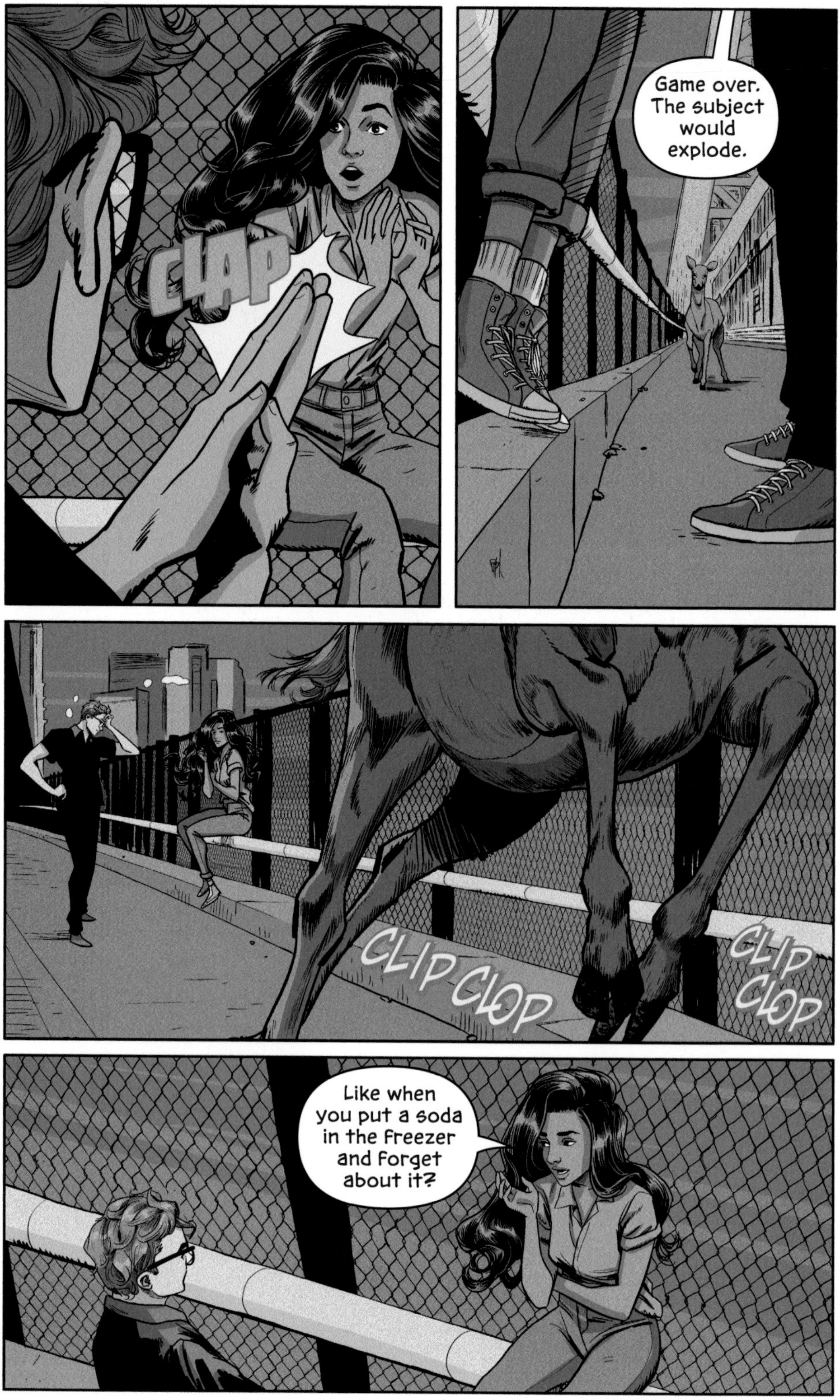
CLAP
Game over. The subject would explode.
CLIP CLOP
CLIP CLOP
Like when you put a soda in the freezer and forget about it?

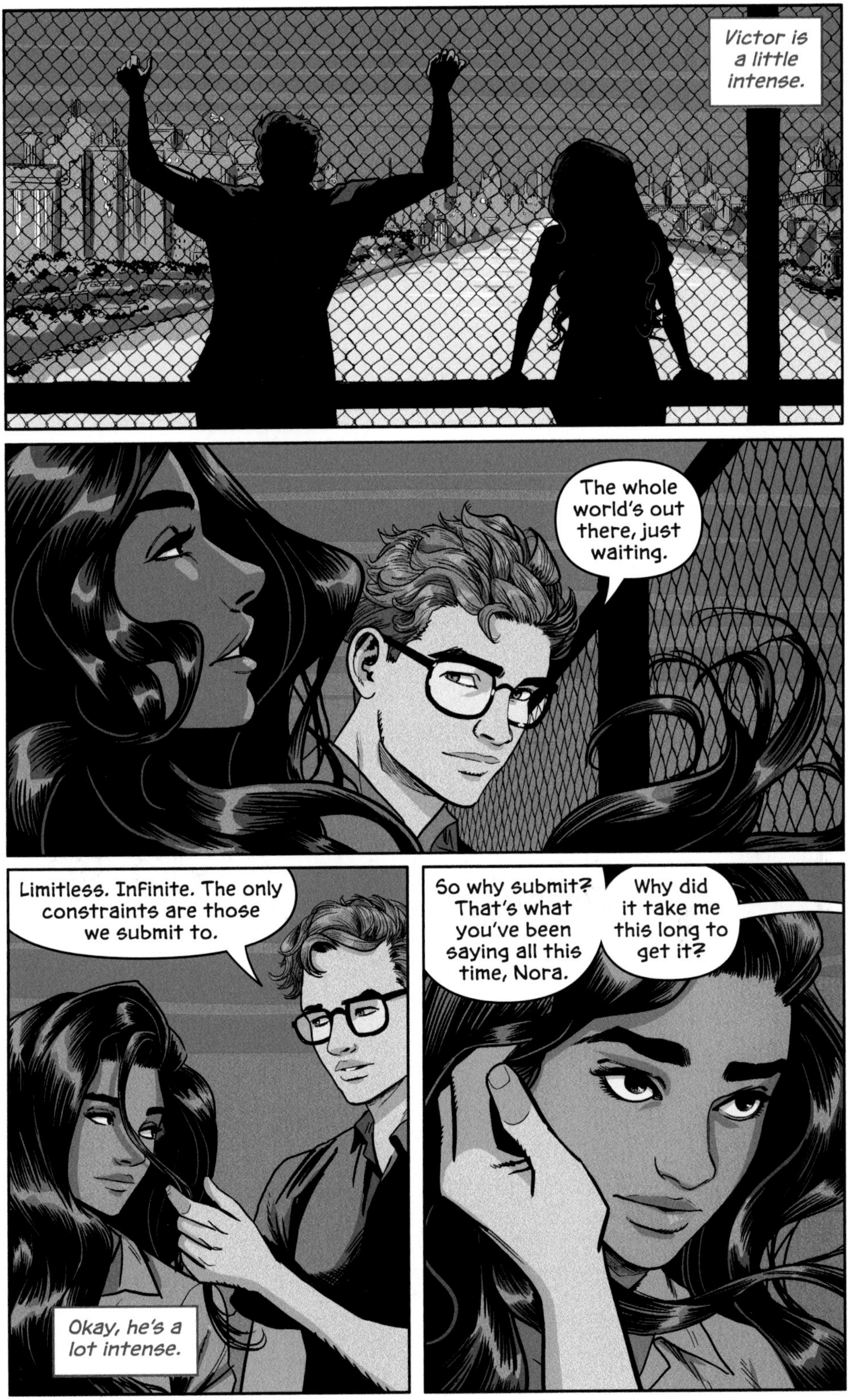
Victor is a little intense.
The whole world's out there, just waiting.
Limitless. Infinite. The only constraints are those we submit to.
Okay, he's a lot intense.
So why submit? That's what you've been saying all this time, Nora.
Why did it take me this long to get it?

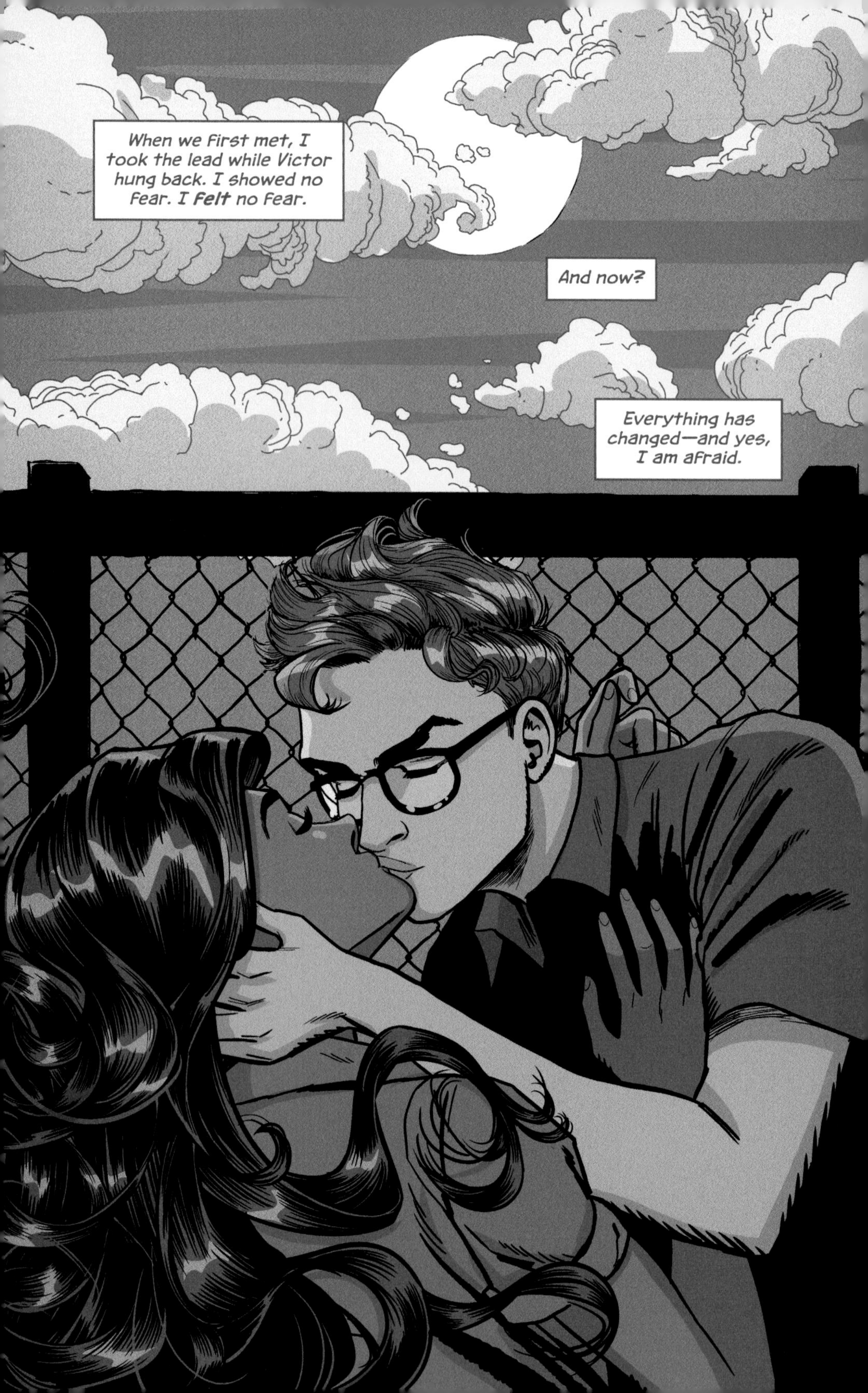
When we first met, I took the lead while Victor hung back. I showed no fear. I **felt** no fear.
And now?
Everything has changed—and yes, I am afraid.

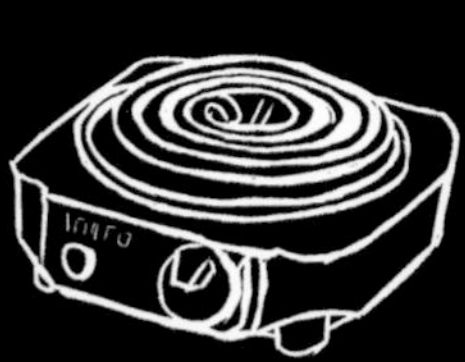

The Boy Who Doesn't Like Makeovers

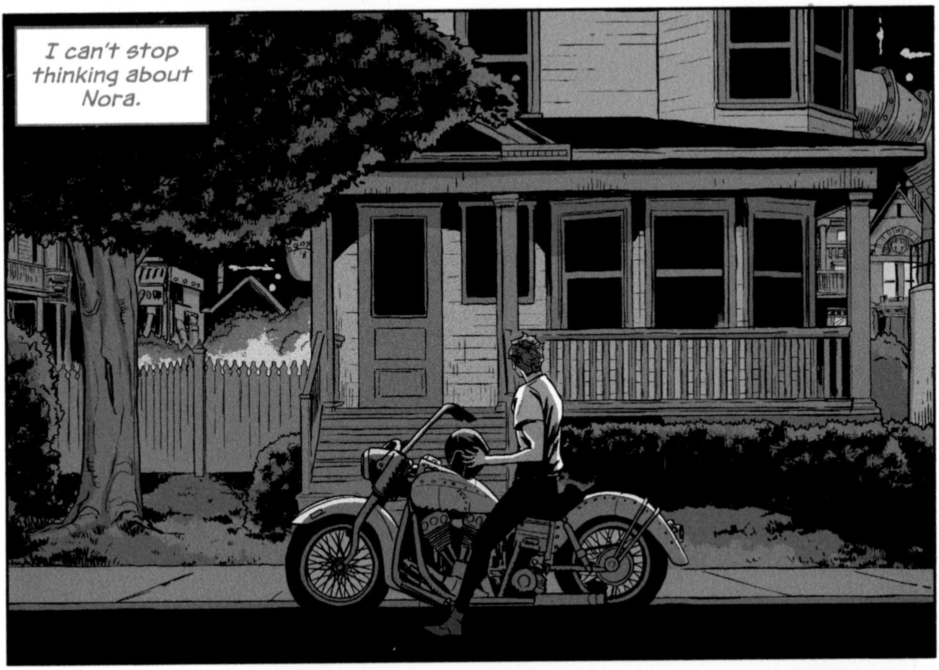
I can't stop thinking about Nora.

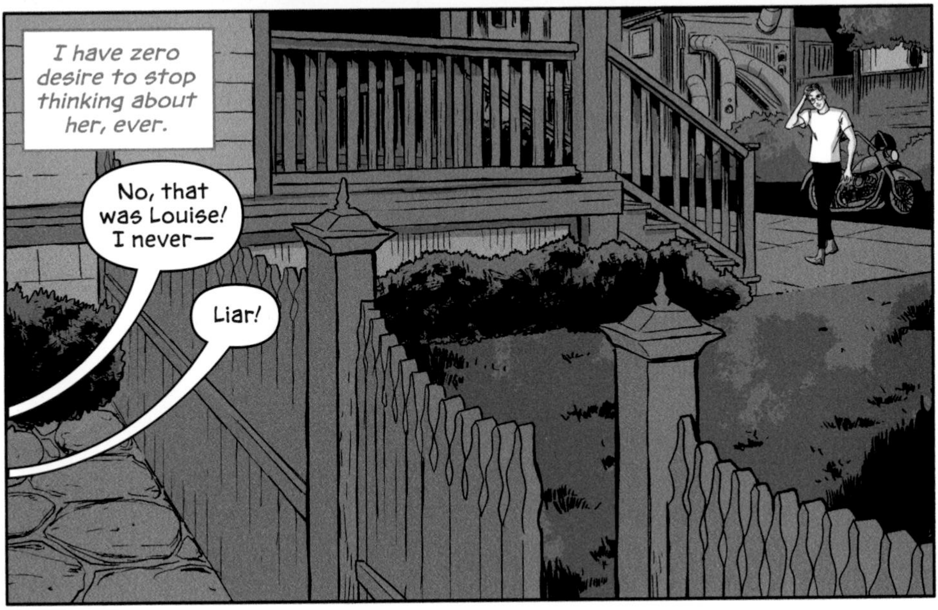
I have zero desire to stop thinking about her, ever.
No, that was Louise! I never—
Liar!

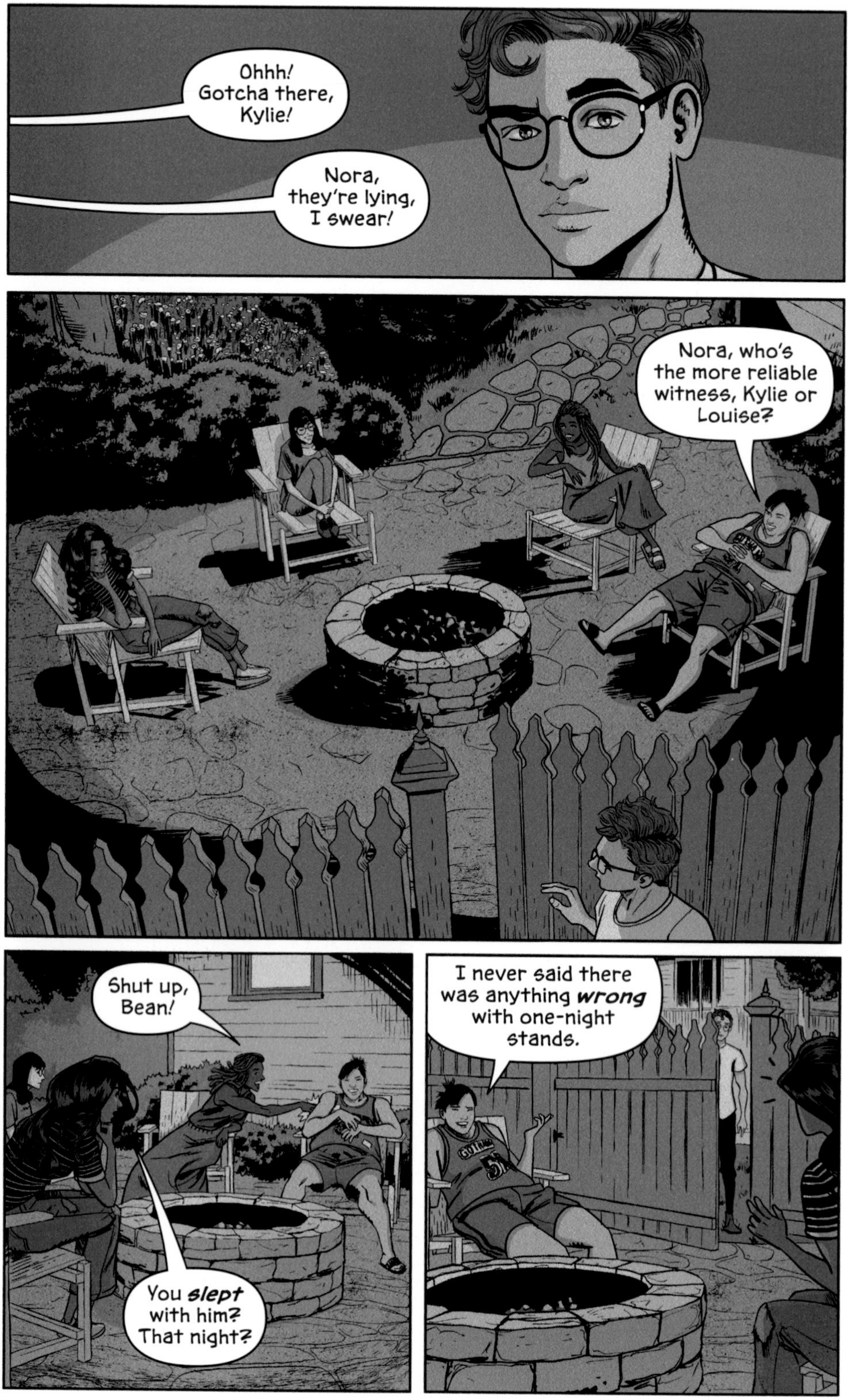
Ohhh! Gotcha there, Kylie!
Nora, they're lying, I swear!
Nora, who's the more reliable witness, Kylie or Louise?
Shut up, Bean!
You *slept* with him? That night?
I never said there was anything *wrong* with one-night stands.

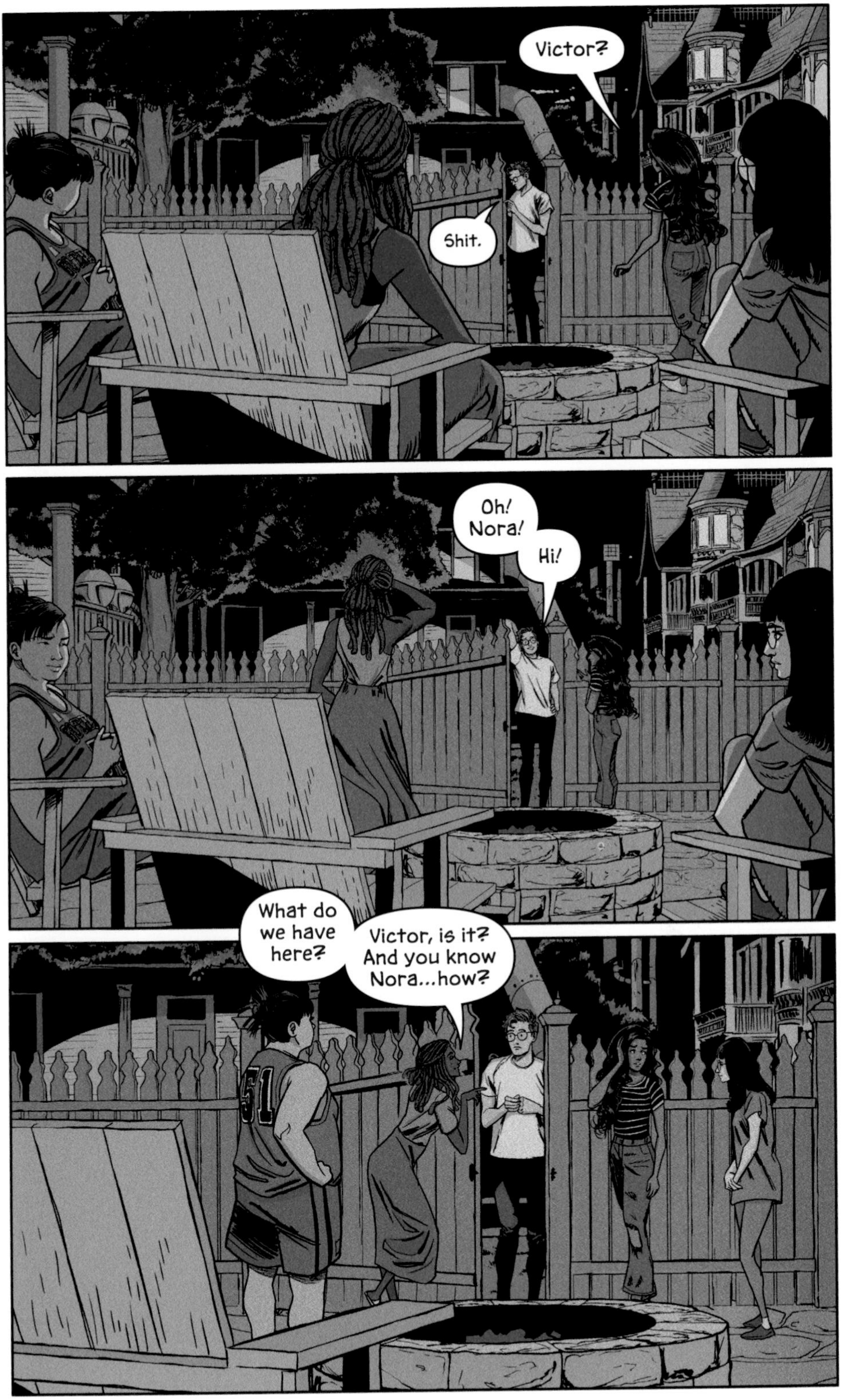
Victor?
Shit.
Oh! Nora!
Hi!
What do we have here?
Victor, is it? And you know Nora...how?

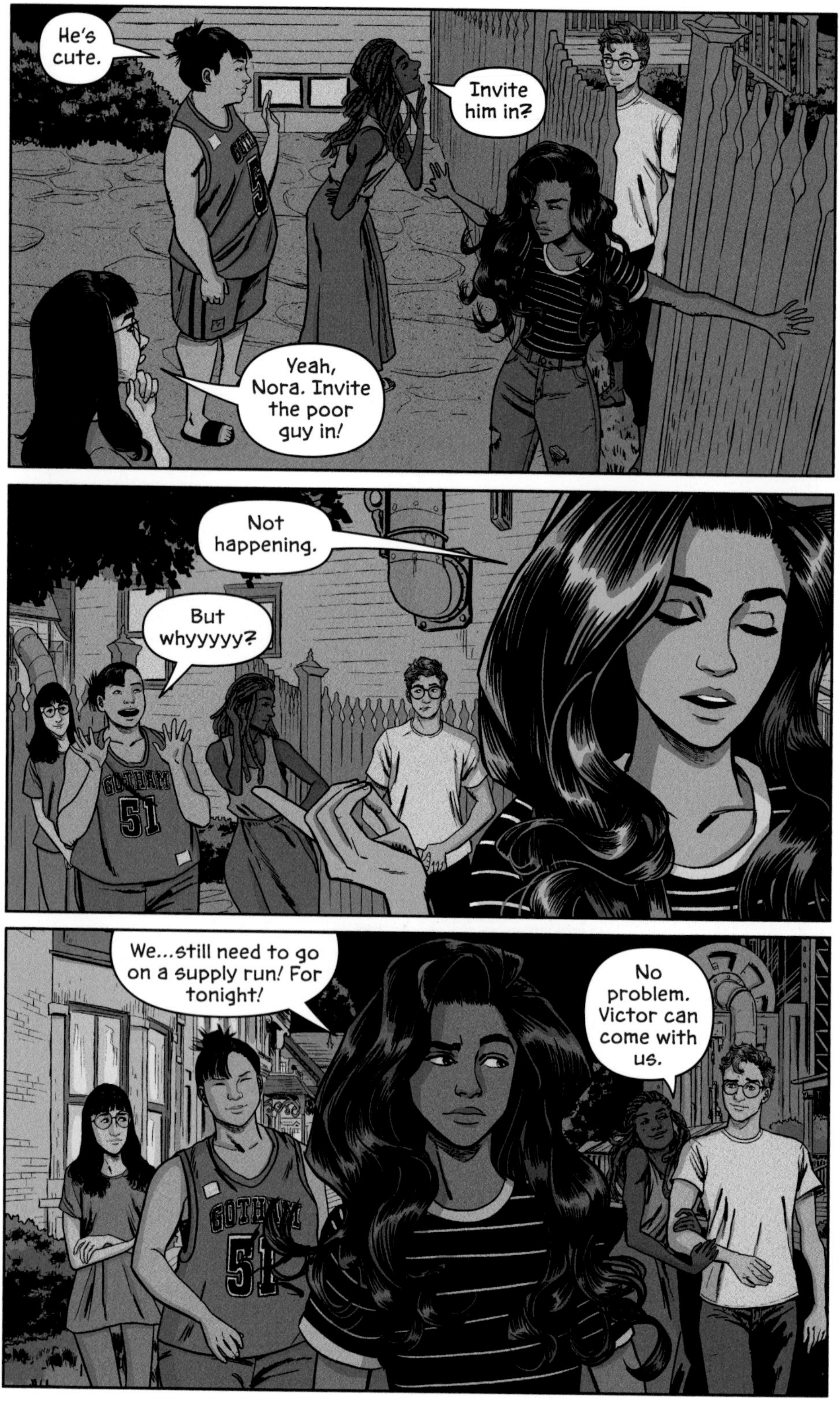
He's cute.
Invite him in?
Yeah, Nora. Invite the poor guy in!
Not happening.
But whyyyyy?
We...still need to go on a supply run! For tonight!
No problem. Victor can come with us.

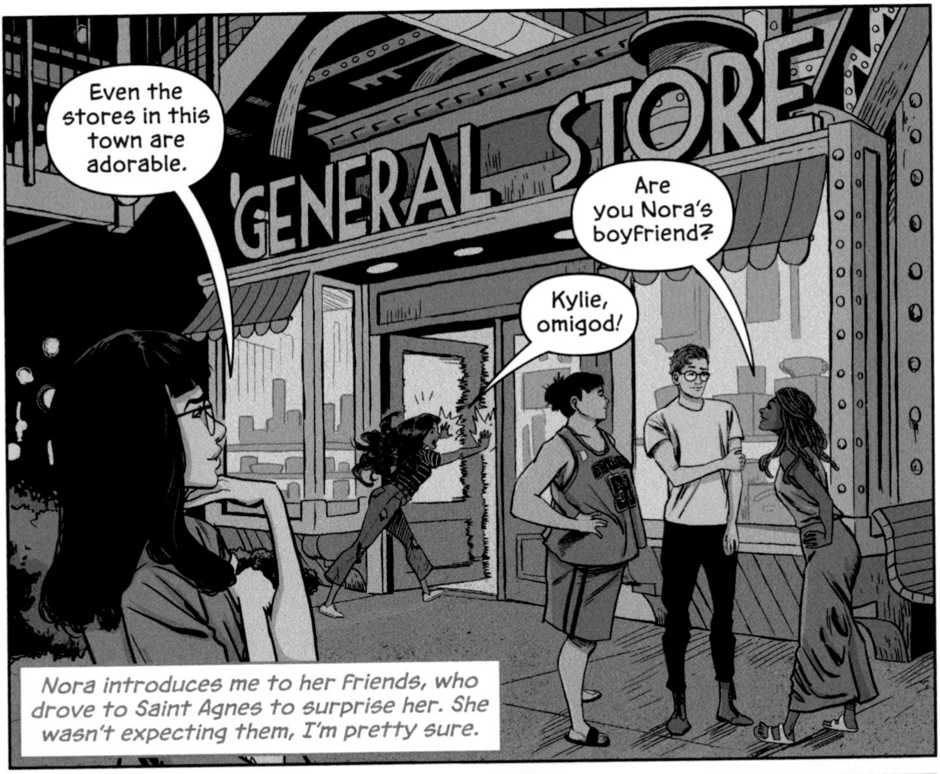
GENERAL STORE
Even the stores in this town are adorable.
Are you Nora's boyfriend?
Kylie, omigod!
Nora introduces me to her friends, who drove to Saint Agnes to surprise her. She wasn't expecting them, I'm pretty sure.

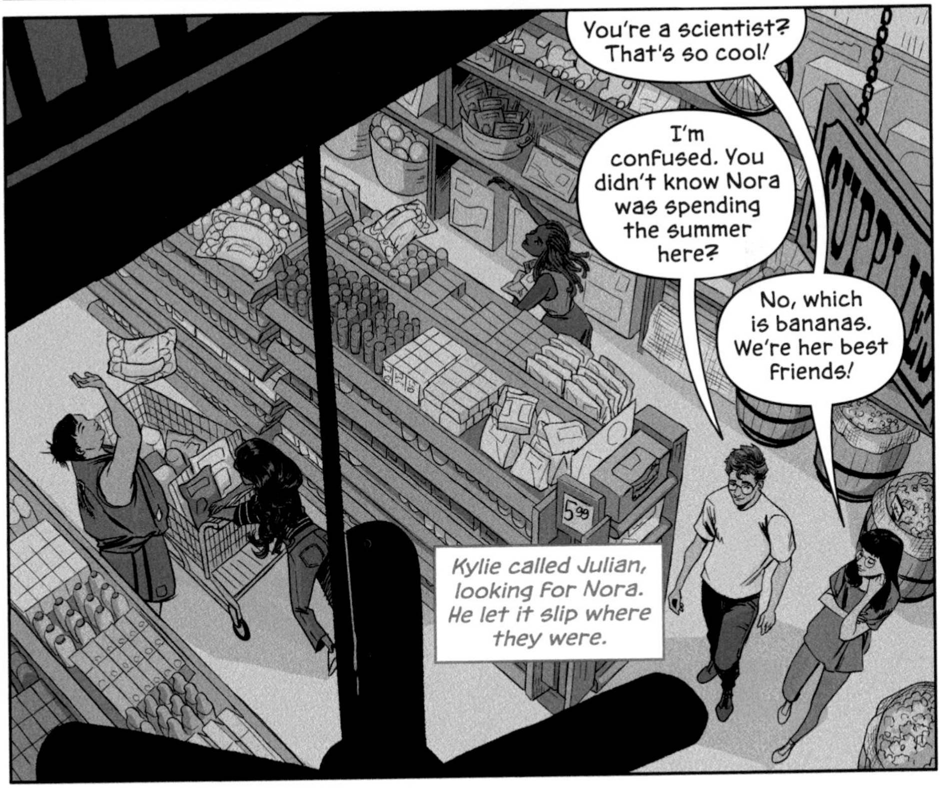
You're a scientist? That's so cool!
I'm confused. You didn't know Nora was spending the summer here?
No, which is bananas. We're her best friends!
5.99
Kylie called Julian, looking for Nora. He let it slip where they were.

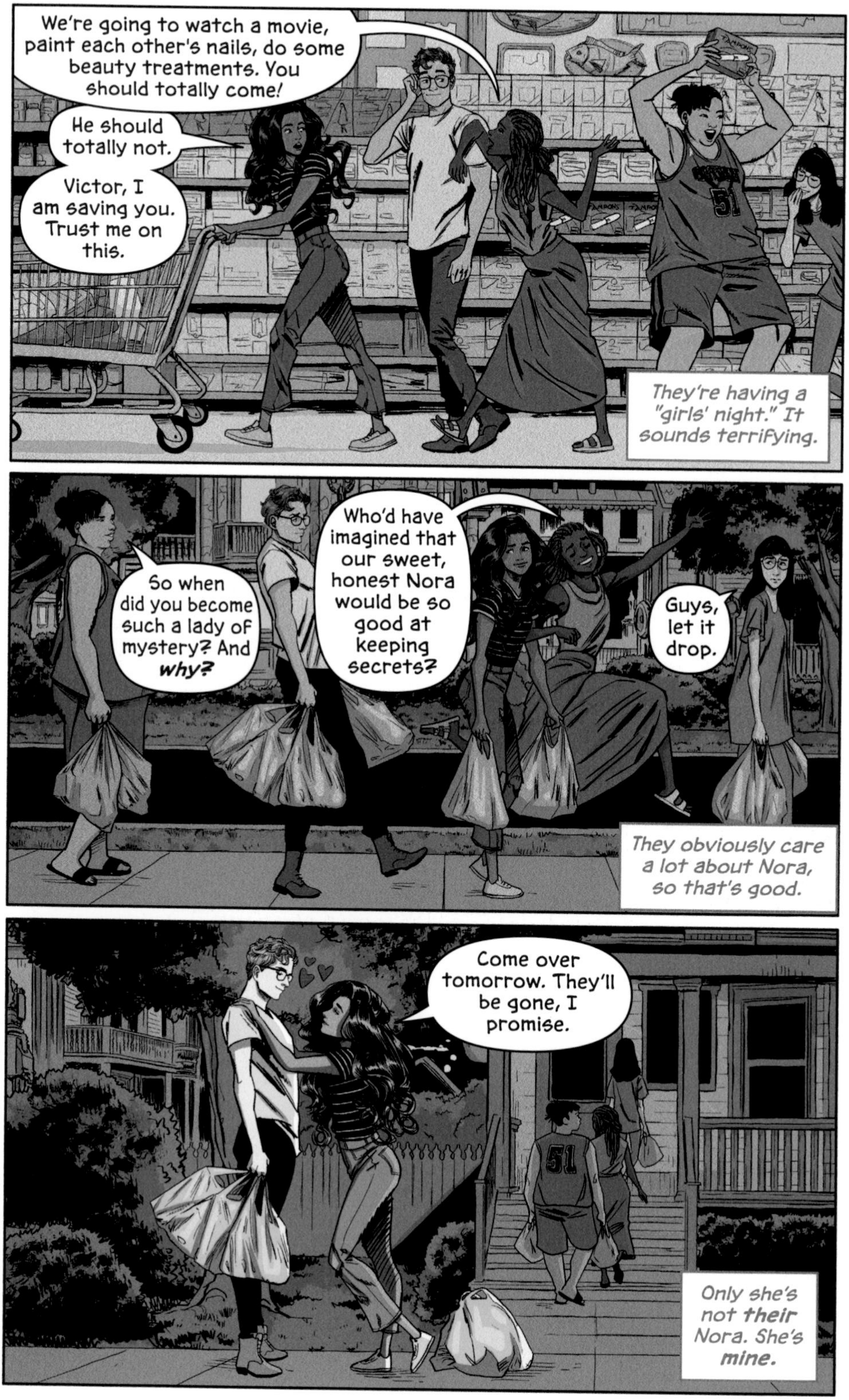
We're going to watch a movie, paint each other's nails, do some beauty treatments. You should totally come!
He should totally not.
Victor, I am saving you. Trust me on this.
They're having a "girls' night." It sounds terrifying.
So when did you become such a lady of mystery? And *why?*
Who'd have imagined that our sweet, honest Nora would be so good at keeping secrets?
Guys, let it drop.
They obviously care a lot about Nora, so that's good.
Come over tomorrow. They'll be gone, I promise.
Only she's not *their* Nora. She's *mine.*

The Girl Who's Always Hot

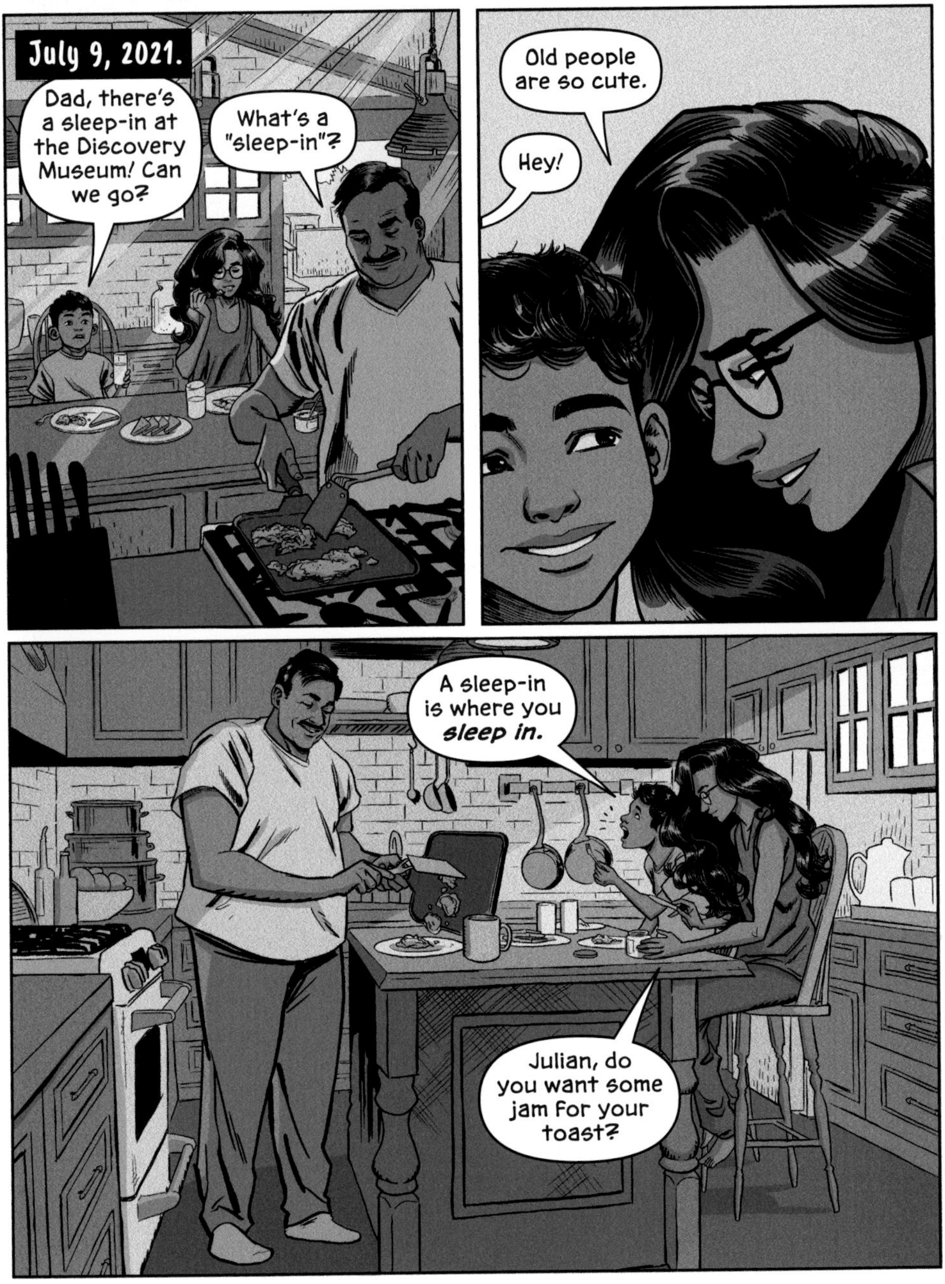
July 9, 2021.
Dad, there's a sleep-in at the Discovery Museum! Can we go?
What's a "sleep-in"?
Old people are so cute.
Hey!
A sleep-in is where you *sleep in.*
Julian, do you want some jam for your toast?

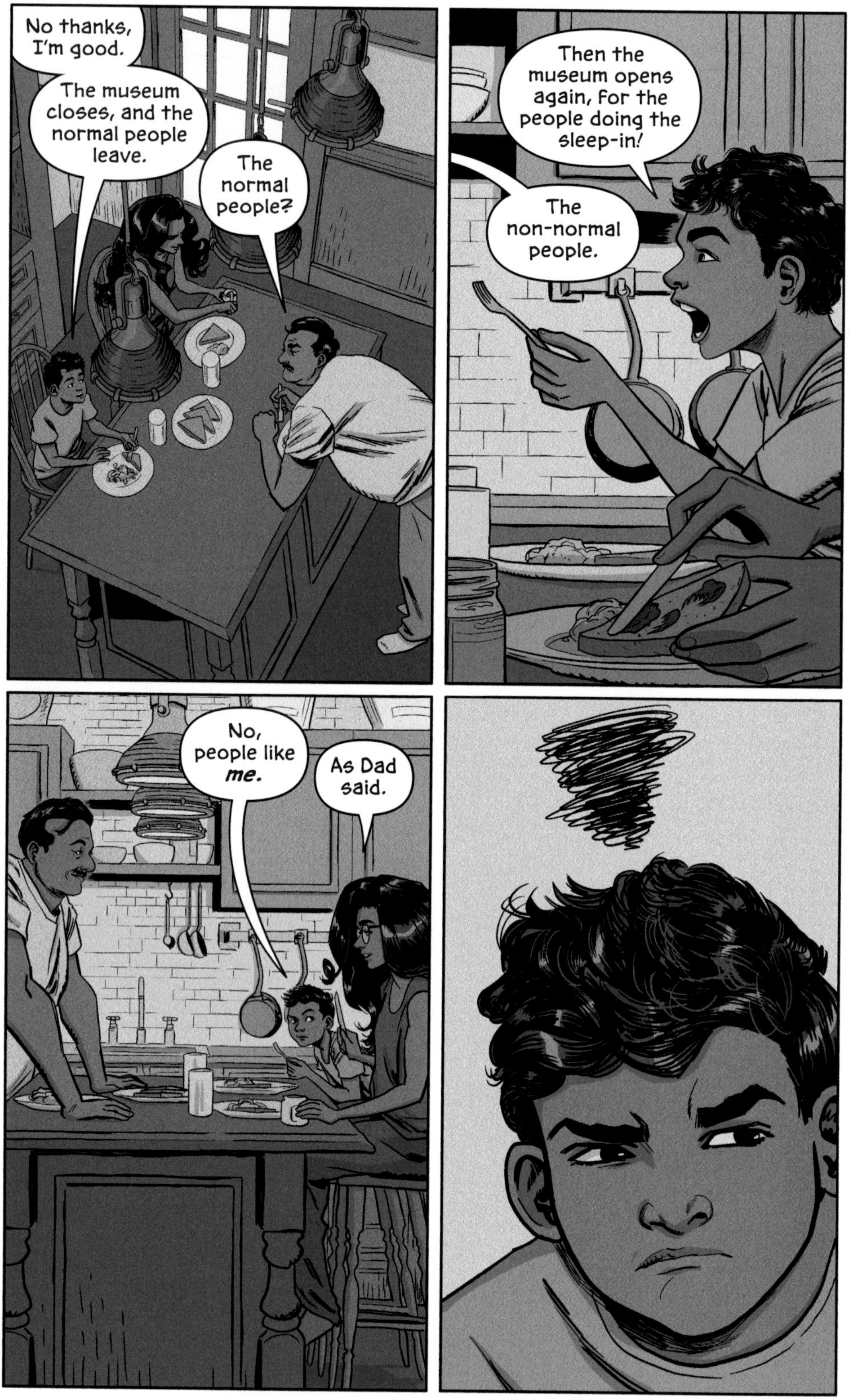
No thanks, I'm good.
The museum closes, and the normal people leave.
The normal people?
Then the museum opens again, for the people doing the sleep-in!
The non-normal people.
No, people like *me.*
As Dad said.

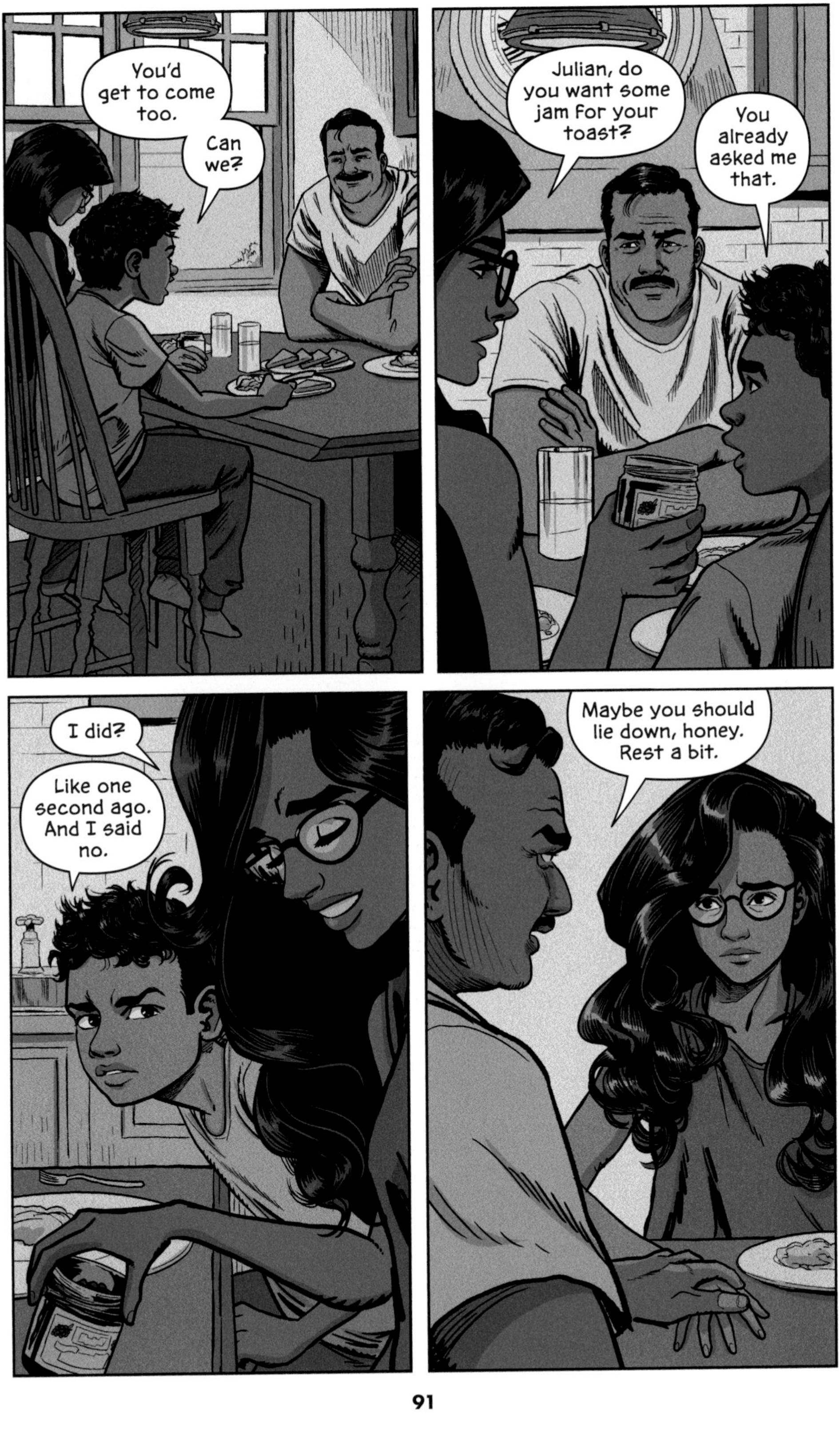
You'd get to come too.
Can we?
Julian, do you want some jam for your toast?
You already asked me that.
I did?
Like one second ago. And I said no.
Maybe you should lie down, honey. Rest a bit.

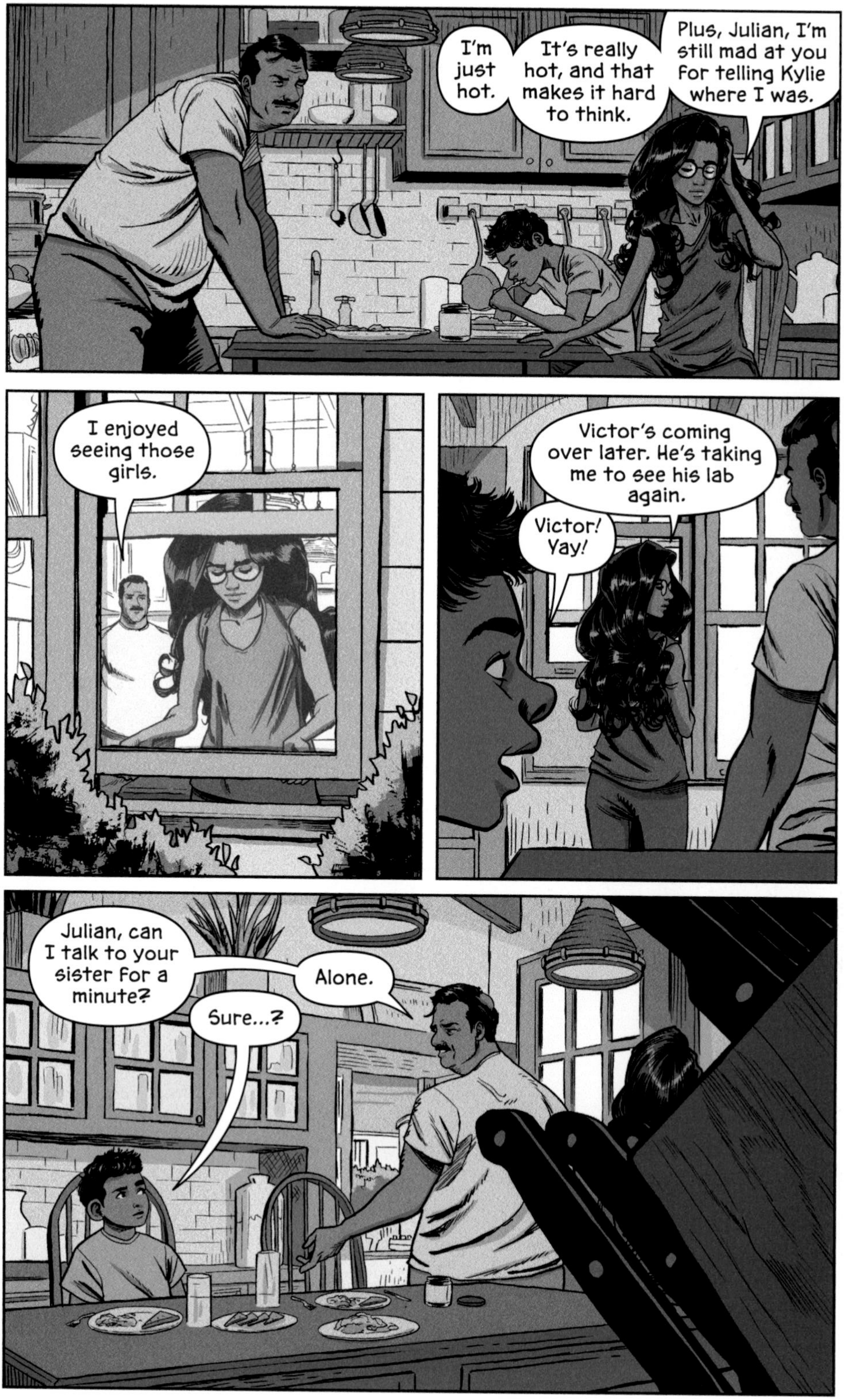
I'm just hot.
It's really hot, and that makes it hard to think.
Plus, Julian, I'm still mad at you for telling Kylie where I was.
I enjoyed seeing those girls.
Victor's coming over later. He's taking me to see his lab again.
Victor! Yay!
Julian, can I talk to your sister for a minute?
Alone.
Sure...?

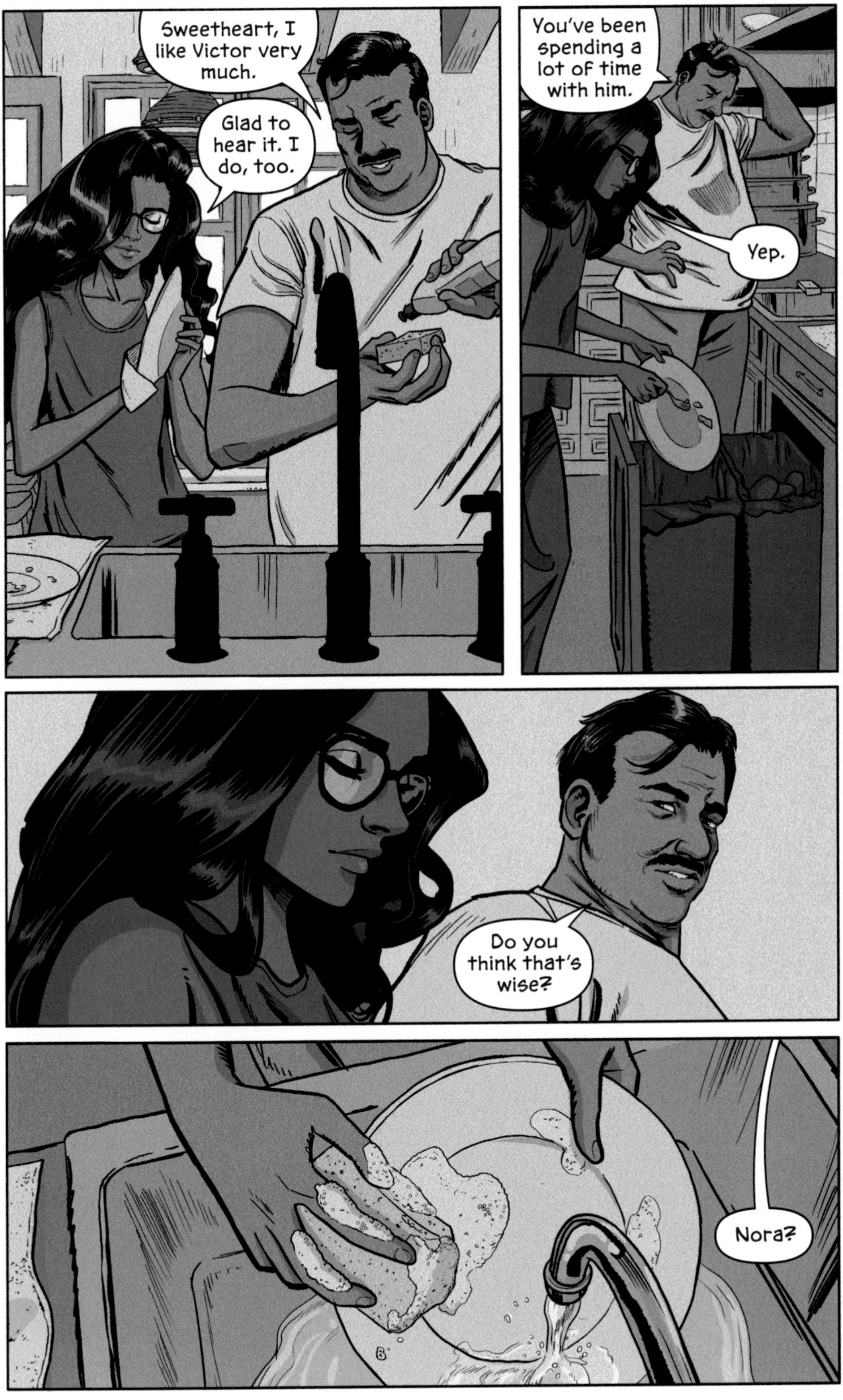
Sweetheart, I like Victor very much.
Glad to hear it. I do, too.
You've been spending a lot of time with him.
Yep.
Do you think that's wise?
Nora?

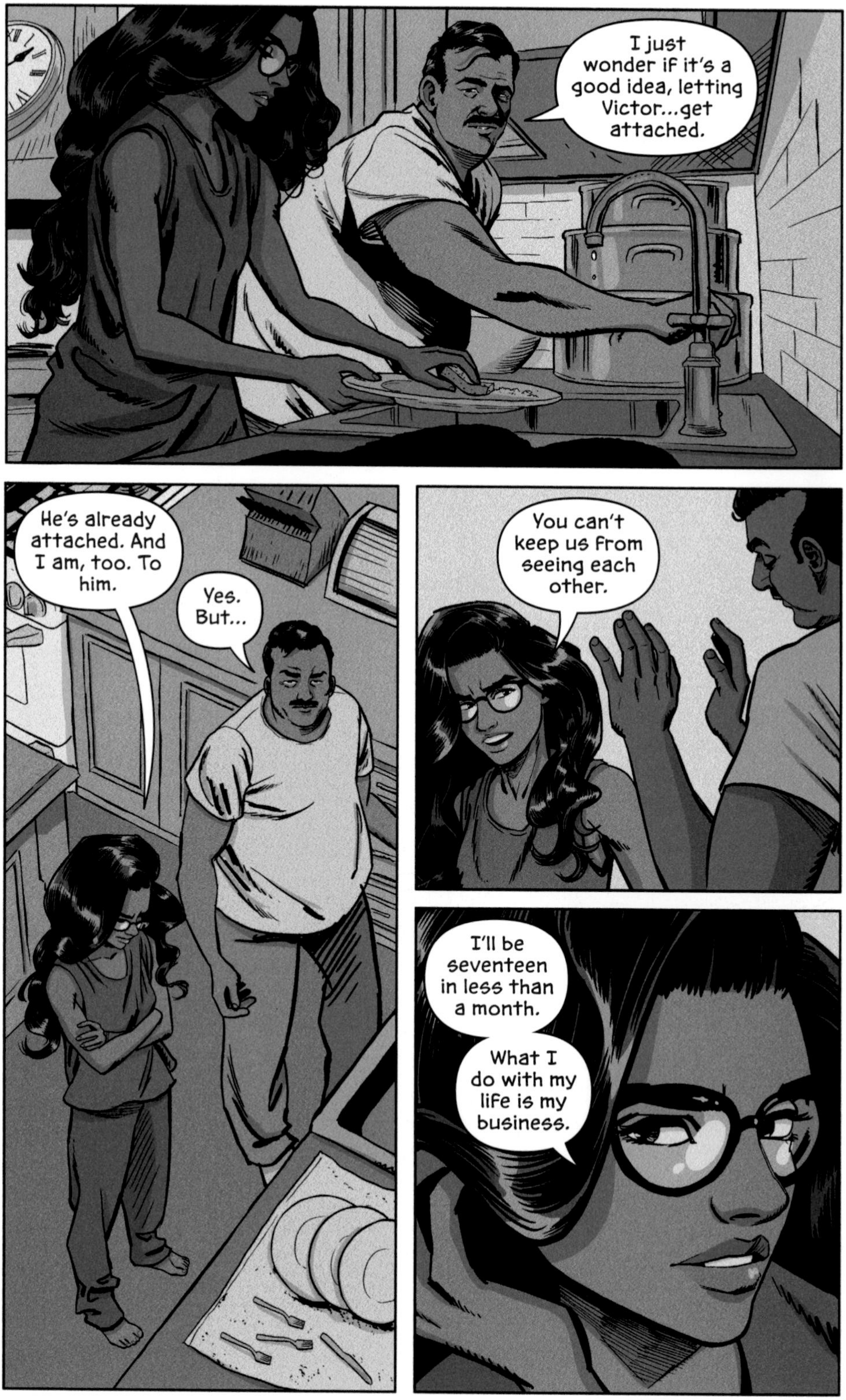
I just wonder if it's a good idea, letting Victor...get attached.
He's already attached. And I am, too. To him.
Yes. But...
You can't keep us from seeing each other.
I'll be seventeen in less than a month.
What I do with my life is my business.

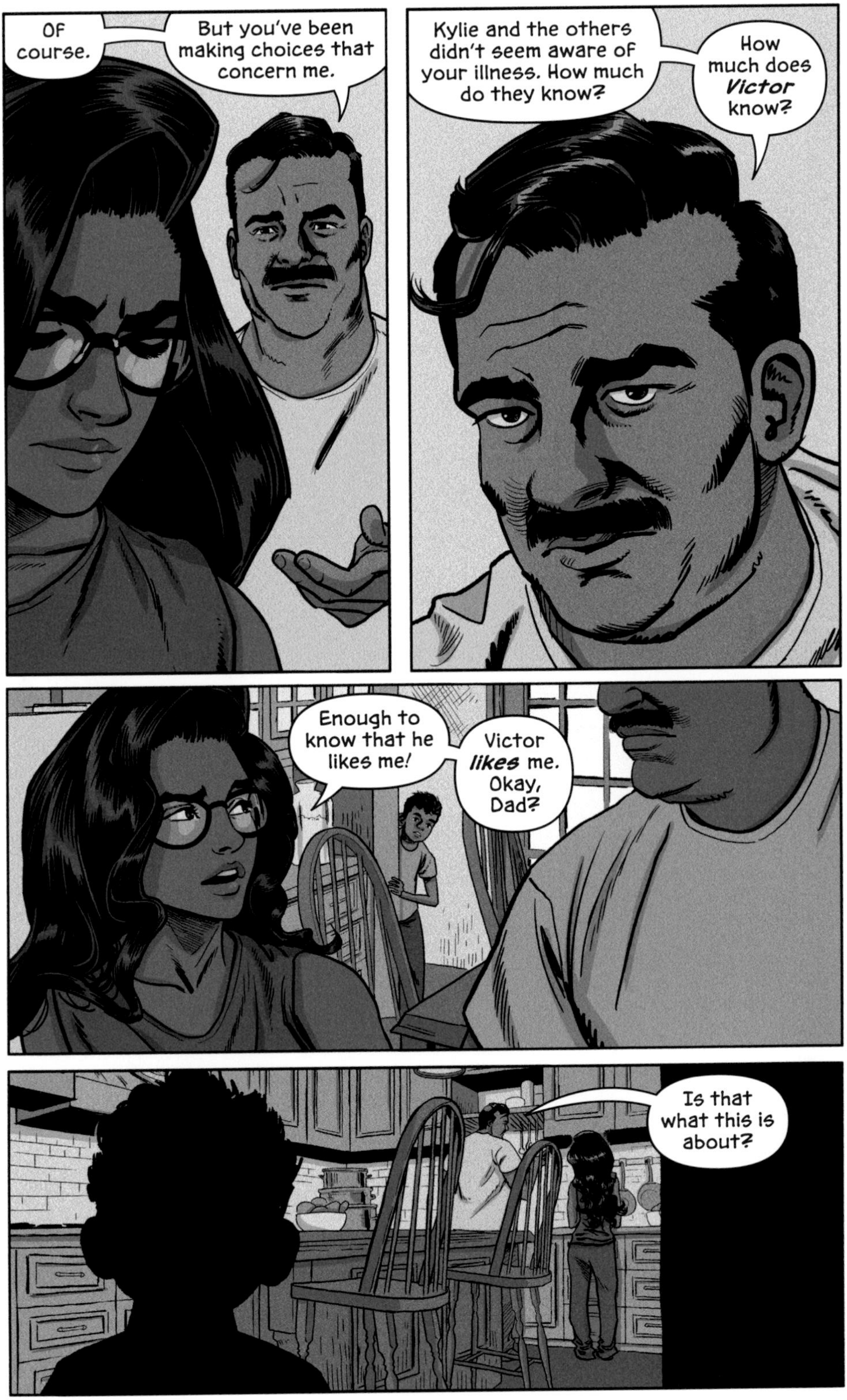
Of course.
But you've been making choices that concern me.
Kylie and the others didn't seem aware of your illness. How much do they know?
How much does *Victor* know?
Enough to know that he likes me!
Victor *likes* me. Okay, Dad?
Is that what this is about?

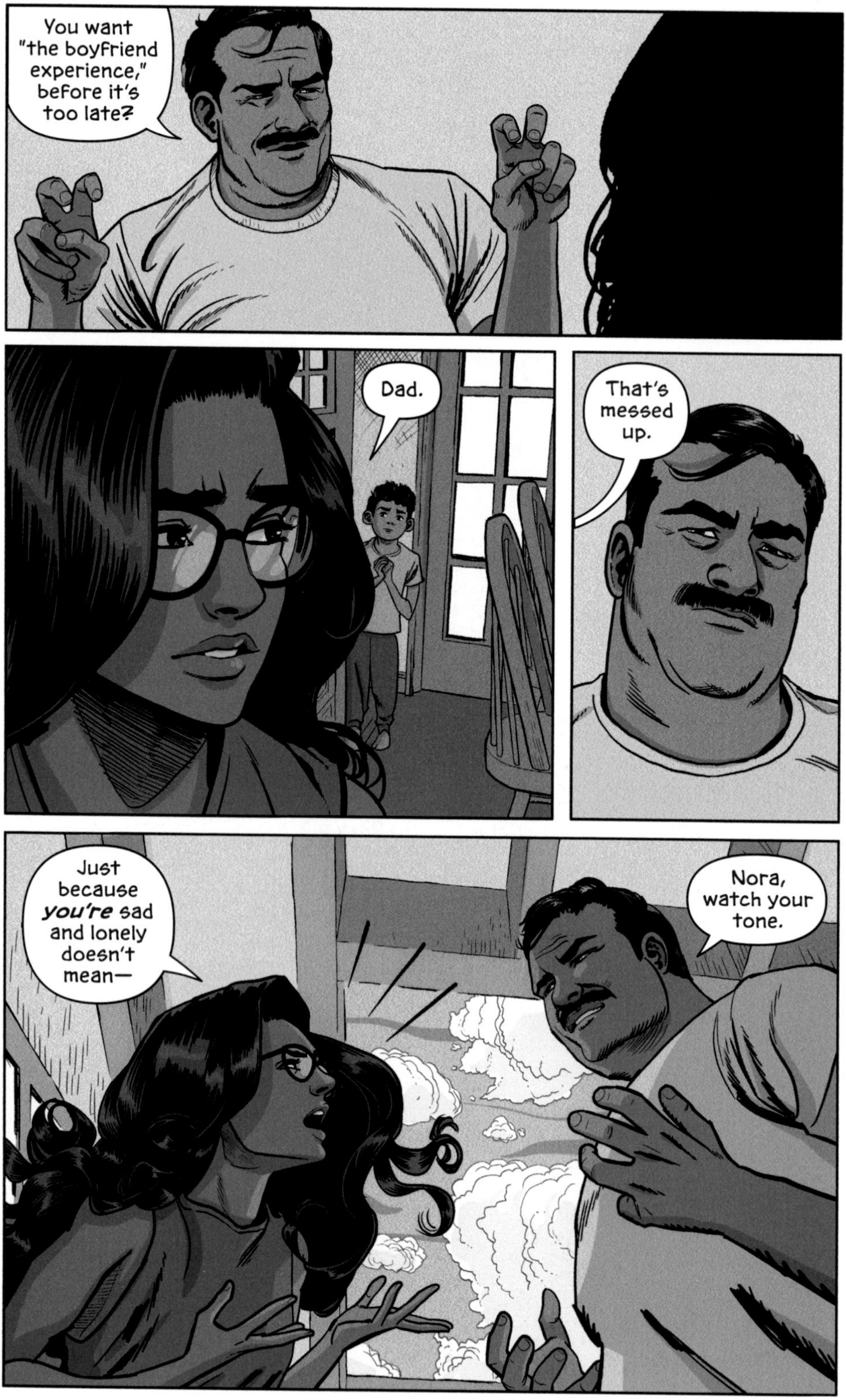
You want "the boyfriend experience," before it's too late?
Dad.
That's messed up.
Just because *you're* sad and lonely doesn't mean—
Nora, watch your tone.

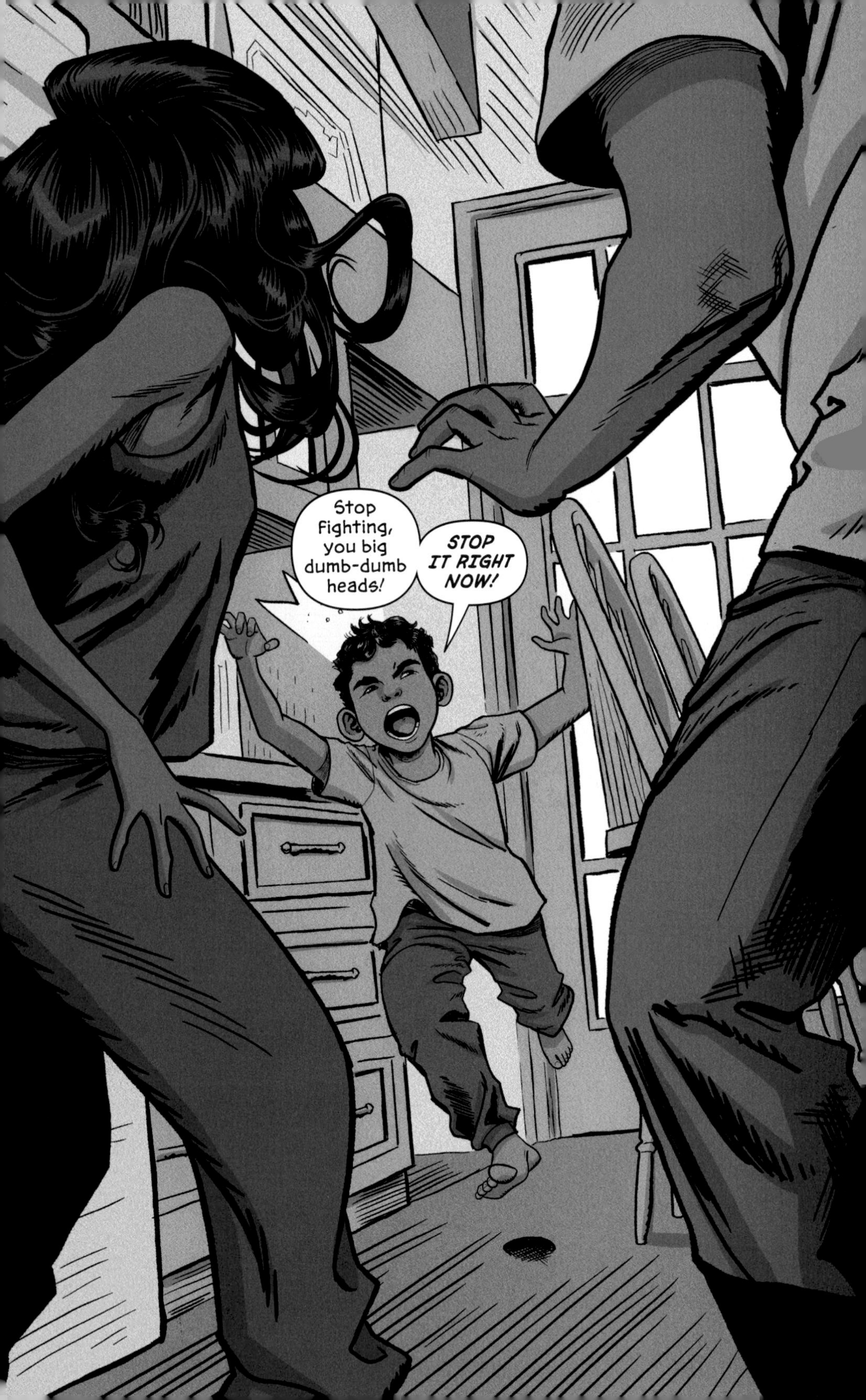
Stop fighting, you big dumb-dumb heads!
STOP IT RIGHT NOW!

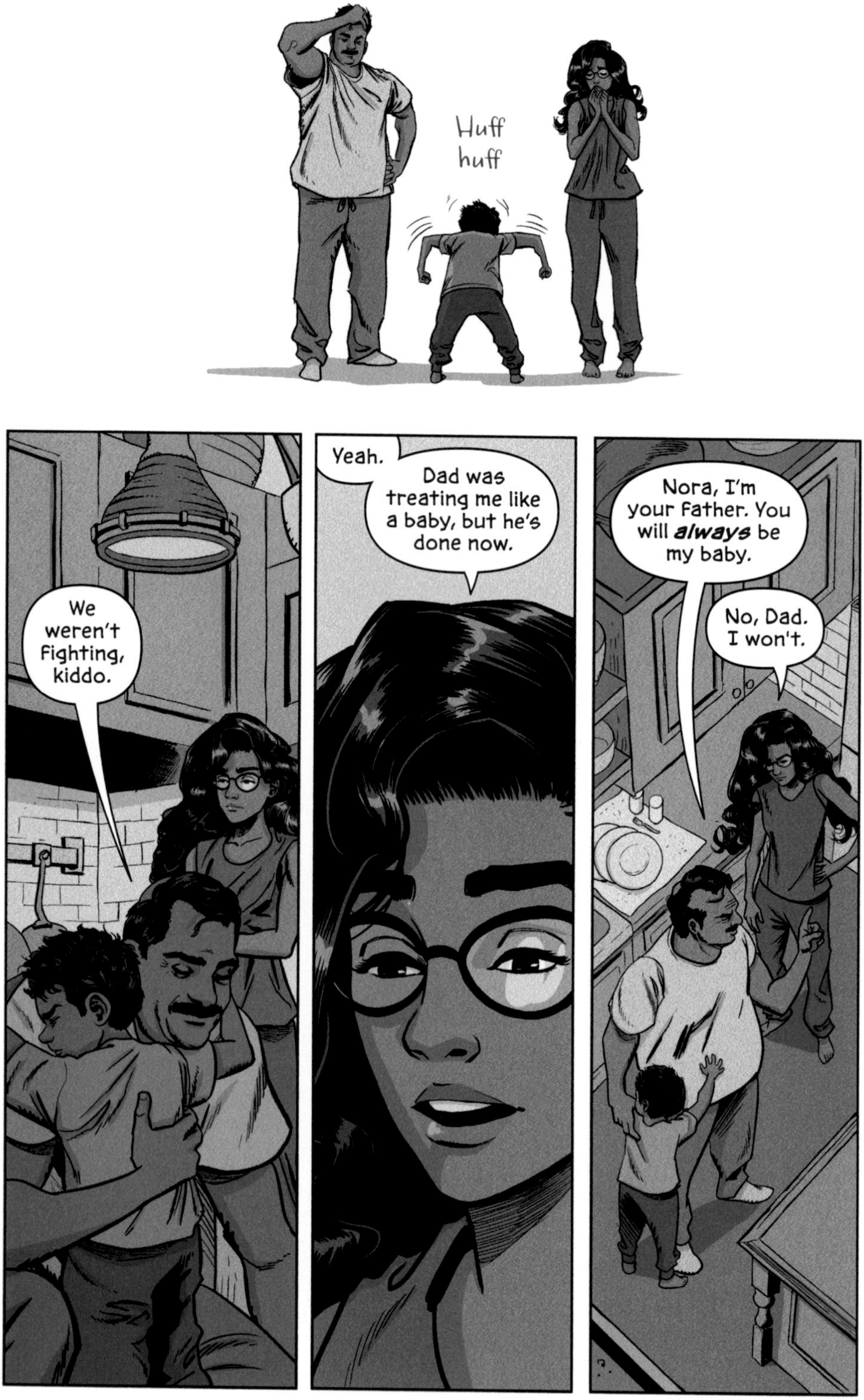
Huff huff
We weren't fighting, kiddo.
Yeah.
Dad was treating me like a baby, but he's done now.
Nora, I'm your father. You will *always* be my baby.
No, Dad. I won't.

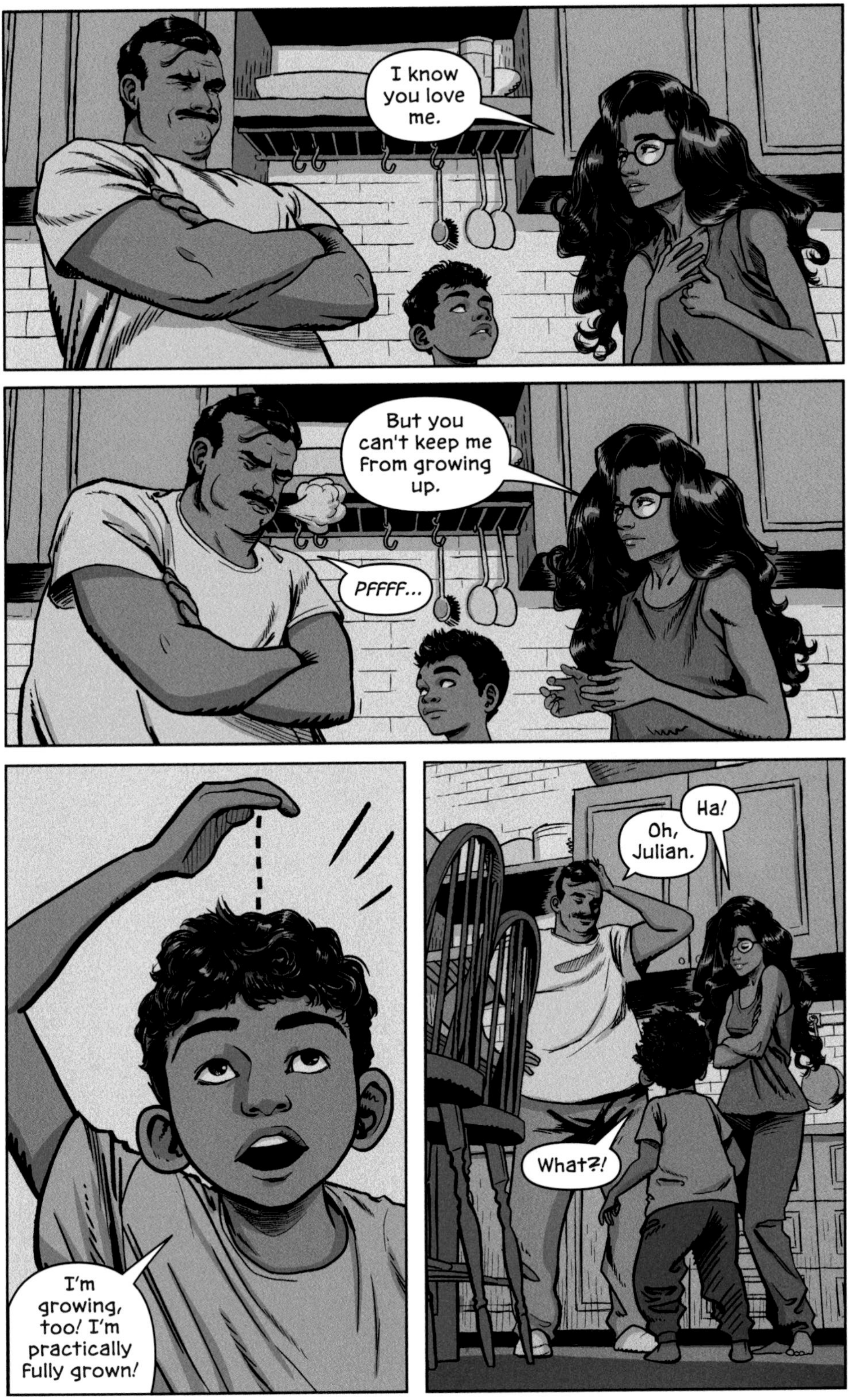
I know you love me.
But you can't keep me from growing up.
PFFFF...
I'm growing, too! I'm practically fully grown!
Ha!
Oh, Julian.
What?!

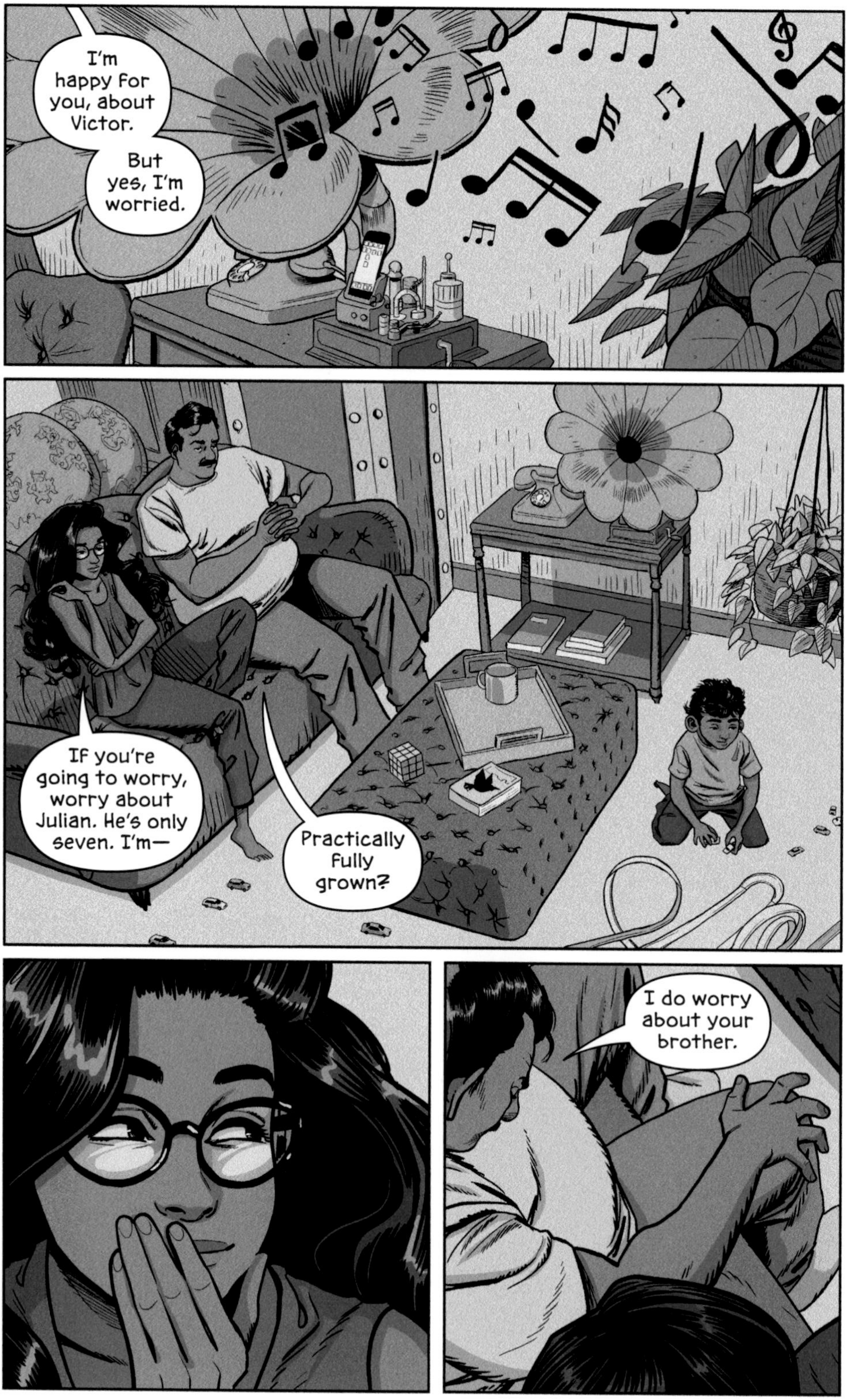
I'm happy for you, about Victor.
But yes, I'm worried.
If you're going to worry, worry about Julian. He's only seven. I'm—
Practically fully grown?
I do worry about your brother.

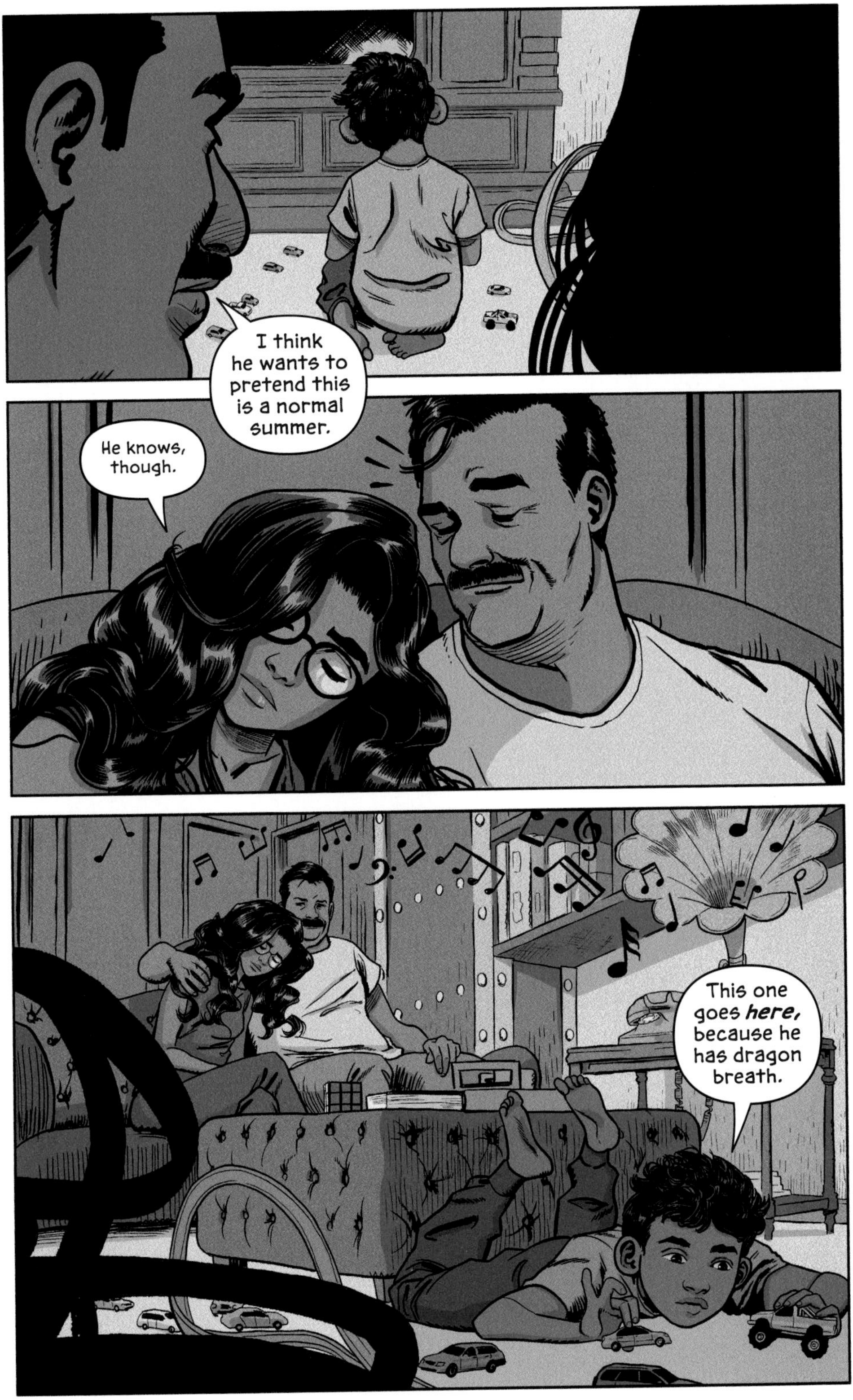
I think he wants to pretend this is a normal summer.
He knows, though.
This one goes ***here,*** because he has dragon breath.

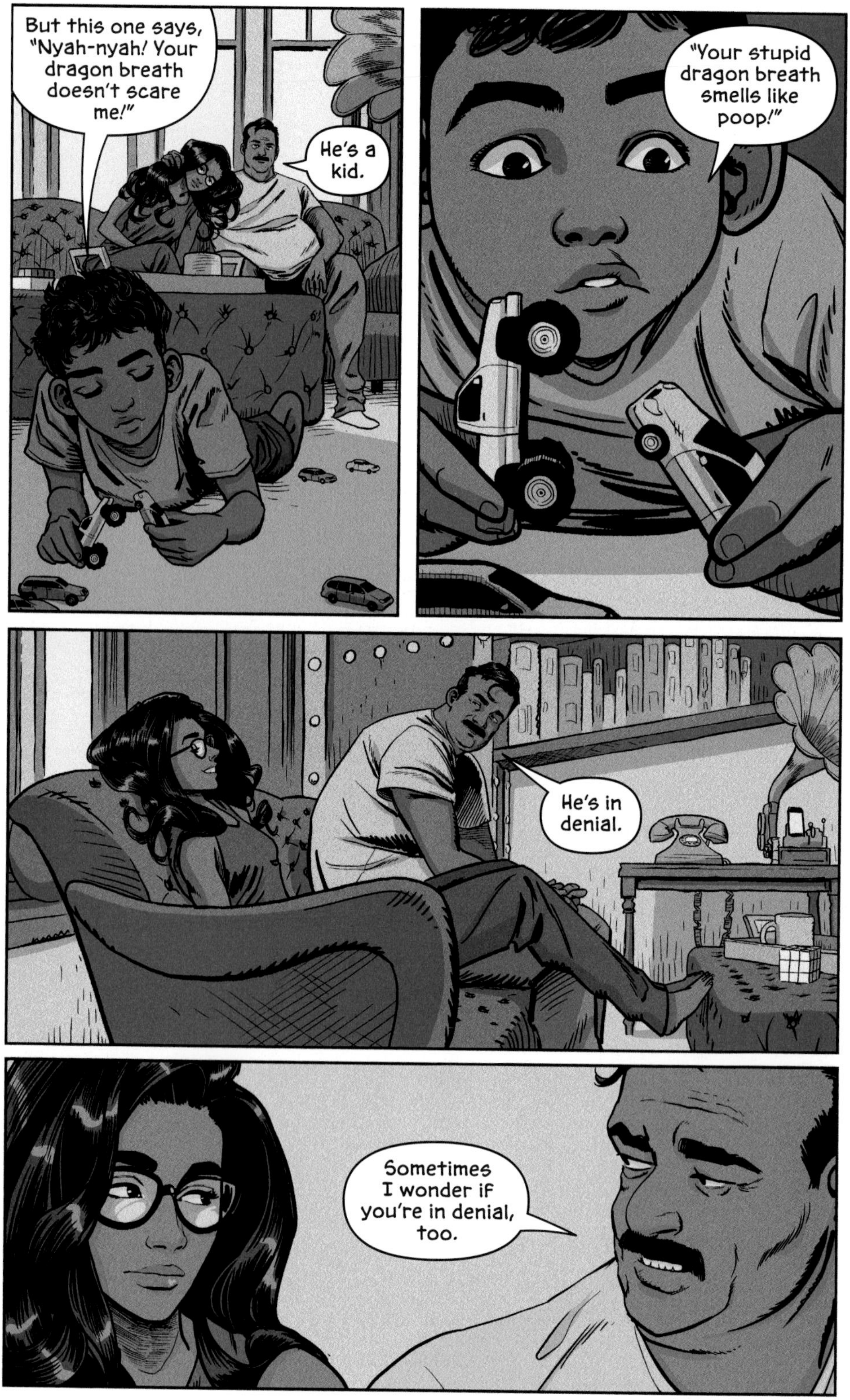

But this one says, "Nyah-nyah! Your dragon breath doesn't scare me!"
He's a kid.
"Your stupid dragon breath smells like poop!"
He's in denial.
Sometimes I wonder if you're in denial, too.

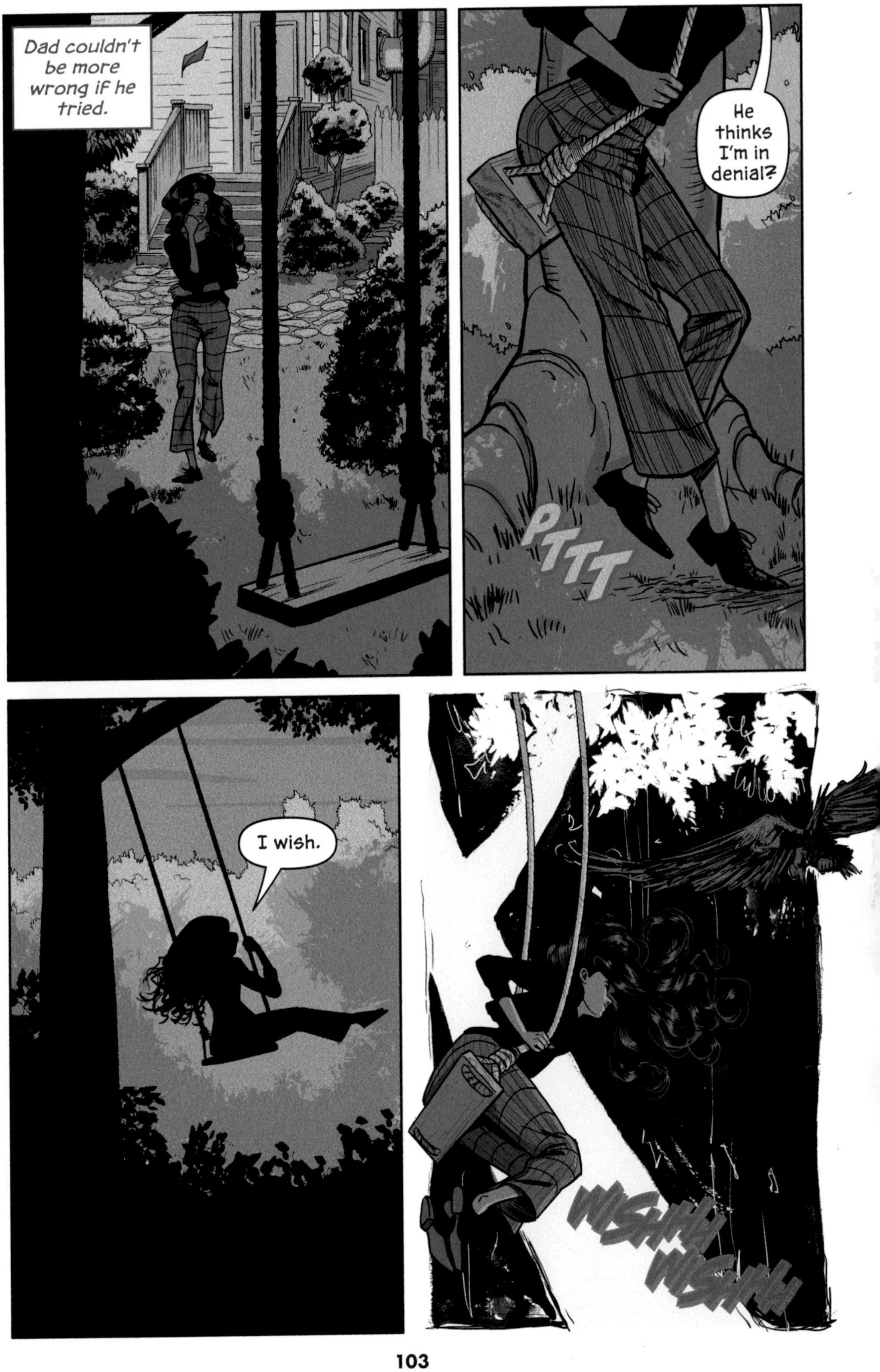

Dad couldn't be more wrong if he tried.
He thinks I'm in denial?
PTTT
I wish.
WSHHH WSHHH

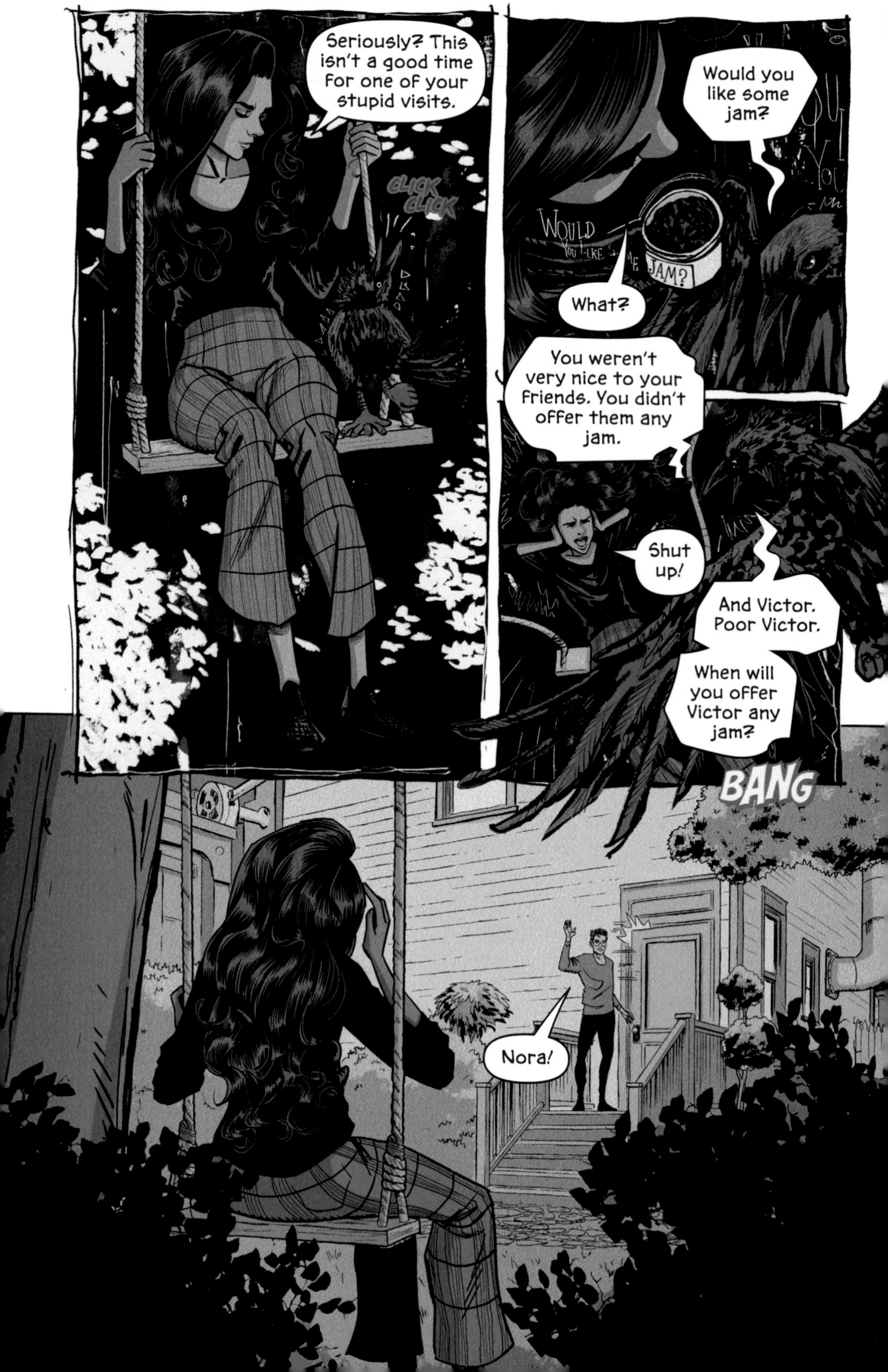
Seriously? This isn't a good time for one of your stupid visits.
CLICK CLICK
Would you like some jam?
WOULD YOU LIKE SOME JAM?
What?
You weren't very nice to your friends. You didn't offer them any jam.
Shut up!
And Victor. Poor Victor.
When will you offer Victor any jam?
BANG
Nora!

The Boy Who Learns to Love

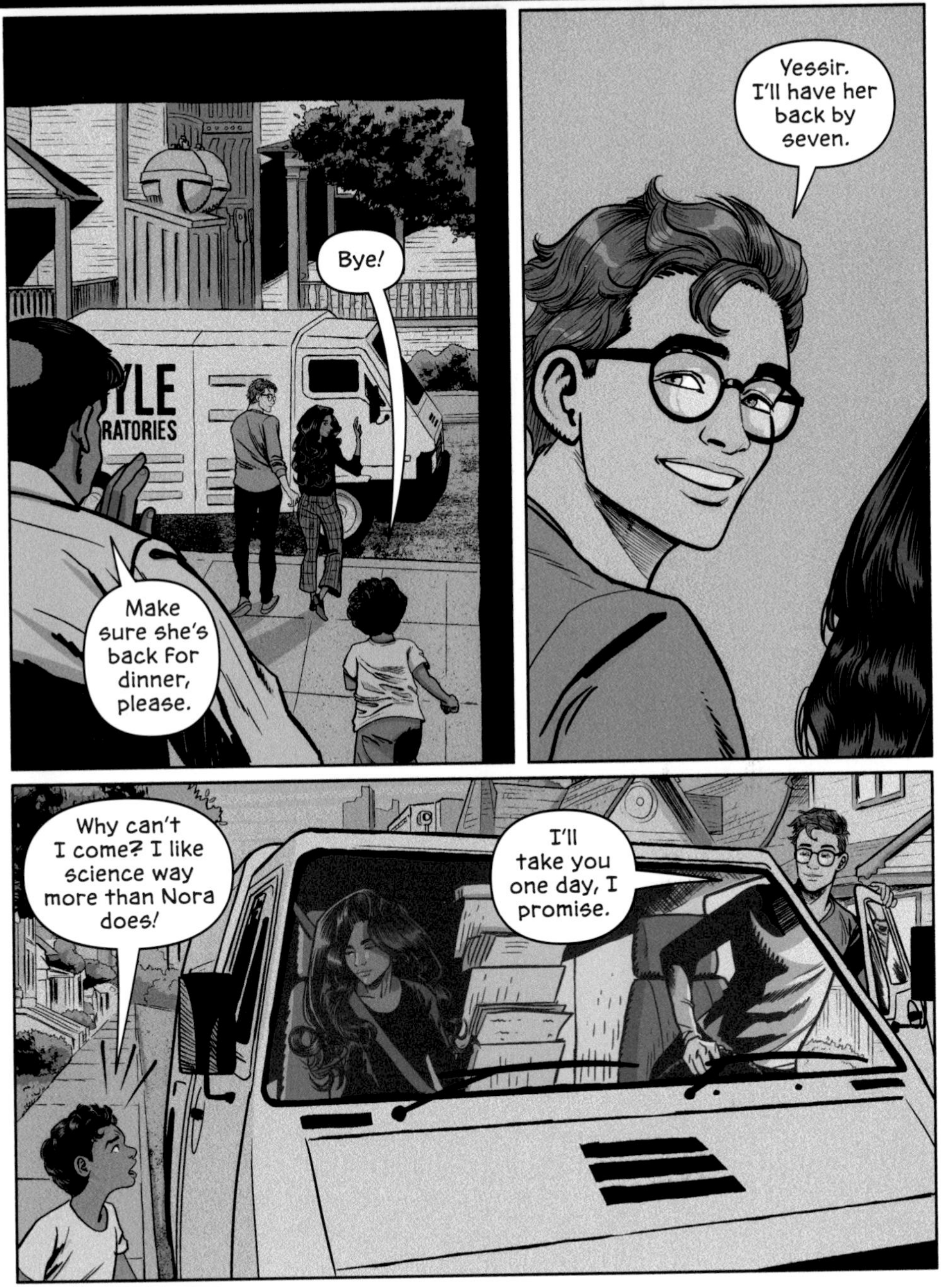
Bye!
Make sure she's back for dinner, please.
Yessir. I'll have her back by seven.
Why can't I come? I like science way more than Nora does!
I'll take you one day, I promise.

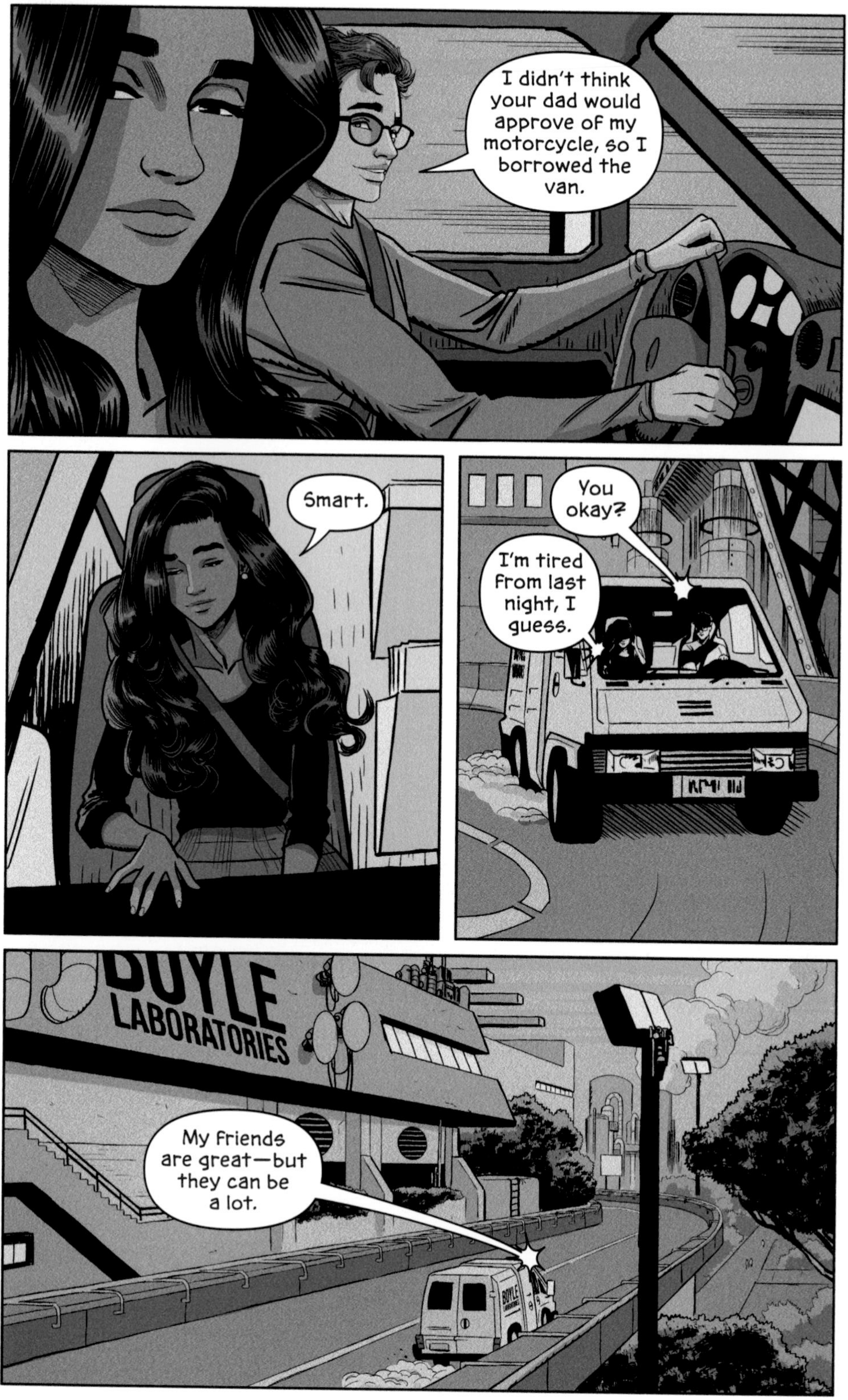
I didn't think your dad would approve of my motorcycle, so I borrowed the van.
Smart.
You okay?
I'm tired from last night, I guess.
BOYLE LABORATORIES
My friends are great—but they can be a lot.

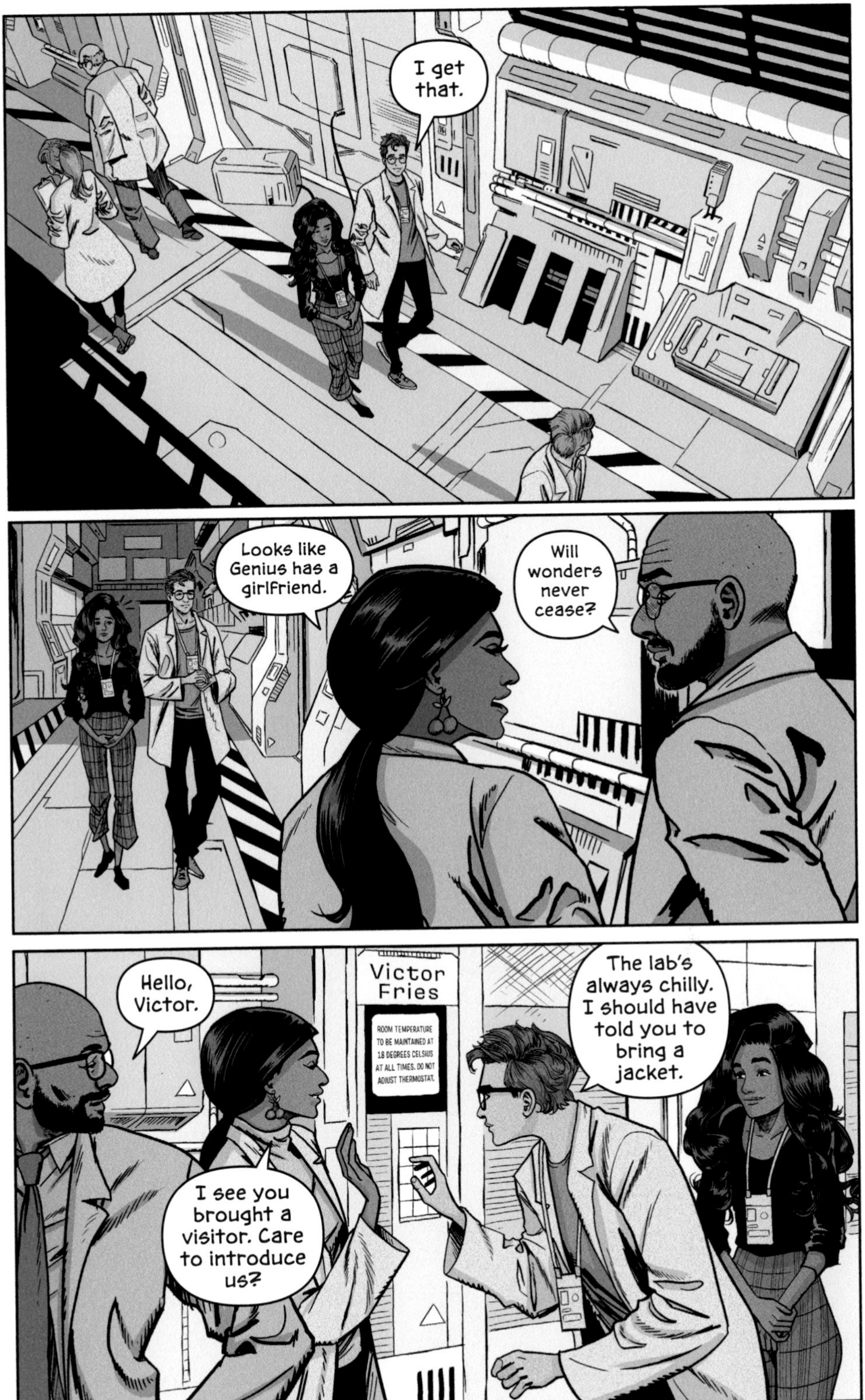
I get that.
Looks like Genius has a girlfriend.
Will wonders never cease?
Hello, Victor.
Victor Fries
ROOM TEMPERATURE TO BE MAINTAINED AT 18 DEGREES CELSIUS AT ALL TIMES. DO NOT ADJUST THERMOSTAT.
I see you brought a visitor. Care to introduce us?
The lab's always chilly. I should have told you to bring a jacket.

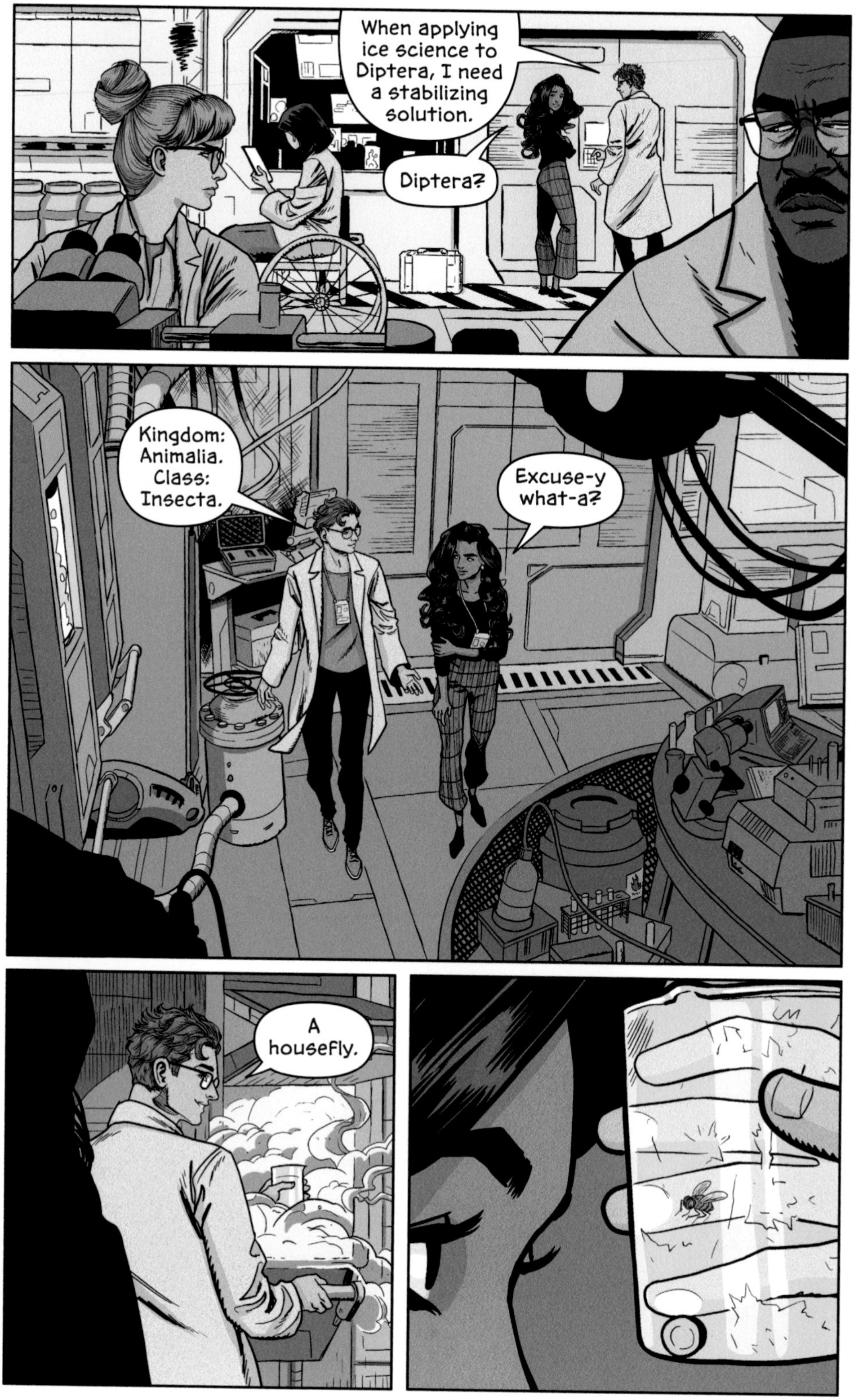

When applying ice science to Diptera, I need a stabilizing solution.
Diptera?
Kingdom: Animalia. Class: Insecta.
Excuse-y what-a?
A housefly.

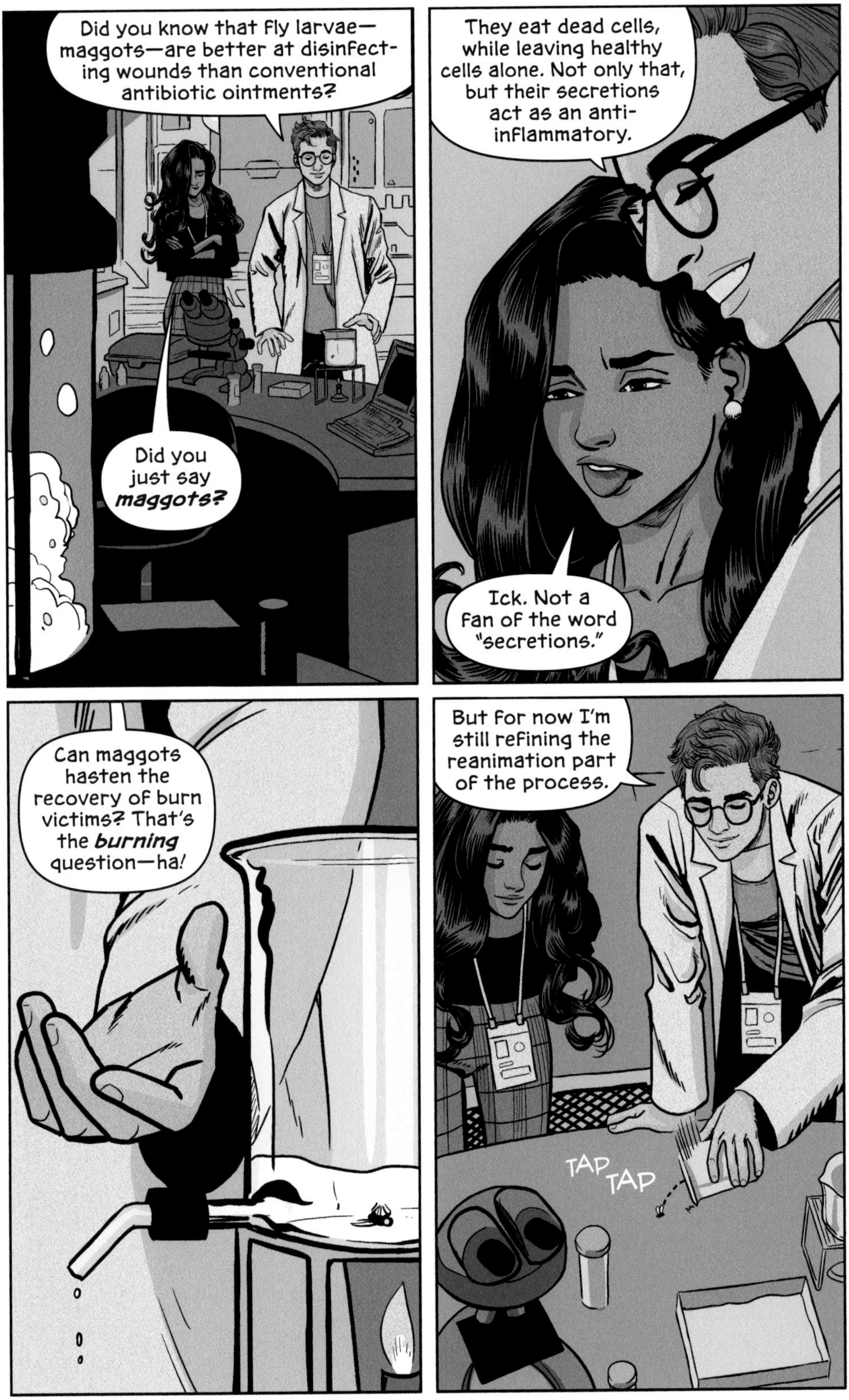

Did you know that fly larvae—maggots—are better at disinfecting wounds than conventional antibiotic ointments?
Did you just say *maggots?*
They eat dead cells, while leaving healthy cells alone. Not only that, but their secretions act as an anti-inflammatory.
Ick. Not a fan of the word "secretions."
Can maggots hasten the recovery of burn victims? That's the *burning* question—ha!
But for now I'm still refining the reanimation part of the process.
TAP TAP

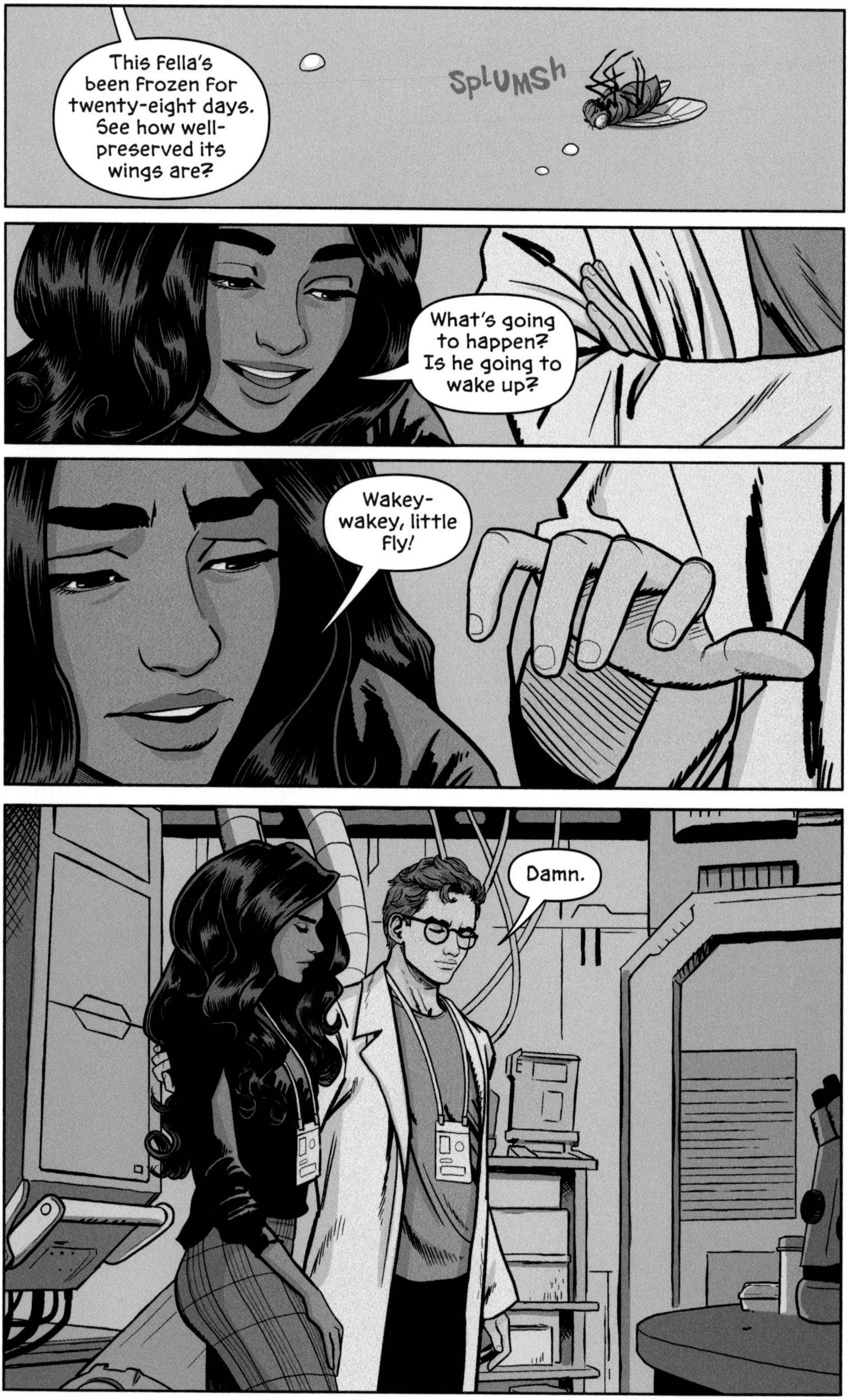
This fella's been frozen for twenty-eight days. See how well-preserved its wings are?
SPLUMSH
What's going to happen? Is he going to wake up?
Wakey-wakey, little fly!
Damn.

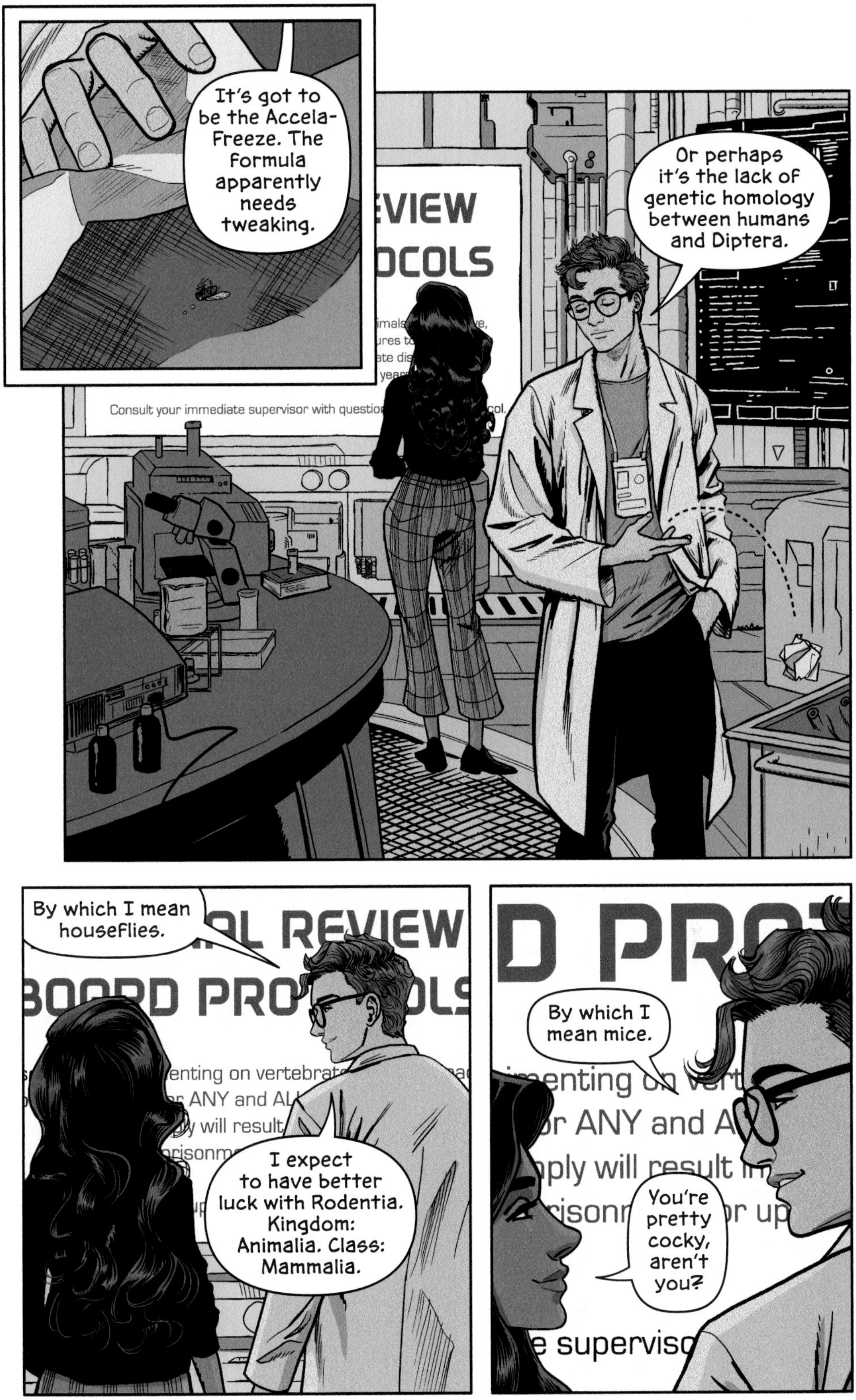
It's got to be the Accela-Freeze. The formula apparently needs tweaking.
Or perhaps it's the lack of genetic homology between humans and Diptera.
By which I mean houseflies.
I expect to have better luck with Rodentia. Kingdom: Animalia. Class: Mammalia.
By which I mean mice.
You're pretty cocky, aren't you?

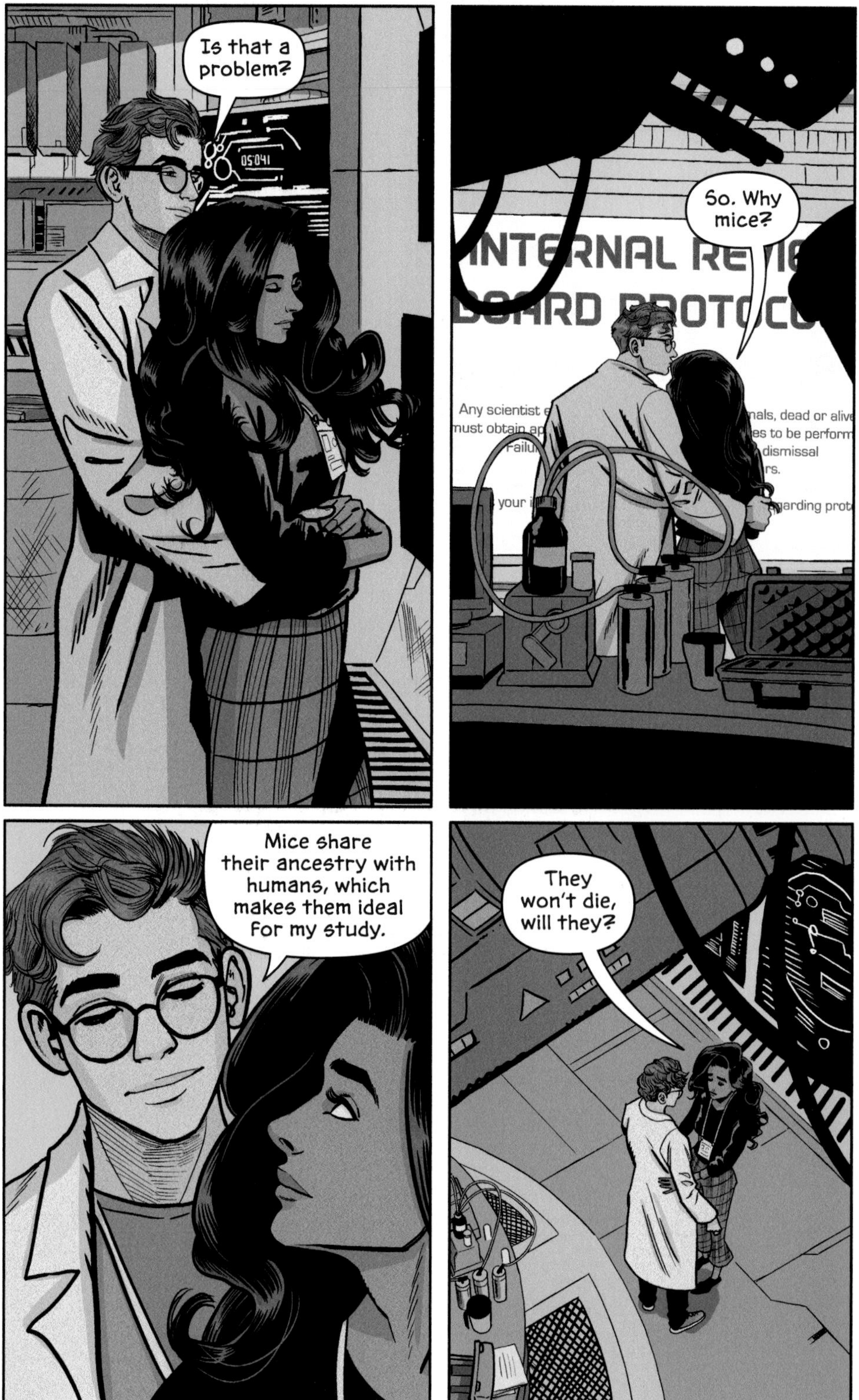
Is that a problem?
So. Why mice?
Mice share their ancestry with humans, which makes them ideal for my study.
They won't die, will they?

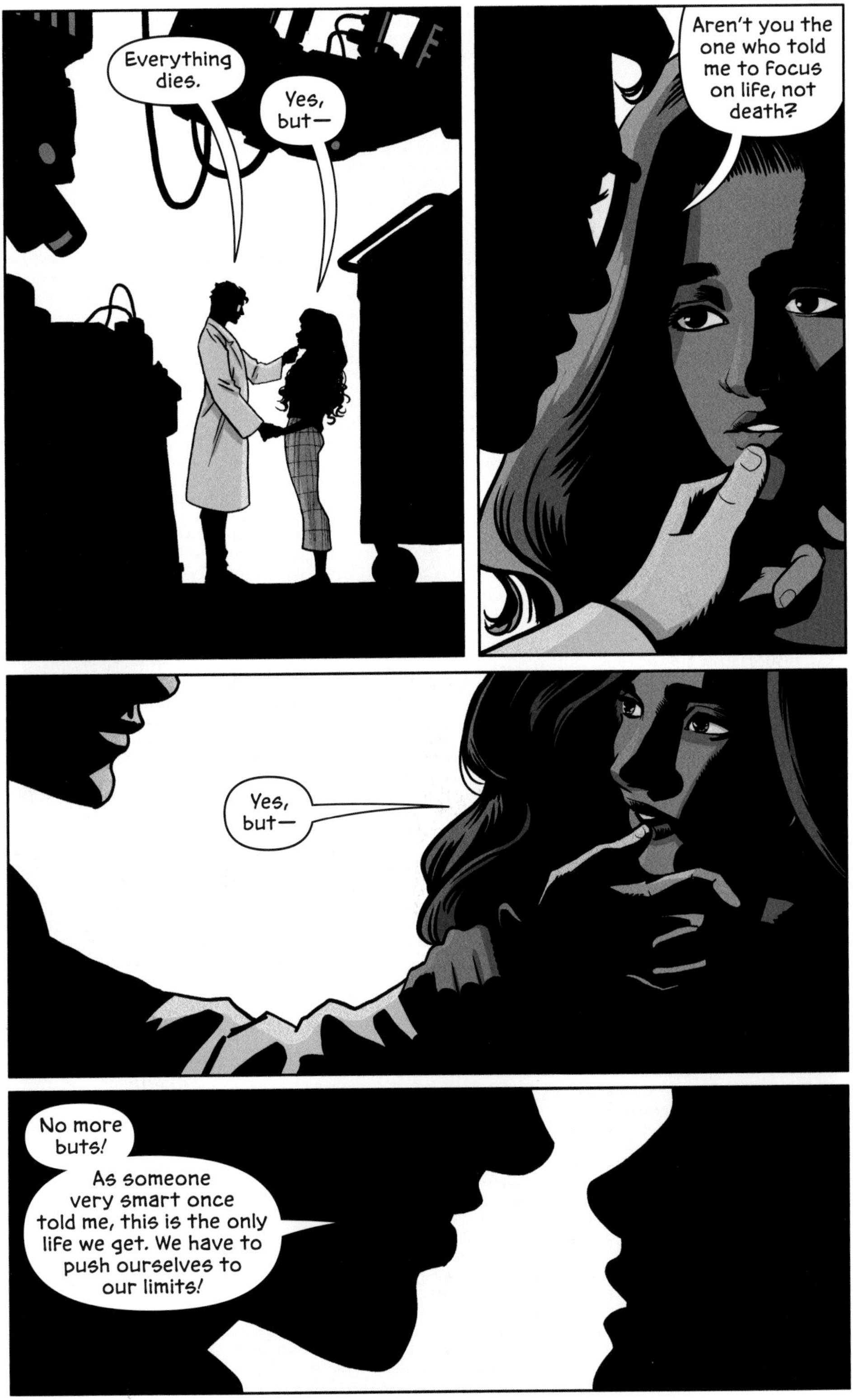
Everything dies.
Yes, but—
Aren't you the one who told me to focus on life, not death?
Yes, but—
No more buts!
As someone very smart once told me, this is the only life we get. We have to push ourselves to our limits!

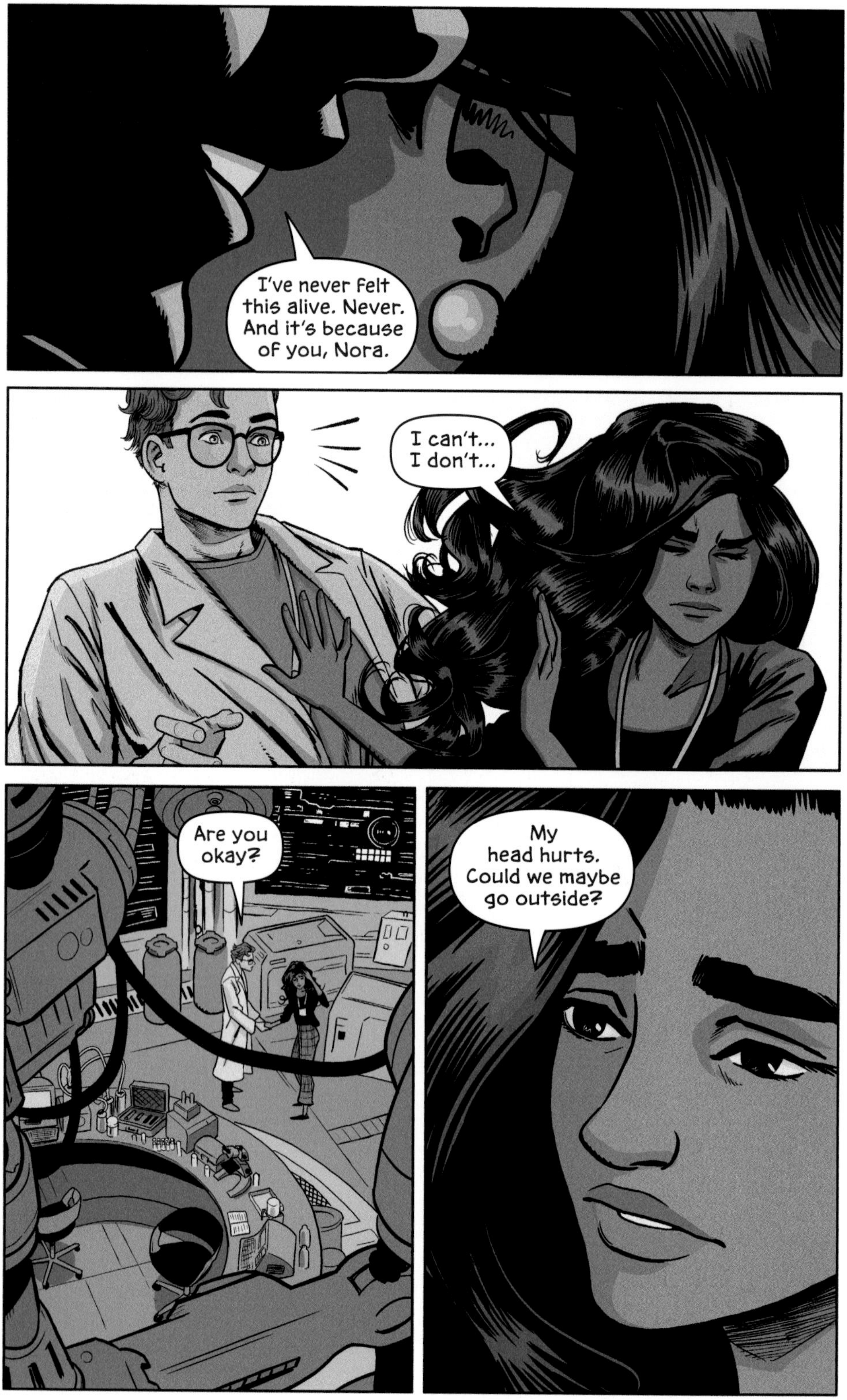
I've never felt this alive. Never. And it's because of you, Nora.
I can't... I don't...
Are you okay?
My head hurts. Could we maybe go outside?

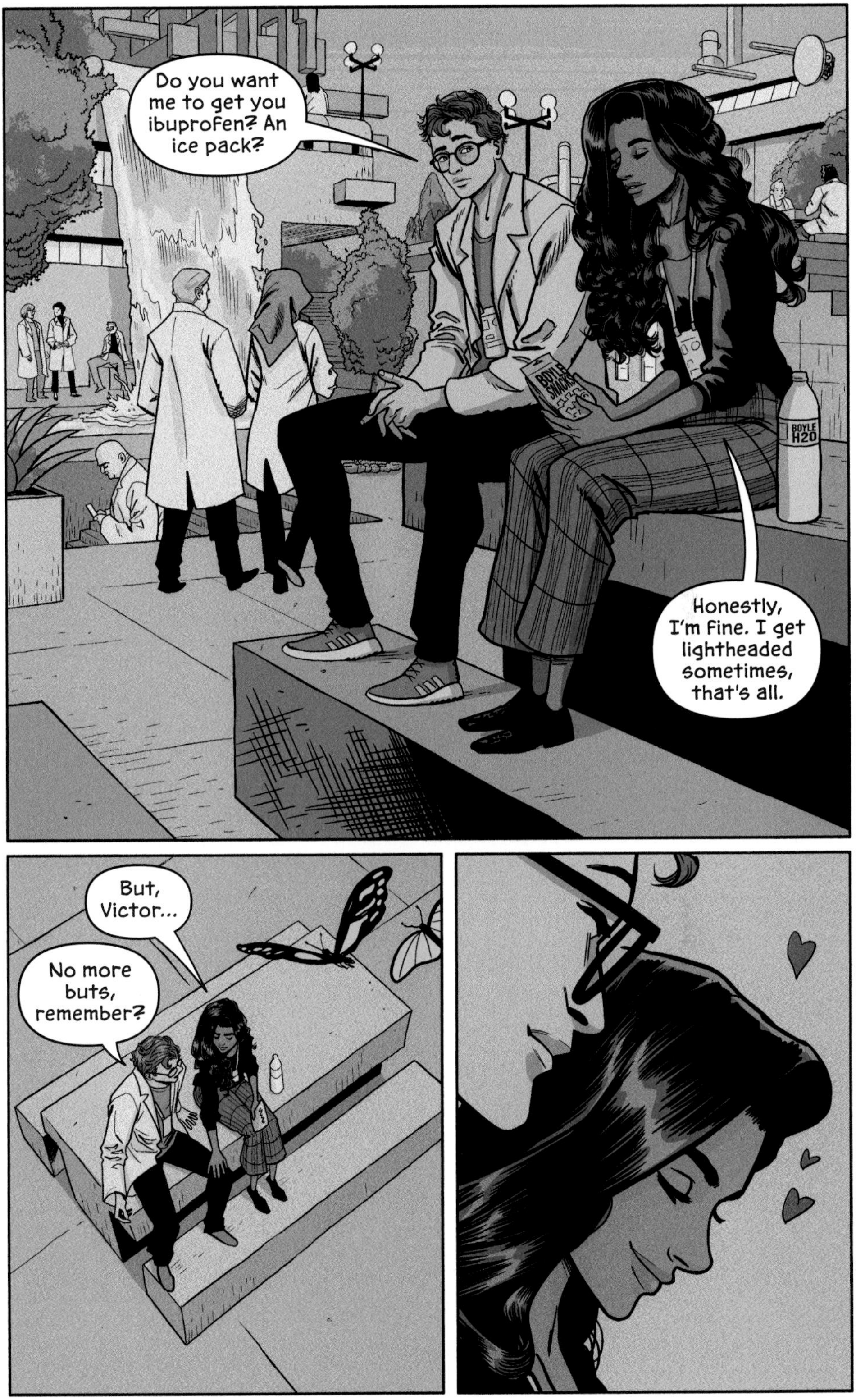
Do you want me to get you ibuprofen? An ice pack?
BOYLE SNACKS
BOYLE H2O
Honestly, I'm fine. I get lightheaded sometimes, that's all.
But, Victor...
No more buts, remember?

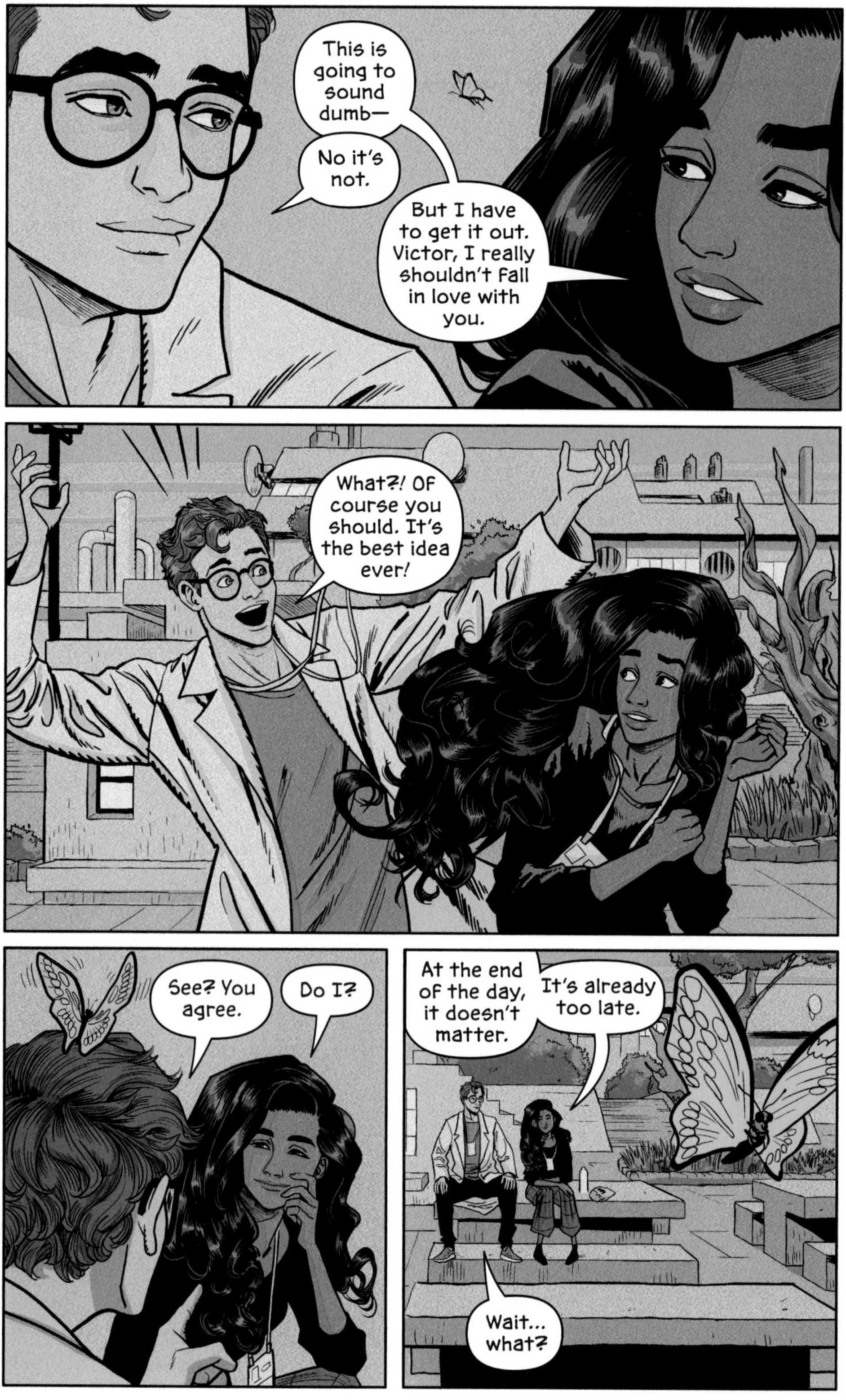
This is going to sound dumb—
No it's not.
But I have to get it out. Victor, I really shouldn't fall in love with you.
What?! Of course you should. It's the best idea ever!
See? You agree.
Do I?
At the end of the day, it doesn't matter.
It's already too late.
Wait... what?

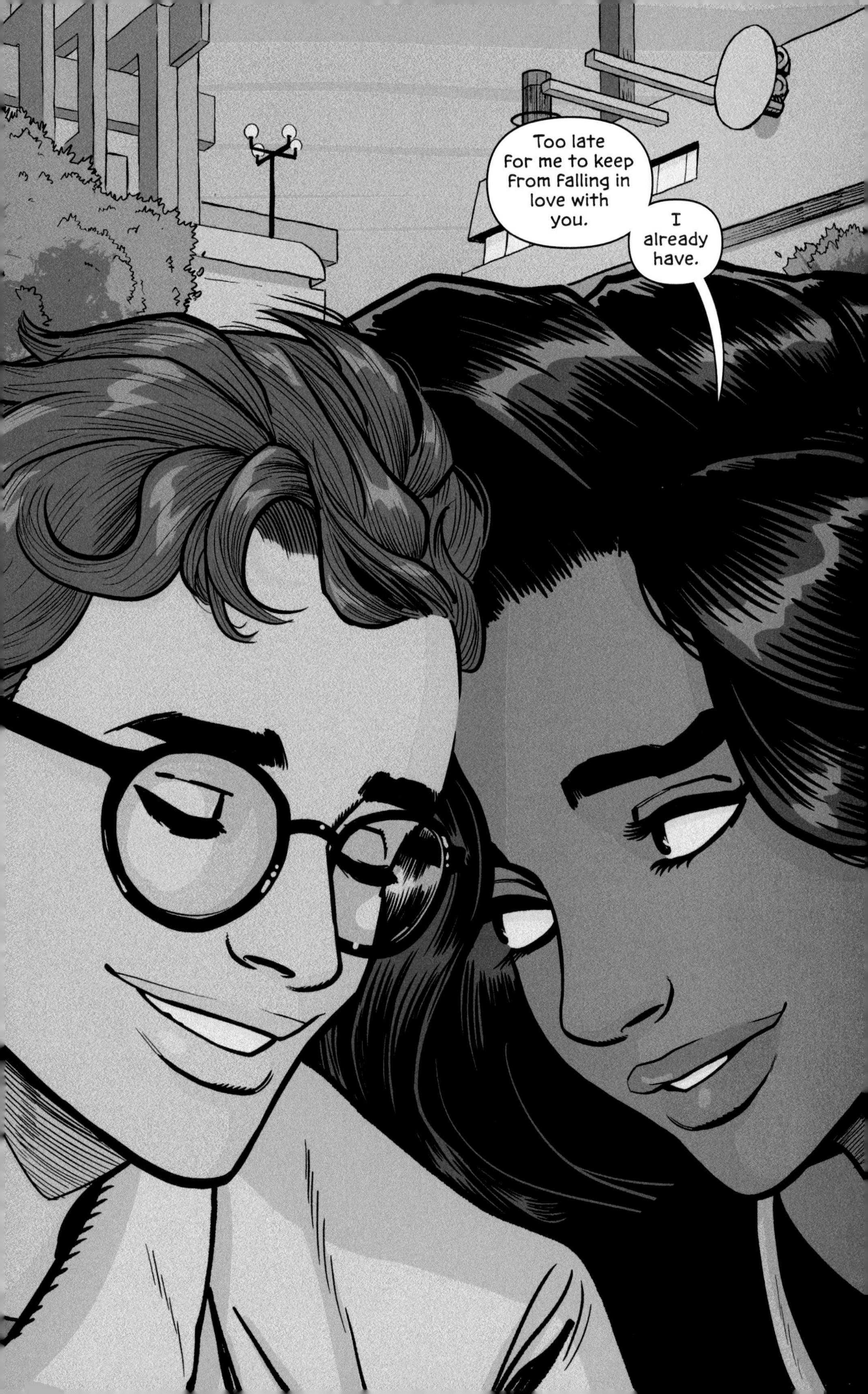
Too late for me to keep from falling in love with you.
I already have.

The Girl Who Sometimes Cries

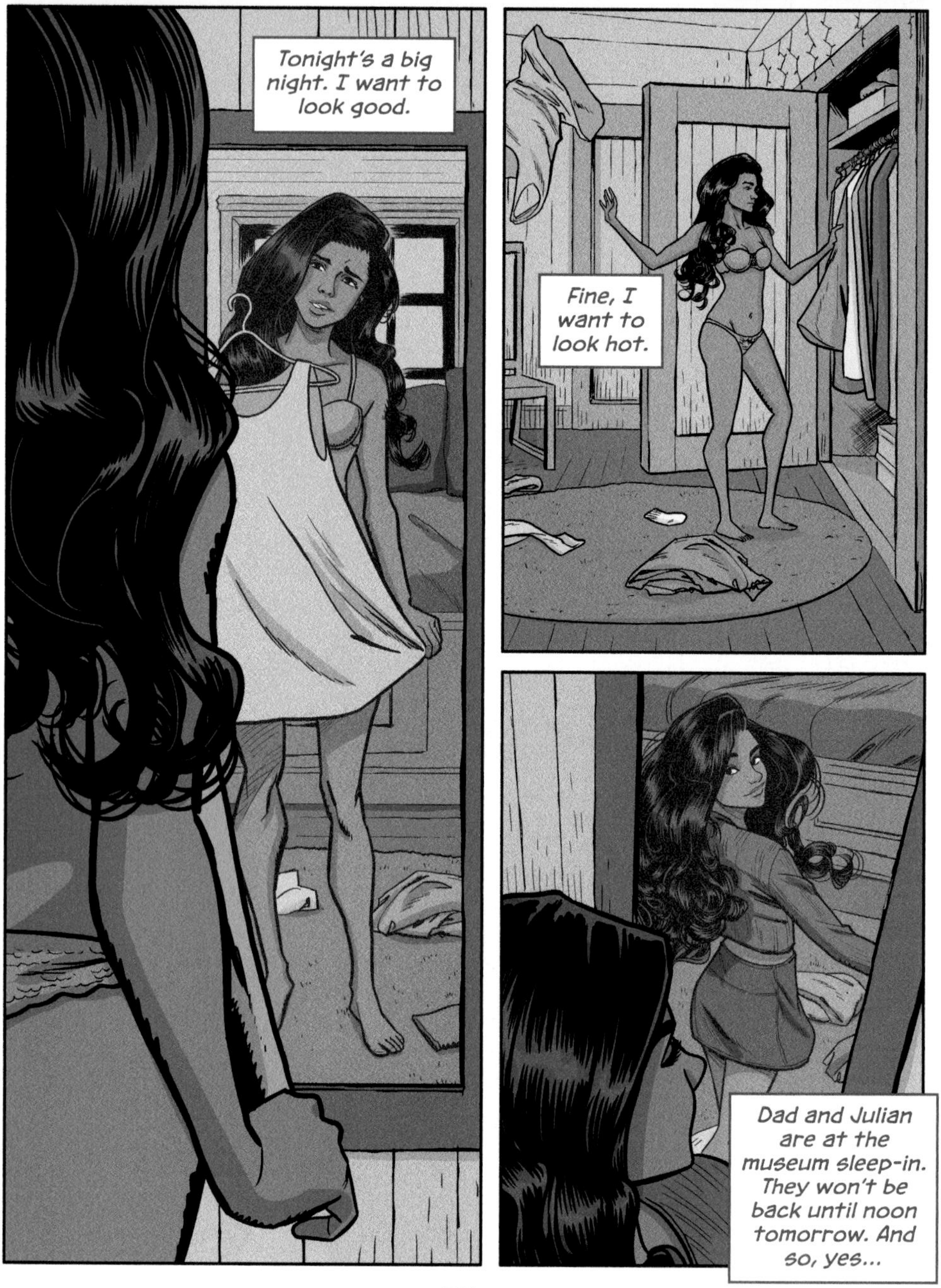
Tonight's a big night. I want to look good.
Fine, I want to look hot.
Dad and Julian are at the museum sleep-in. They won't be back until noon tomorrow. And so, yes...

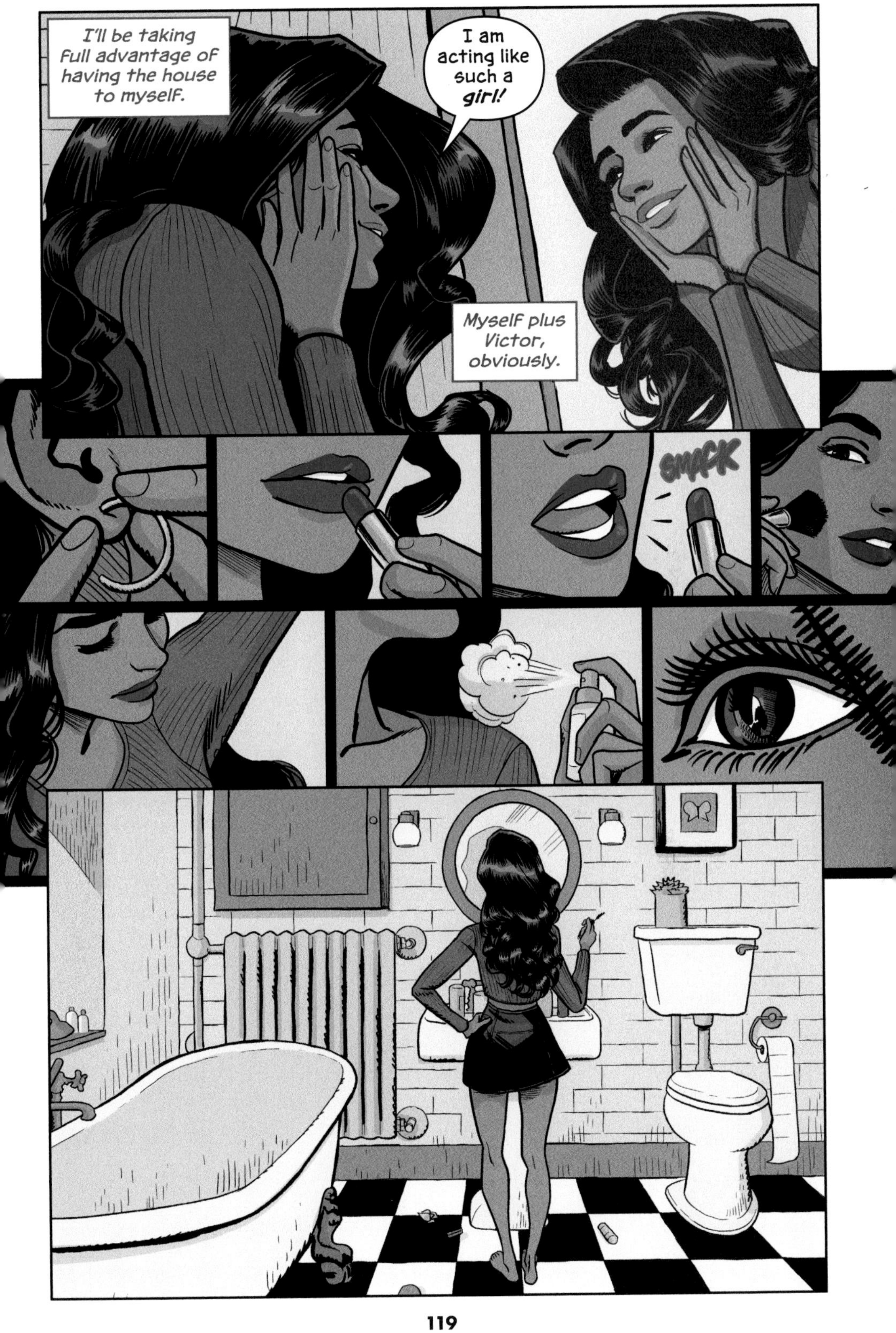
I'll be taking full advantage of having the house to myself.
I am acting like such a ***girl!***
Myself plus Victor, obviously.
SMACK

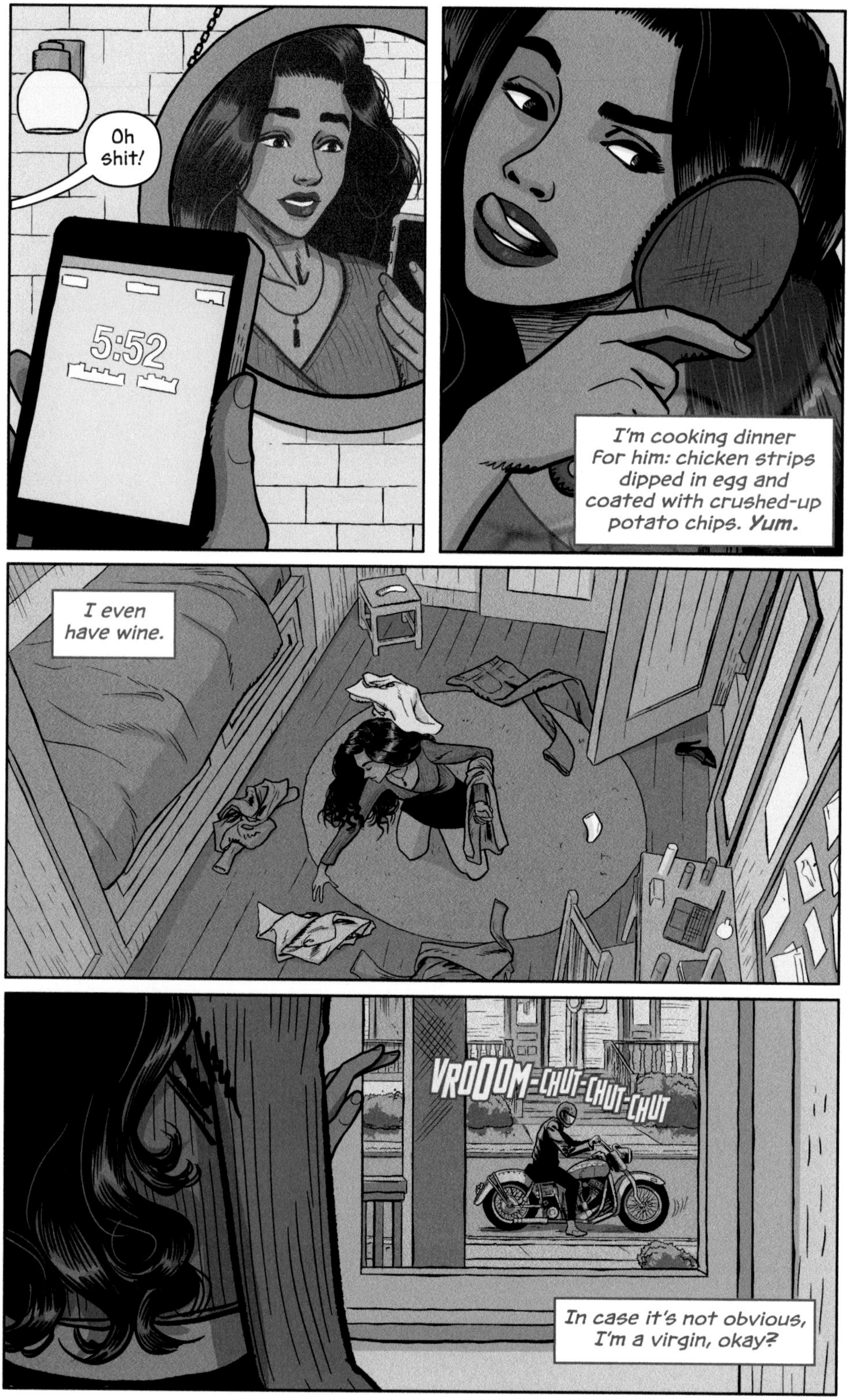

Oh shit!
5:52
I'm cooking dinner for him: chicken strips dipped in egg and coated with crushed-up potato chips. **Yum.**
I even have wine.
VROOOM-CHUT-CHUT-CHUT
In case it's not obvious, I'm a virgin, okay?

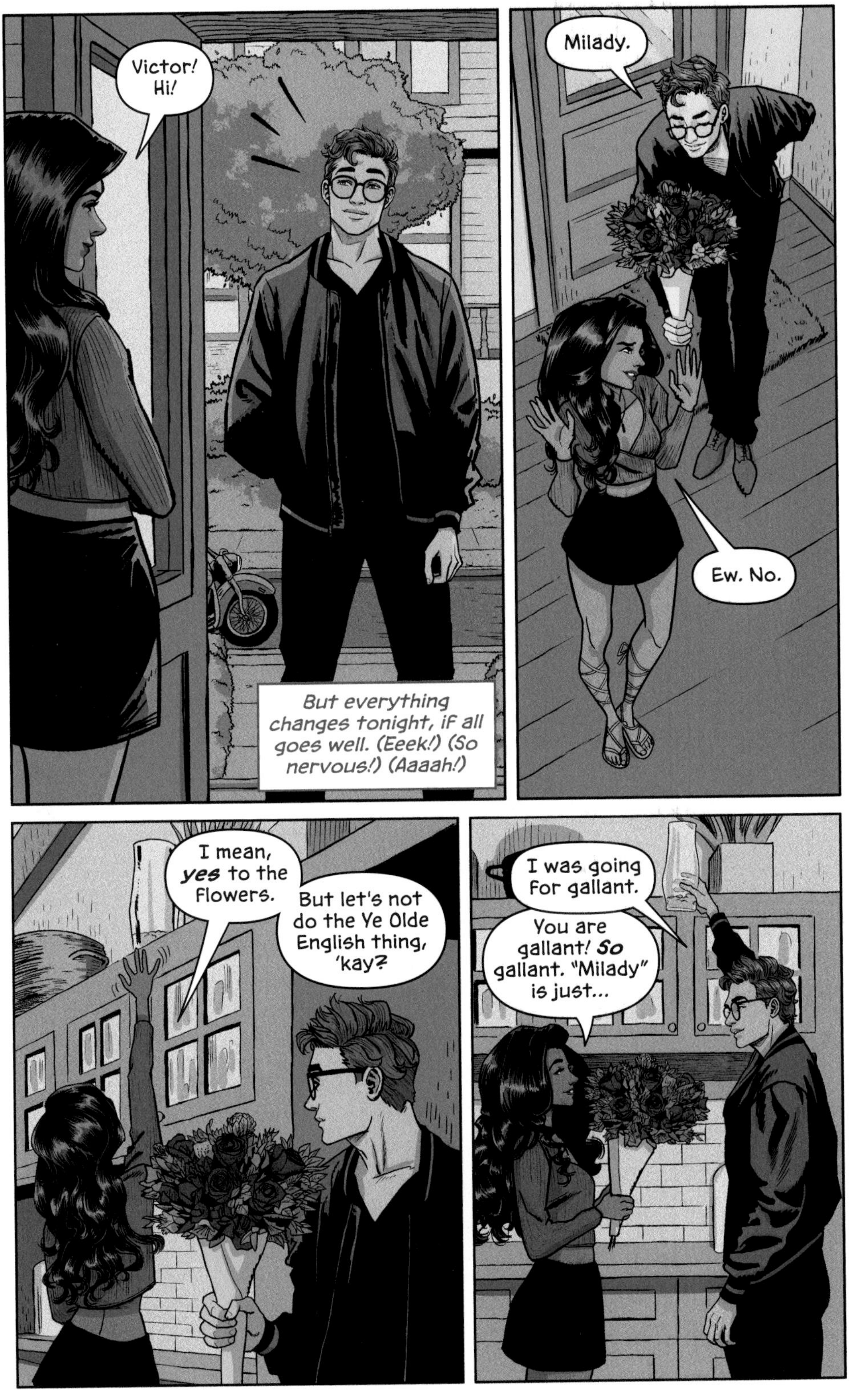
Victor! Hi!
But everything changes tonight, if all goes well. (Eeek!) (So nervous!) (Aaaah!)
Milady.
Ew. No.
I mean, *yes* to the flowers.
But let's not do the Ye Olde English thing, 'kay?
I was going for gallant.
You are gallant! *So* gallant. "Milady" is just...

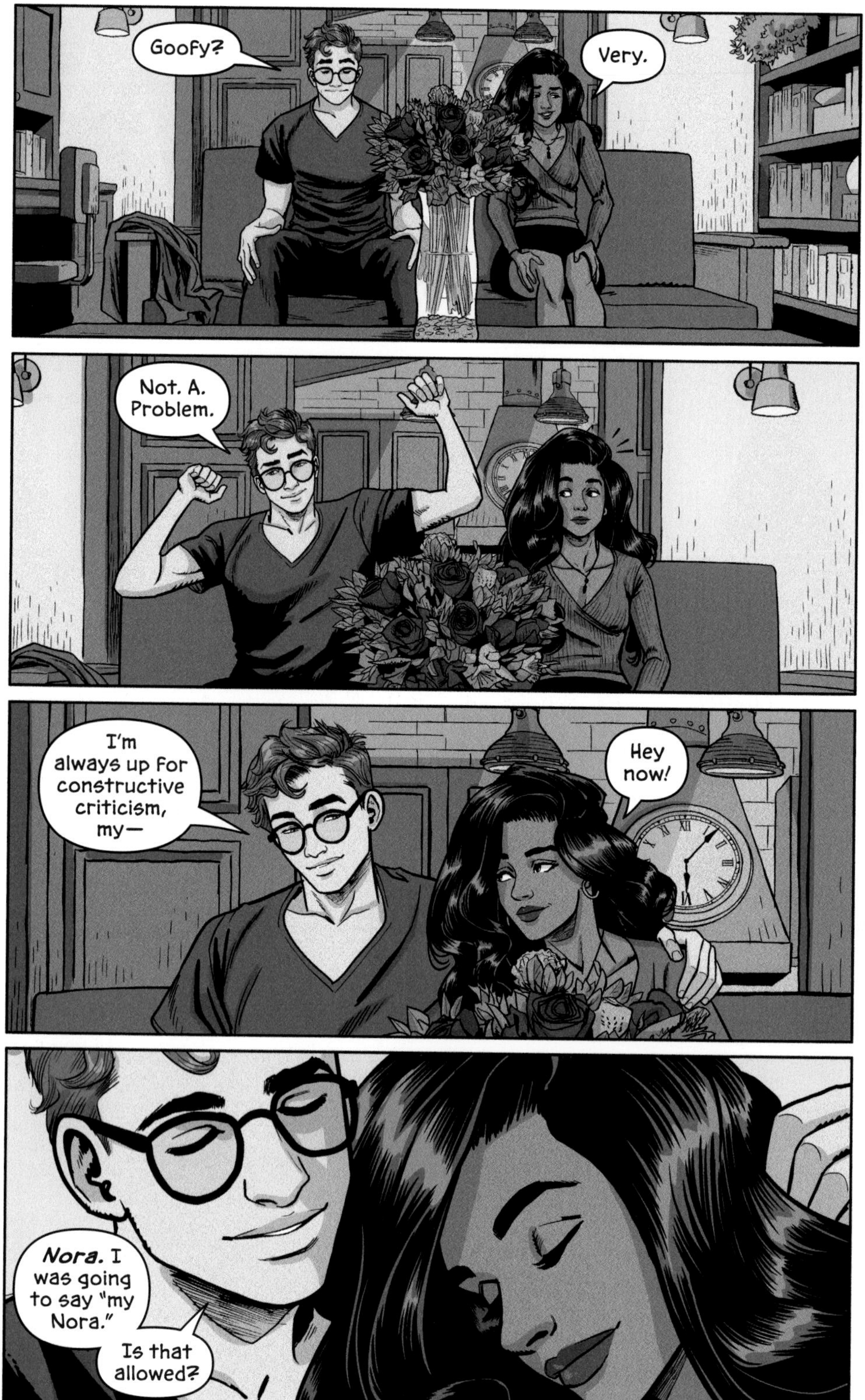
Goofy?
Very.
Not. A. Problem.
I'm always up for constructive criticism, my—
Hey now!
Nora. I was going to say "my Nora."
Is that allowed?

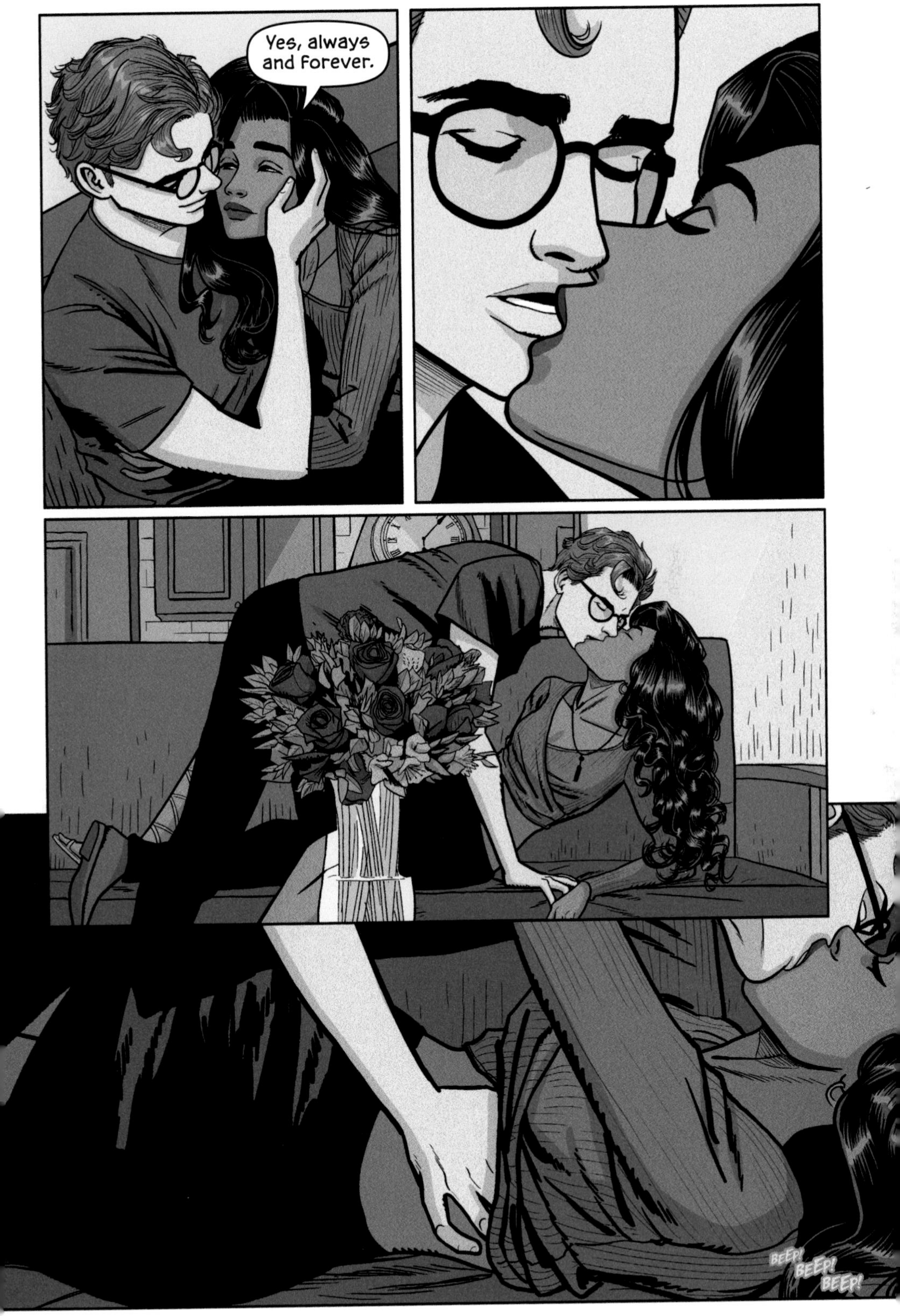
Yes, always and forever.
BEEP! BEEP! BEEP!

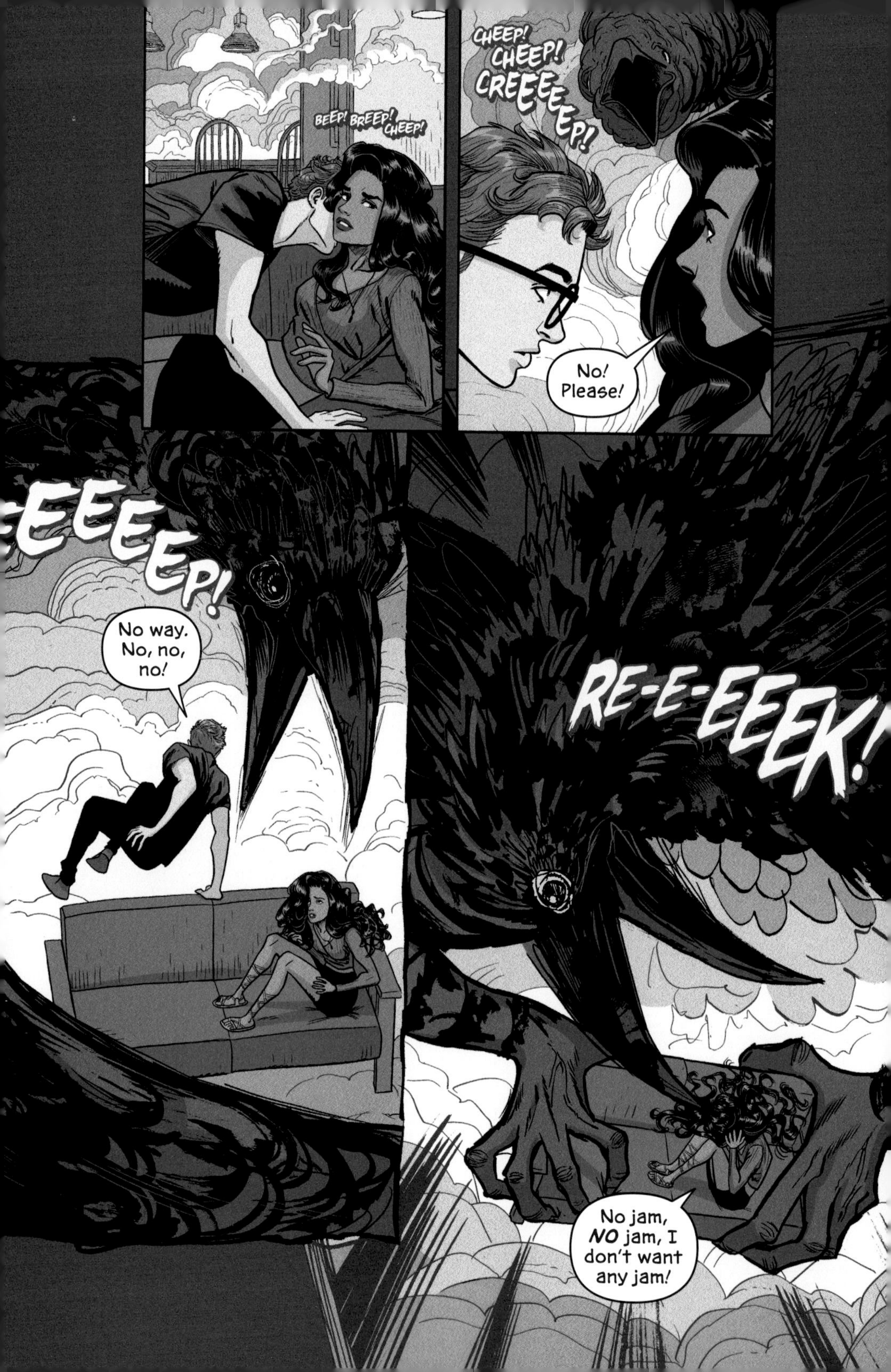
BEEP! BREEP! CHEEP!
CHEEP! CHEEP! CREEEEEEP!
No! Please!
EEEEEP!
No way. No, no, no!
RE-E-EEEEK!
No jam, NO jam, I don't want any jam!

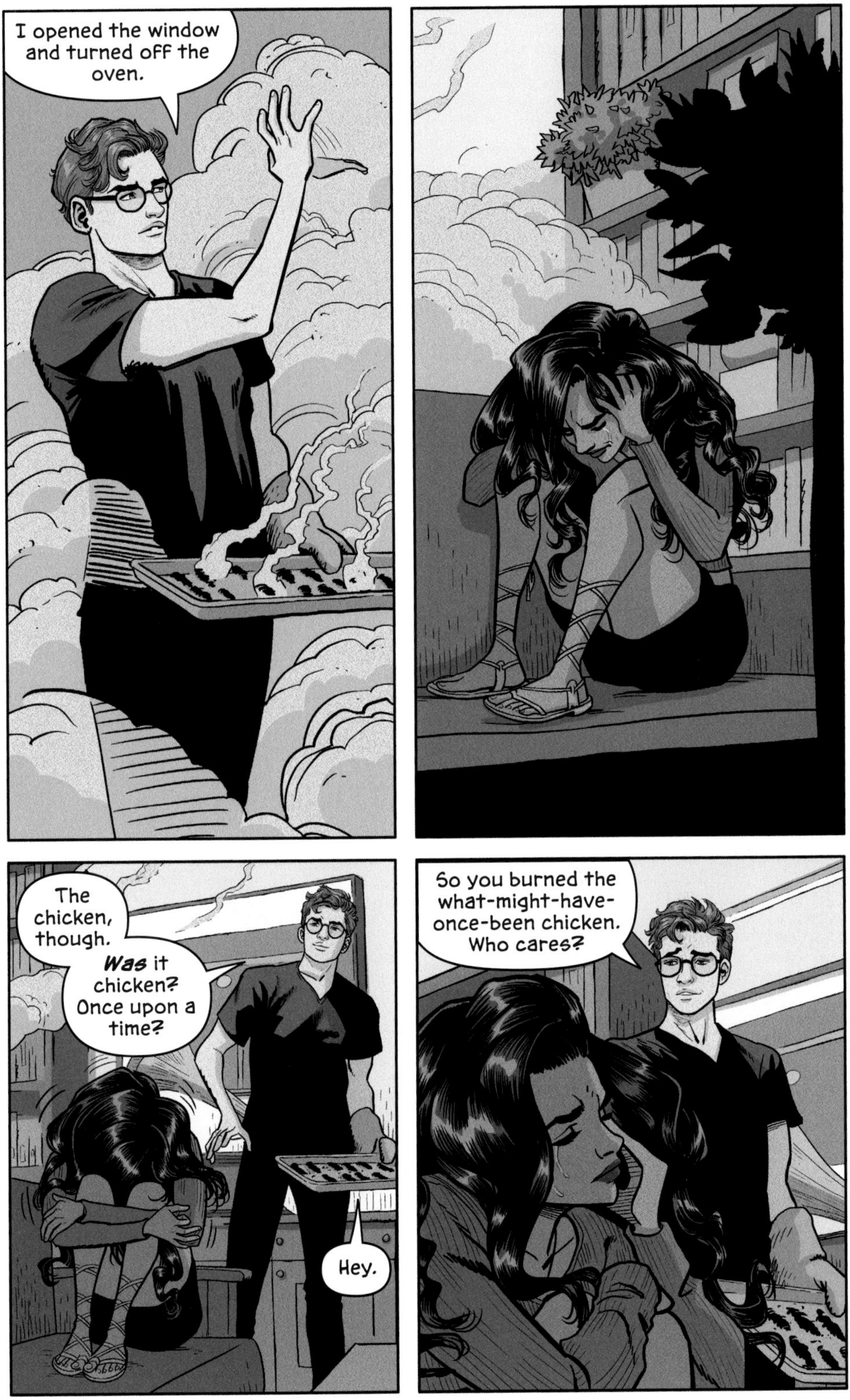
I opened the window and turned off the oven.
The chicken, though.
Was it chicken? Once upon a time?
Hey.
So you burned the what-might-have-once-been chicken. Who cares?

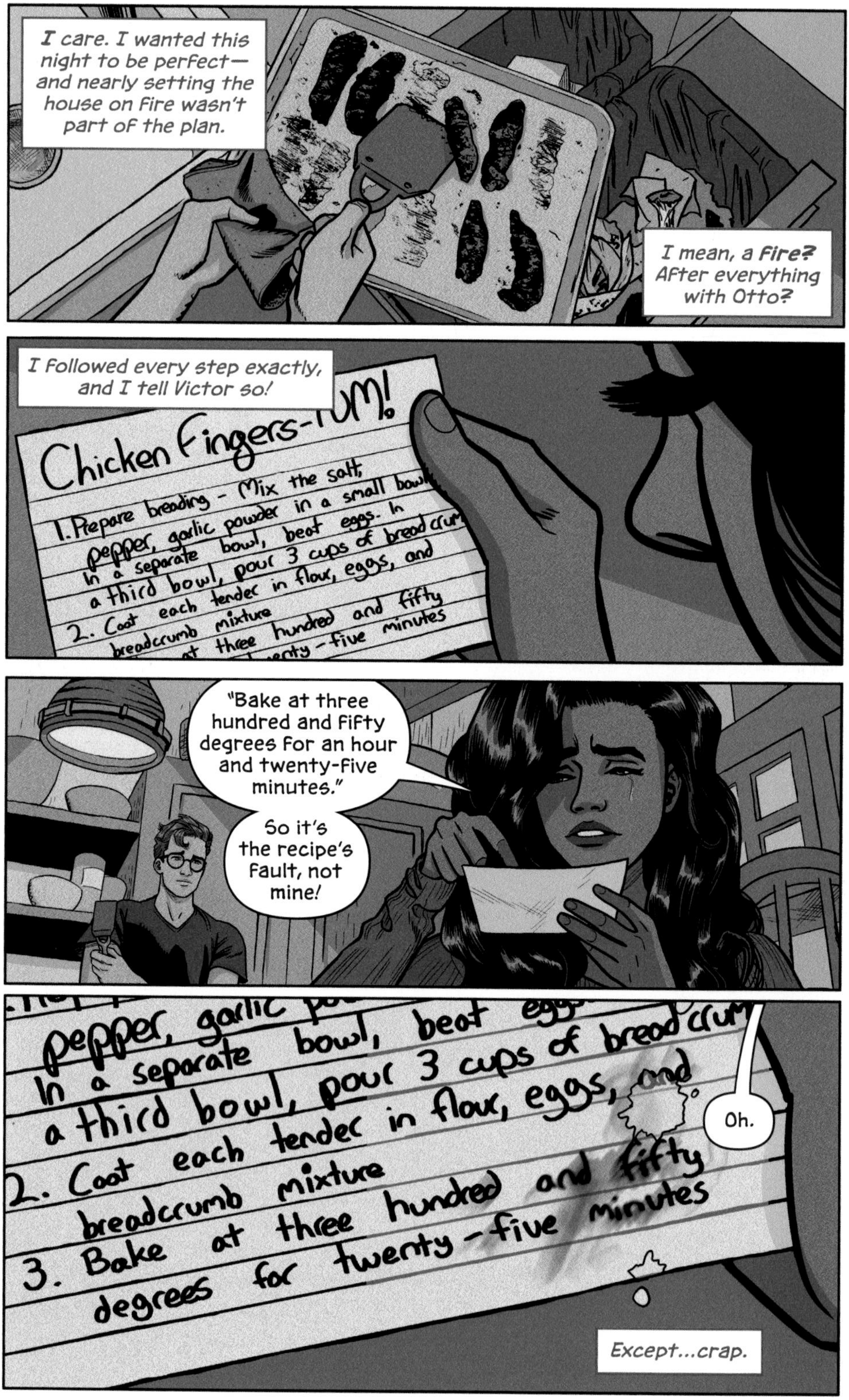
I care. I wanted this night to be perfect—and nearly setting the house on fire wasn't part of the plan.
I mean, a fire? After everything with Otto?
I followed every step exactly, and I tell Victor so!
"Bake at three hundred and fifty degrees for an hour and twenty-five minutes."
So it's the recipe's fault, not mine!
Oh.
Except...crap.

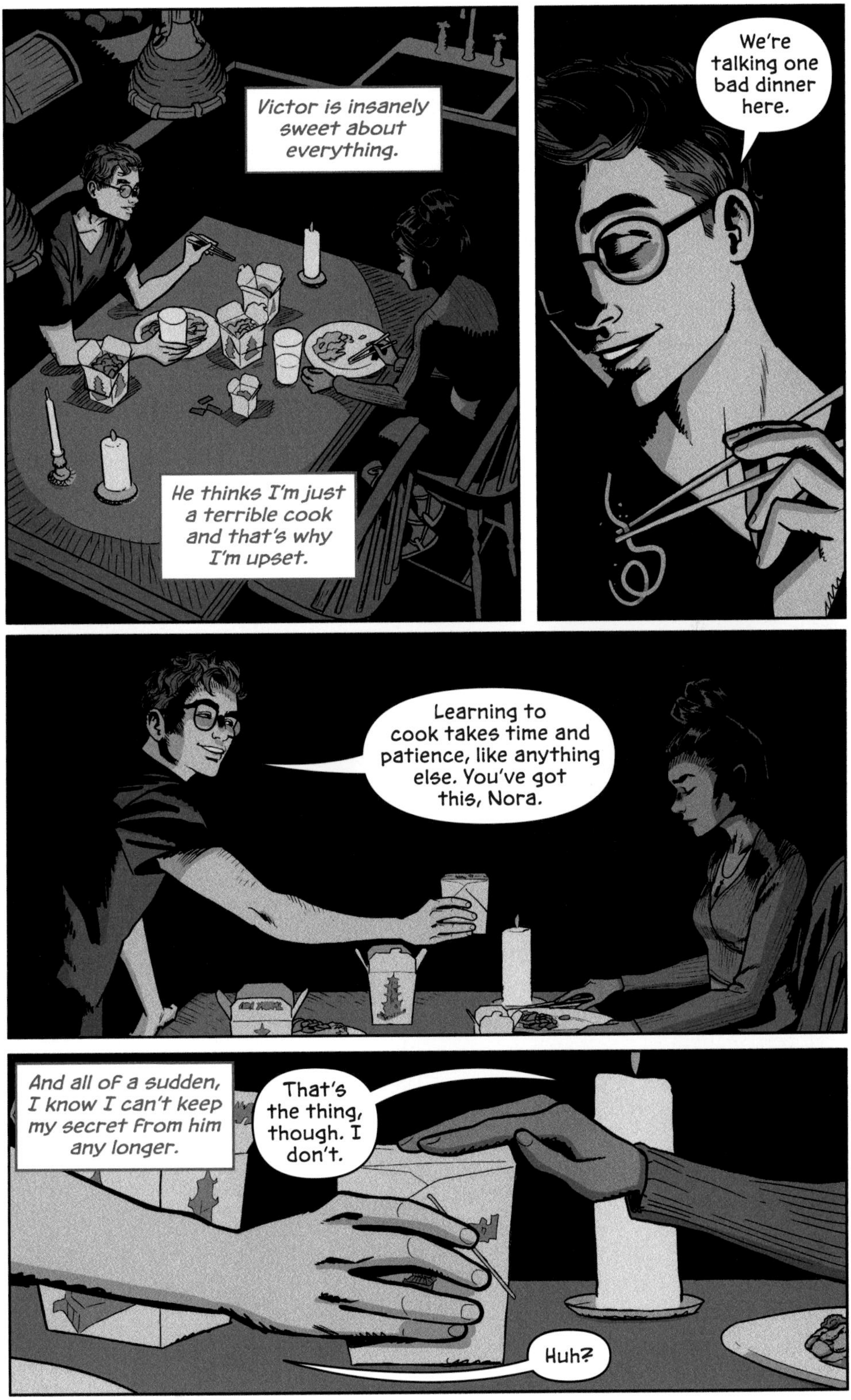
Victor is insanely sweet about everything.
He thinks I'm just a terrible cook and that's why I'm upset.
We're talking one bad dinner here.
Learning to cook takes time and patience, like anything else. You've got this, Nora.
And all of a sudden, I know I can't keep my secret from him any longer.
That's the thing, though. I don't.
Huh?

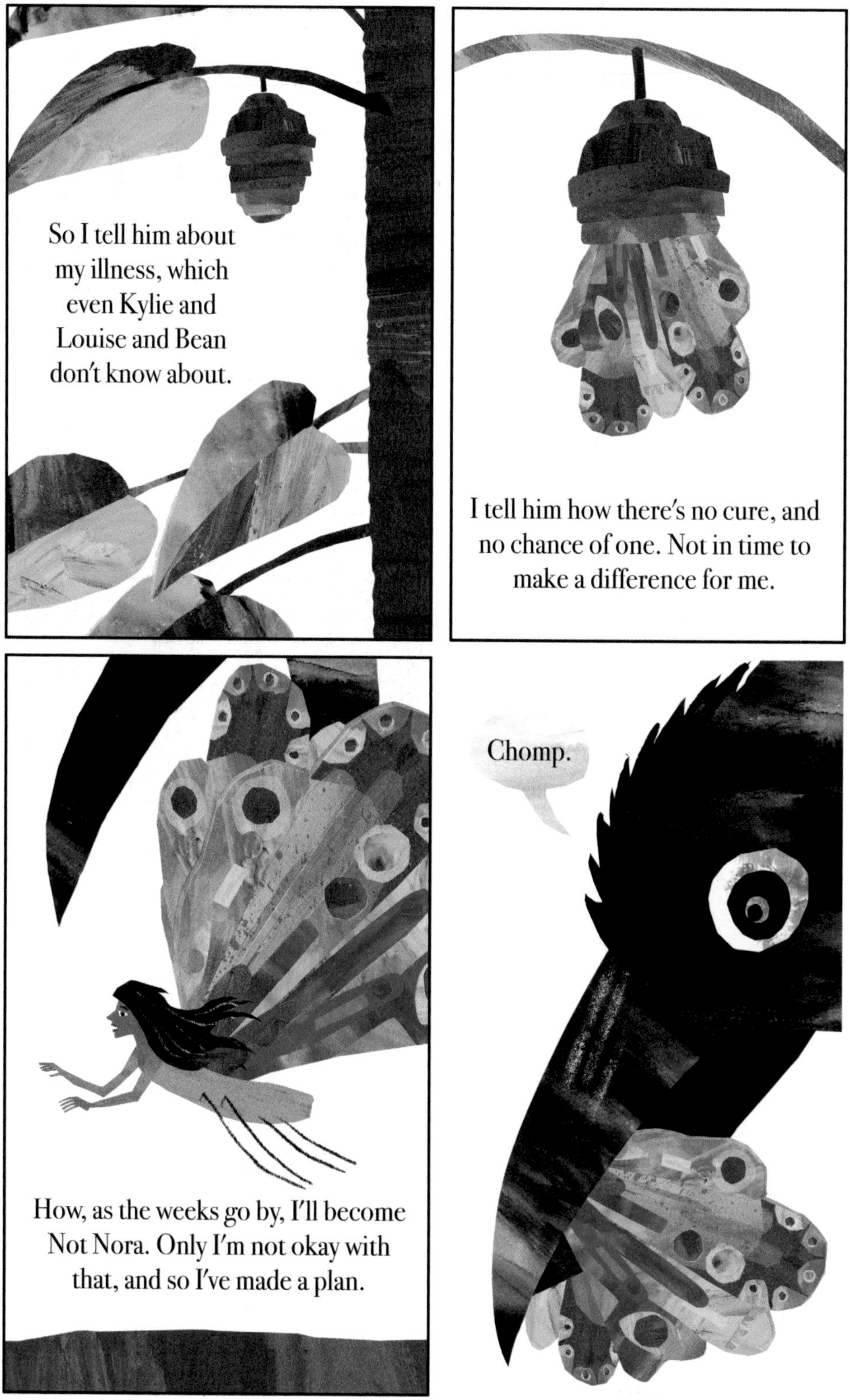
So I tell him about my illness, which even Kylie and Louise and Bean don't know about.
I tell him how there's no cure, and no chance of one. Not in time to make a difference for me.
How, as the weeks go by, I'll become Not Nora. Only I'm not okay with that, and so I've made a plan.
Chomp.

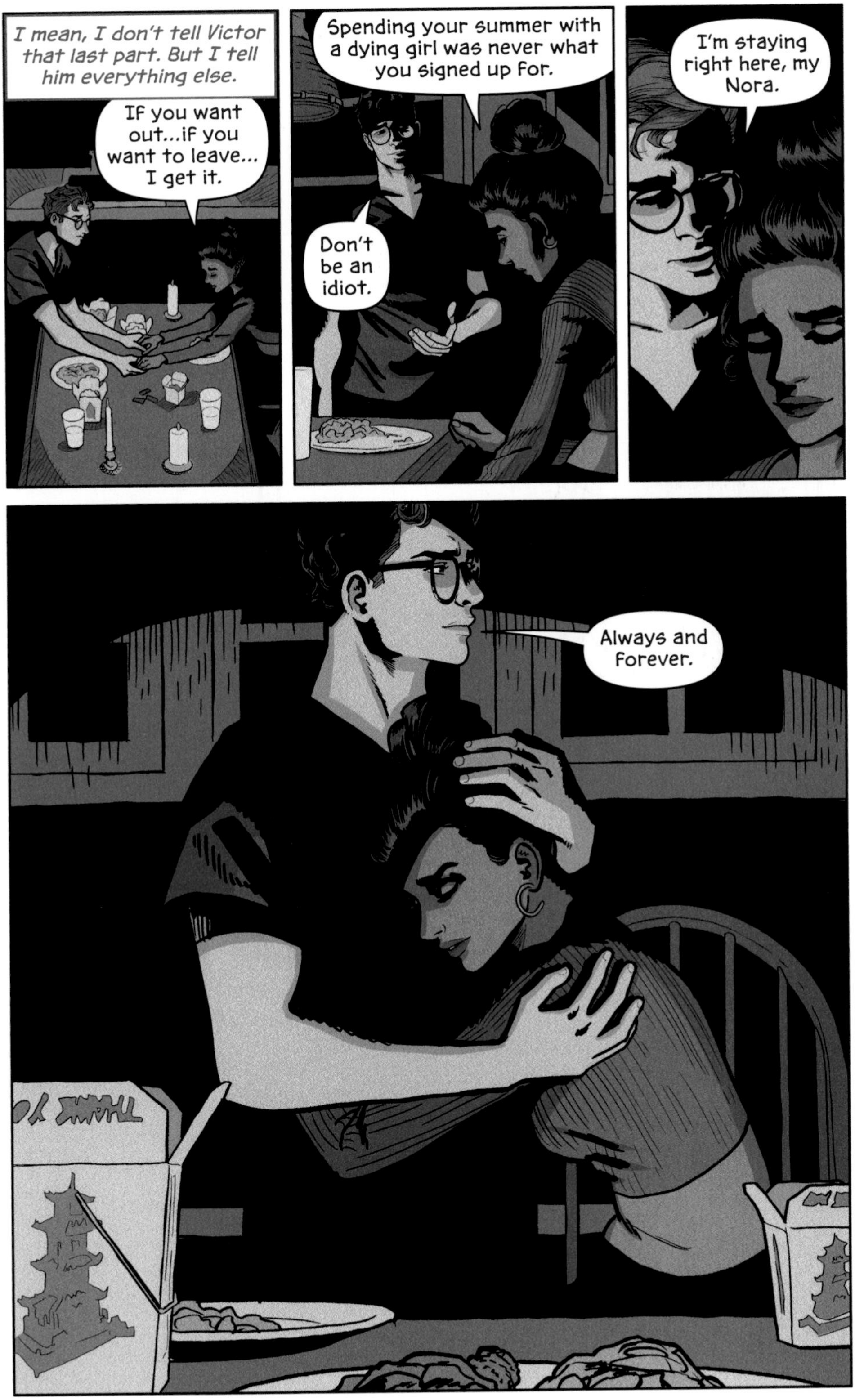
I mean, I don't tell Victor that last part. But I tell him everything else.
If you want out...if you want to leave... I get it.
Spending your summer with a dying girl was never what you signed up for.
Don't be an idiot.
I'm staying right here, my Nora.
Always and forever.

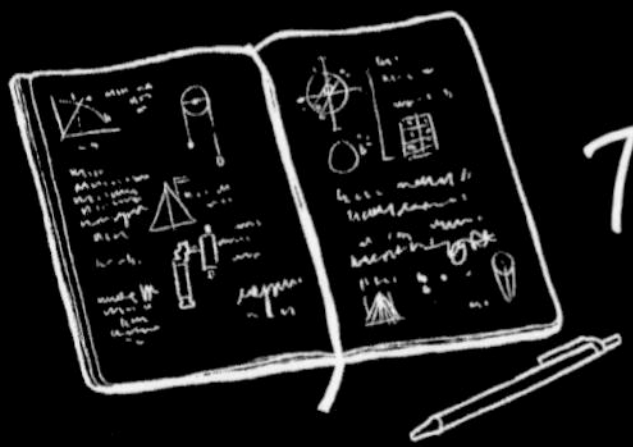

The Boy Who Rides a Motorcycle

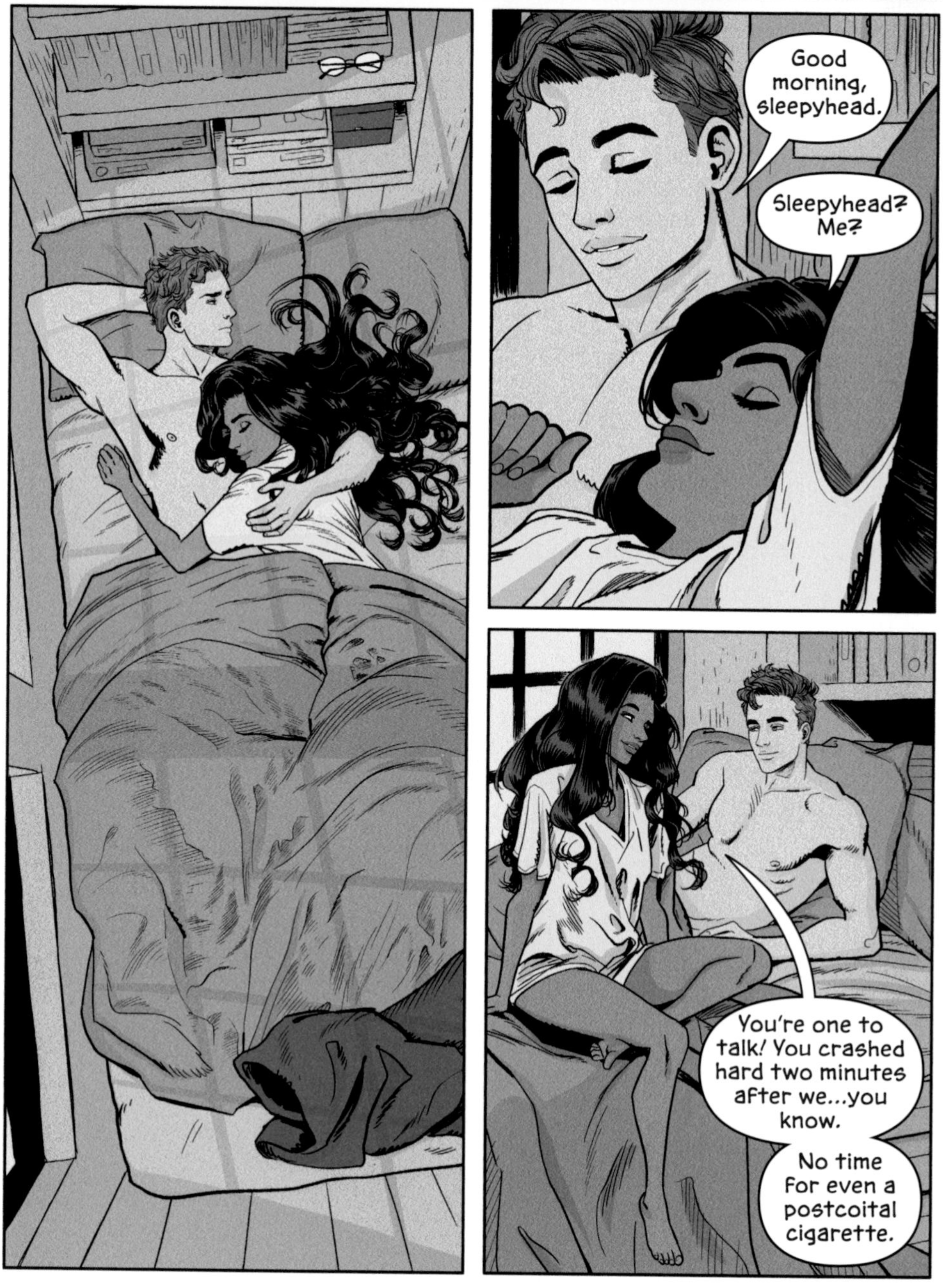
Good morning, sleepyhead.
Sleepyhead? Me?
You're one to talk! You crashed hard two minutes after we...you know.
No time for even a postcoital cigarette.

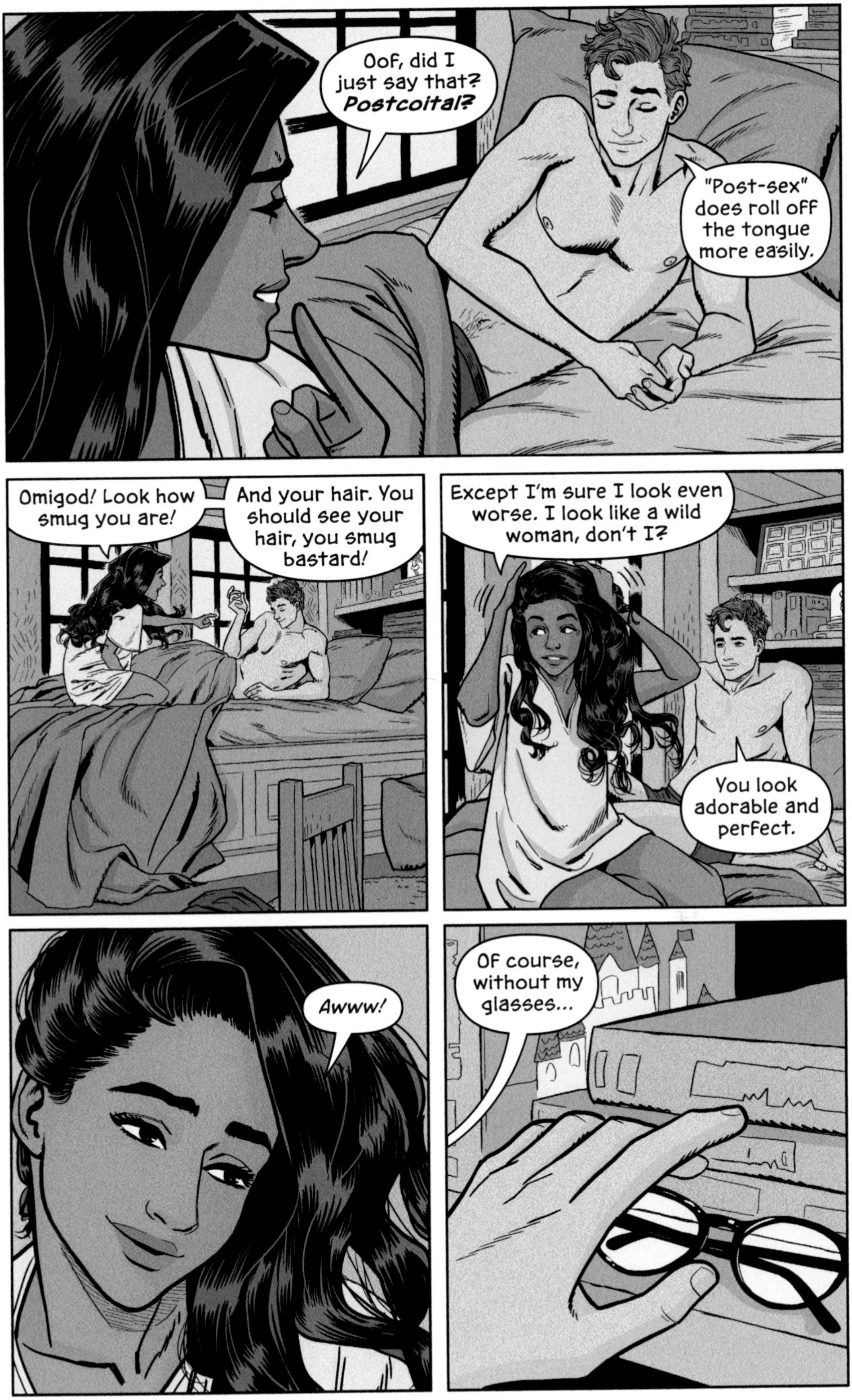
Oof, did I just say that? *Postcoital?*
"Post-sex" does roll off the tongue more easily.
Omigod! Look how smug you are!
And your hair. You should see your hair, you smug bastard!
Except I'm sure I look even worse. I look like a wild woman, don't I?
You look adorable and perfect.
Awww!
Of course, without my glasses...

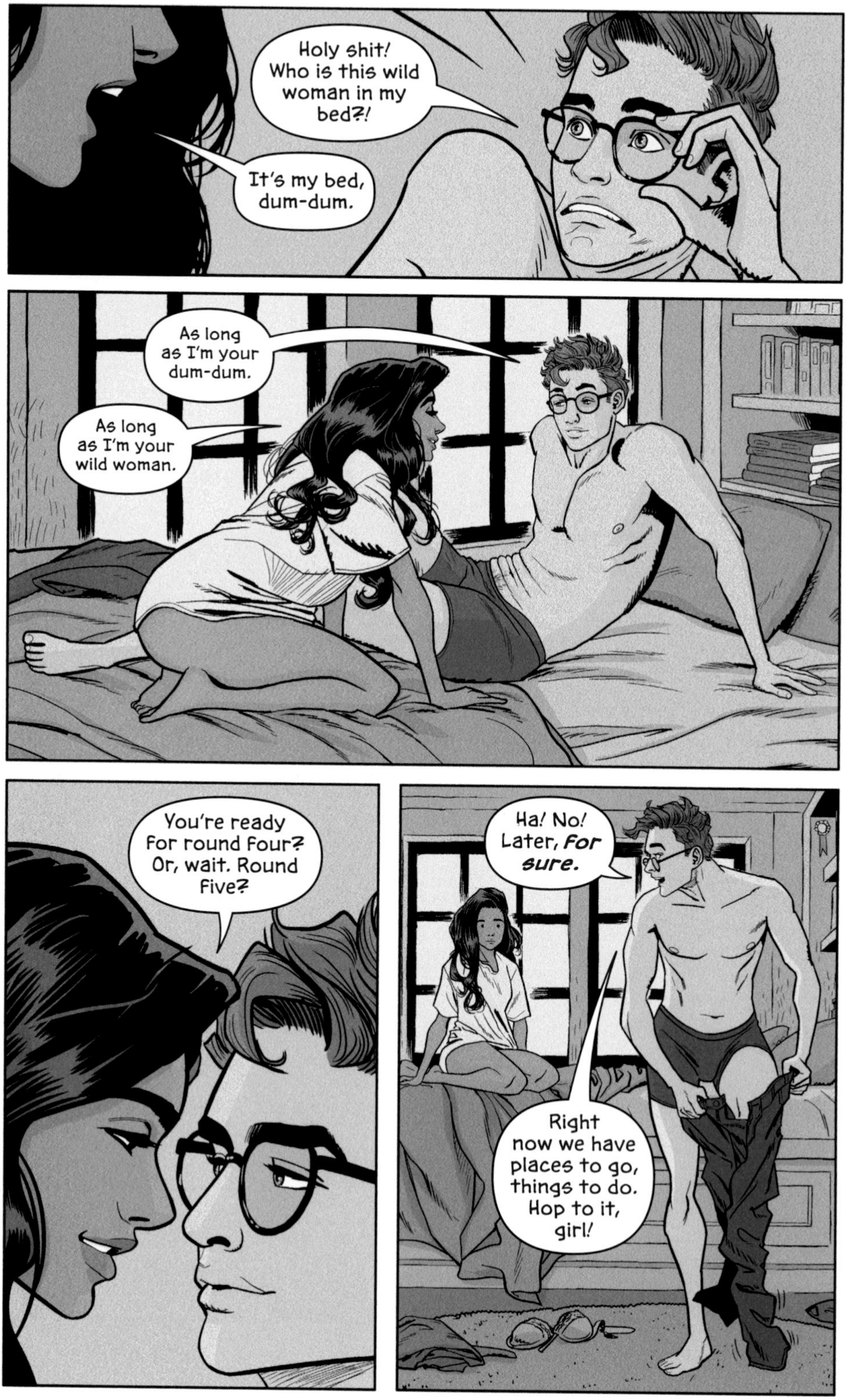
Holy shit! Who is this wild woman in my bed?!
It's my bed, dum-dum.
As long as I'm your dum-dum.
As long as I'm your wild woman.
You're ready for round four? Or, wait. Round five?
Ha! No! Later, *for sure.*
Right now we have places to go, things to do. Hop to it, girl!

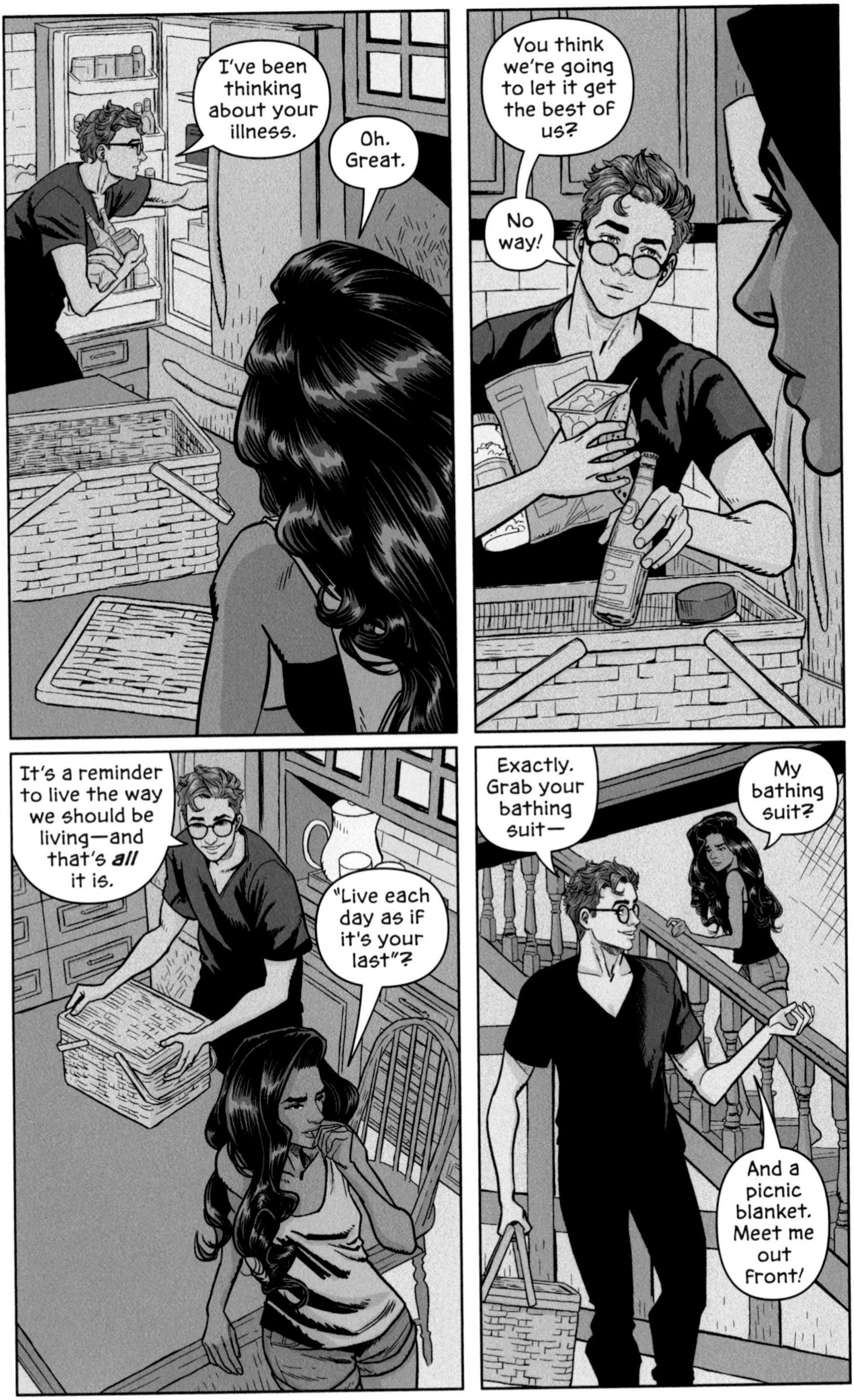
I've been thinking about your illness.
Oh. Great.
You think we're going to let it get the best of us?
No way!
It's a reminder to live the way we should be living—and that's *all* it is.
"Live each day as if it's your last"?
Exactly. Grab your bathing suit—
My bathing suit?
And a picnic blanket. Meet me out front!

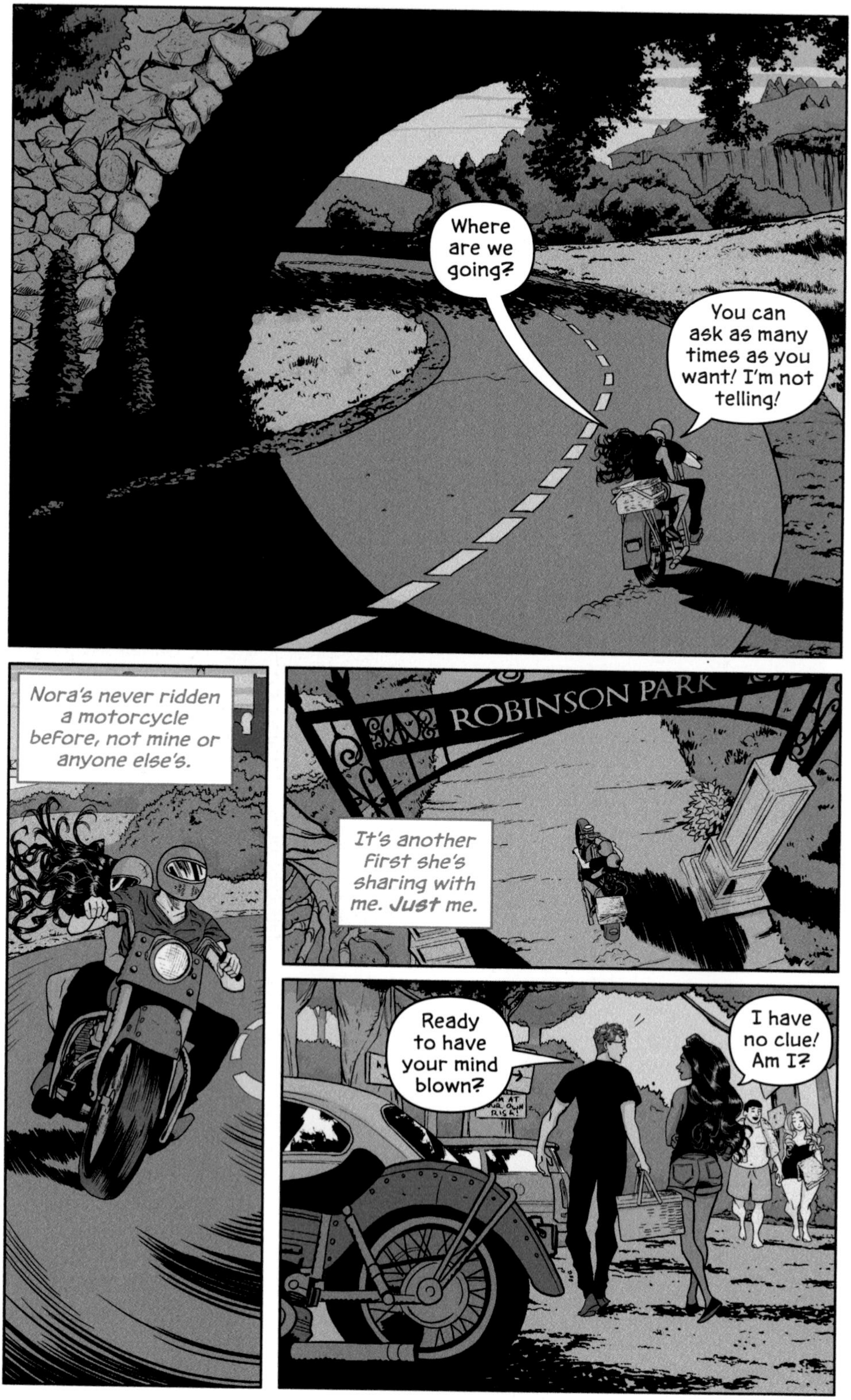
Where are we going?
You can ask as many times as you want! I'm not telling!
Nora's never ridden a motorcycle before, not mine or anyone else's.
ROBINSON PARK
It's another first she's sharing with me. *Just* me.
Ready to have your mind blown?
I have no clue! Am I?

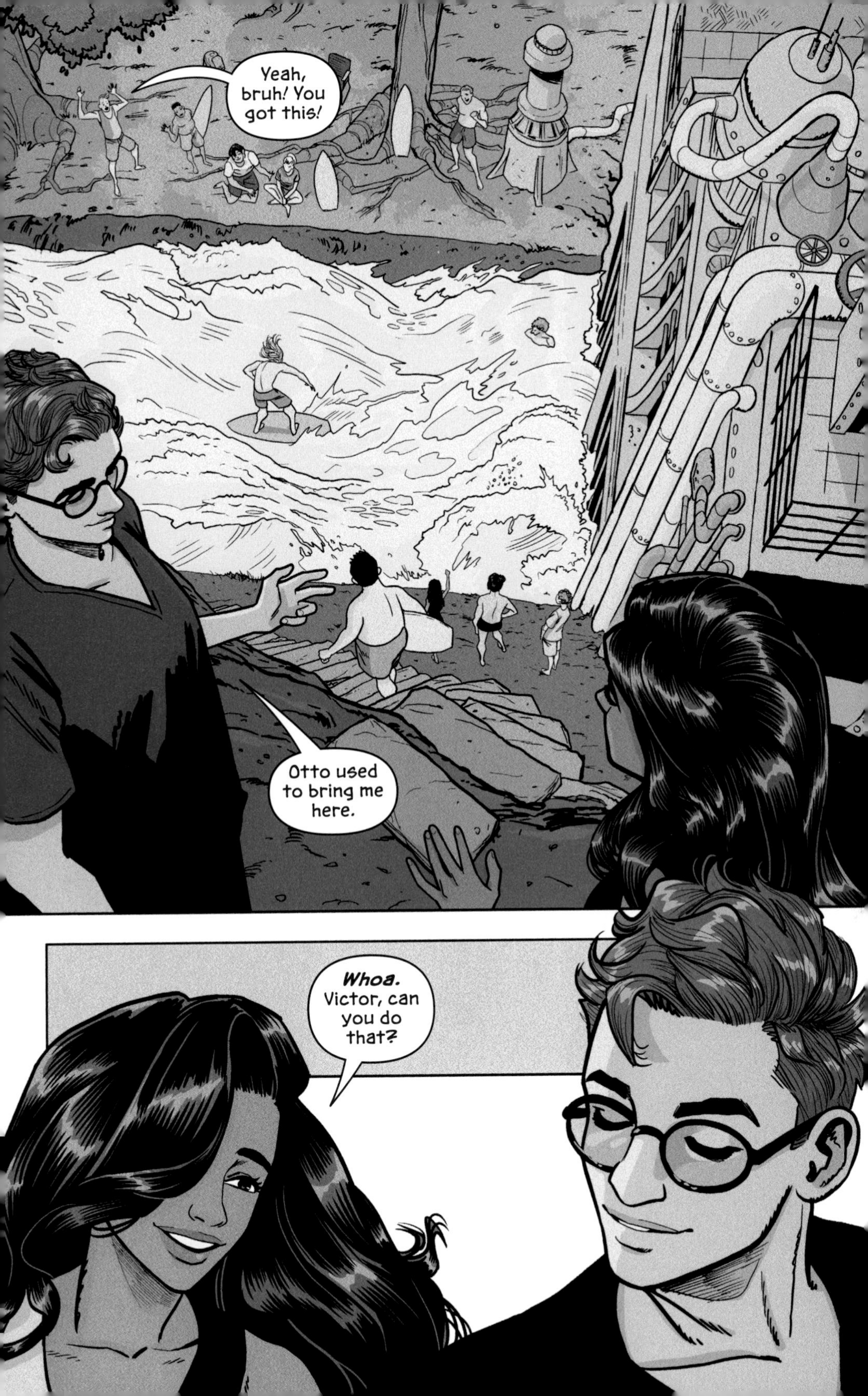
Yeah, bruh! You got this!
Otto used to bring me here.
Whoa. Victor, can you do that?

The Girl Who Goes Along for the Ride

Victor used to river surf with his brother.

This is his first time back since Otto died.

He needs to lean forward, to lower his center of gravity.

So no pressure, right? Just another day in the life!

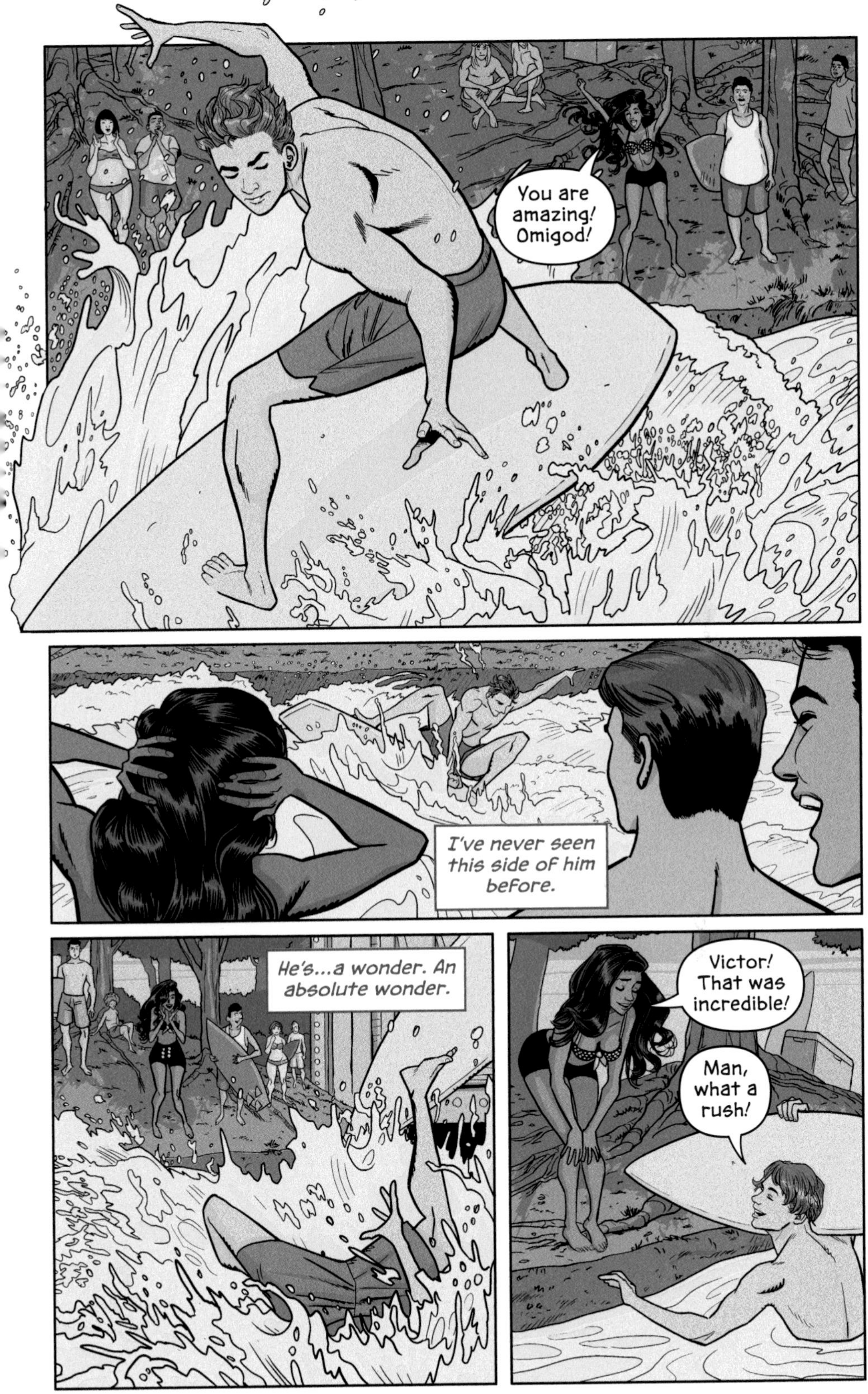
You are amazing! Omigod!
I've never seen this side of him before.
He's...a wonder. An absolute wonder.
Victor! That was incredible!
Man, what a rush!

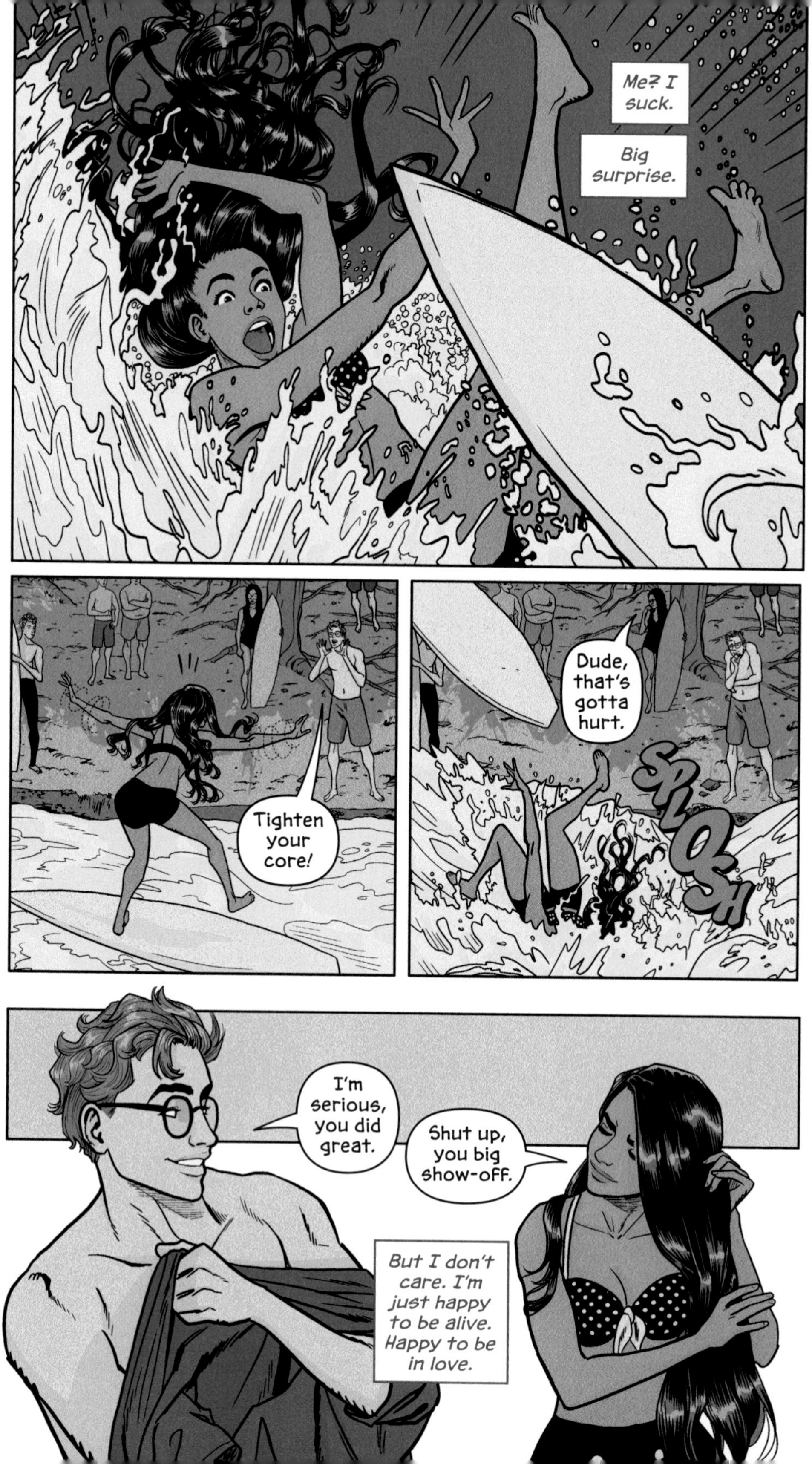
Me? I suck.
Big surprise.
Tighten your core!
Dude, that's gotta hurt.
SPLOSH
I'm serious, you did great.
Shut up, you big show-off.
But I don't care. I'm just happy to be alive. Happy to be in love.

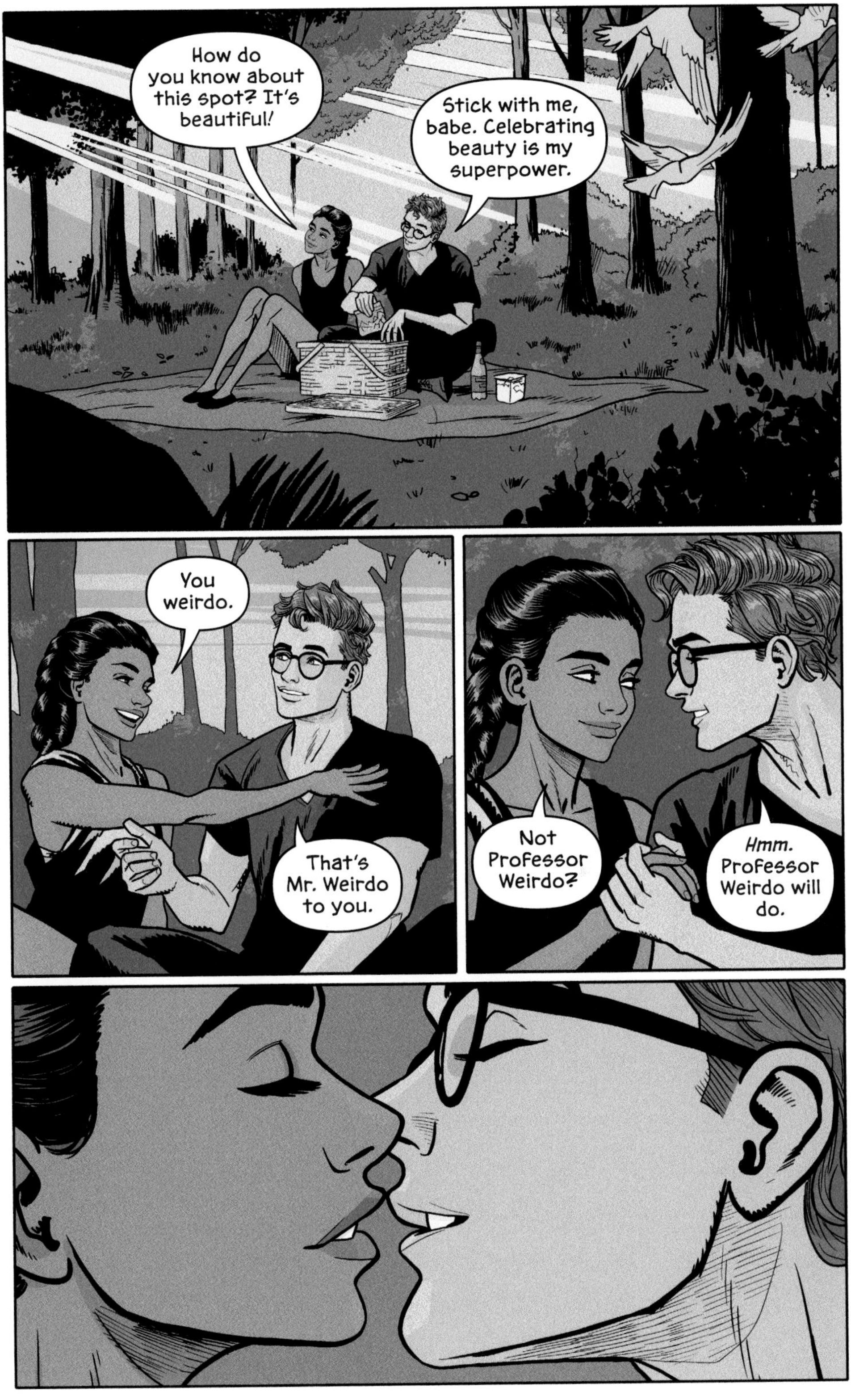
How do you know about this spot? It's beautiful!
Stick with me, babe. Celebrating beauty is my superpower.
You weirdo.
That's Mr. Weirdo to you.
Not Professor Weirdo?
Hmm. Professor Weirdo will do.

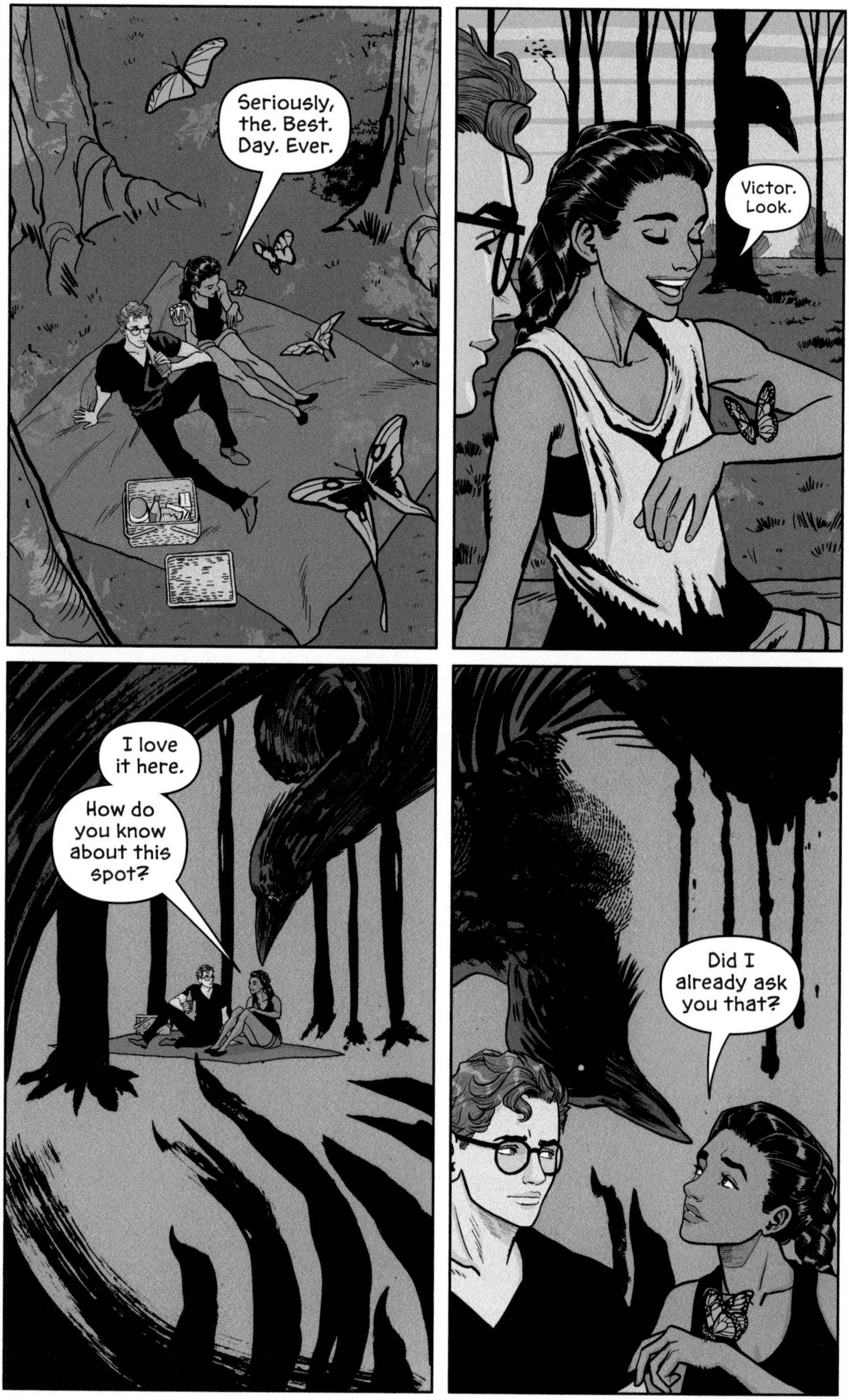
Seriously, the. Best. Day. Ever.
Victor. Look.
I love it here.
How do you know about this spot?
Did I already ask you that?

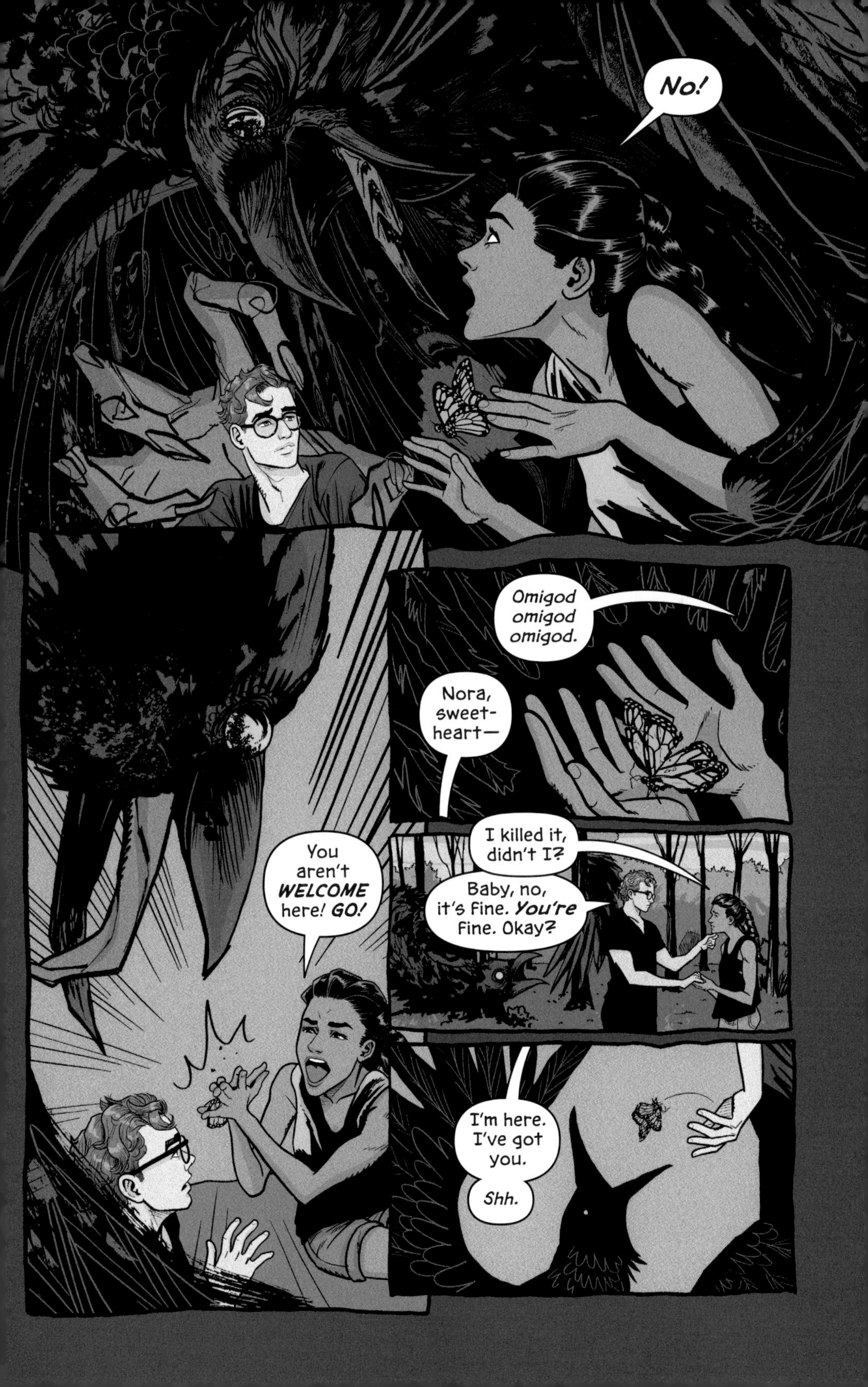
No!
You aren't WELCOME here! GO!
Omigod omigod omigod.
Nora, sweet-heart—
I killed it, didn't I?
Baby, no, it's fine. You're fine. Okay?
I'm here. I've got you.
Shh.

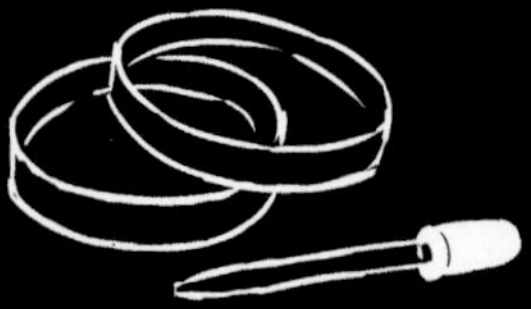

The Boy Whose Heart Is a Flame

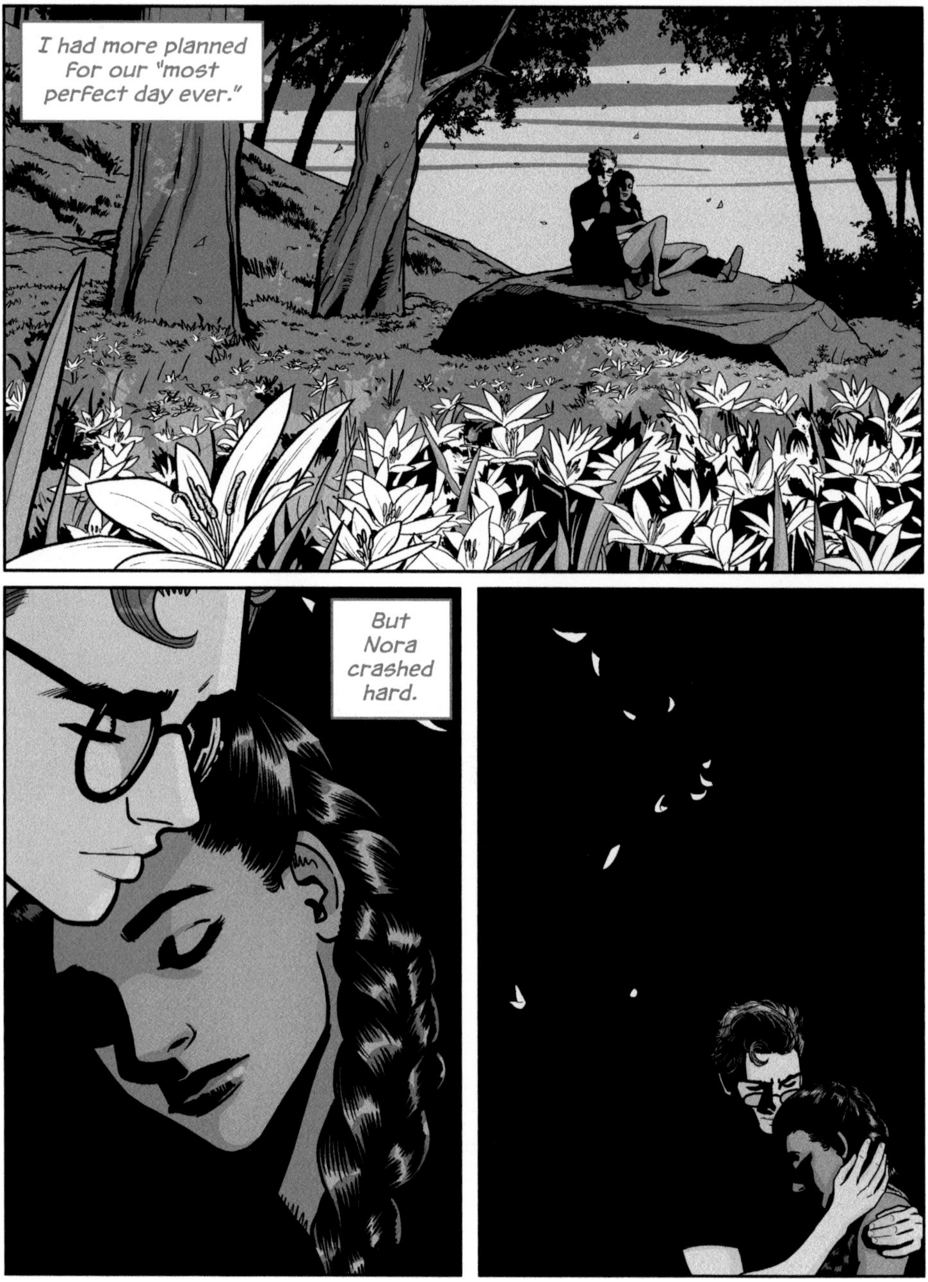
I had more planned for our "most perfect day ever."
But Nora crashed hard.

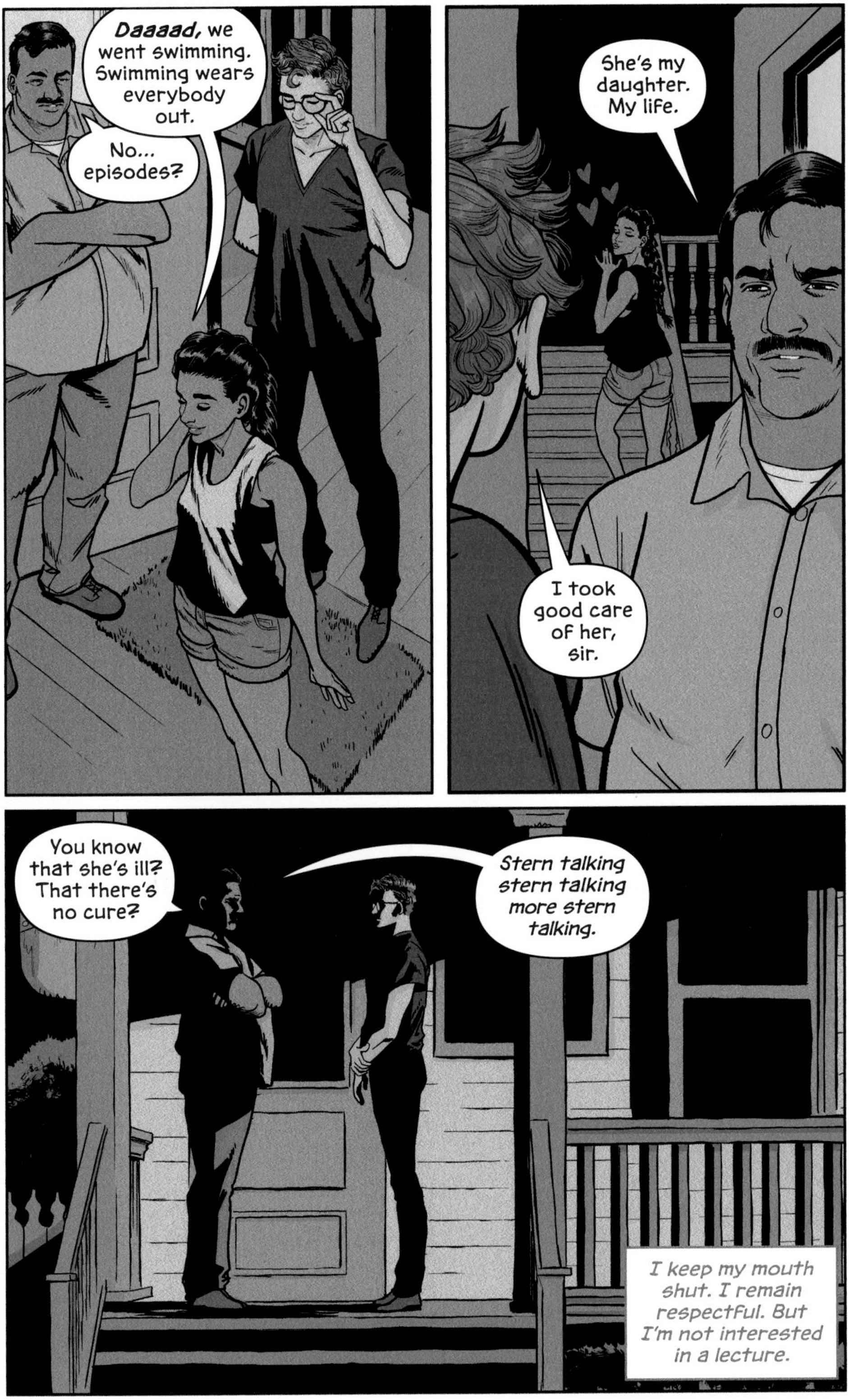
Daaaad, we went swimming. Swimming wears everybody out.
No... episodes?
She's my daughter. My life.
I took good care of her, sir.
You know that she's ill? That there's no cure?
Stern talking stern talking more stern talking.
I keep my mouth shut. I remain respectful. But I'm not interested in a lecture.

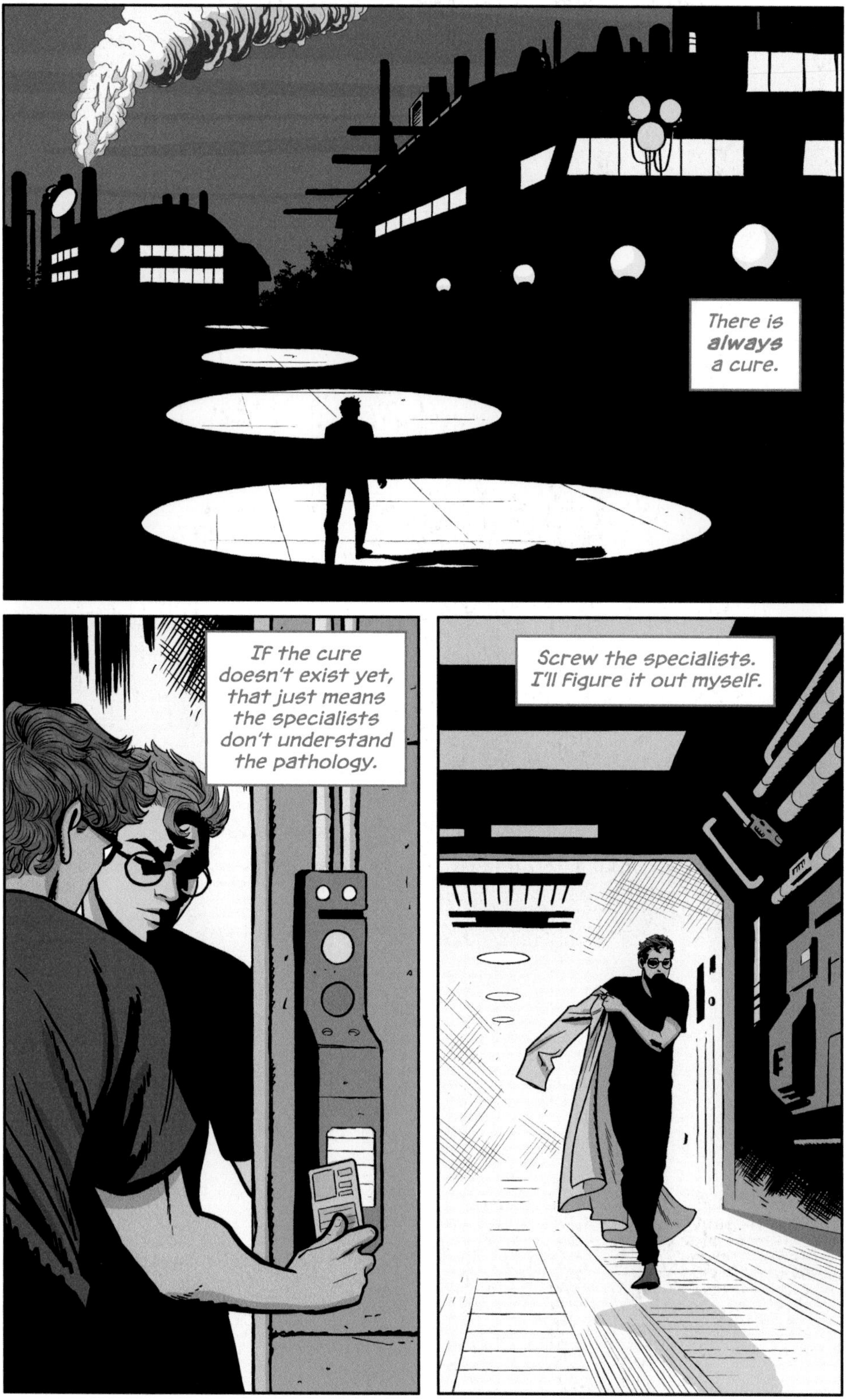
There is always a cure.
If the cure doesn't exist yet, that just means the specialists don't understand the pathology.
Screw the specialists. I'll figure it out myself.

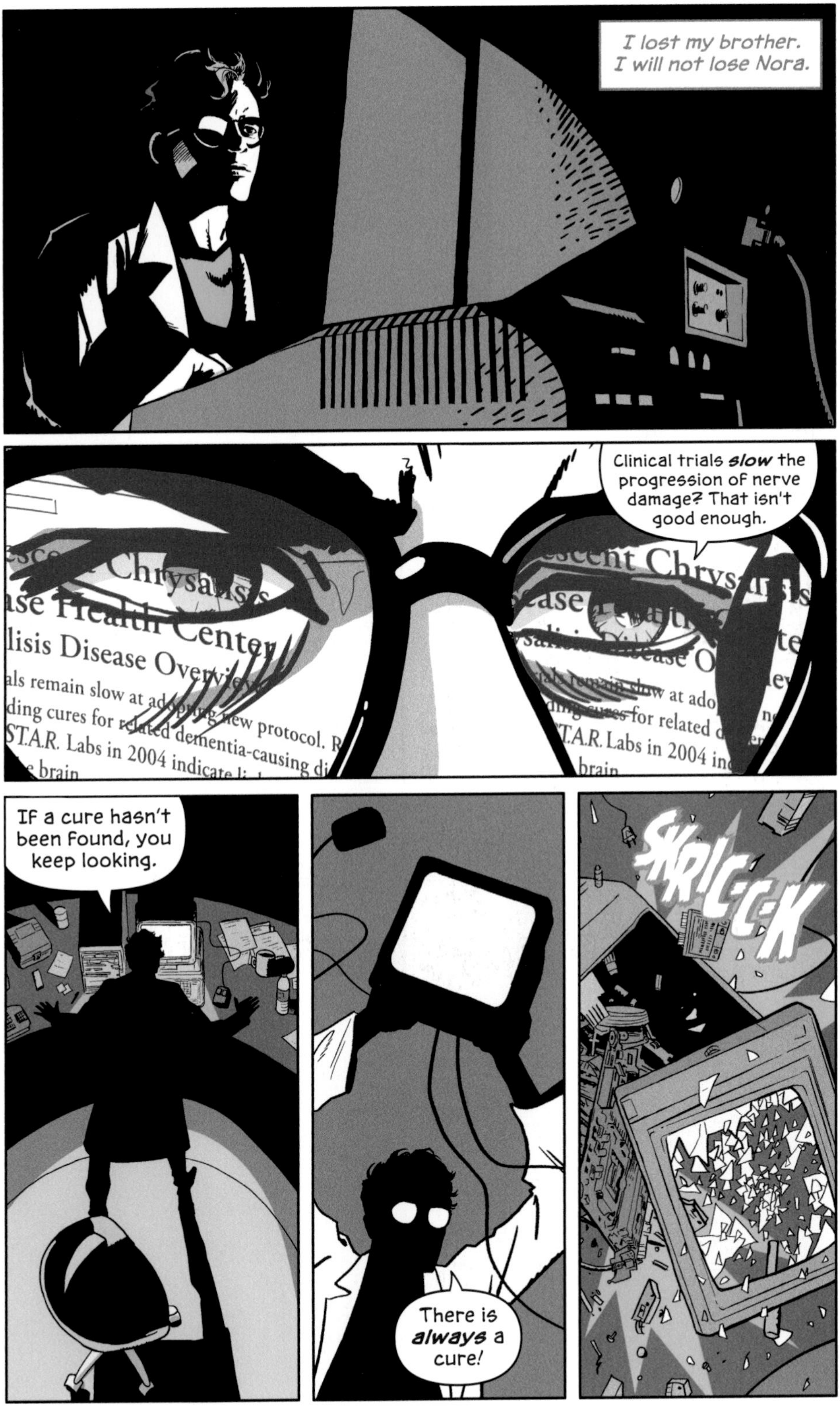
I lost my brother. I will not lose Nora.
Clinical trials *slow* the progression of nerve damage? That isn't good enough.
If a cure hasn't been found, you keep looking.
There is *always* a cure!
SKRIC-C-K

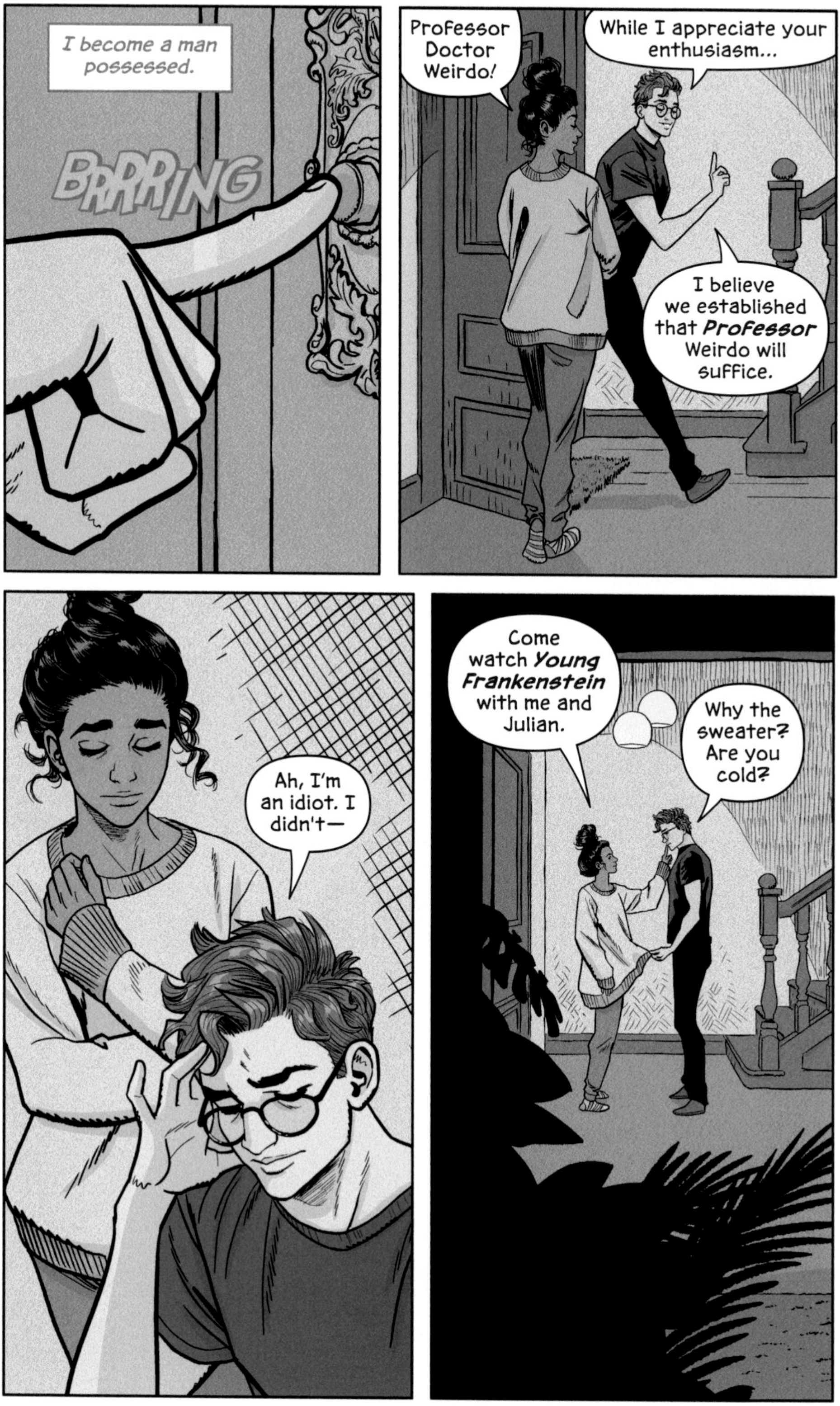

I become a man possessed.
BRRRING
Professor Doctor Weirdo!
While I appreciate your enthusiasm...
I believe we established that *Professor* Weirdo will suffice.
Ah, I'm an idiot. I didn't—
Come watch *Young Frankenstein* with me and Julian.
Why the sweater? Are you cold?

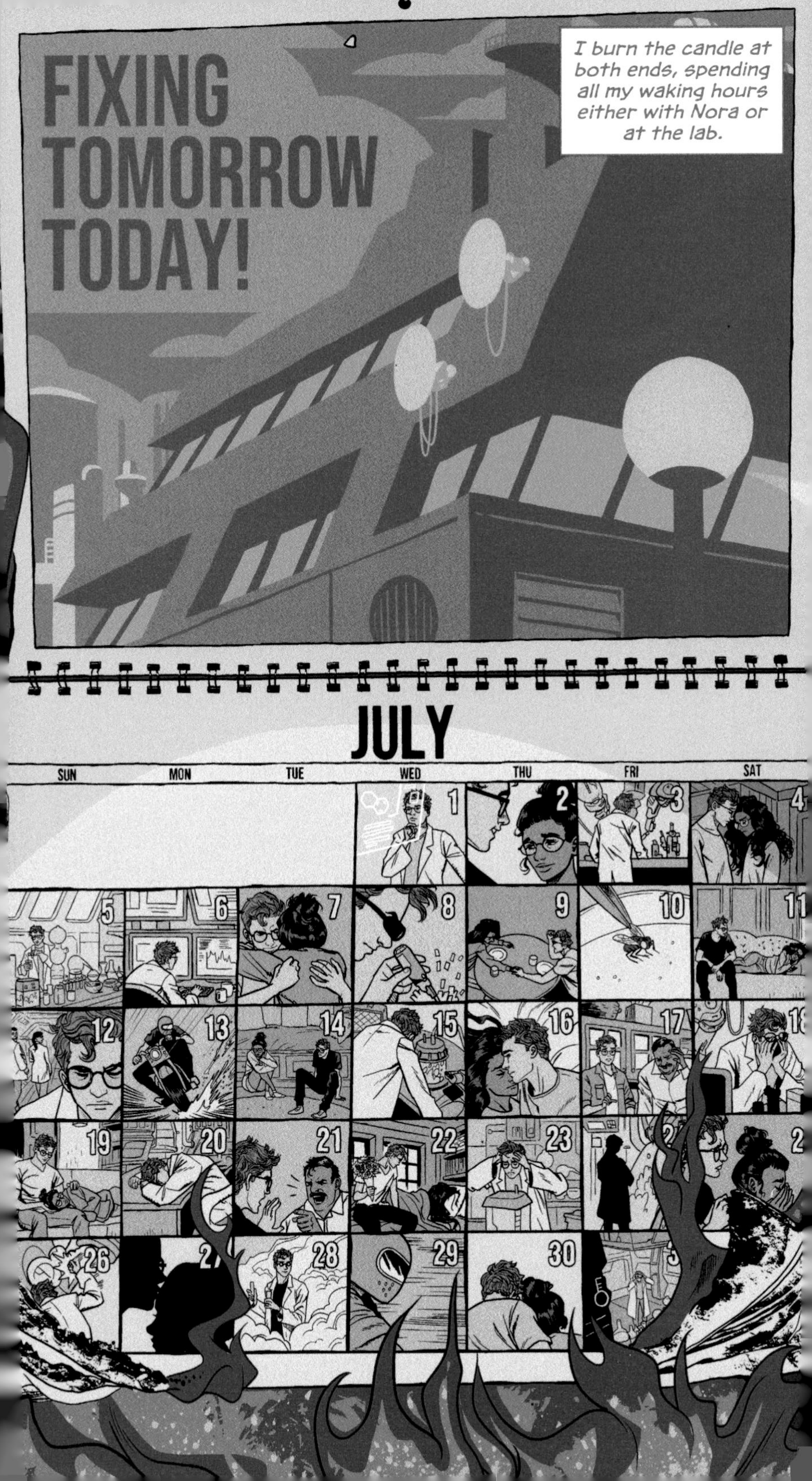
FIXING TOMORROW TODAY!
I burn the candle at both ends, spending all my waking hours either with Nora or at the lab.
JULY
SUN
MON
TUE
WED
THU
FRI
SAT
1
2
3
4
5
6
7
8
9
10
11
12
13
14
15
16
17
18
19
20
21
22
23
28
29
30

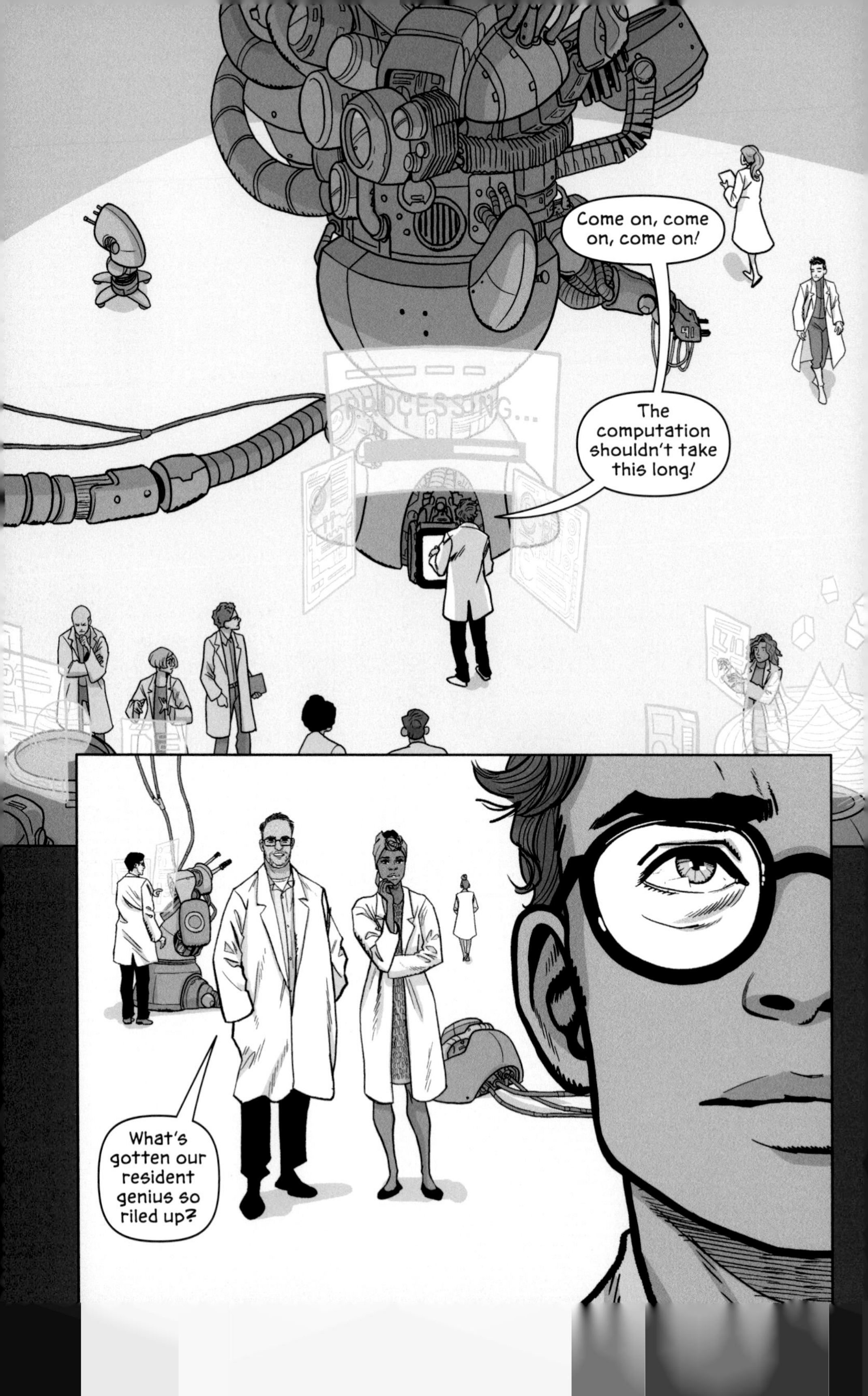
Come on, come on, come on!
The computation shouldn't take this long!
What's gotten our resident genius so riled up?

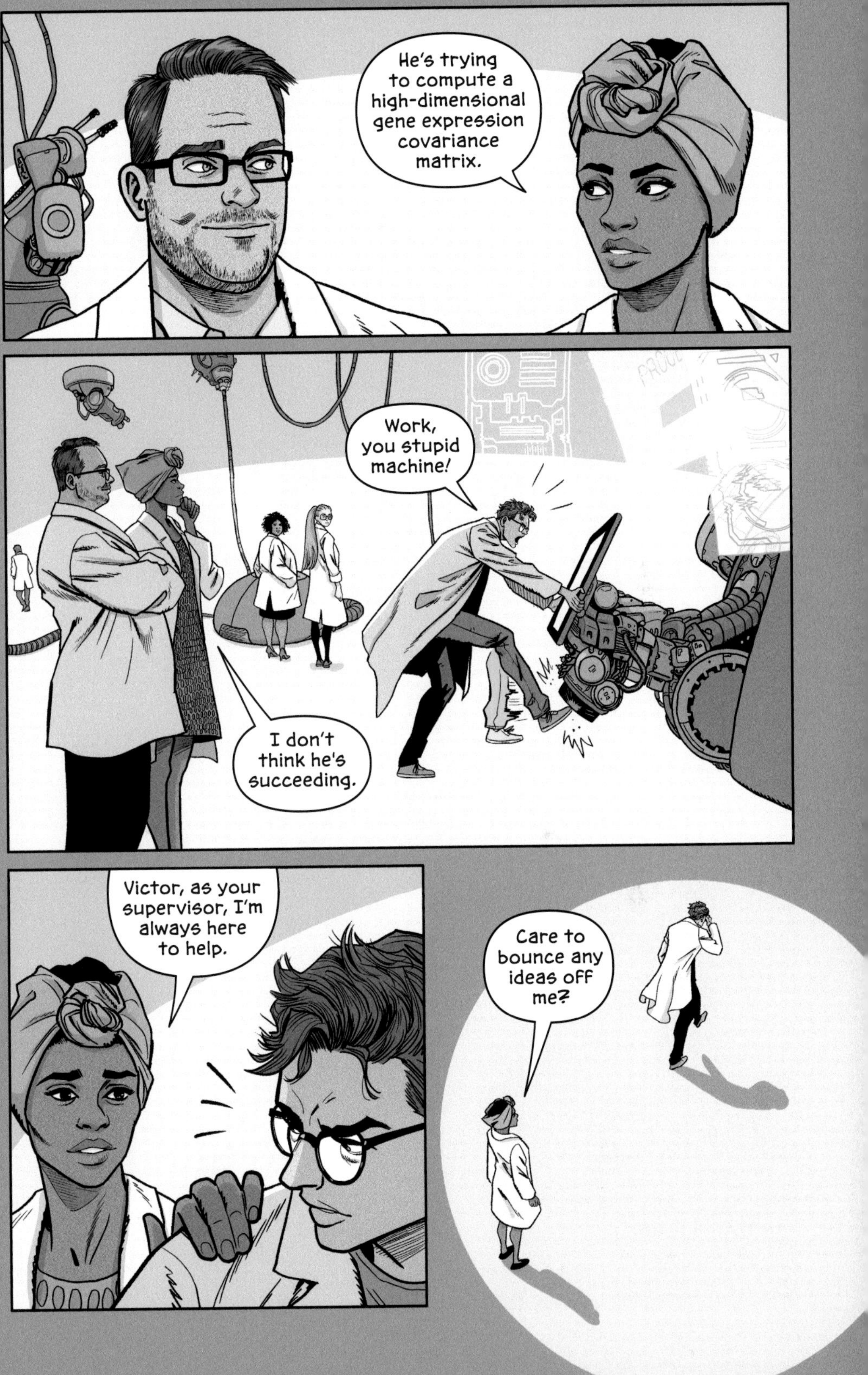
He's trying to compute a high-dimensional gene expression covariance matrix.
Work, you stupid machine!
I don't think he's succeeding.
Victor, as your supervisor, I'm always here to help.
Care to bounce any ideas off me?

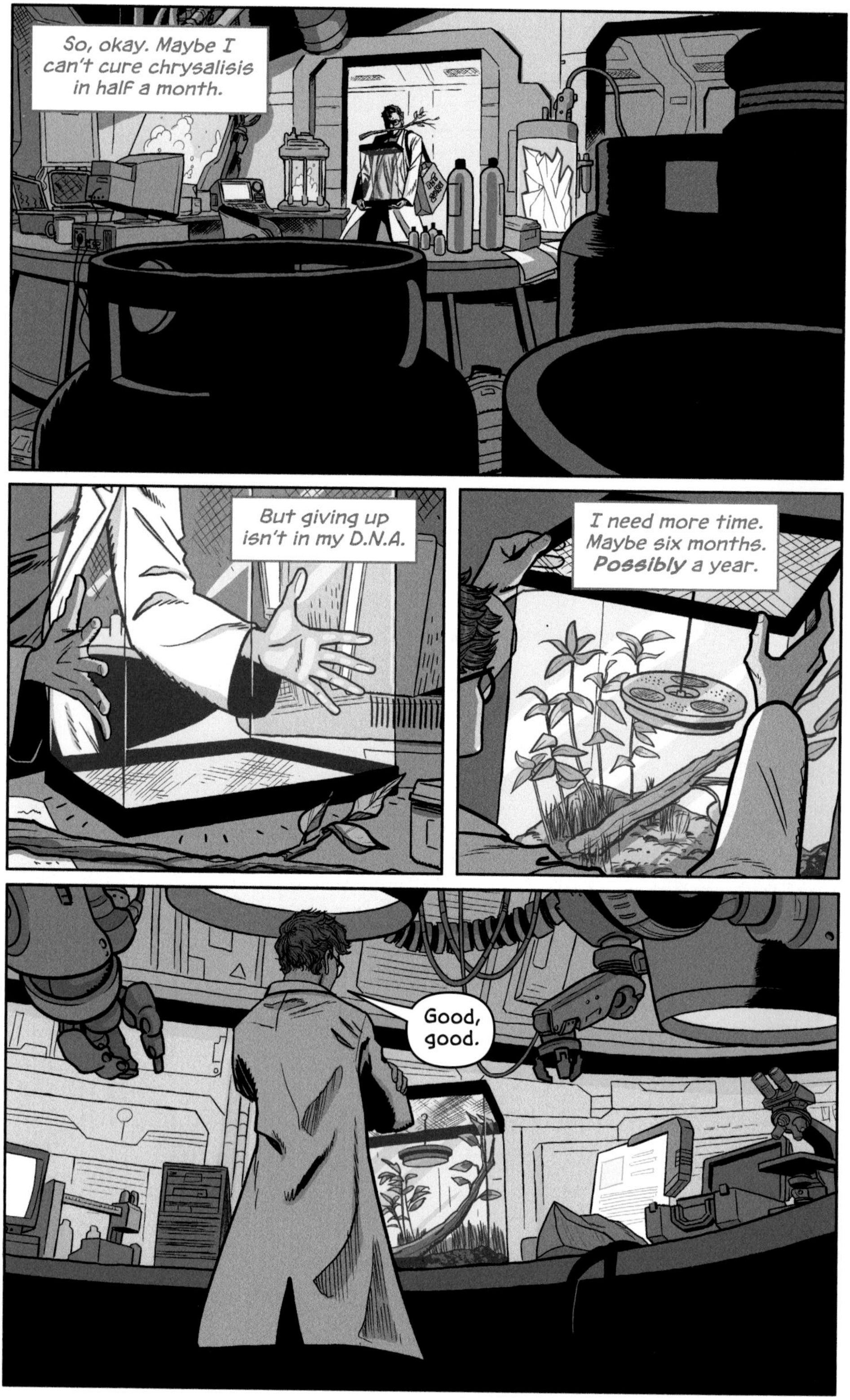
So, okay. Maybe I can't cure chrysalisis in half a month.
But giving up isn't in my D.N.A.
I need more time. Maybe six months. **Possibly** a year.
Good, good.

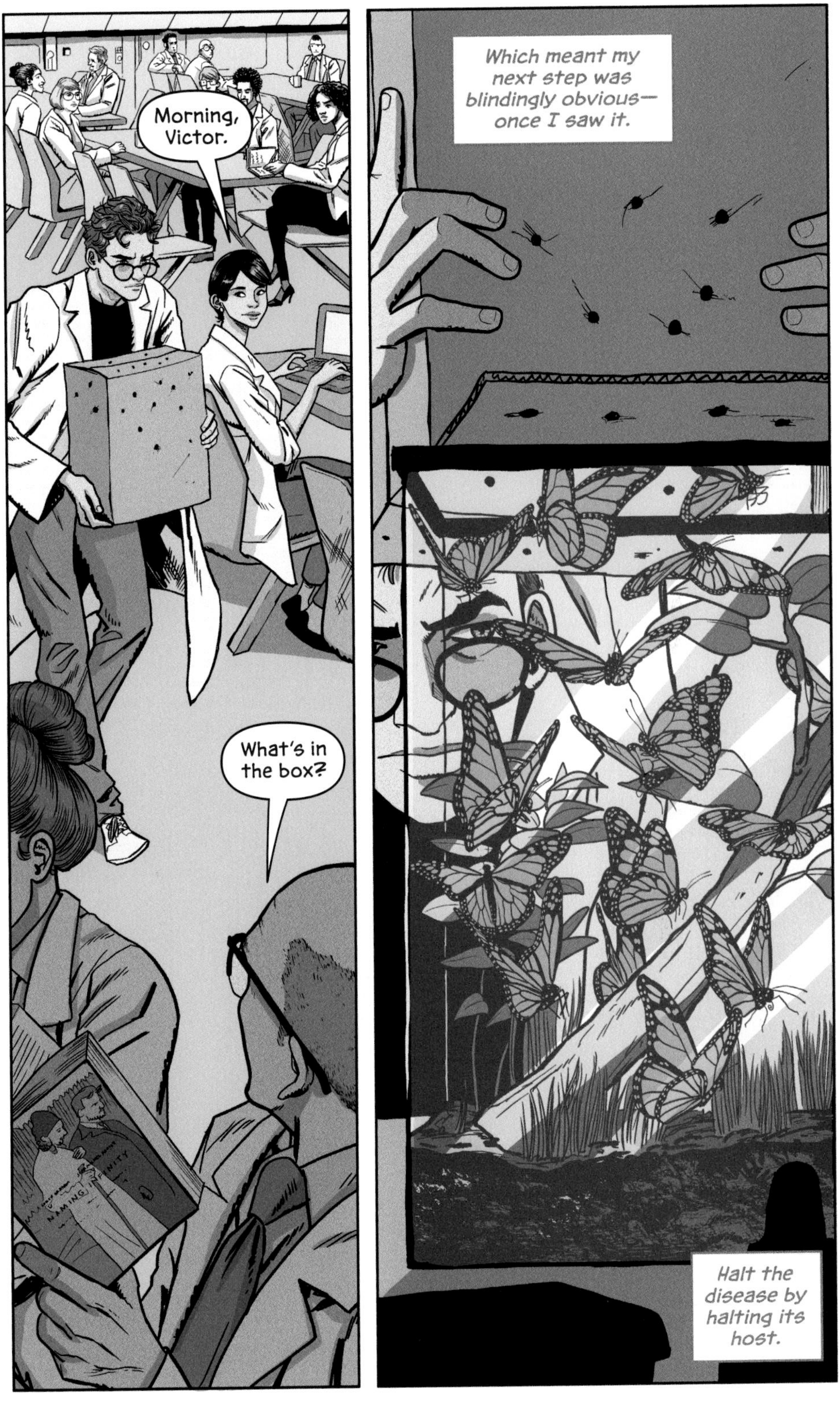
Morning, Victor.
What's in the box?
Which meant my next step was blindingly obvious—once I saw it.
Halt the disease by halting its host.

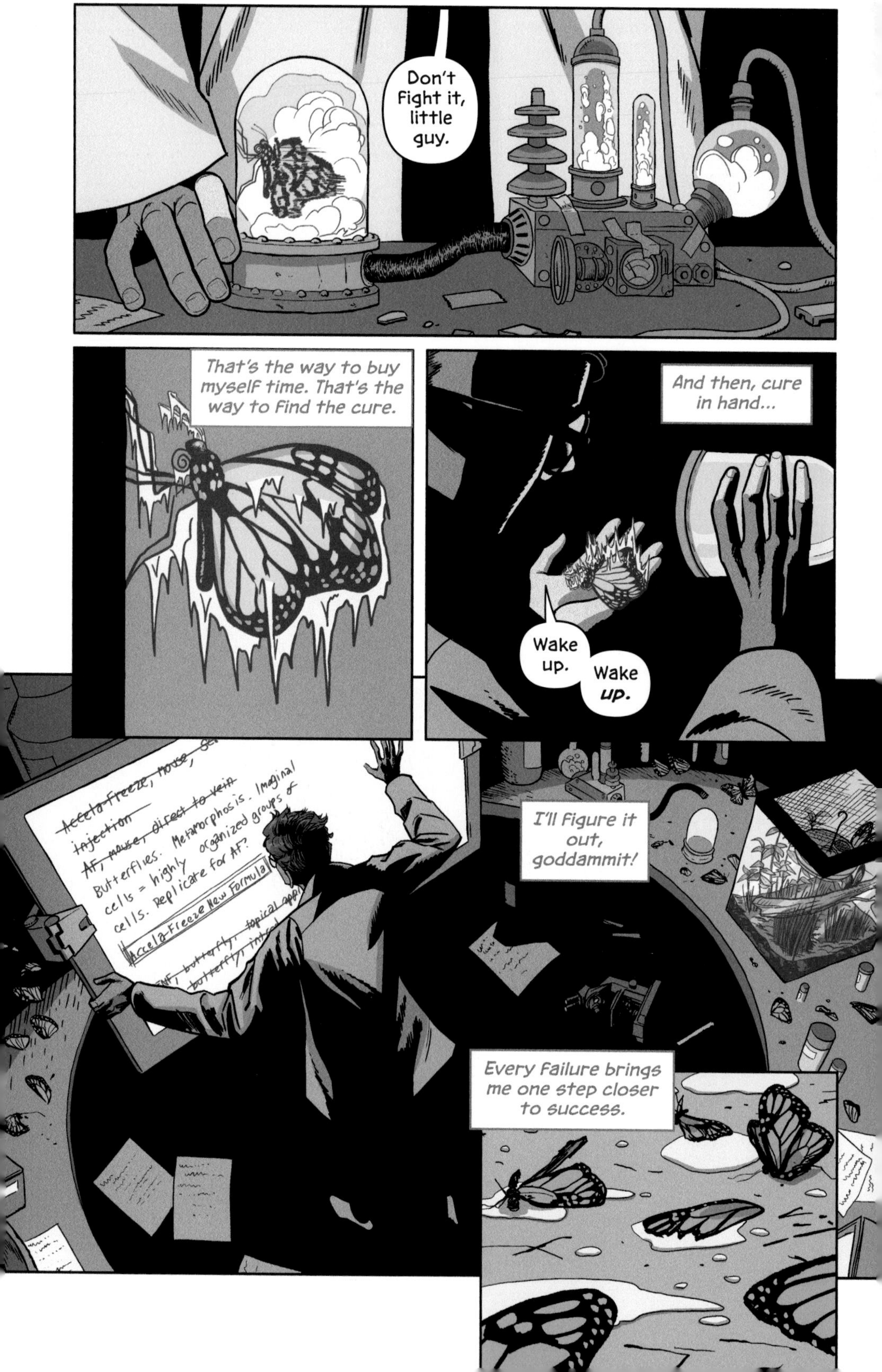
Don't fight it, little guy.
That's the way to buy myself time. That's the way to find the cure.
And then, cure in hand...
Wake up.
Wake up.
Accela-Freeze, mouse,
injection
AF, mouse, direct to vein
Butterflies. Metamorphosis. Imaginal cells = highly organized groups of cells. Replicate for AF?
Accela-Freeze New Formula
I'll figure it out, goddammit!
Every failure brings me one step closer to success.

The Girl Whose Light Is Dimming

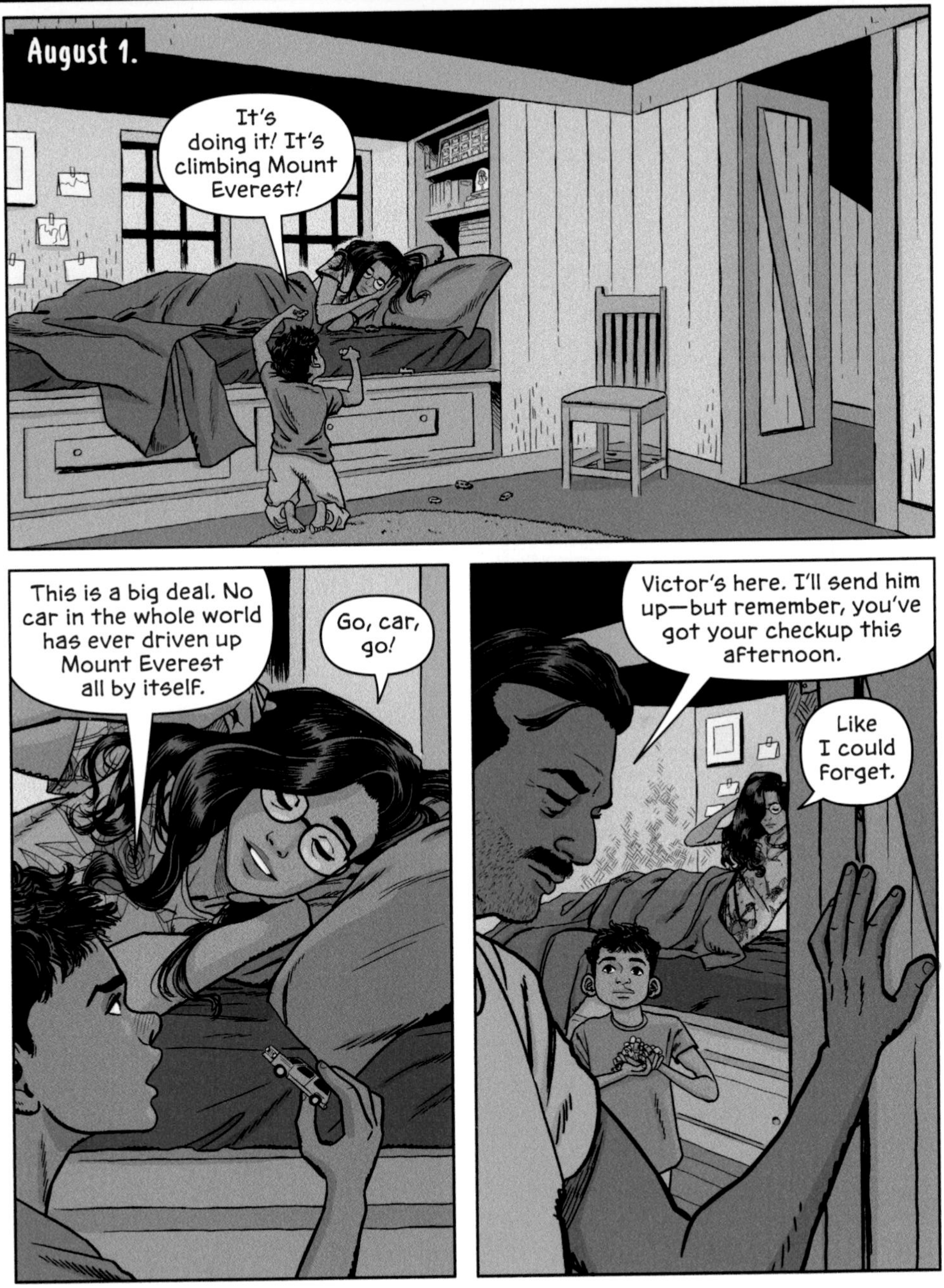
August 1.
It's doing it! It's climbing Mount Everest!
This is a big deal. No car in the whole world has ever driven up Mount Everest all by itself.
Go, car, go!
Victor's here. I'll send him up—but remember, you've got your checkup this afternoon.
Like I could forget.

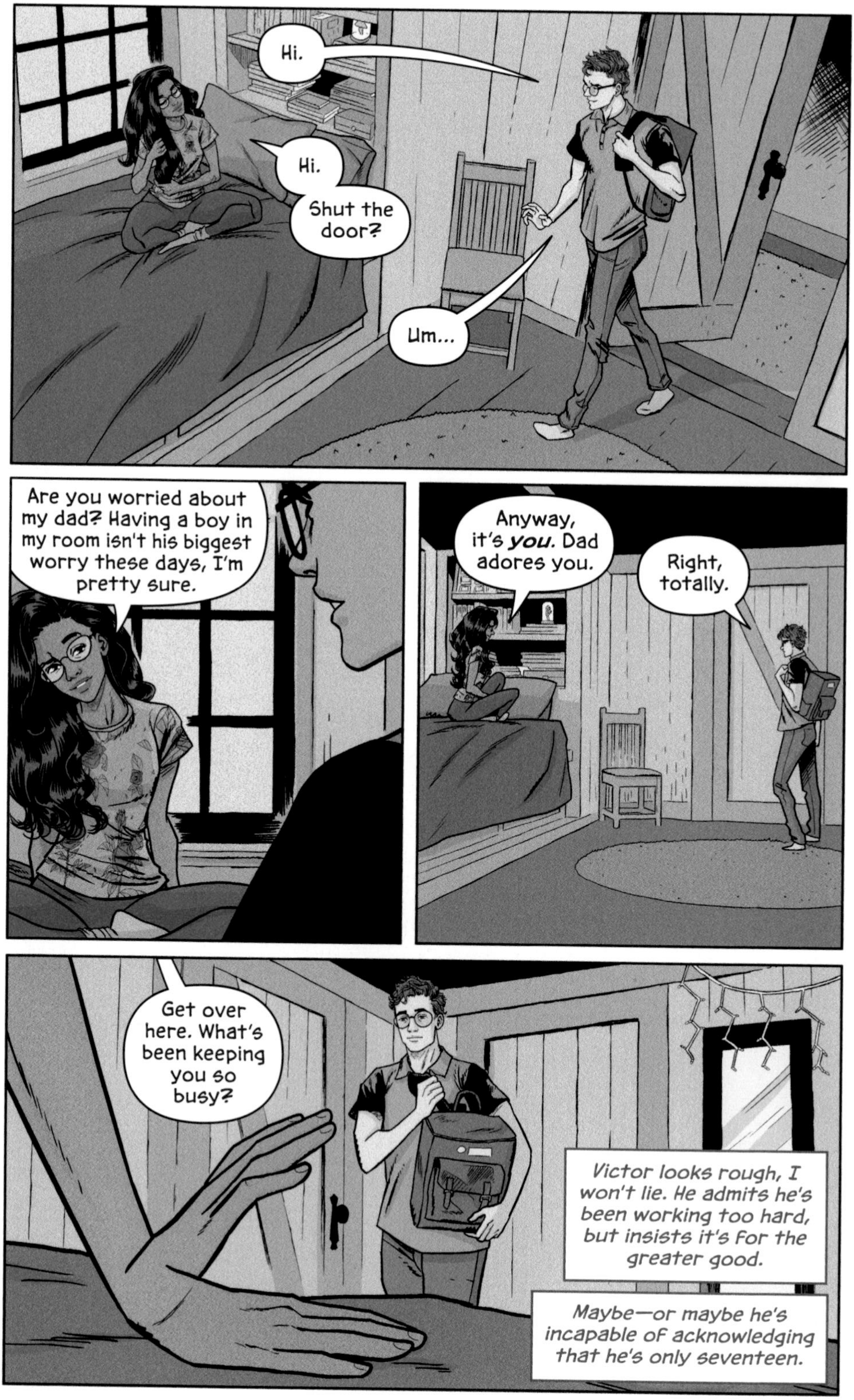
Hi.
Hi.
Shut the door?
Um...
Are you worried about my dad? Having a boy in my room isn't his biggest worry these days, I'm pretty sure.
Anyway, it's *you*. Dad adores you.
Right, totally.
Get over here. What's been keeping you so busy?
Victor looks rough, I won't lie. He admits he's been working too hard, but insists it's for the greater good.
Maybe—or maybe he's incapable of acknowledging that he's only seventeen.

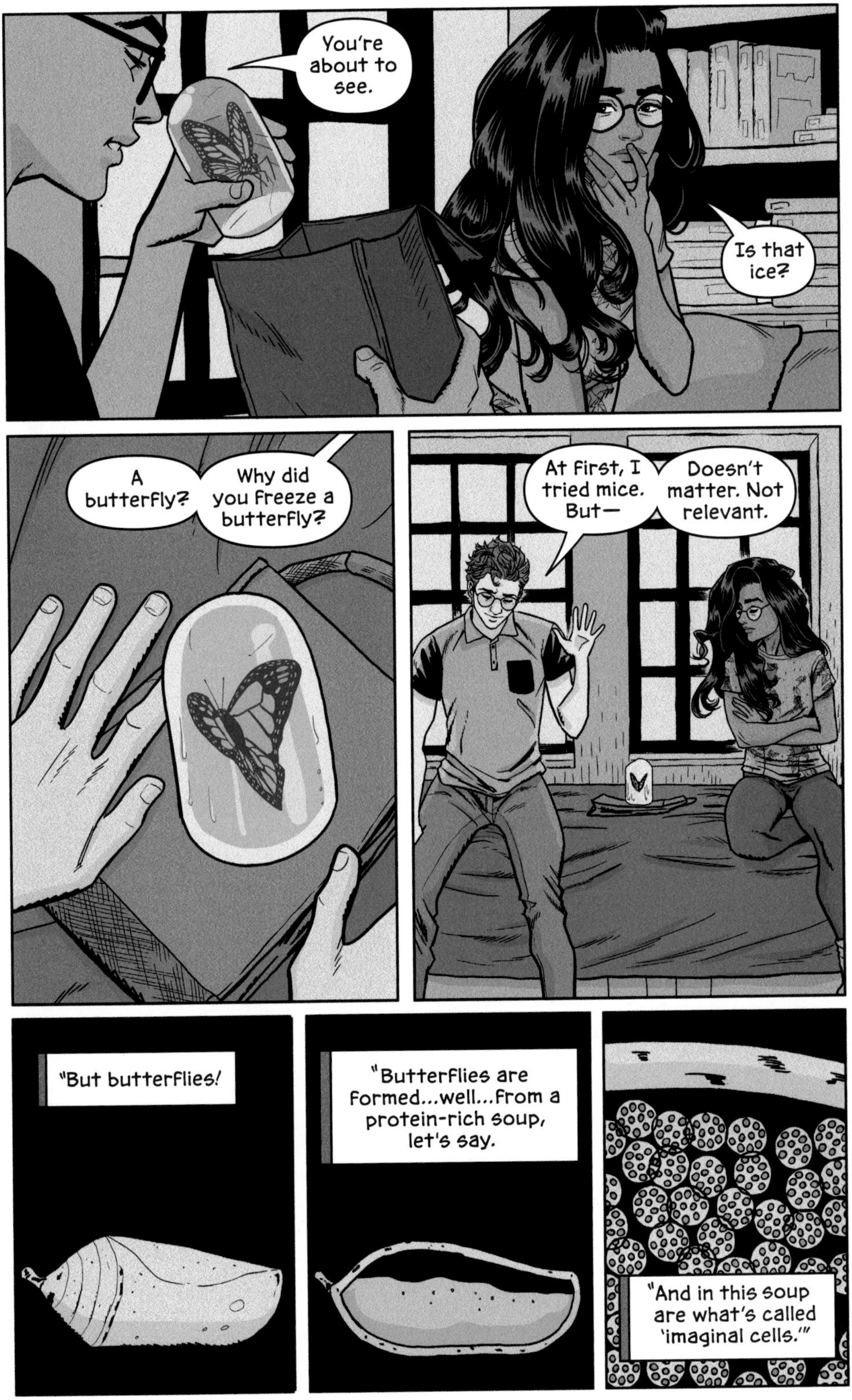
You're about to see.
Is that ice?
A butterfly?
Why did you freeze a butterfly?
At first, I tried mice. But—
Doesn't matter. Not relevant.
"But butterflies!
"Butterflies are formed...well...from a protein-rich soup, let's say.
"And in this soup are what's called 'imaginal cells.'"

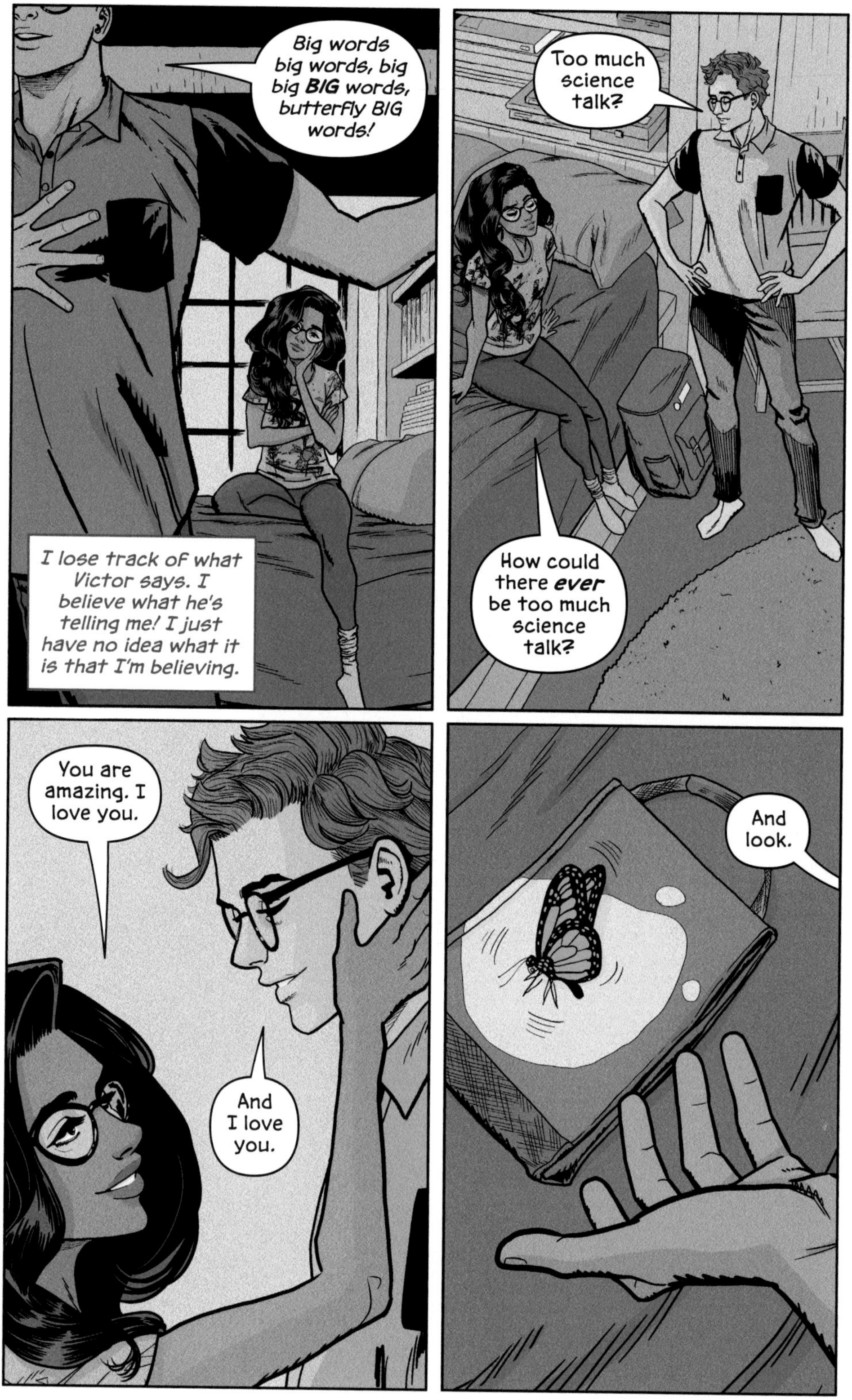
Big words big words, big big BIG words, butterfly BIG words!
I lose track of what Victor says. I believe what he's telling me! I just have no idea what it is that I'm believing.
Too much science talk?
How could there ever be too much science talk?
You are amazing. I love you.
And I love you.
And look.

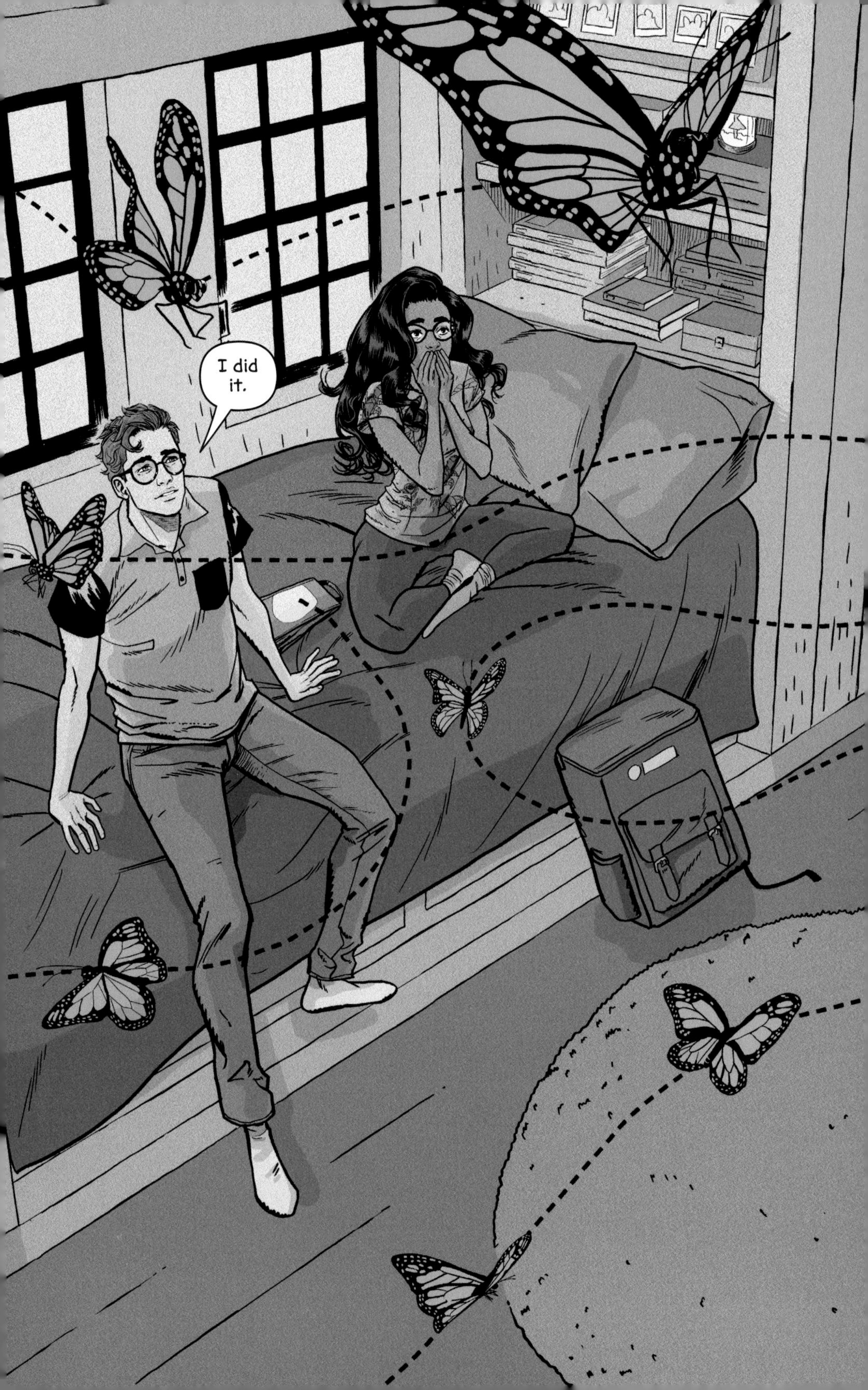
I did it.

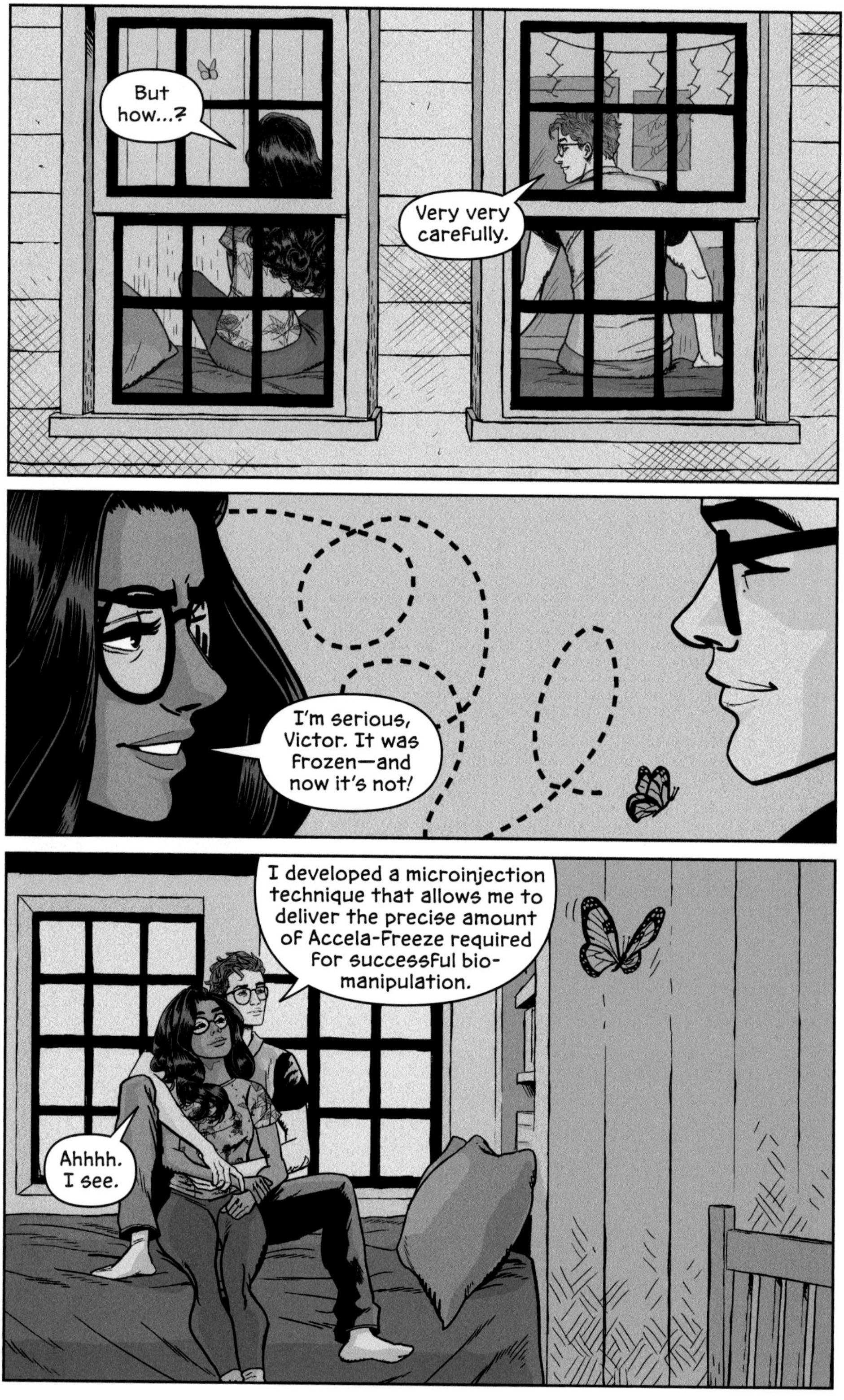
But how...?
Very very carefully.
I'm serious, Victor. It was frozen—and now it's not!
I developed a microinjection technique that allows me to deliver the precise amount of Accela-Freeze required for successful bio-manipulation.
Ahhhh. I see.

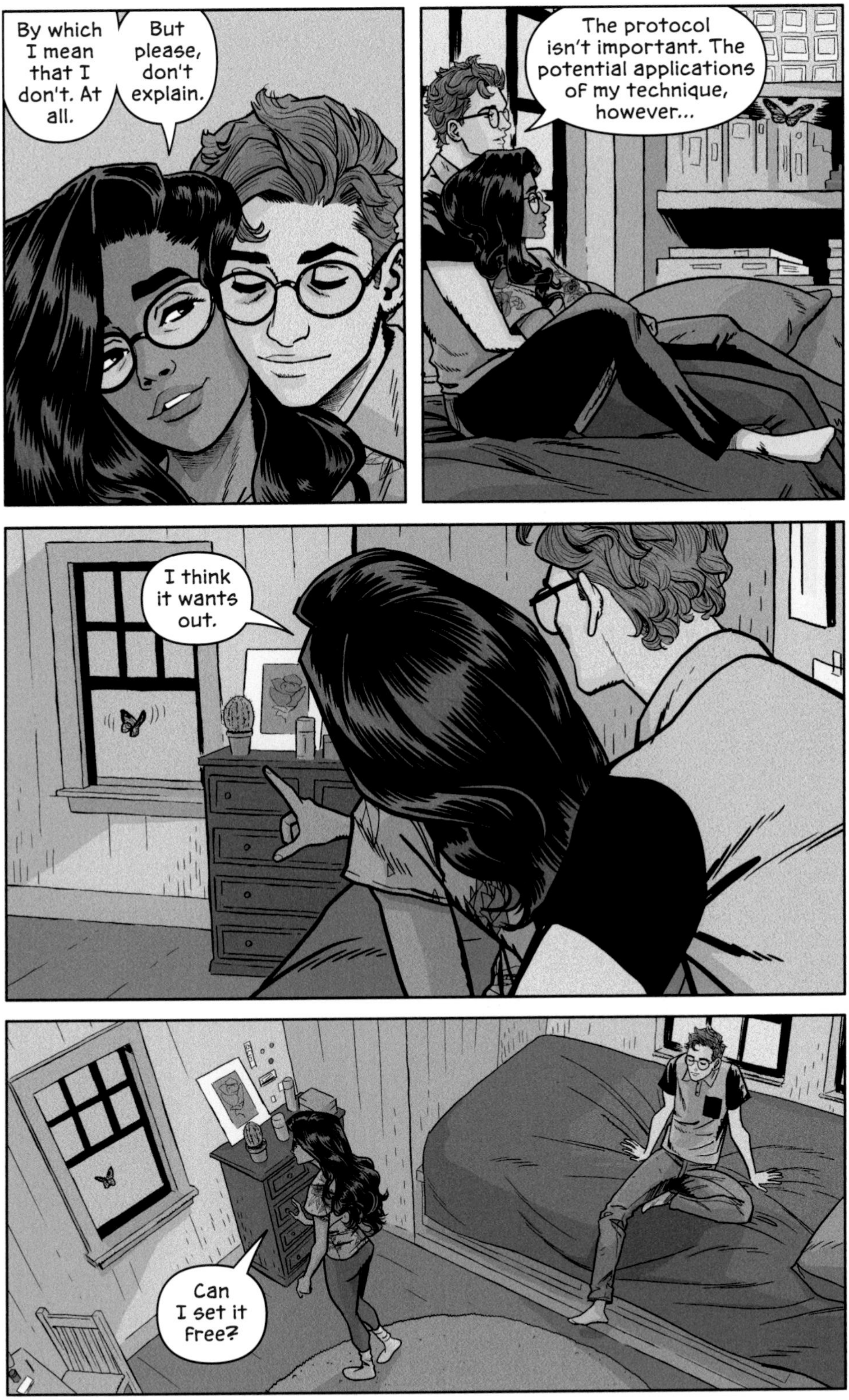
By which I mean that I don't. At all.
But please, don't explain.
The protocol isn't important. The potential applications of my technique, however...
I think it wants out.
Can I set it free?

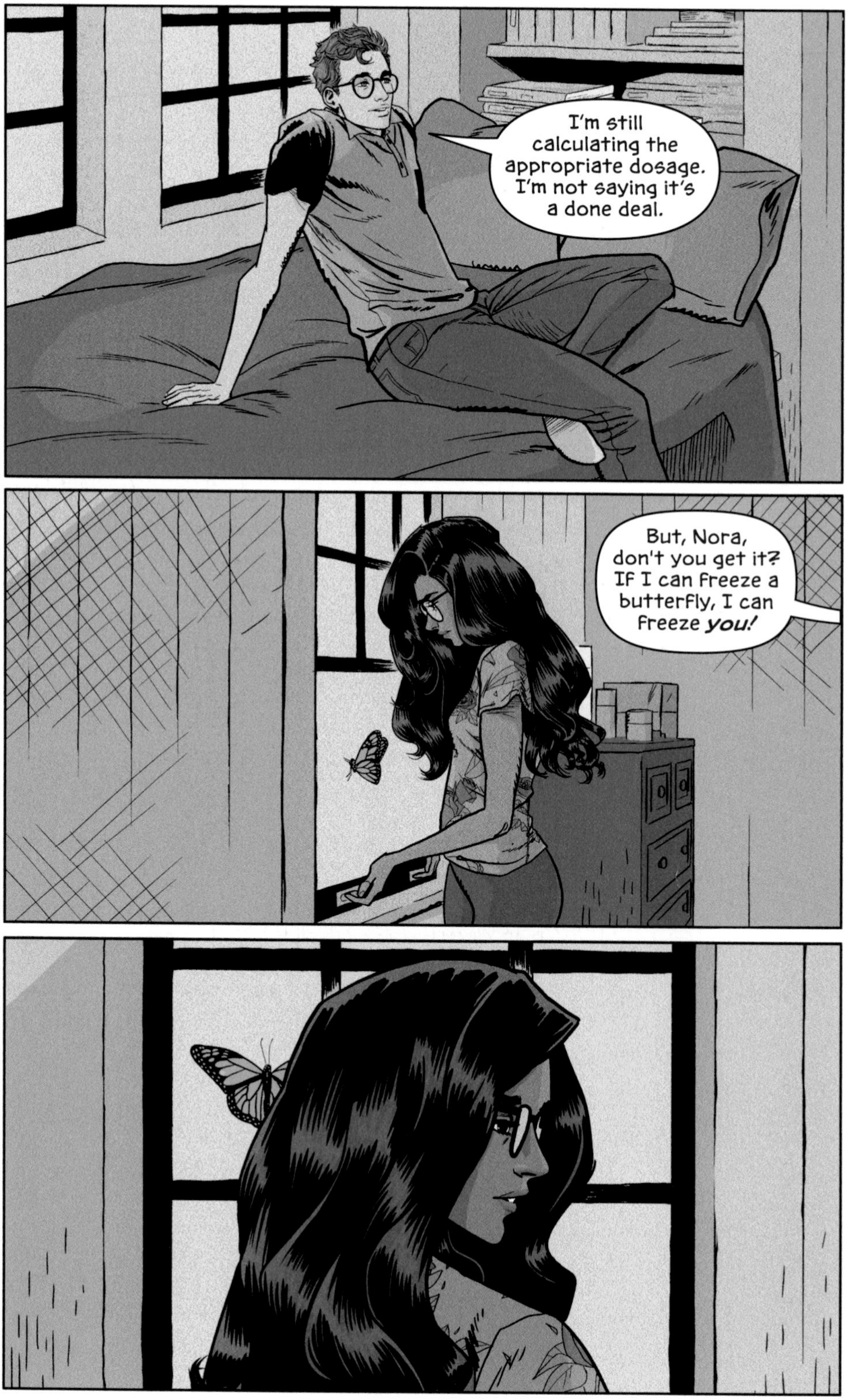
I'm still calculating the appropriate dosage. I'm not saying it's a done deal.
But, Nora, don't you get it? If I can freeze a butterfly, I can freeze *you!*

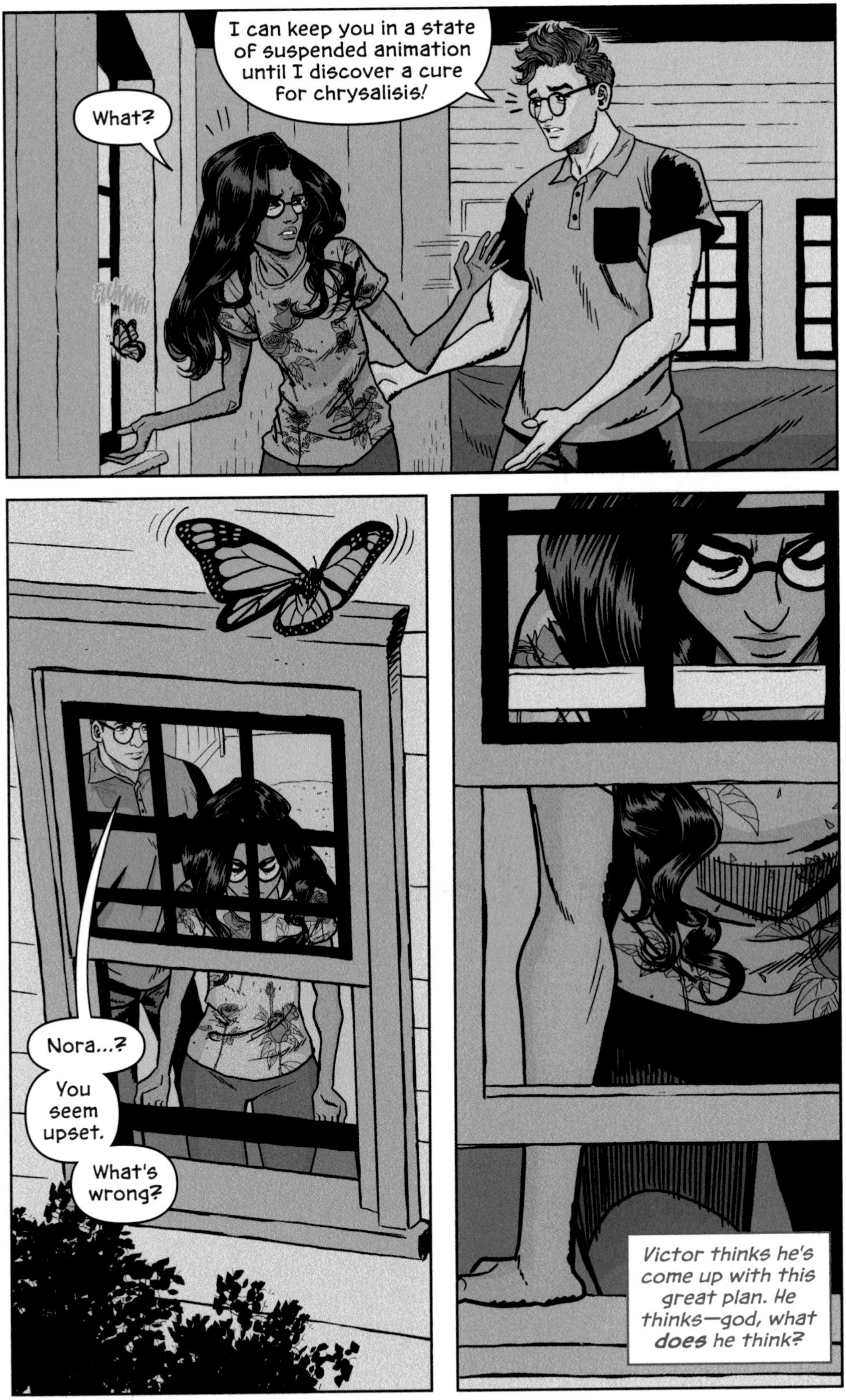
I can keep you in a state of suspended animation until I discover a cure for chrysalisis!
What?
FLUMWAH
Nora...?
You seem upset.
What's wrong?
Victor thinks he's come up with this great plan. He thinks—god, what **does** he think?

That I'm his doll to play with, like Frankenstein's poor, dumb monster?
He keeps talking. "Explaining."
What unsettles me most, I think, is that Victor, the boy I love, **thinks his plan makes sense.**
Long ago, we talked about our "worst ways to die."
And now I know. This. ***This*** is my absolute worst way to die.

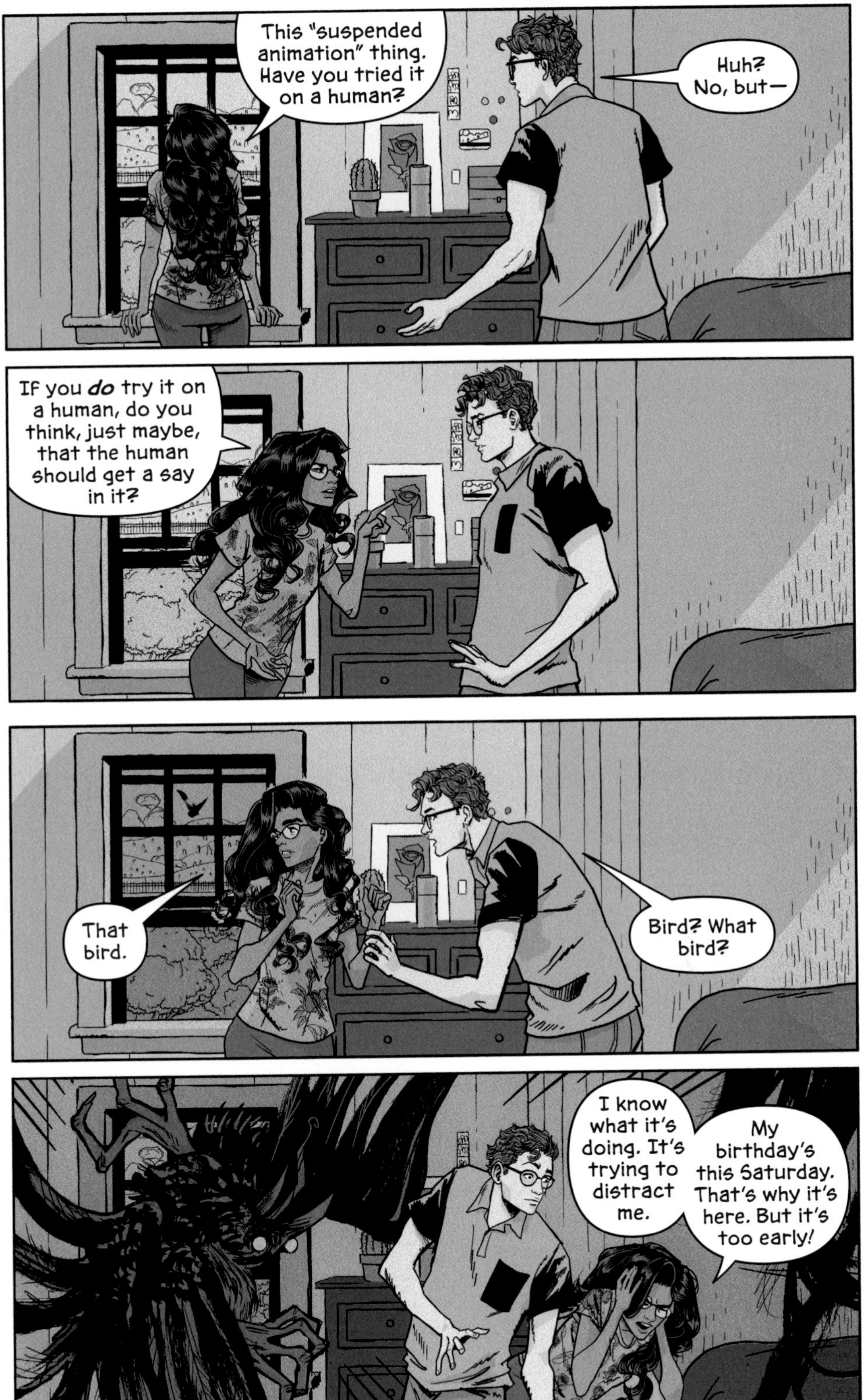
This "suspended animation" thing. Have you tried it on a human?
Huh? No, but—
If you *do* try it on a human, do you think, just maybe, that the human should get a say in it?
That bird.
Bird? What bird?
I know what it's doing. It's trying to distract me.
My birthday's this Saturday. That's why it's here. But it's too early!

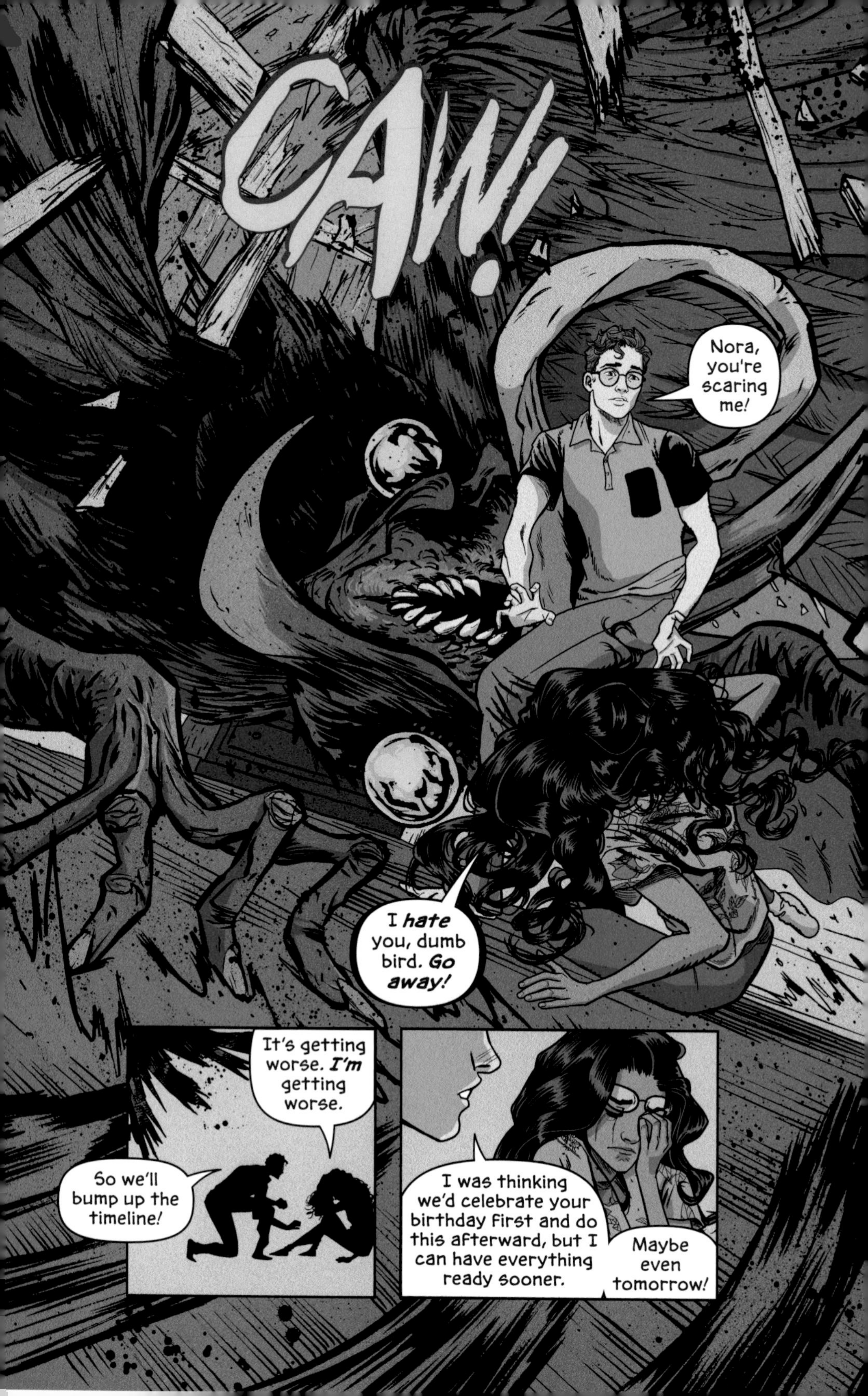
CAW!
Nora, you're scaring me!
I *hate* you, dumb bird. *Go away!*
It's getting worse. *I'm* getting worse.
So we'll bump up the timeline!
I was thinking we'd celebrate your birthday first and do this afterward, but I can have everything ready sooner.
Maybe even tomorrow!

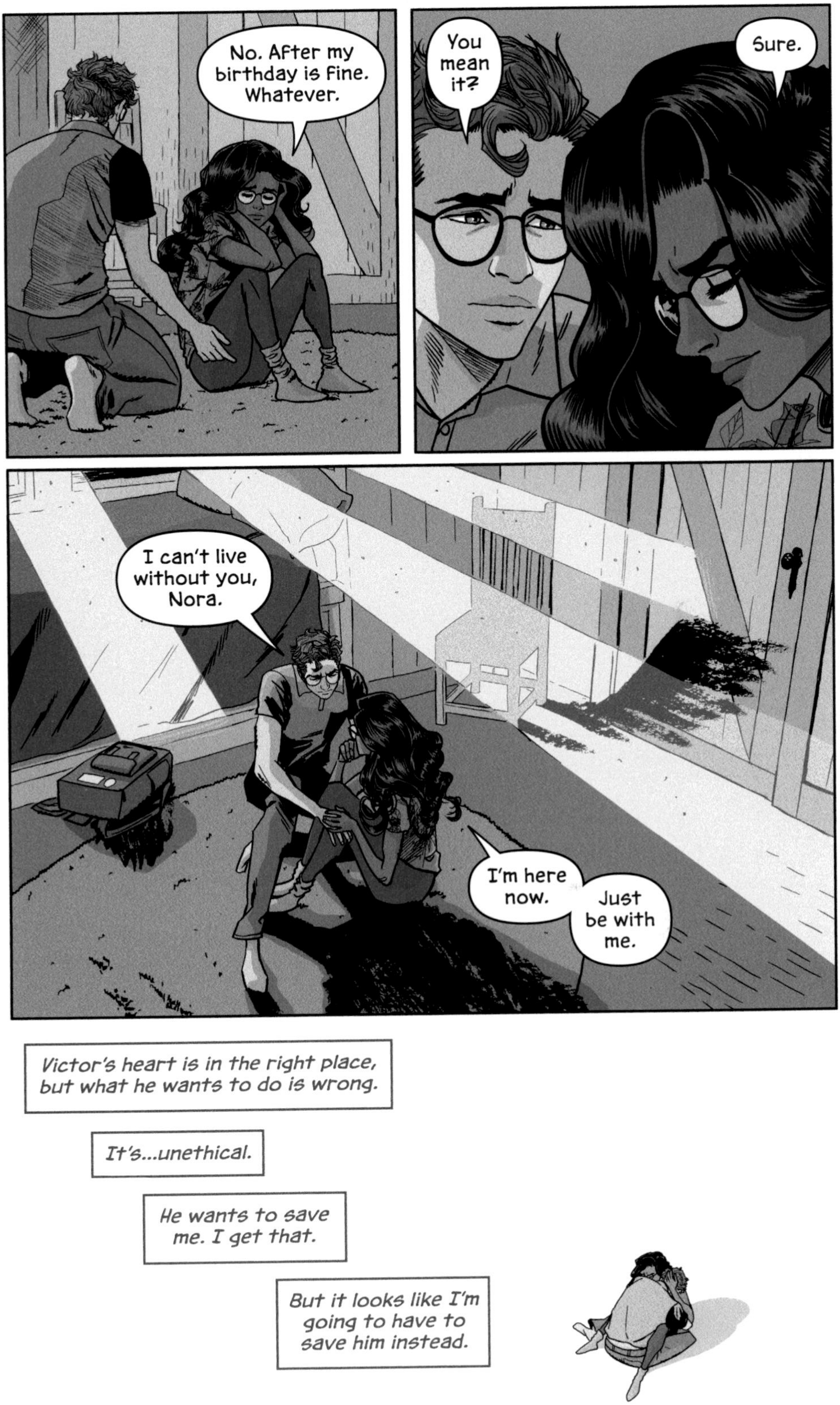
No. After my birthday is fine. Whatever.
You mean it?
Sure.
I can't live without you, Nora.
I'm here now.
Just be with me.
Victor's heart is in the right place, but what he wants to do is wrong.
It's...unethical.
He wants to save me. I get that.
But it looks like I'm going to have to save him instead.

The Boy Who Refuses to Play Dice with the Universe

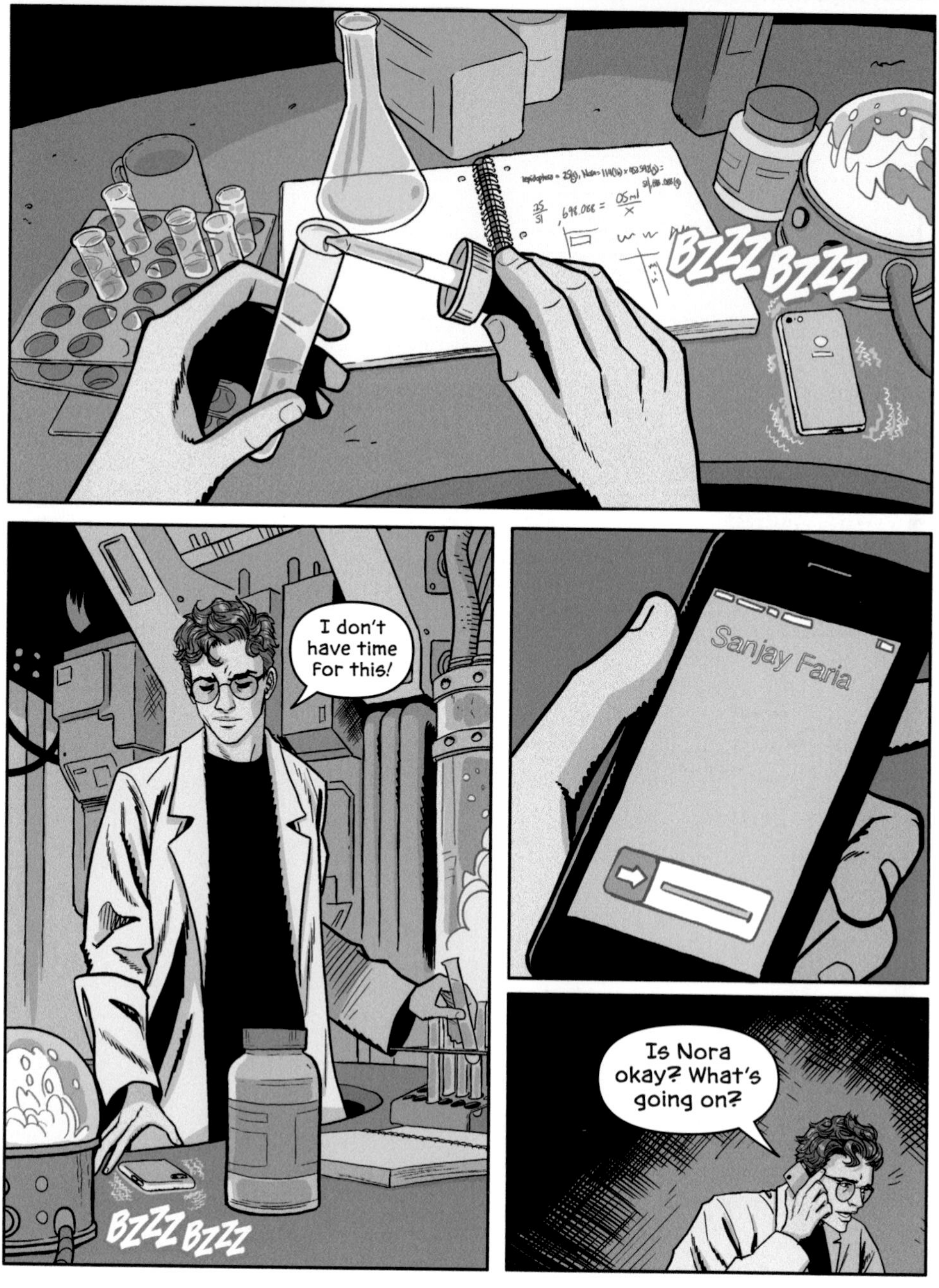
BZZZ BZZZ
I don't have time for this!
BZZZ BZZZ
Sanjay Faria
Is Nora okay? What's going on?

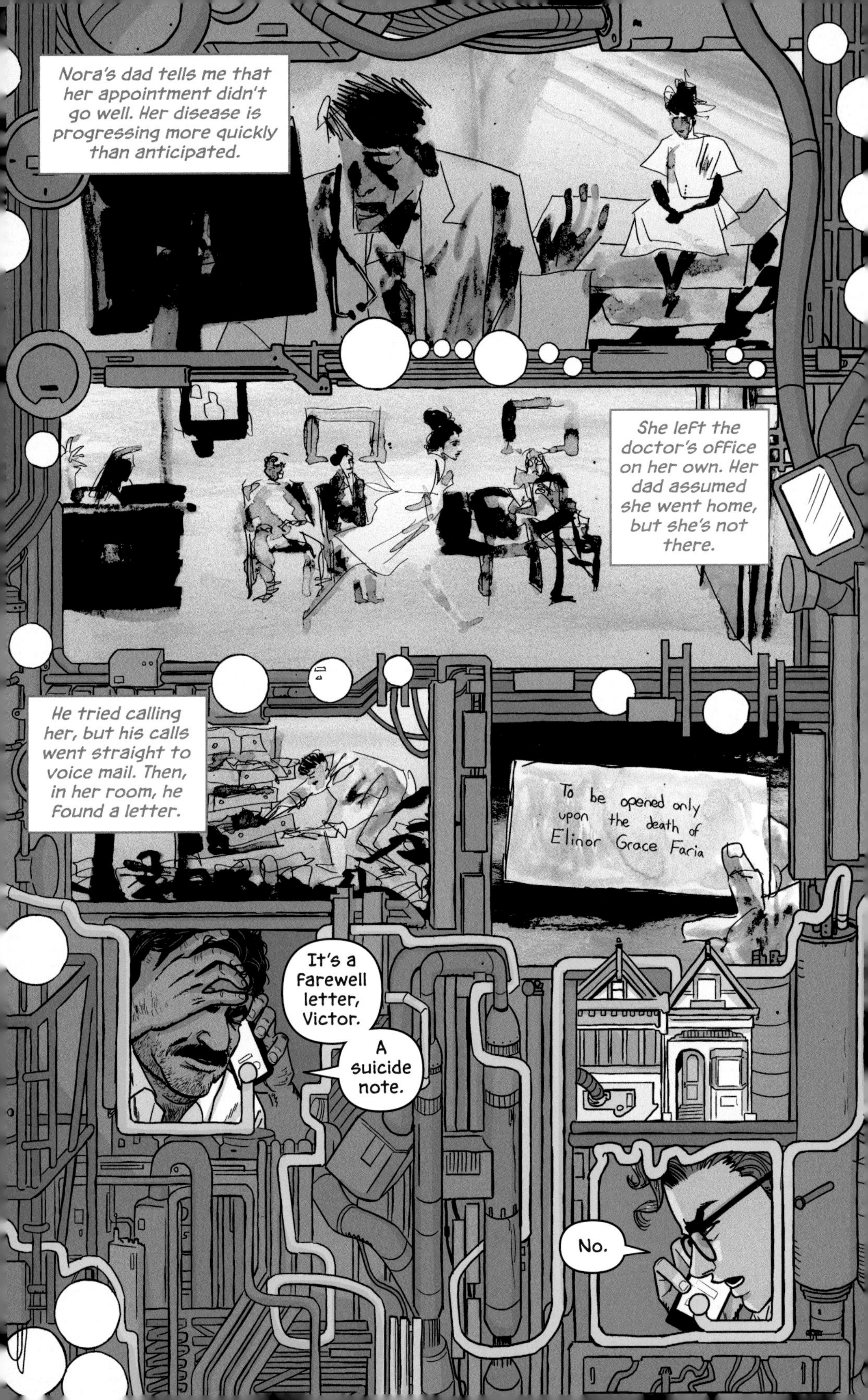

Nora's dad tells me that her appointment didn't go well. Her disease is progressing more quickly than anticipated.
She left the doctor's office on her own. Her dad assumed she went home, but she's not there.
He tried calling her, but his calls went straight to voice mail. Then, in her room, he found a letter.
To be opened only upon the death of Elinor Grace Facia
It's a farewell letter, Victor.
A suicide note.
No.

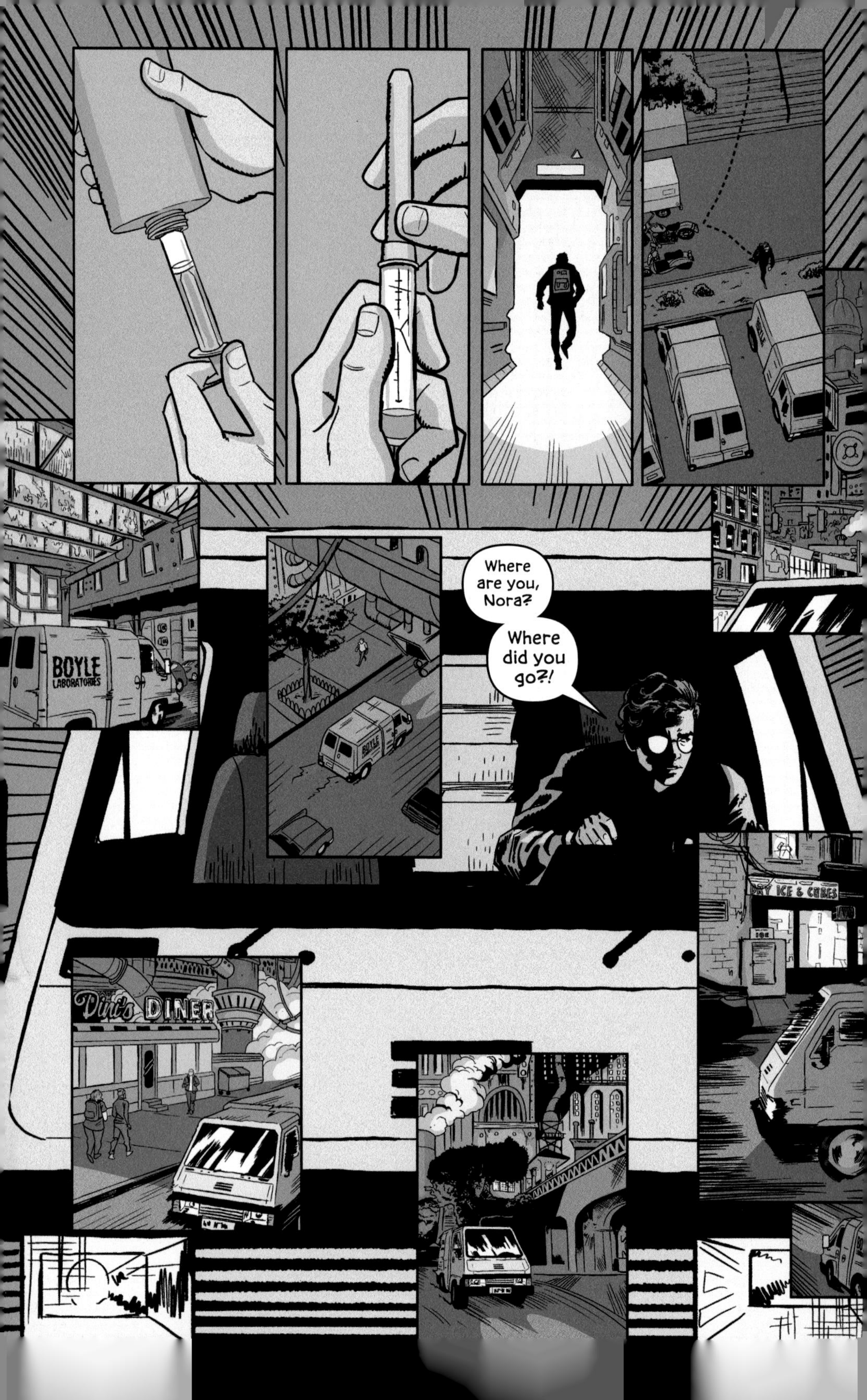
BOYLE LABORATORIES
Where are you, Nora?
Where did you go?!
DRY ICE & CUBES
Dini's DINER

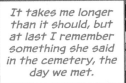

It takes me longer than it should, but at last I remember something she said in the cemetery, the day we met.

"IF I were going to kill myself, I'd go out big."

"It's a two-hundred-meter fall. That's high enough."

She said it so casually, like dropping a penny into a well—or a girl into a river, far below.

The Girl Who Grabs Hold of Fate

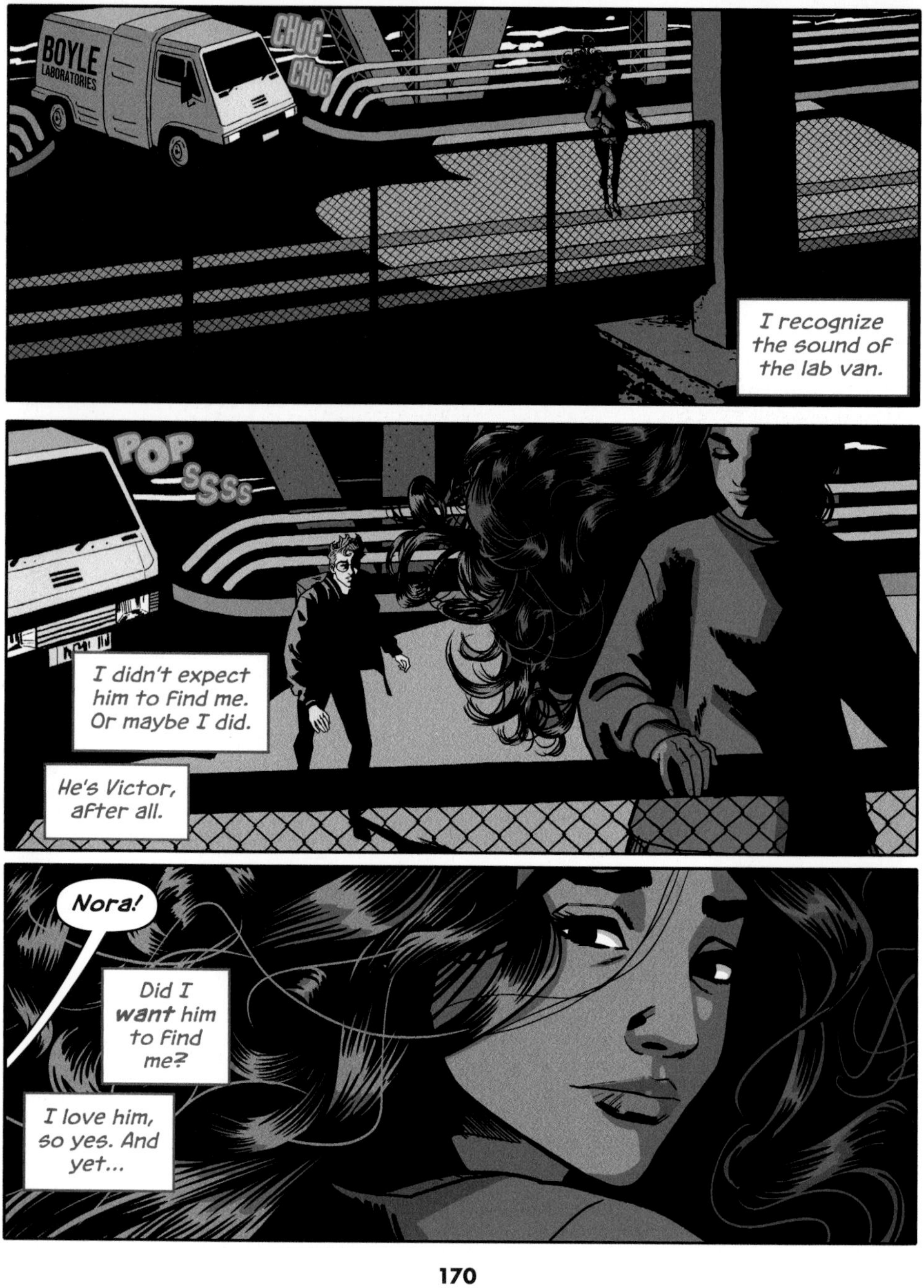
BOYLE LABORATORIES
CHUG CHUG
I recognize the sound of the lab van.
POP SSSS
I didn't expect him to find me. Or maybe I did.
He's Victor, after all.
Nora!
Did I **want** him to find me?
I love him, so yes. And yet...

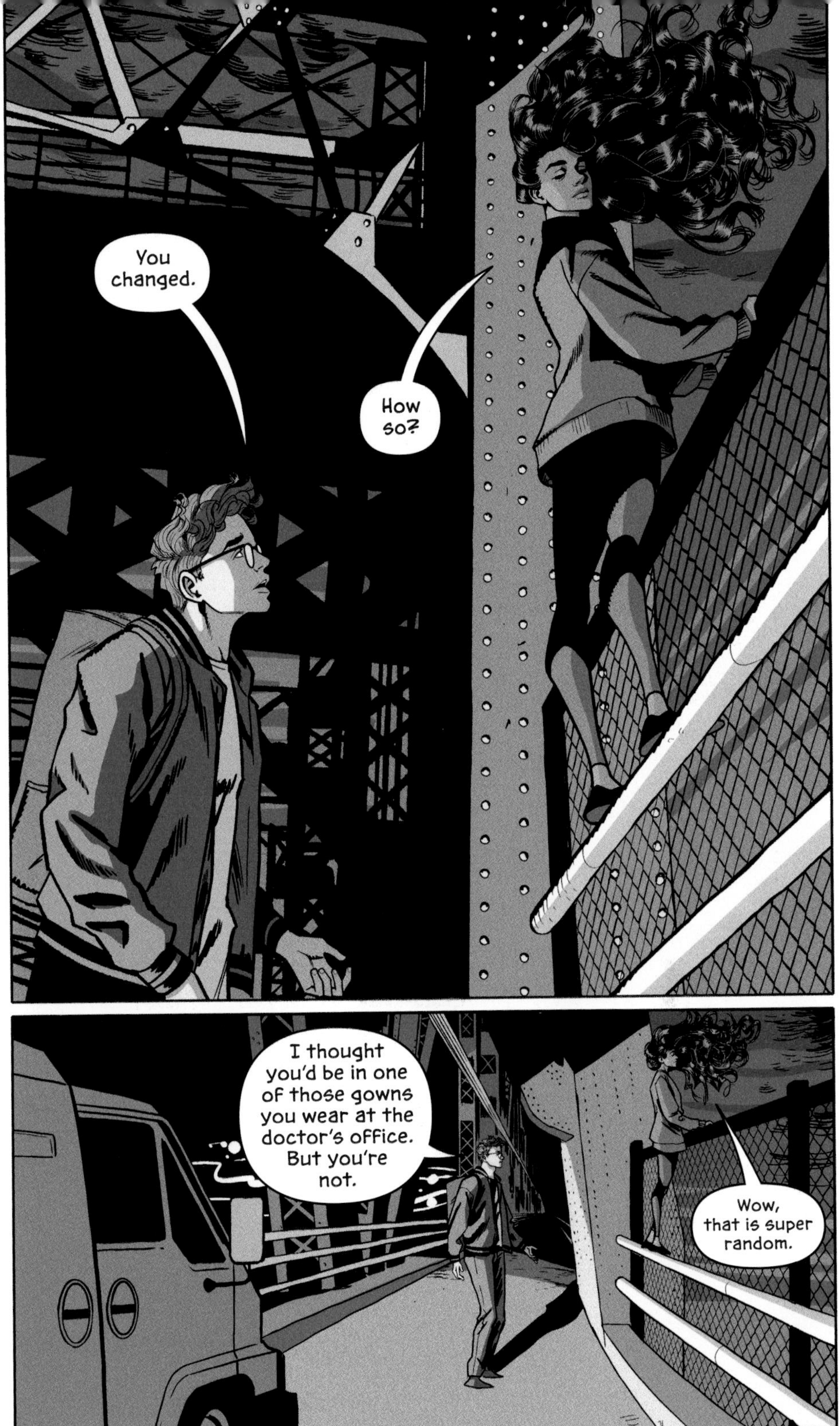
You changed.
How so?
I thought you'd be in one of those gowns you wear at the doctor's office. But you're not.
Wow, that is super random.

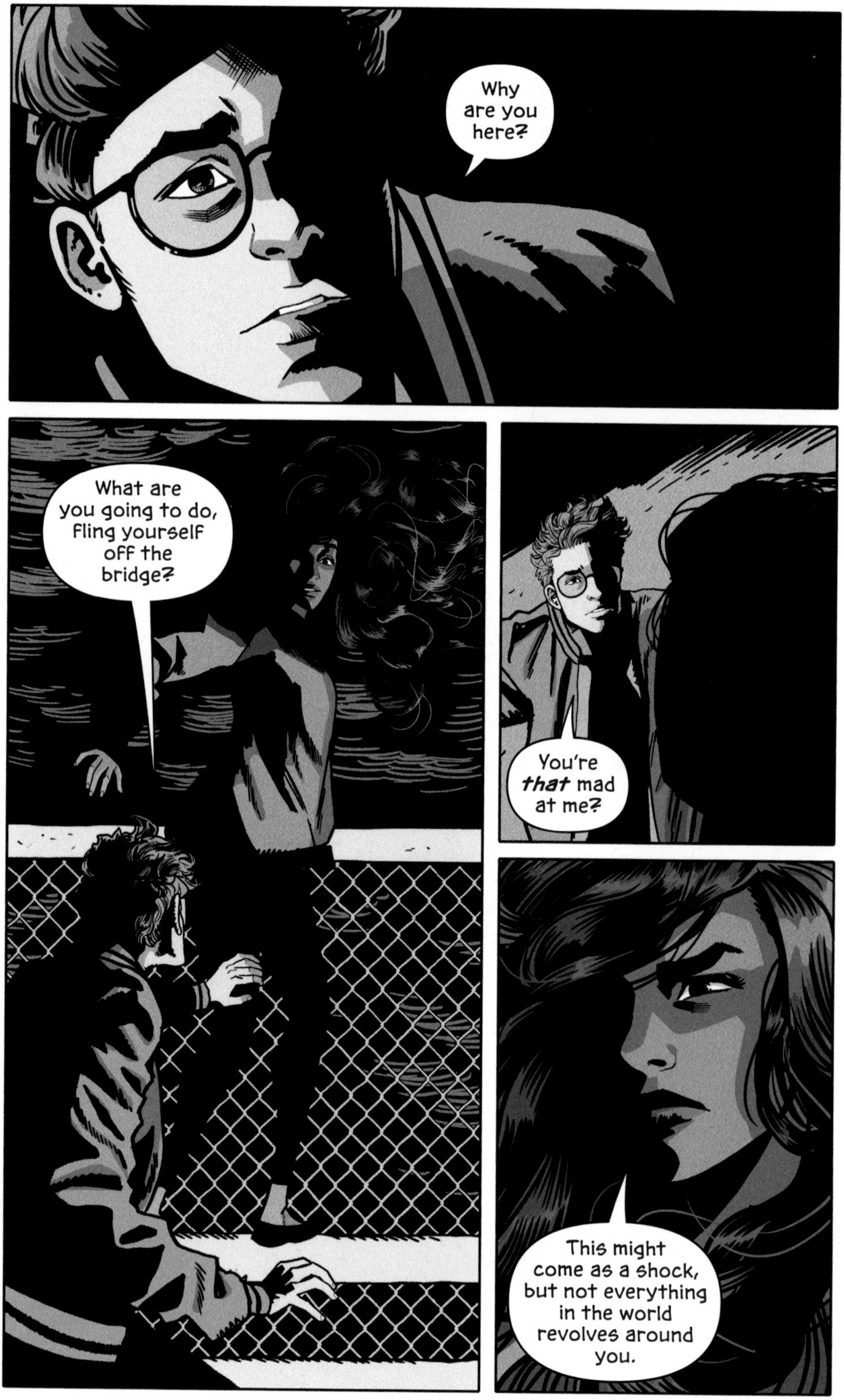
Why are you here?
What are you going to do, fling yourself off the bridge?
You're *that* mad at me?
This might come as a shock, but not everything in the world revolves around you.

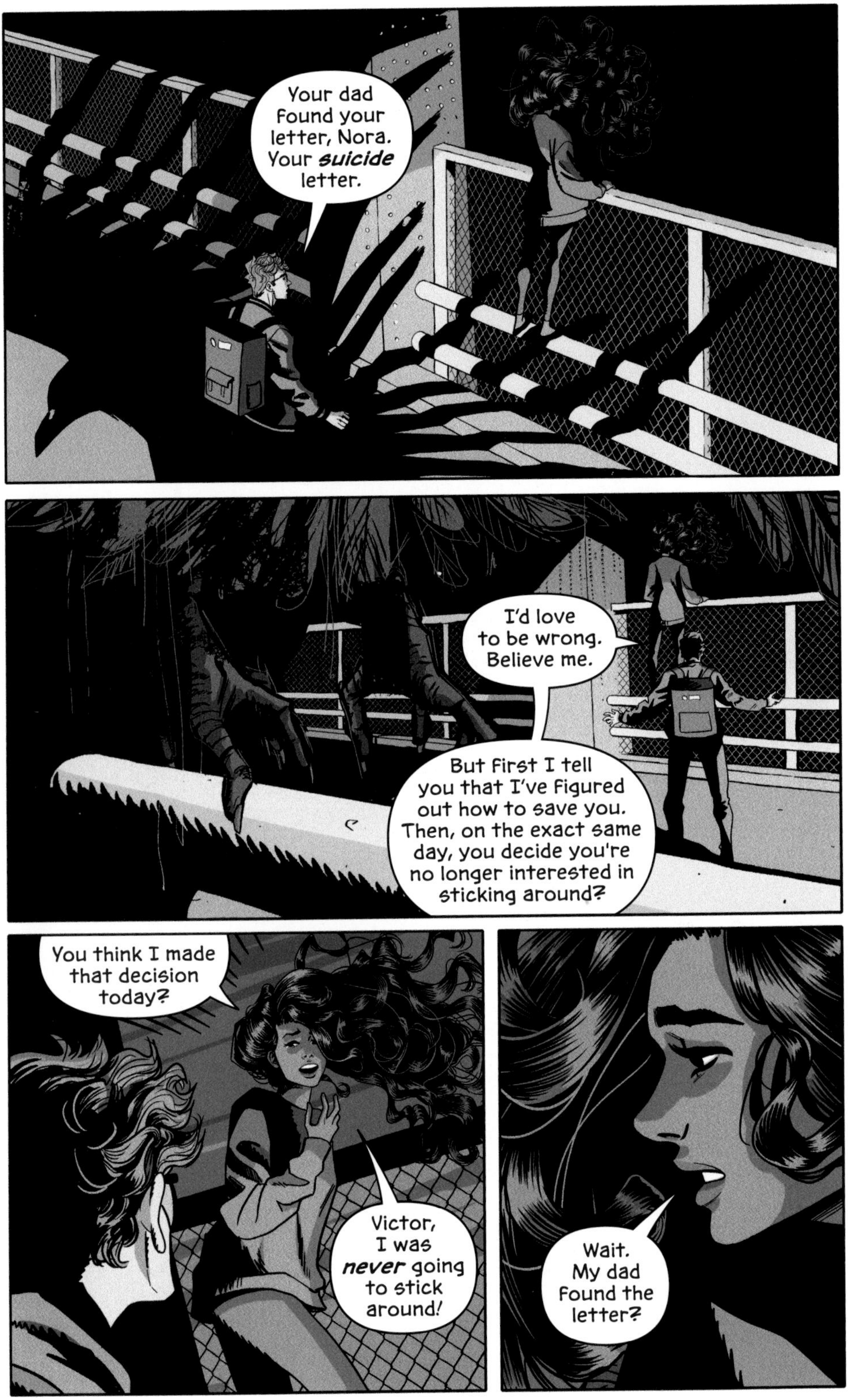
Your dad found your letter, Nora. Your *suicide* letter.
I'd love to be wrong. Believe me.
But first I tell you that I've figured out how to save you. Then, on the exact same day, you decide you're no longer interested in sticking around?
You think I made that decision today?
Victor, I was *never* going to stick around!
Wait. My dad found the letter?

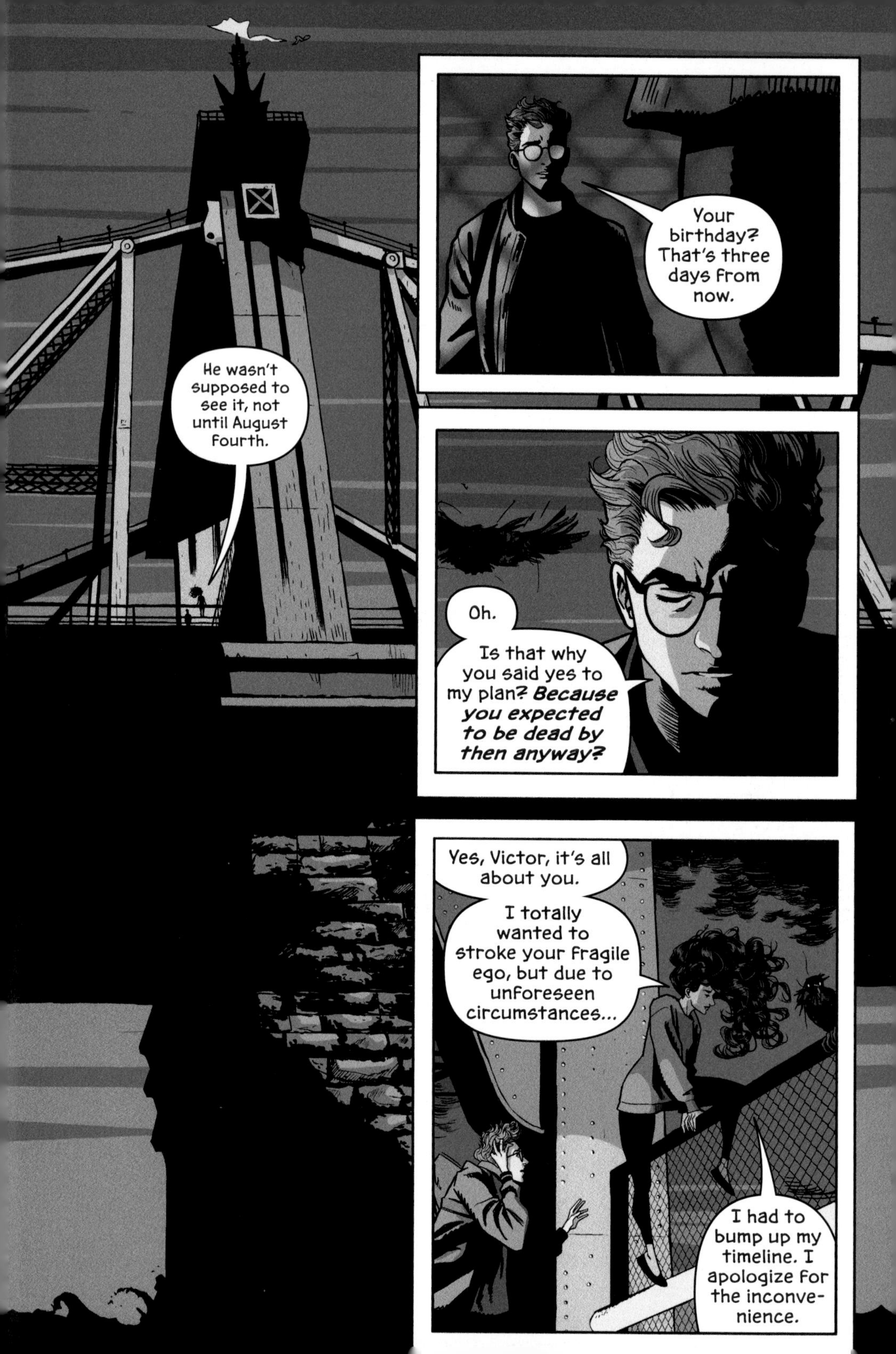
He wasn't supposed to see it, not until August fourth.
Your birthday? That's three days from now.
Oh.
Is that why you said yes to my plan? *Because you expected to be dead by then anyway?*
Yes, Victor, it's all about you.
I totally wanted to stroke your fragile ego, but due to unforeseen circumstances...
I had to bump up my timeline. I apologize for the inconvenience.

The Boy Who Freezes Time

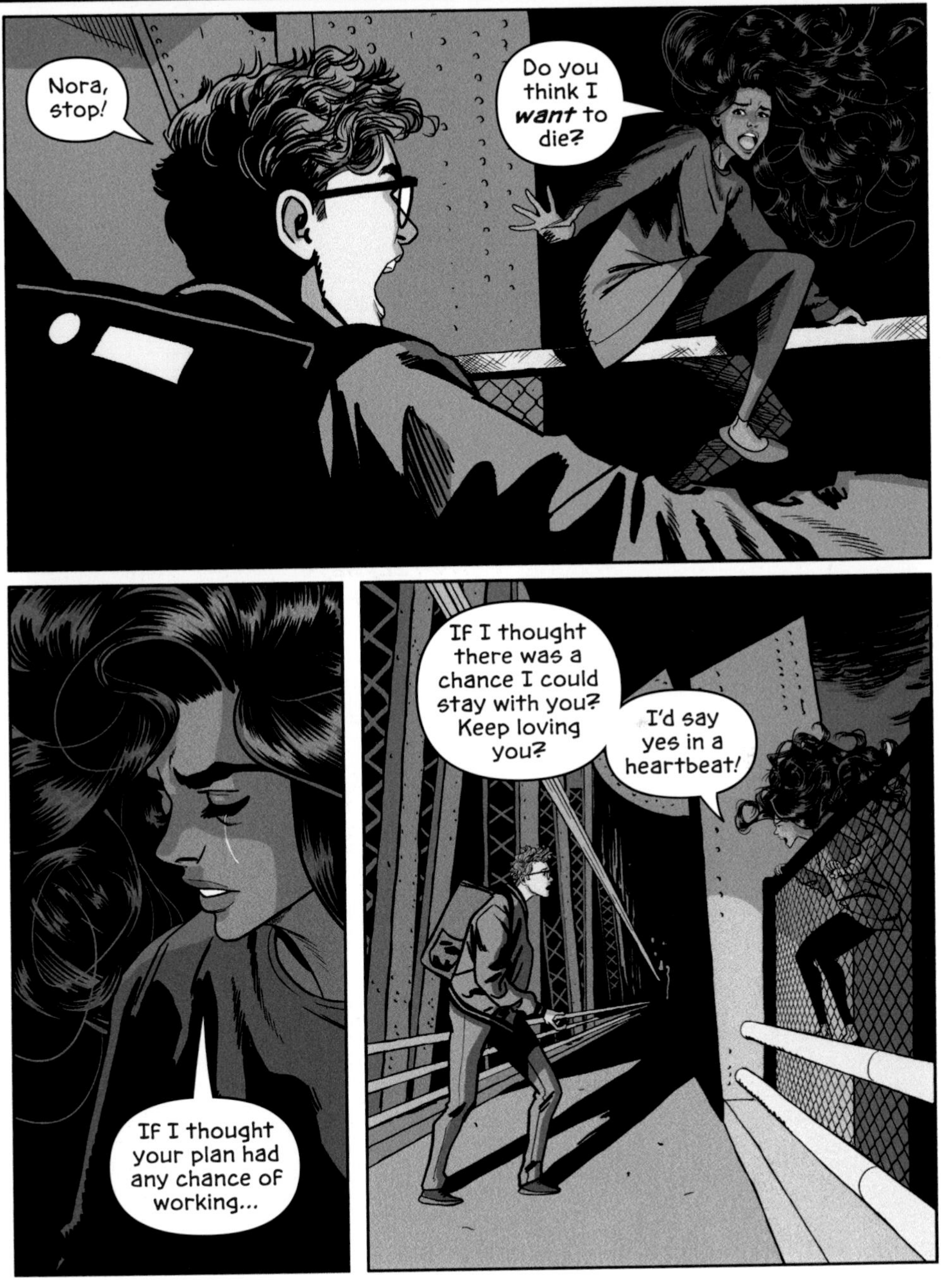
Nora, stop!
Do you think I *want* to die?
If I thought your plan had any chance of working...
If I thought there was a chance I could stay with you? Keep loving you?
I'd say yes in a heartbeat!

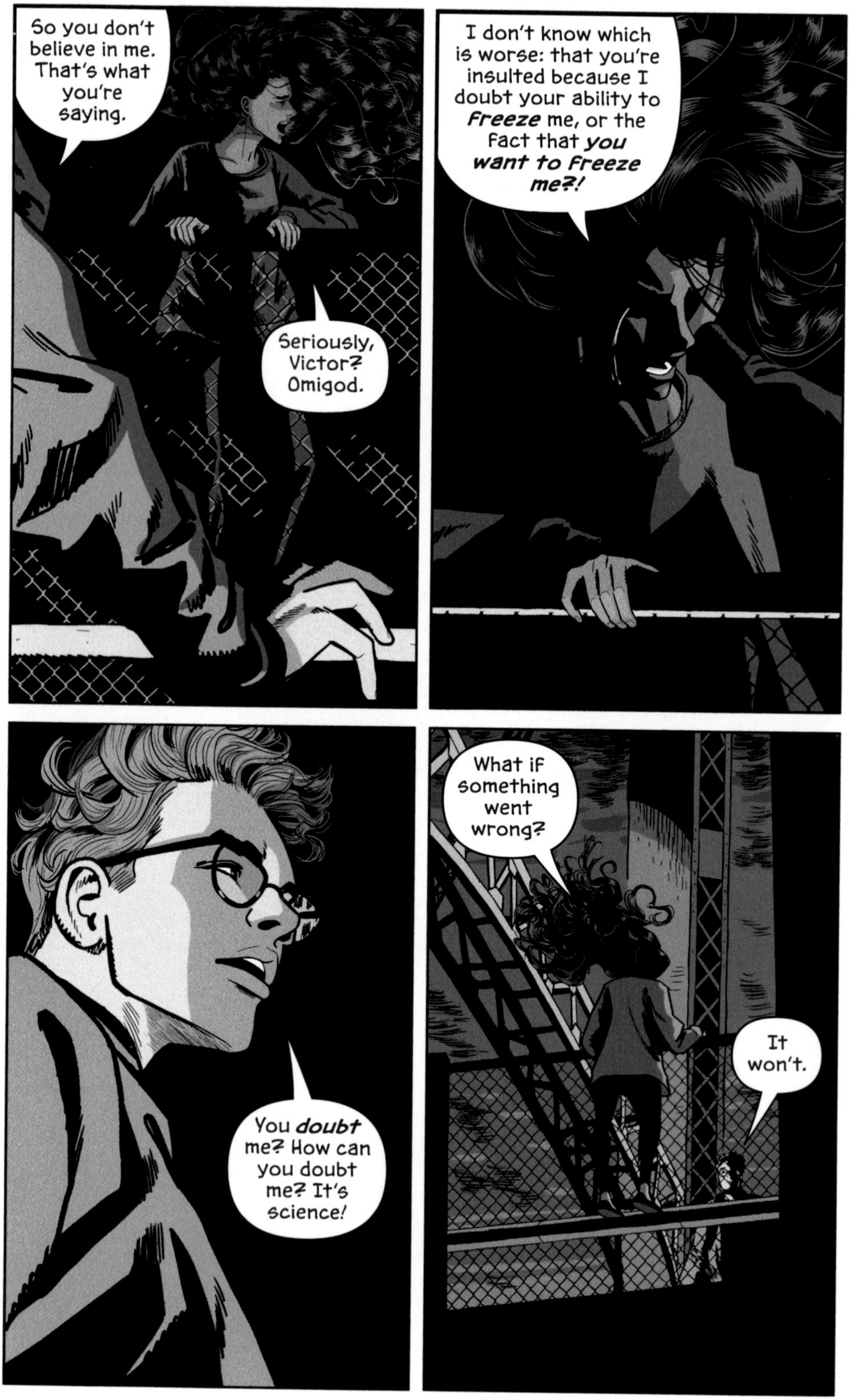
So you don't believe in me. That's what you're saying.
Seriously, Victor? Omigod.
I don't know which is worse: that you're insulted because I doubt your ability to *freeze* me, or the fact that *you want to freeze me?!*
You *doubt* me? How can you doubt me? It's science!
What if something went wrong?
It won't.

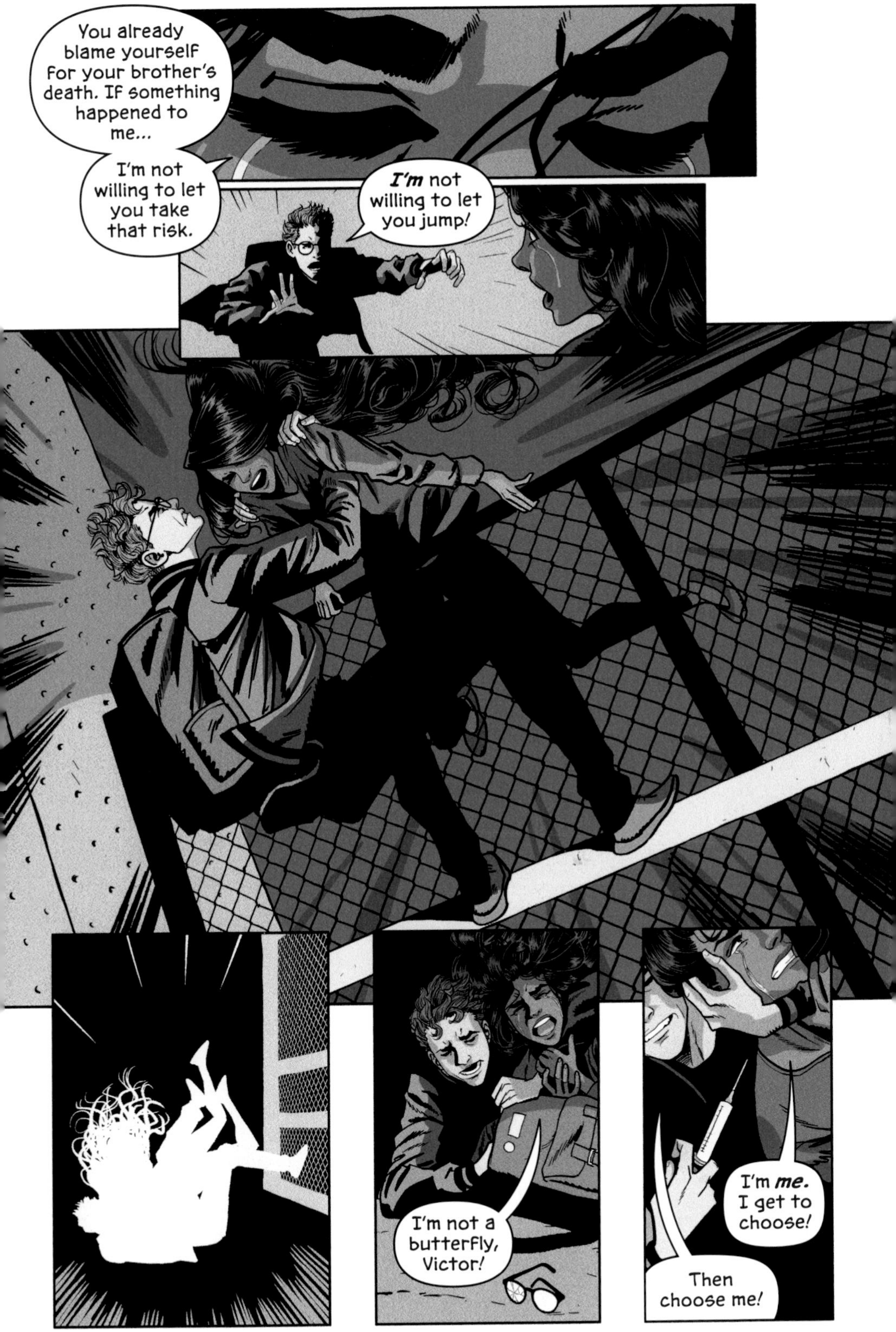
You already blame yourself for your brother's death. If something happened to me...
I'm not willing to let you take that risk.
I'm not willing to let you jump!
I'm not a butterfly, Victor!
I'm me. I get to choose!
Then choose me!

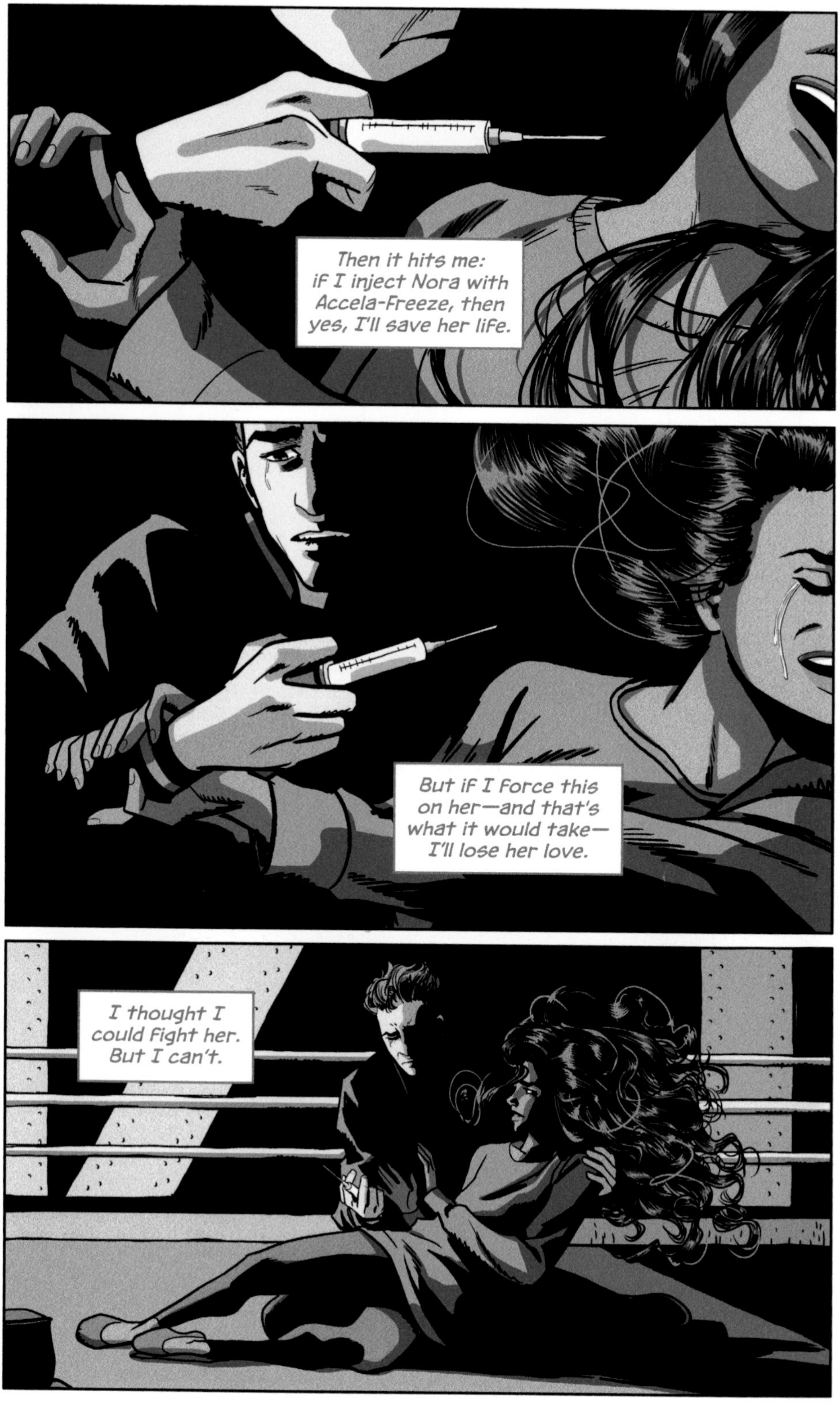
Then it hits me: if I inject Nora with Accela-Freeze, then yes, I'll save her life.
But if I force this on her—and that's what it would take—I'll lose her love.
I thought I could fight her. But I can't.

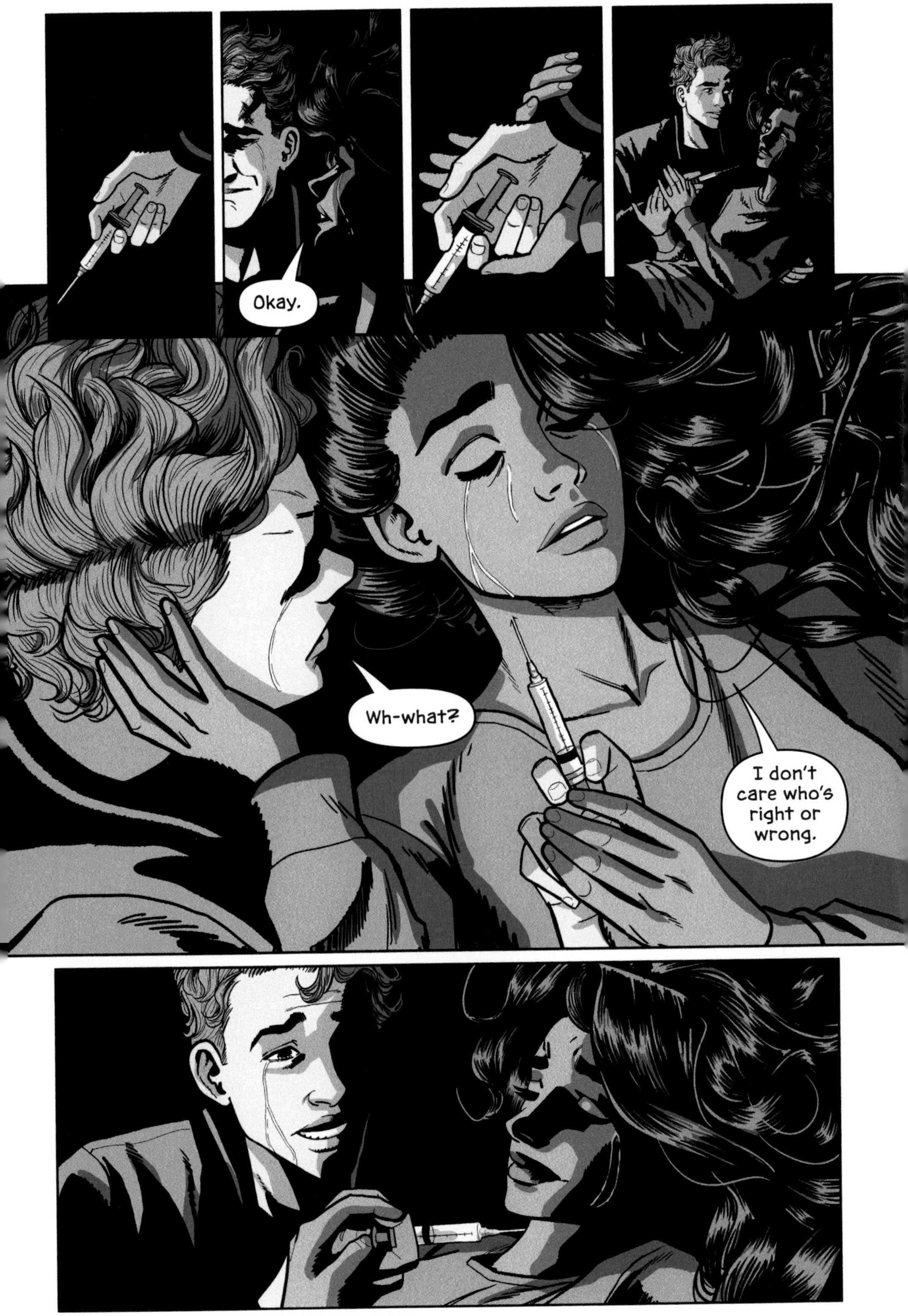
Okay.
Wh-what?
I don't care who's right or wrong.

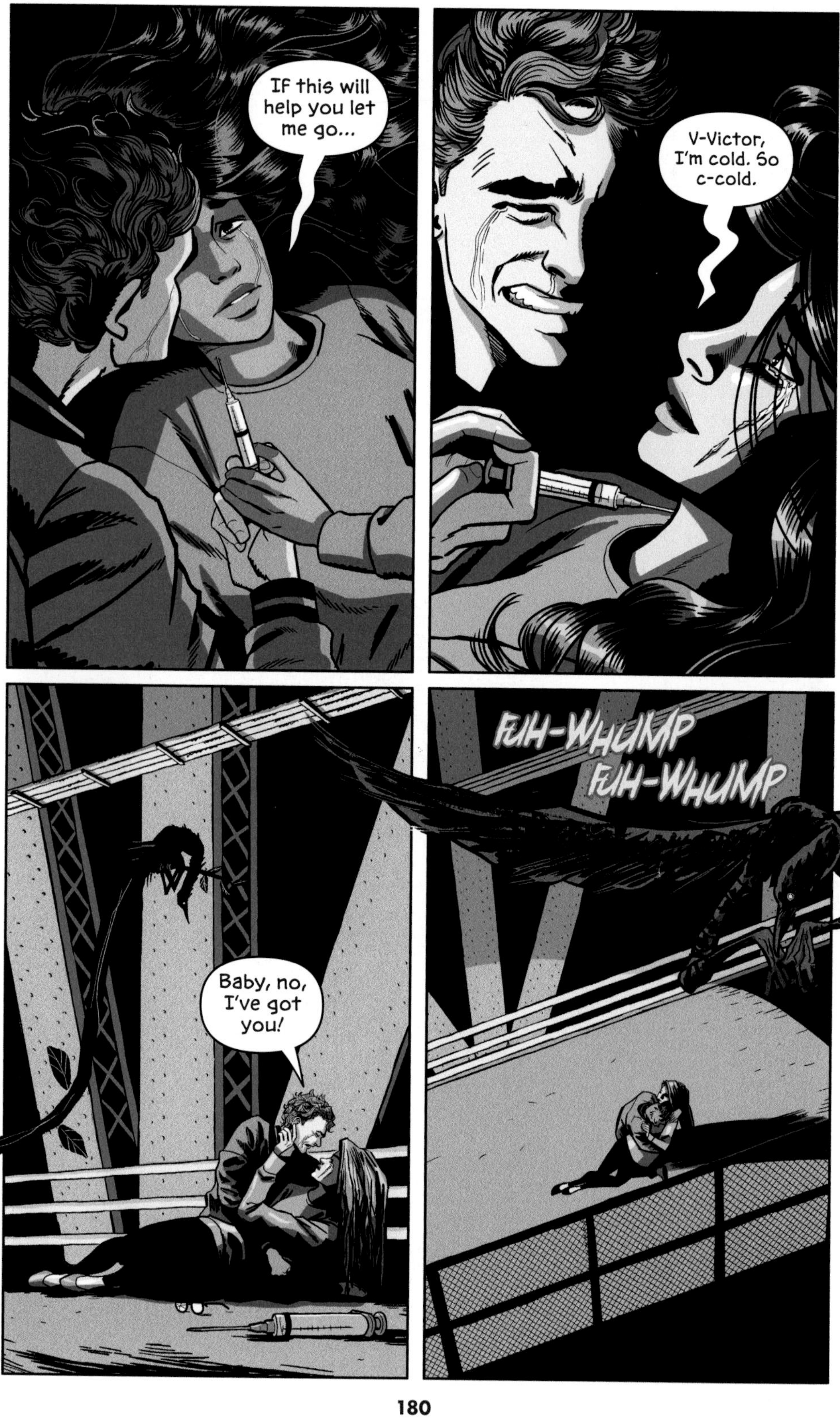
If this will help you let me go...
V-Victor, I'm cold. So c-cold.
Baby, no, I've got you!
FUH-WHUMP
FUH-WHUMP

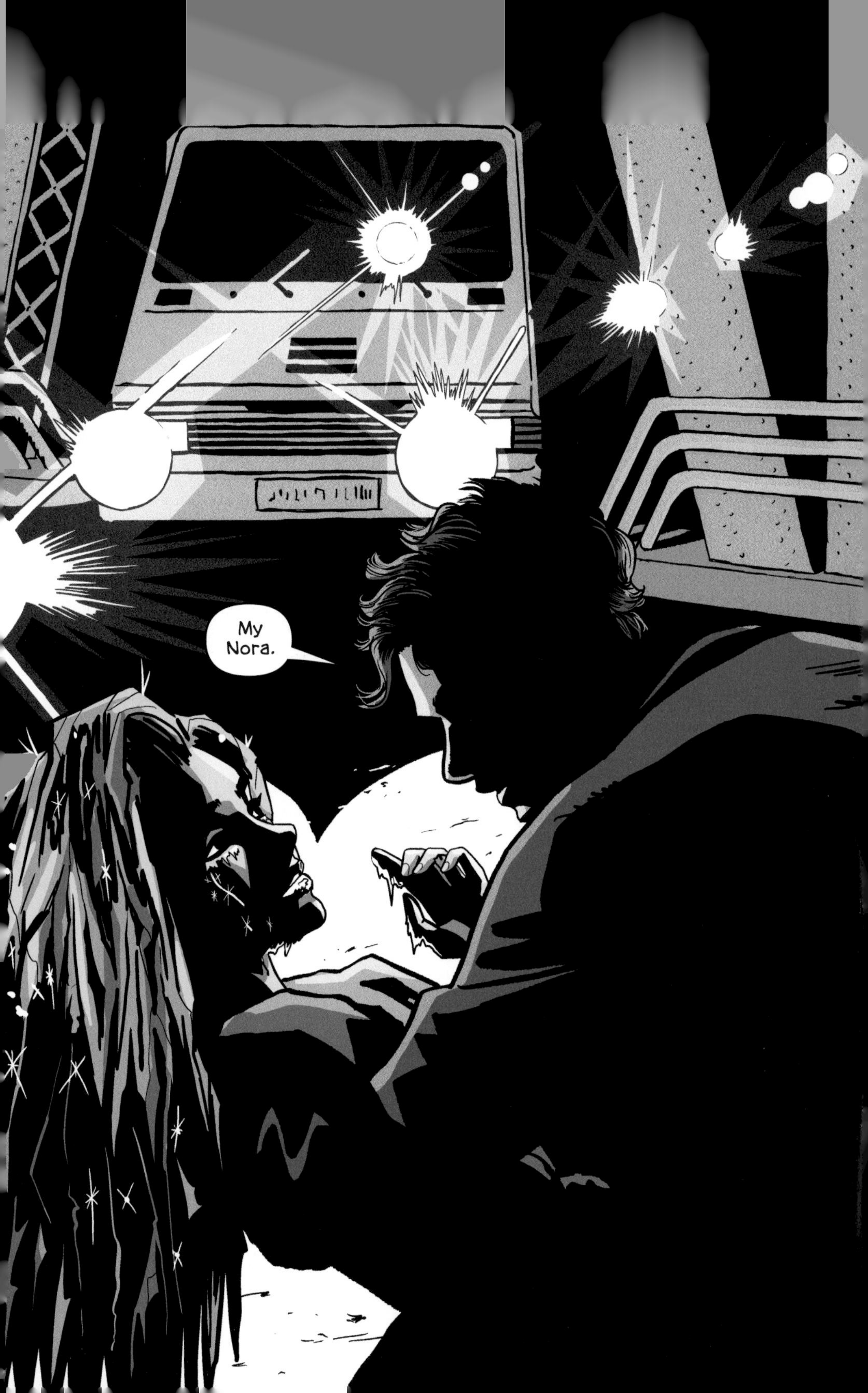
My Nora.

Dad, you will think your heart is broken. It's not. Don't let it be.

Think of that poem I like, about how hope is the thing with feathers.

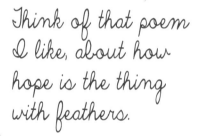

Only give me wings instead, okay? Feathers, they're fine, but they sometimes creep me out!

Tell Louise and Bean and Kylie that I love them. Tell them if a butterfly flits past or a moth! Ha!—it's me, just checking in.

But, Dad, I couldn't stick around getting sicker and sicker. I couldn't become Not Nora. Please, please try to understand.

Vroomedy-vroom!

Death is a mystery. Life, even more so. And I think, maybe, a space exists between the two?

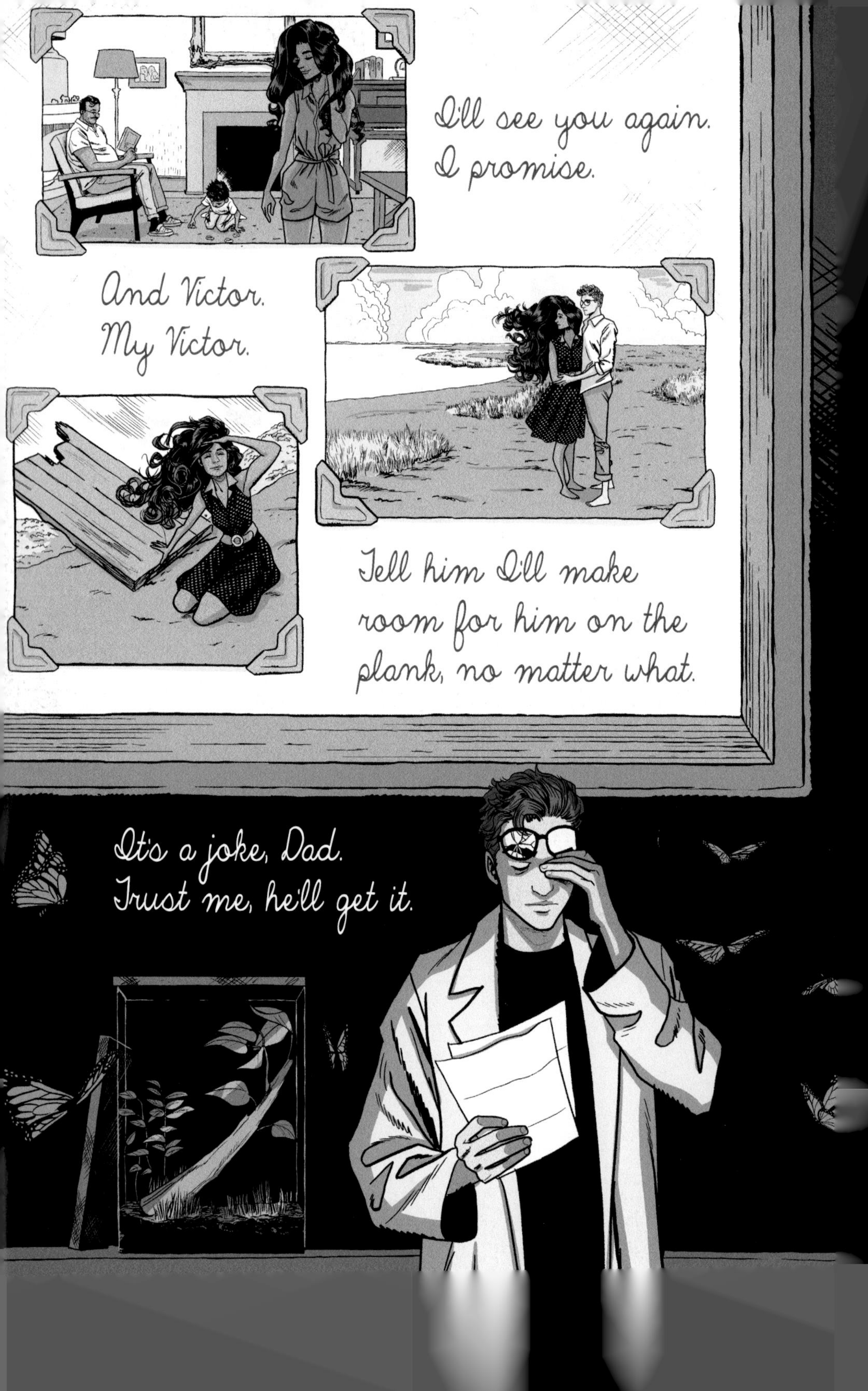
I'll see you again.
I promise.
And Victor.
My Victor.
Tell him I'll make
room for him on the
plank, no matter what.
It's a joke, Dad.
Trust me, he'll get it.

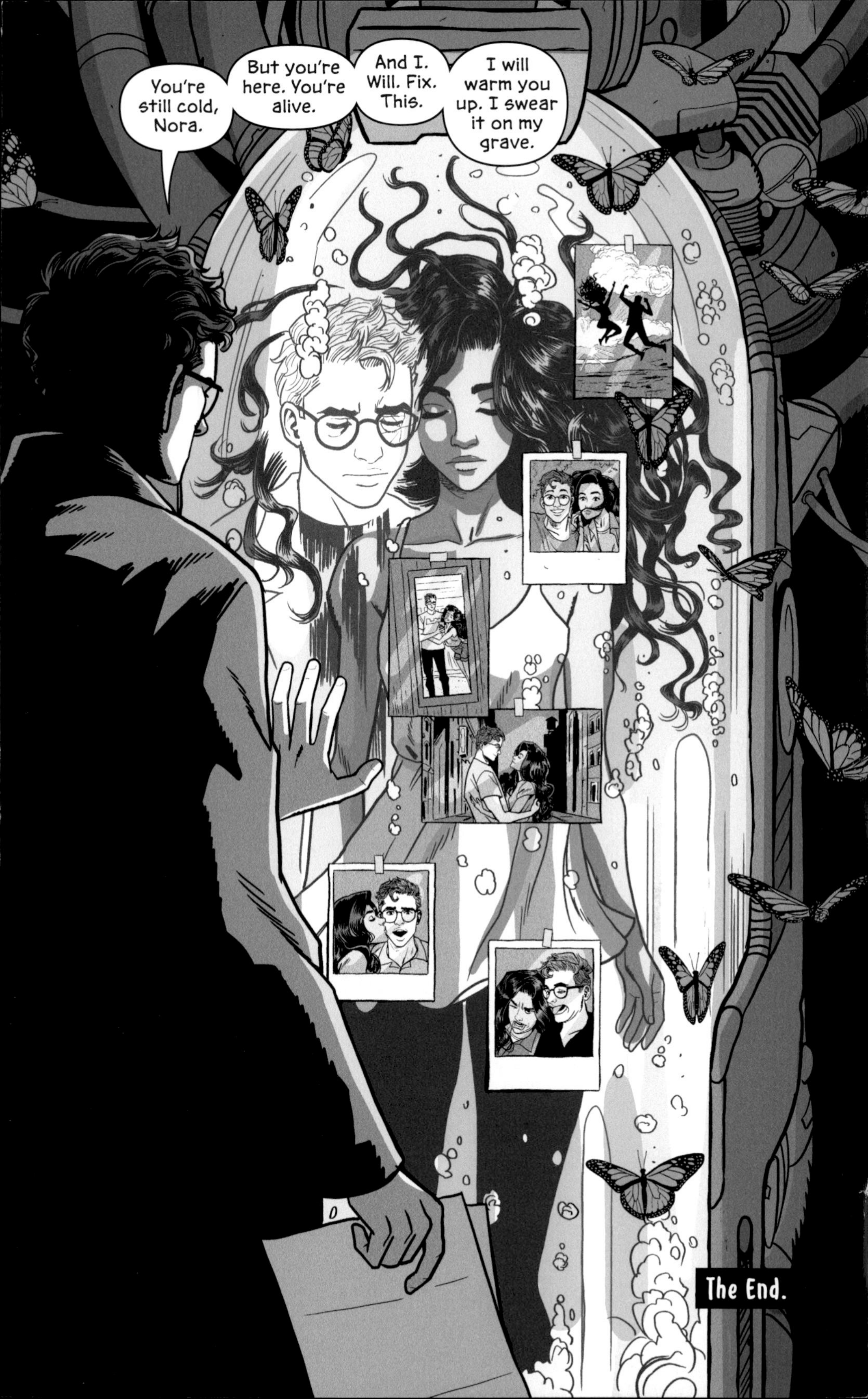
You're still cold, Nora.
But you're here. You're alive.
And I. Will. Fix. This.
I will warm you up. I swear it on my grave.
The End.

RESOURCES

If you, or a loved one, need help in any way, you do not need to act alone. Below is a list of resources that may be helpful to you. If you are in immediate danger, please call emergency services in your area (9-1-1 in the U.S.) or go to your nearest hospital emergency room.

National Suicide Prevention Lifeline
Available 24 hours a day, 7 days a week.
Phone: 1-800-273-8255
Website: suicidepreventionlifeline.org
Online chat: chat.suicidepreventionlifeline.org/gethelp/lifelinechat.aspx

The Jed Foundation
A nonprofit that exists to protect emotional health and prevent suicide for our nation's teens and young adults. Text "START" to 741-741 or call 1-800-273-TALK (8255). Website: jedfoundation.org

International Hotlines
The above hotlines are based in the U.S. and Canada. A list of international suicide hotlines is listed at suicide.org/international-suicide-hotlines.html, compiled by suicide.org. Another list can be found at iasp.info/index.php, compiled by the International Association for Suicide Prevention.

Shatterproof
A national nonprofit organization dedicated to ending the devastation addiction causes families. Visit shatterproof.org for more information.

Safe Horizon
The largest provider of comprehensive services for domestic violence survivors and victims of all crime and abuse including rape and sexual assault, human trafficking, stalking, youth homelessness, and violent crimes committed against a family member or within communities. If you need help, call their 24-hour hotline at 1-800-621-HOPE (4673) or visit safehorizon.org.

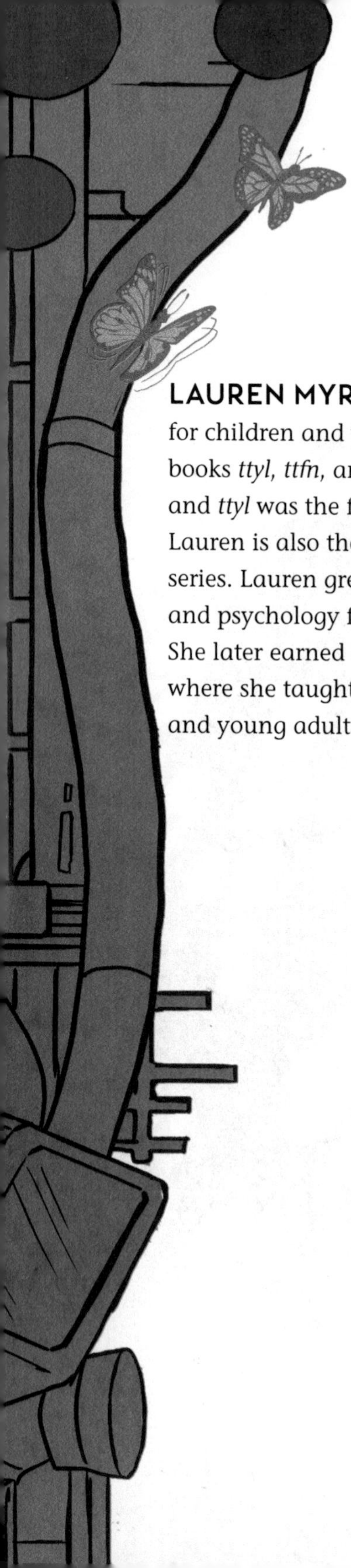

LAUREN MYRACLE is the bestselling author of many books for children and young adults, including the acclaimed Internet Girls books *ttyl, ttfn,* and *l8r, g8r. ttyl* and *ttfn* are *New York Times* bestsellers, and *ttyl* was the first book to be written entirely in instant message. Lauren is also the author of the popular Winnie Years middle grade series. Lauren grew up in Atlanta, Georgia, and earned a BA in English and psychology from the University of North Carolina at Chapel Hill. She later earned an MA in English from Colorado State University, where she taught for two years, and an MFA in writing for children and young adults from Vermont College.

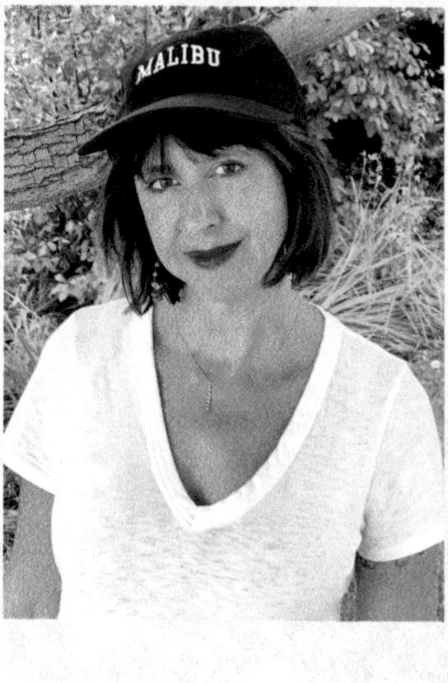
MALIBU

PHOTO BY RANDY BARTELS

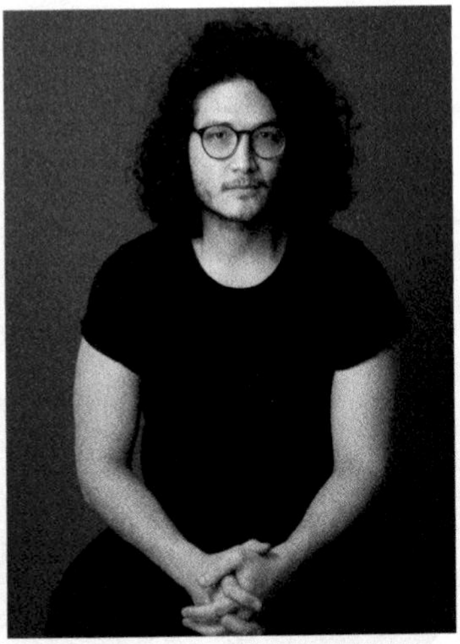

PHOTO BY CECILE VACCARO

ISAAC GOODHART got his start in comics in 2014 as one of the winners of the Top Cow Talent Hunt. After drawing *Artifacts* #38, he moved on to illustrating Matt Hawkins's *Postal* for 26 consecutive issues. He recently illustrated *Under the Moon: A Catwoman Tale,* written by Lauren Myracle and published by DC Comics.

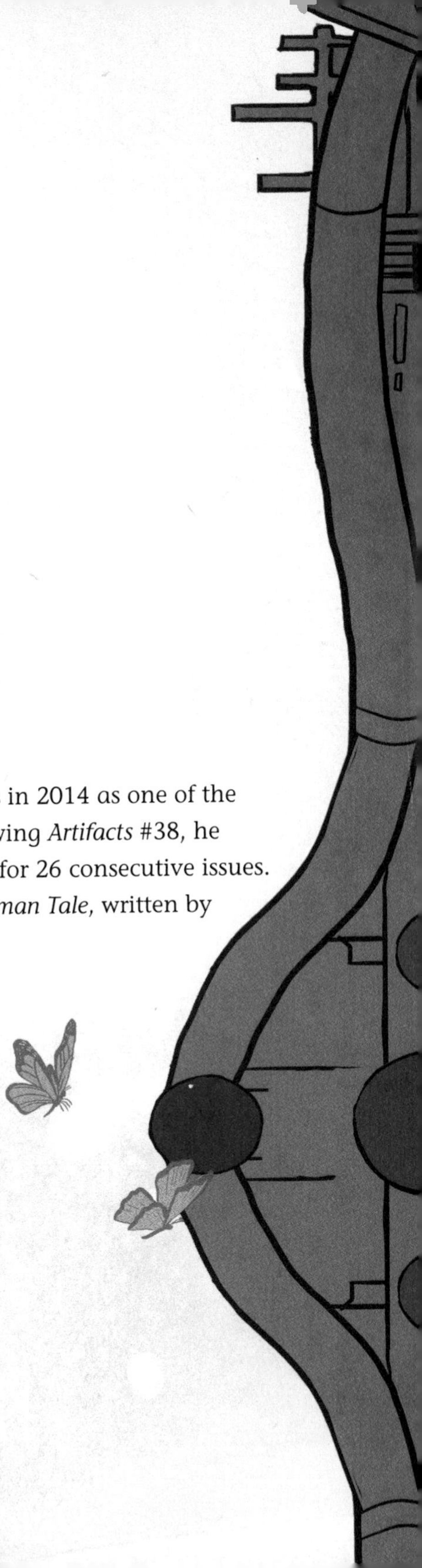

When twin brothers Alec and Walker Holland find themselves spending the summer in rural Virginia with their cousins before heading off to college, Alec's plant experiments expand beyond what he'd ever imagined. But will his experiment consume him to the point of no return?

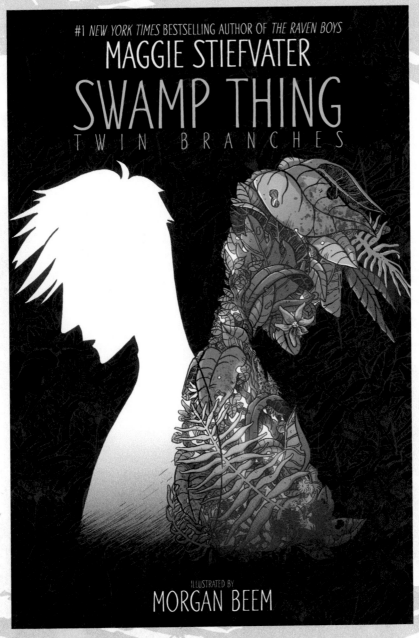

#1 *NEW YORK TIMES* BESTSELLING AUTHOR OF *THE RAVEN BOYS*
MAGGIE STIEFVATER
SWAMP THING
TWIN BRANCHES

ILLUSTRATED BY
MORGAN BEEM

From *#1 New York Times* bestselling author **Maggie Stiefvater** (the Raven Cycle series) and artist **Morgan Beem** comes a story about the primal power of memory and how it twists the bond between two brothers. Turn the page for a sneak peek!

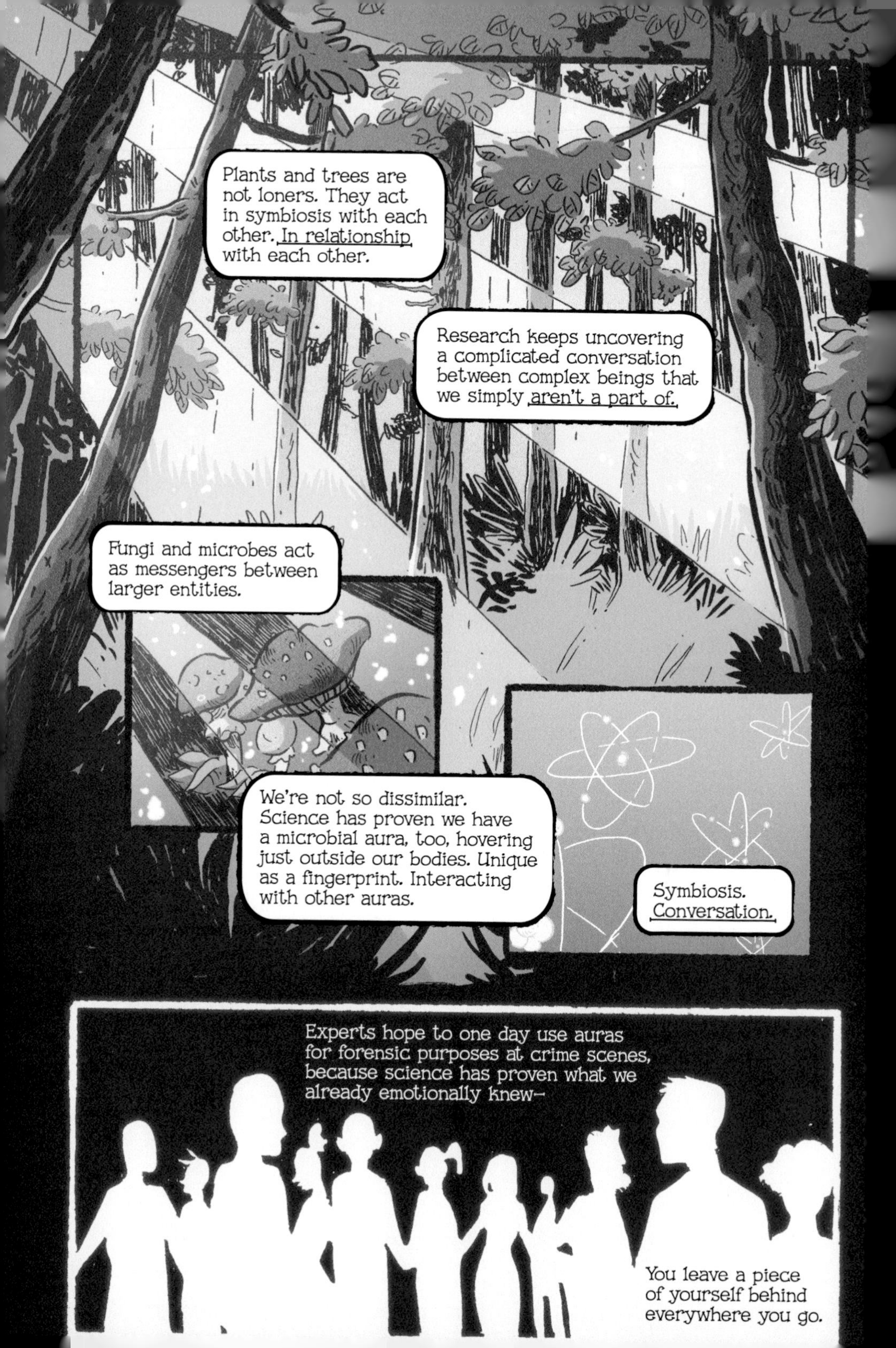
Plants and trees are not loners. They act in symbiosis with each other. In relationship with each other.
Research keeps uncovering a complicated conversation between complex beings that we simply aren't a part of.
Fungi and microbes act as messengers between larger entities.
We're not so dissimilar. Science has proven we have a microbial aura, too, hovering just outside our bodies. Unique as a fingerprint. Interacting with other auras.
Symbiosis. Conversation.
Experts hope to one day use auras for forensic purposes at crime scenes, because science has proven what we already emotionally knew—
You leave a piece of yourself behind everywhere you go.

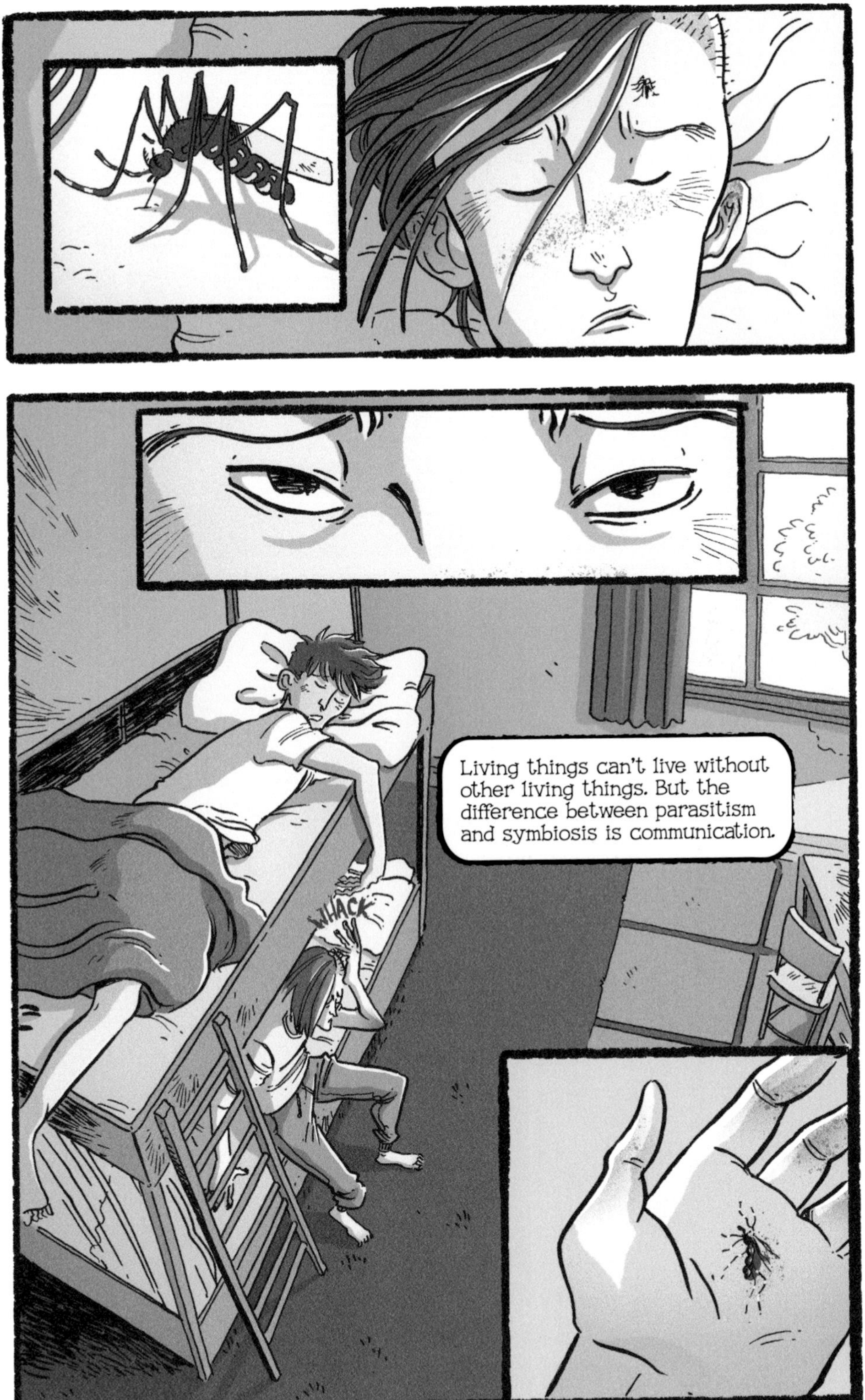
Living things can't live without other living things. But the difference between parasitism and symbiosis is communication.
WHACK

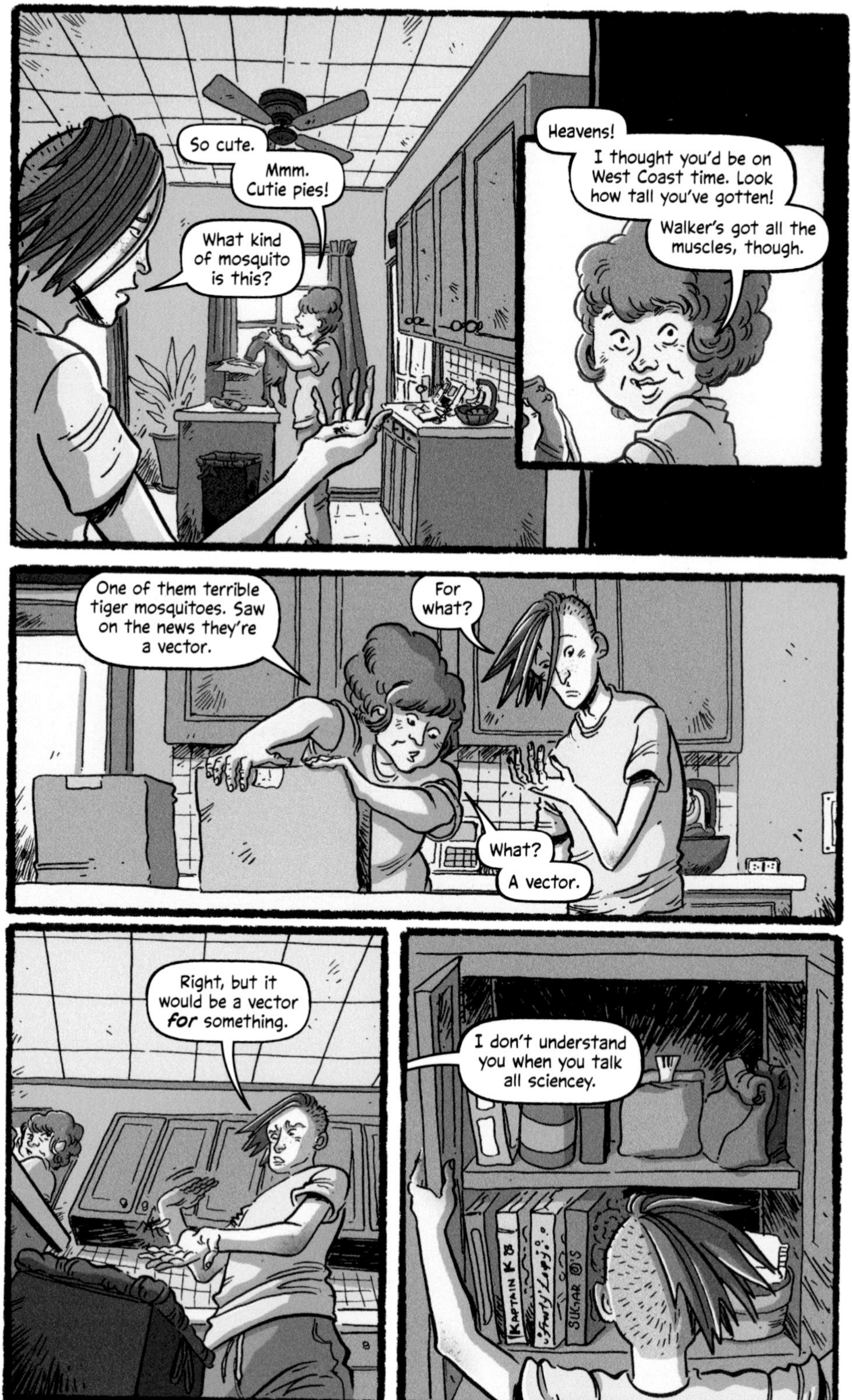
So cute.
Mmm. Cutie pies!
What kind of mosquito is this?
Heavens!
I thought you'd be on West Coast time. Look how tall you've gotten!
Walker's got all the muscles, though.
One of them terrible tiger mosquitoes. Saw on the news they're a vector.
For what?
What?
A vector.
Right, but it would be a vector *for* something.
I don't understand you when you talk all sciencey.
KAPTAIN K
SUGAR

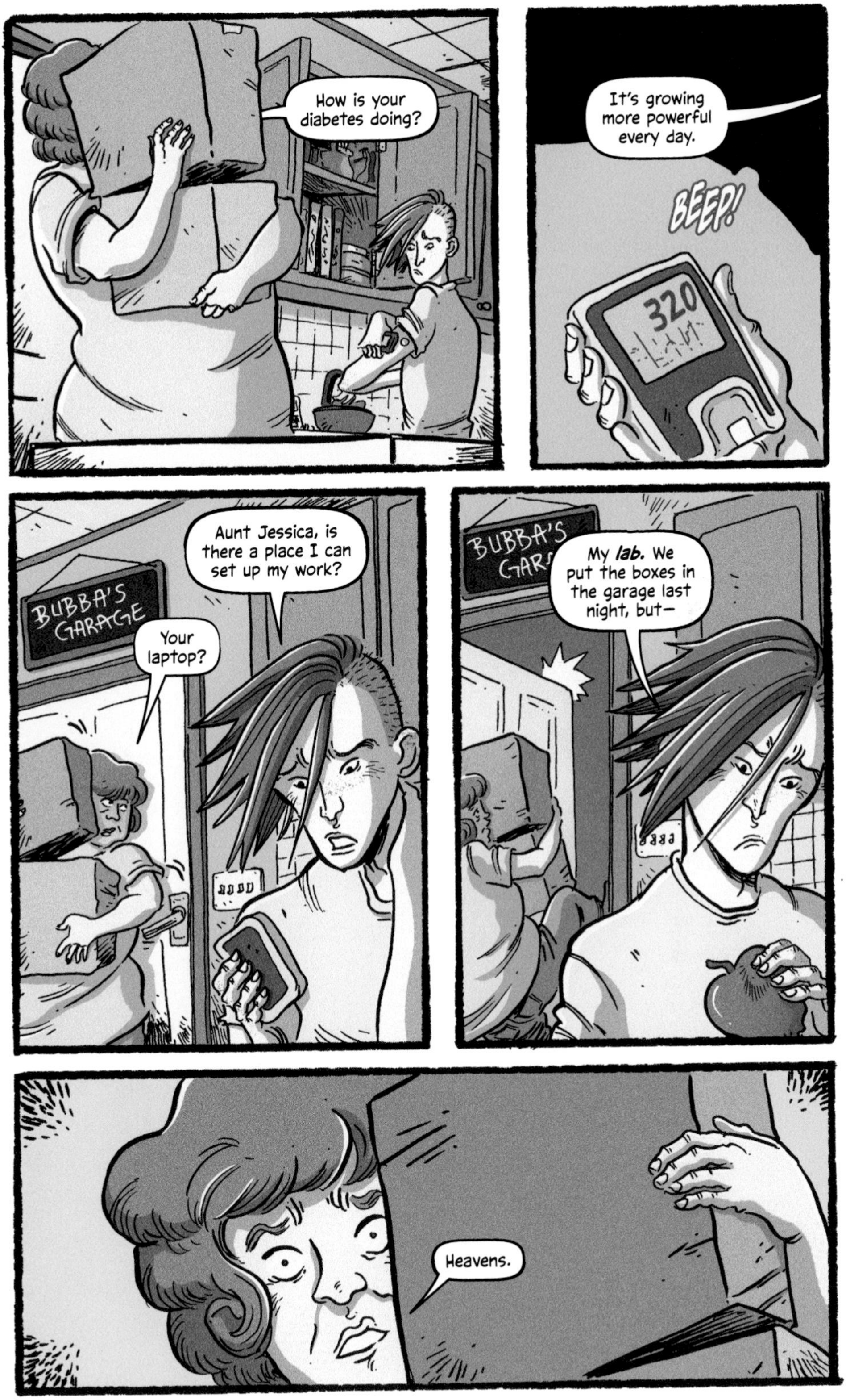
How is your diabetes doing?
It's growing more powerful every day.
BEEP!
320
Aunt Jessica, is there a place I can set up my work?
BUBBA'S GARAGE
Your laptop?
My *lab.* We put the boxes in the garage last night, but—
Heavens.

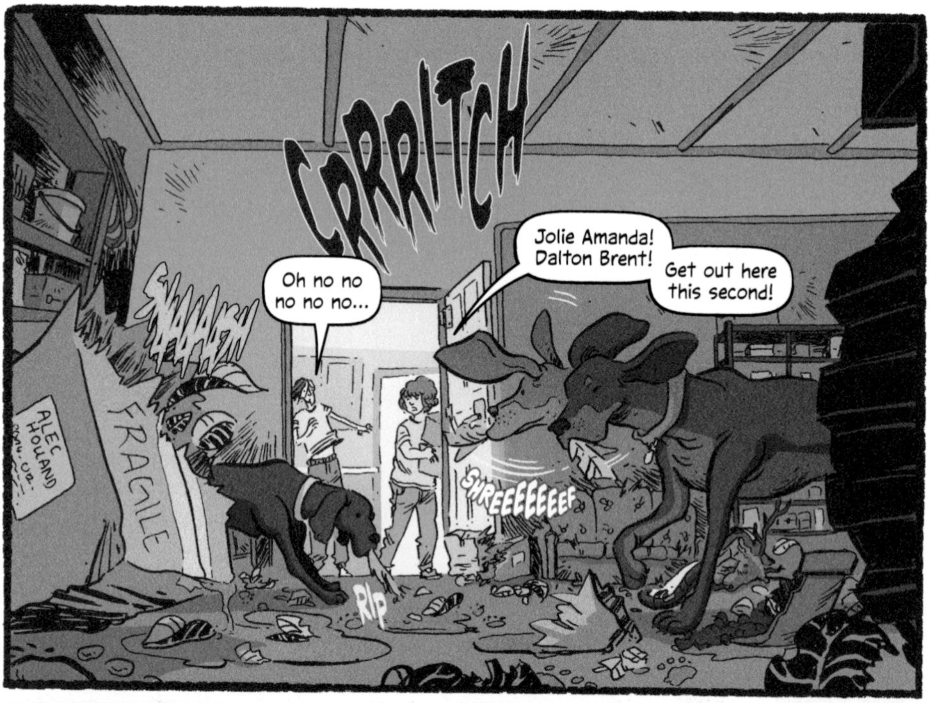
CRRRITCH
SNAAASH
ALEC HOLLAND
FRAGILE
Oh no no no no no...
Jolie Amanda! Dalton Brent!
Get out here this second!
SHREEEEEEEF
RIP

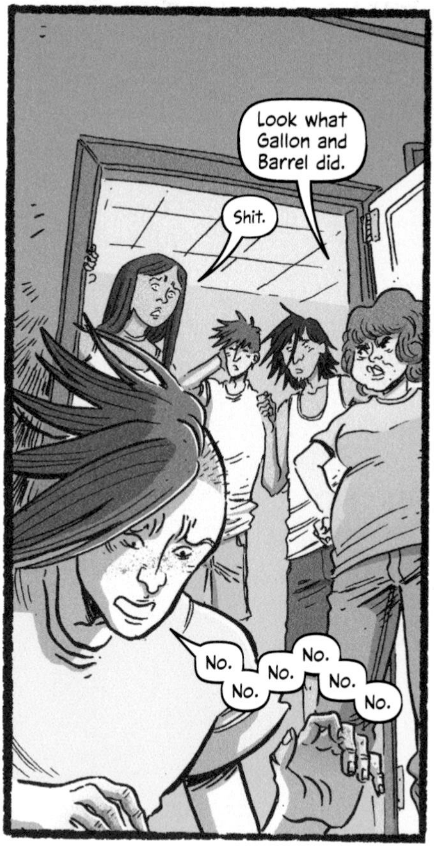
Look what Gallon and Barrel did.
Shit.
No. No. No. No. No. No.

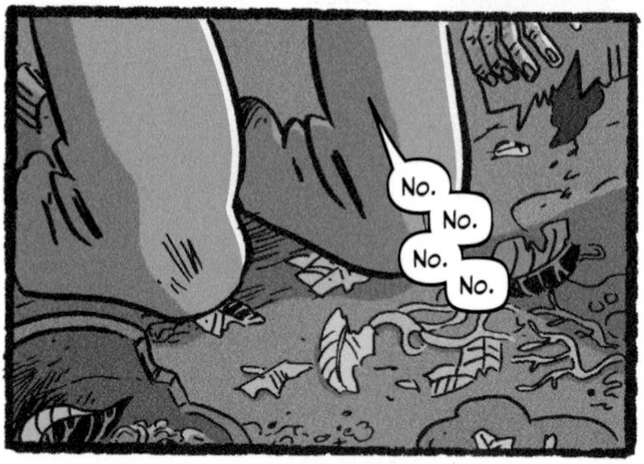
No. No. No. No.

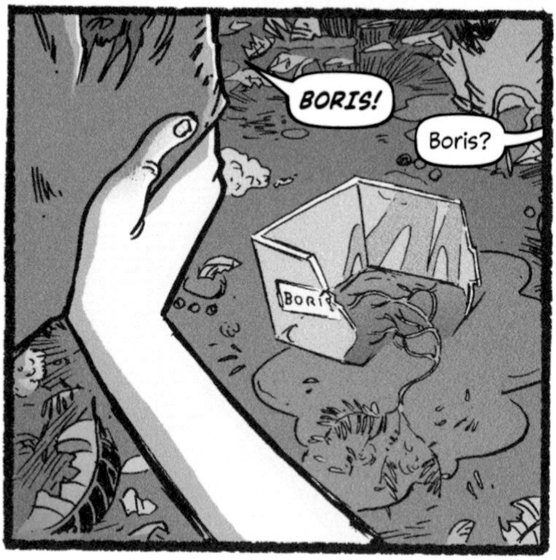
BORIS!
Boris?
BORIS

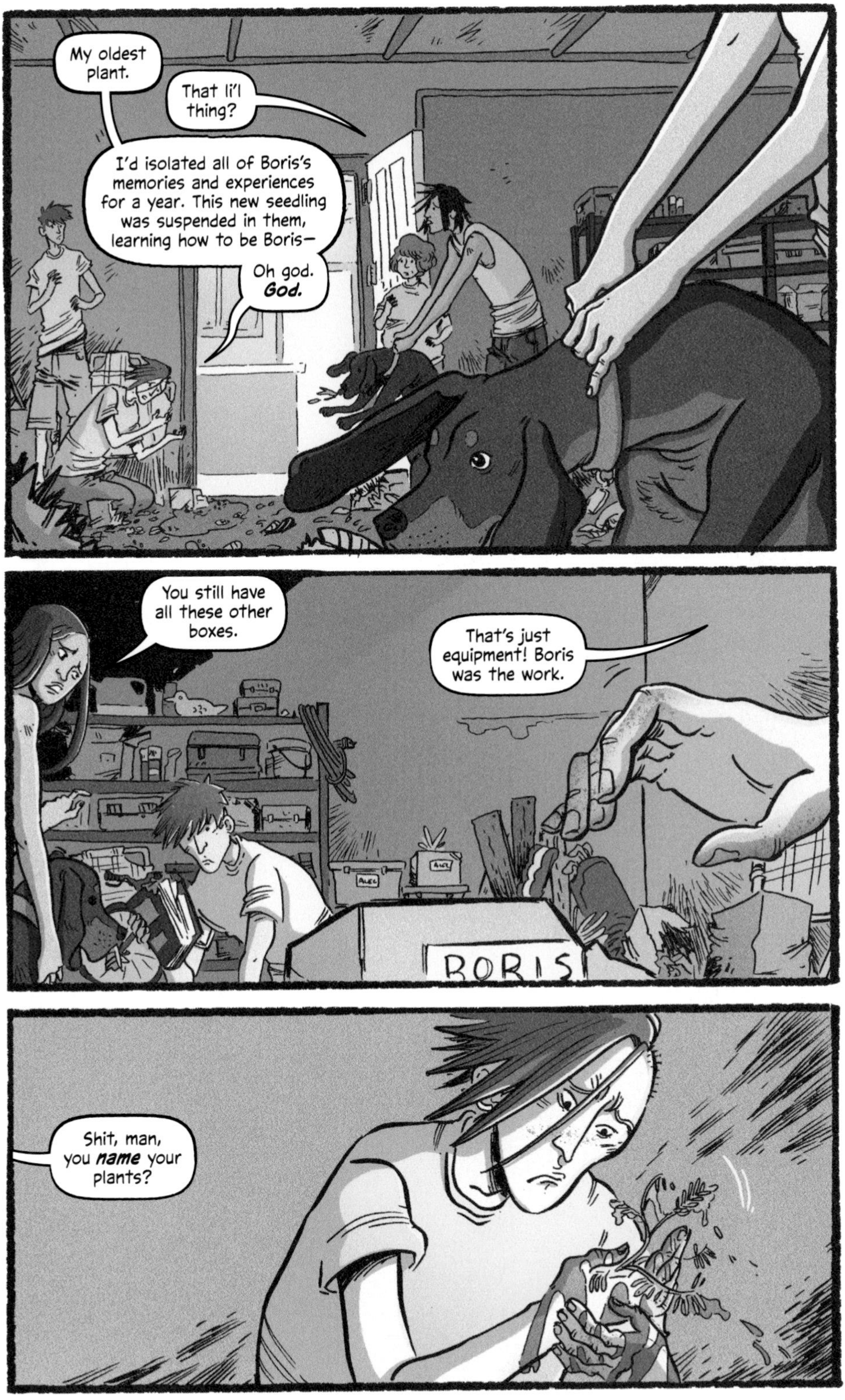
My oldest plant.
That li'l thing?
I'd isolated all of Boris's memories and experiences for a year. This new seedling was suspended in them, learning how to be Boris—
Oh god. ***God.***
You still have all these other boxes.
That's just equipment! Boris was the work.
BORIS
Shit, man, you ***name*** your plants?

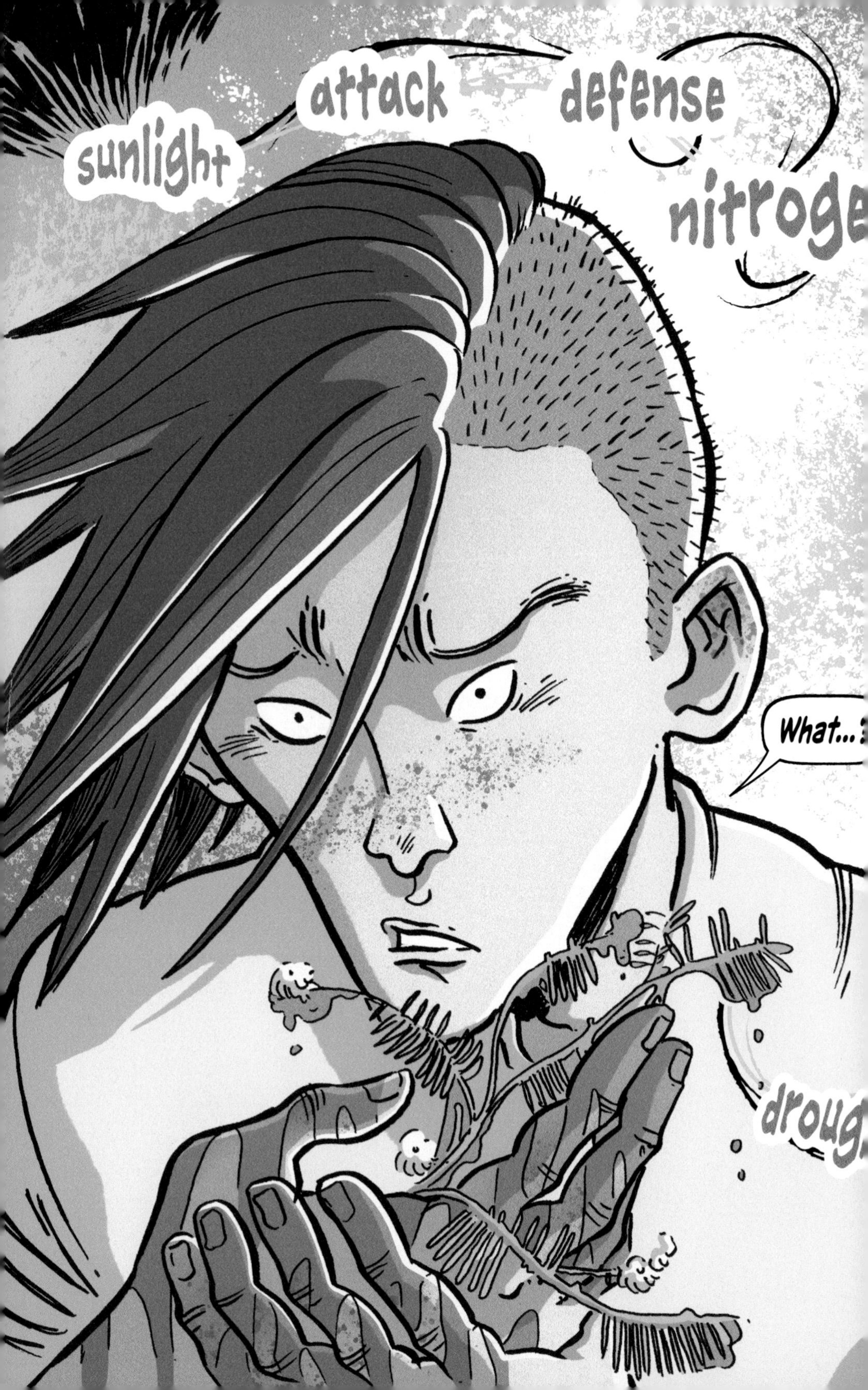
sunlight
attack
defense
nitroge
What...
droug

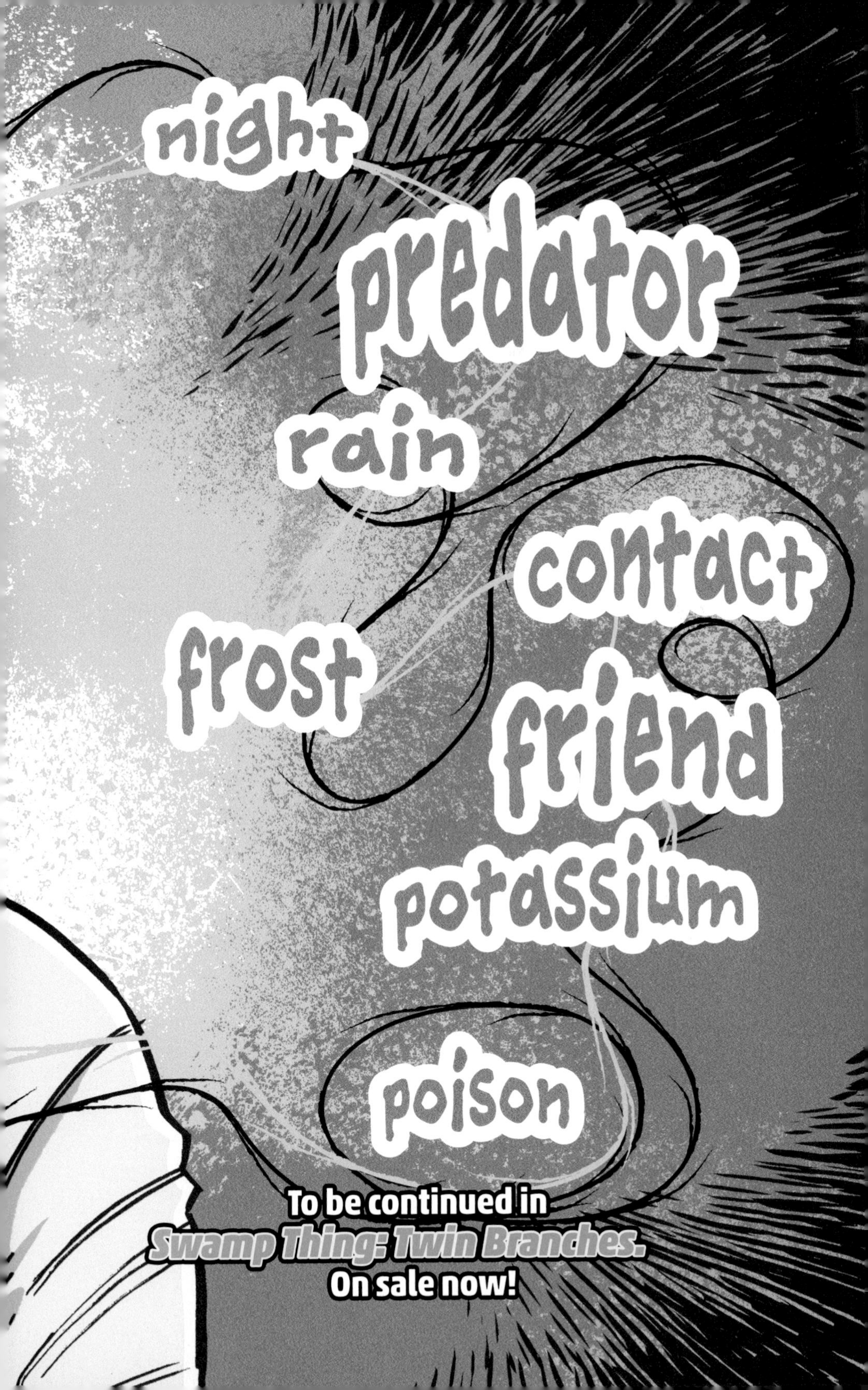
night
predator
rain
contact
frost
friend
potassium
poison
To be continued in
Swamp Thing: Twin Branches.
On sale now!